DATE DUE

Demco, Inc. 38-293

THE OAKEN THRONE

BOOK TWO OF THE DEPTFORD HISTORIES

THE OAKEN THRONE

BOOK TWO OF THE DEPTFORD HISTORIES

BY ROBIN JARVIS

A PETER GLASSMAN BOOK
SEASTAR BOOKS
SAN FRANCISCO

First published in the United States in 2005
by Chronicle Books LLC.

Text © 1993, 2005 by Robin Jarvis.
Jacket Illustration © 2005 by Leonid Gore.
All rights reserved.

First published in Great Britain in 1993.
Reprinted under license from Hodder Children's Books,
a division of Hodder Headline Limited.

Production assistance by DC Typography, San Francisco.
Typeset in Walbaum Book.
Manufactured in the United States of America.

SeaStar is an imprint of Chronicle Books LLC.

Library of Congress Cataloging-in-Publication Data
Jarvis, Robin, 1963-
The oaken throne / by Robin Jarvis.
p. cm.
"Originally published in the United Kingdom in 1993
by Hodder Children's Books."
Summary: As a series of dark wars between the bats and the squirrels rage,
Vesper, a young bat, and the squirrel maiden Ysabelle are unaware of
the devastating events that are unfolding, but they will soon be drawn
into a nightmarish journey and a desperate attempt to save
their lands from destruction.
ISBN 1-58717-277-1
[1. Bats–Fiction. 2. Squirrels–Fiction. 3. Supernatural–Fiction.] I. Title.
PZ7.J2965Oak 2005   [Fic]–dc22   2004026188

Distributed in Canada by Raincoast Books
9050 Shaughnessy Street, Vancouver, British Columbia V6P 6E5

10 9 8 7 6 5 4 3 2 1

Chronicle Books LLC
85 Second Street, San Francisco, California 94105

www.chroniclekids.com

CONTENTS

VESPERTILIO

The city of London sheltered snugly behind its strong, girdling walls. The pale light of the afternoon was already growing dim, and soft lilac shadows were now stealing over the stonework, reaching up to the high towers that rose above the narrow, straw-strewn streets.

By the Eastern Gate, the wardens sealed the entrance and set up watch until the next morning. A tall turret reared up on either side of the gateway. One of them was used as a guardroom and holding jail, but the other had fallen into disrepair and the roof had collapsed long ago. For many years, no one had dared climb the crumbling stairway, and the arrow slits, which stared out at the great river, were blank and empty.

Around the abandoned tower the weak rays of the setting sun gently curved, coloring the broken stones, turning them into glowing coals, and transforming the clinging mosses into livid flames.

And then the sun sank behind the wooded hills and the tower turned cold and dull once more, a bleak ruin robbed of its fiery plumage. When the moon rose in the night sky, its crooked silhouette was stark and severe, the jagged shape of its crown cast ugly shadows across the city, and God-fearing souls would not raise their eyes to look on it. Whispers hissed rumors of ghosts, and there were those who had heard strange noises coming from that place in the dead of night.

Yet, upon one of the cracked stones of that grim, high place, a small figure sat, watching the bright arc of the moon as it climbed the heavens.

From some remote part of the dense forests that encroached upon the city, a wolf threw back its head and howled. Its mournful voice was taken up by the night, and the hollow lament echoed between the frosty stars.

A stifled cry blurted from the mouth of the figure on the tower as a desperate wish consumed his entire body.

"It is not fair!" he wailed, stamping his feet as bitter tears spiked down his cheeks.

Vespertilio—or just plain Vesper—covered his face and his knees buckled beneath the weight of his leaden heart.

For several hours, he had sat there, watching the afternoon fail and the evening draw in. From his lofty vantage point he had seen the distant hills grow dim while, below him, the streets and lanes emptied. Silence covered all, and with each second that passed, his young spirit had diminished inside him.

"This night, all will be ended," he sighed. "No hopes are left unto me now, and the dawn shall see the curtain fall upon each of my dreams."

Drawing himself up to his full height, Vesper stared intently over the brink of the narrow ledge.

The ground stretched far below, and he closed his eyes in misery. Never had there been so wretched a soul as he—after tonight, his life would creep painfully by, without honor and with no chance to prove himself. Everything he had always thirsted for would be eternally out of his reach—life was almost not worth living.

Vesper raised one foot in the air, then, with a shout, he leaped from the tower.

Down he plunged, plummeting through the night like a stone. The wind screamed in his ears, and his eyes snapped open to behold the terrible fate that raced to greet him. Soon his body would be smashed, broken upon the cobbles below, and he would know no more—all his fears and troubles would be over.

A scream rent the night as Vesper hurtled down; the eaves of the stables shot by, and then, even as his death rushed toward him, the scream changed to a gurgle that in turn became a high, grim laugh.

"Not yet!" Vesper yelled. "I'll not be quenched so easily."

And, with that, the young bat opened his wings and skilfully skimmed over the ground, tapping the paving with his toes. Then, beating the air, Vesper soared high over the thatched rooftops once more.

He was an expert at catching the slightest breath of a breeze in his leathery wings, and could outpace any of the other weanlings. Stretching out his fingers, Vesper hovered for a moment over the battlements and drank in the scents of the newborn spring. The night was full of excitements, and for a brief moment he forgot his woes.

But as he gazed out to where the river twisted and was hidden behind wooded banks, the fears returned, and, with an unhappy groan, the bat flitted wearily back to the ruined tower.

Returning to the ledge, Vesper stood and took up a small bag.

He was a fine young bat, with large, pointed ears and eyes that gleamed like tiny black gems. He had a handsome, furry face that had been known to break into the warmest, slightly toothy grin. His nostrils were wide, and they thrilled to the green fragrance that came with the spring. Upon his chin fine wisps had started to sprout that in time, his mother had assured him, would grown into a wiry bramble bush of a beard like that of his late father.

The corners of his mouth drooped sadly. If only he could really take after his father—if only he was old enough to begin the training that would make him a Knight of the Moon.

Vesper slung the bag over his shoulder and glanced upward, to where that bright crescent shone frostily amid the faint stars.

"Is what I ask too great?" he murmured. "Is it my lot to be shamed for all time?" Shaking his head, he let out a forlorn sigh and bowed solemnly. "Whatever my Lady wills, I shall serve her."

Taking a last look at the world around him, he hopped along the ledge, crawled through a chink in the stonework, and passed inside the broken tower.

The way was dark at first, but Vesper clicked his tongue and sensed the fallen masonry around him; there was the shattered beam that sliced through the floor ahead, and he could feel the curving wall at his side. In the pitch blackness, he expertly avoided these obstacles and, feeling dejected and downhearted, turned the corner to join one of the main passageways of the bat realm.

Candlelight now flickered over the walls, and the clicks faded from Vesper's tongue as he ambled home.

It was a cramped, stuffy place. Vesper's kind had taken possession of the tower some time after the roof had collapsed, and many of their halls and chambers were formed from the slanting walkways and tilting floors. Most of the habitable areas were taken up by the living quarters, but the larger spaces were reserved for special gatherings, and he miserably reflected that soon they would all be full to overflowing.

Near the top of the tower, Vesper shared a pokey little room with his mother, Indith, and it was this the young bat was making for.

Flitting along a steeply sloping gantry, he looked keenly about him. The air was charged with anticipation and excitement—it was a momentous time for his people. He could hear their babbling voices talking of nothing but the coming night, and his stomach lurched sickeningly to think of it.

Suddenly a bat younger than himself came charging down the gantry, half running, half flying. In his grasp, he held a bundle of empty pouches, and his joy-filled eyes fixed accusingly upon Vesper.

"Ho," he cried, "whither hast thou been? Thy mother hath looked for thee." The youngster flew in circles about Vesper's head and waved the pouches roughly in his face. "Mark these well," he sniggered, "for yea, I am in the service of those who fly with the fire eggs! One day I shall be as they. Soon I will begin the training and go to battle!"

Vesper pushed the gloating child away with his wings and managed a disbelieving chuckle. "Hah!" he scoffed. "You are as addled as that which they carry. Breca—you are far too young to join the pouch bombers. They have made a game of you!"

Breca wheeled around in a high arc and stuck his sharp nose in the air. "Time will tell!" he retorted. "But what of thee, Vesper? What brave deeds art thou to perform this night? Where will the helm of thy father shine? Not on thy head, I'll wager." He laughed mockingly and pulled at Vesper's hair. "While thou hidest under thy mother's wing, I shall be preparing the pouch bombers for war. Oh, ignoble Vesper, thou shalt only be good for raiding the nest of the chiff-chaff."

At this Vesper growled and flew at Breca, with anger roaring inside him. Only cowards and weaklings were sent on egg raids, and he cuffed the youngster about the head with the bag in his grasp.

Breca dodged and escaped him, spiraling down the passageway, his sneering voice still hooting insults.

Vesper landed back on the gantry with a thud and glared after the swindling pest. "Use what little wit you possess!" he called. "If this will indeed be the end of the wars, then why should you be trained? Don't you see, Breca—we'll never see battle! There will be no more holy wars to fight!" But the other bat had flown down to where the armies would soon be mustering.

"Lackwit!" Vesper muttered before turning to continue on his way. But secretly he envied Breca—at least he would be among the brave legions of the pouch bombers and see them take to the air one last time. He grumbled under his breath, knowing that

11

when the time came, he would be with his mother and the rest of the weanlings, expected to do the mundane, honorless duties—why, he might as well be a nest robber after all.

Presently, the gantry reached a wide thoroughfare where many female bats hurried to and fro. They were all Daughters of the Moon, for it was in Her realm that they freely roamed, spreading their wings beneath the boundless reaches of night and hearing the music of Her darkness. The Lady was revered by each and every one.

Vesper nodded to those who greeted him, but there was still so much to be done that many barged about their business without a thought for anything else. It was the most important time any of them had ever lived through—no mistakes must be made, nothing must go wrong. Everyone had a task to complete before the night was over. Some carried bowls filled with bright pigment, others were busy polishing their husband's war gear, while the wet nurses took care of infants and kept them out of everyone else's way.

As Vesper passed the entrances to private quarters, he caught glimpses of what was happening within. In one darkened chamber, two large matrons were busily preparing weapons for the pouch bombers to take with them. One was engaged in piercing and blowing a wren's egg, while the other poured strange yellow powder into eggs that had already been emptied before sealing both ends with wax.

In another swelling, a large noctule stood grim and fierce with his great wings spread wide as his three daughters scampered round, carefully painting images of flame on the membranes between his massive fingers. He was a great warrior—a Knight of the Moon, whose valor was renowned throughout the twelve colonies. Rohgar was his name, and he had been in countless battles, leading the assault against the hated enemy, bellowing war cries, and meting out justice to those who dared oppose the council and the Lord Hrethel.

Vesper stared at him for a moment, admiring the war banner painted on the huge bat's wings and wishing he could be so heroically decorated. Then, turning aside, he hurried on, away from these glorious sights.

"And so the evil mistresses of the wood did cast an enchantment and all our kind were bereft. The birthright that our grandsires were given by the Lady herself was stolen from us."

The intoning words drifted out of a nursery, where a harassed Daughter of the Moon tried to calm her charges by telling them the old histories. Even the babes sensed the tinkling excitement, and all were agitated and restless.

When Vesper finally ducked under the curtain that covered the entrance to his home, his mother glanced up crossly. "My son!" Indith said sternly. "Many hours have passed since you were sent to fetch more pigment!"

Vesper shrugged and tossed the bag he had been carrying upon the floor.

Indith looked tired. She had been a beauty in her youth, but worry and grief had bent her back and grizzled her fur. She was standing over a bowl of scarlet paint, stirring in the pigment with a short stick. She had stowed other sticks into the loose bun of her unkempt hair but had completely forgotten about this convenient stash and had been forced to go and hunt out another bundle. Around her were a number of bowls similar to the one she labored over, and these contained a rainbow of colors, although a greater variety of hues had splashed upon her face.

"Are you so simple, child?" she scolded her son. "You know how vital was your errand. These pigments are needed most urgently. Our forces must be resplendent as they utter the war cries. The symbols of moon, flame, and eye possess charms of protection. Oh, why didst thou pick this day to dawdle and have naught but wool in your head?"

She seized the bag he had brought and poured its contents into yet another bowl.

Vesper said nothing, but gazed over to one corner of their cramped quarters. There, upon a shelf cut into the stone wall, his father's armor glinted.

As if in a dream, he made his way across the room and, catching his breath, Vesper folded his wings about himself.

Every day, for as long as he could remember, he had seen his mother polish his father's armor. It was the custom for bats to wear fearsome helmets when they went to war. These were meant to instill terror in the hearts of the enemy, for the helmets were crafted into horrific faces, with wide, staring eyes or vicious beaks ringed with teeth of steel. Each of these helmets–or "screechmasks," as they were known–had individual names, chosen by the Knight of the Moon who wore them.

The one belonging to Vesper's father was called Terrorgrin, for it had a long snout that protected the wearer's nose and a hinged lower jaw with a row of sharp fangs that could clang shut about a fleeing enemy's head. Two round eyes sat on either side of the snout, and above these were two pointed horns.

The metal shone like a mirror, and the bright colors of the paints were reflected and thrown back across Vesper's yearning face. He touched the grim object reverently and blinked back the tears that sprang to his eyes.

Beside the Terrorgrin, two armor-plated gauntlets had been carefully placed. Vesper's father had worn these on his feet, for the gauntlets had talons of razor-sharp blades that could slice through the toughest hide.

"I should be taking you into battle," he whispered despondently. "You and I deserve one night of glory, to be tempered in the heat of the fray."

At that moment, the sound of many voices raised in song drifted up from the lower levels. The armies were gathering and were already chanting the victory hymns. For only a short time would the plainsong continue. Once they had called on the Lady to watch over them, the forces would depart.

14

Indith lay the mixing stick down for a moment and wiped her brow, smudging the splotches of paint that had splashed there into lurid swirls. She looked at her son and shook her head sadly.

"Poor Vesper," she said in a gentle voice, "I guess what troubles your heart. This must be very difficult for you."

The young bat whirled round. "Difficult?" he cried. "Mother, do you not understand? Once tonight is over and our armies have vanquished our enemies, there will be nothing left to me!"

"But we must act now," she told him. "Our Lord Hrethel has decreed it. Would you let our chance of victory slip by because you were not old enough to wear your father's armor?"

Vesper stared sullenly at the floor. "Of course not," he mumbled. "I hate the squirrels as much as anyone. If it were not for them, Father might still be alive." He hesitated for a moment before he lifted his head and stared at his mother with hope brimming in his eyes. "Please," he implored, "no one need know. If thou wouldst let me fly with the others, I vow not to get in their way. I only want to be a part of it–somehow!"

"No!" Indith firmly replied. "It is no merry game that General Rohgar leads the might of the twelve colonies into. All have been trained and know their part exactly. The pouch bombers must learn each other's movements to the smallest degree–the slightest deviation from their plotted route would be disastrous. Fire eggs are deadly tools of war, Vesper, not nursery toys, and only the most skilful Moonrider may bear them."

"But Mother!" he begged desperately. "In this, the war to end all wars, I merely want to observe. I want to see those squirrels perish for what they and their Starwife have done to us. They are filthy creatures–would you deny me that?"

"We all despise them, Vesper," Indith replied–her voice trembling with emotion. "Those loathsome savages have inflicted much sorrow upon our kind. How many times have I desired to don the armor of your father and slay some of those tree rats myself?"

She took a deep breath and tried to control the anger that was bubbling inside her. Vesper waited and chewed his wispy beard while his mother calmed herself. Eventually, Indith shook her wings then put them about her son's shoulders.

"Oh, my dear child," she said with a faint smile. "Fear not; there will be other times to prove your mettle."

"Will there?" he asked doubtfully.

Indith hugged him tightly. "Tomorrow you shall know it. Once our warriors have destroyed the Starwife and all her hateful subjects, the enchantment she wrought will be broken forever, and then you will know."

"What will it be like? To have our birthright once more—what manner of things shall we see?"

Vesper's mother closed her eyes and chanted dreamily, her voice blending with the hymns floating up from below. "Prophecy and insight," she cooed, "bestowed upon us by the Heavenly Lady. By Her leave our race may look into the hearts of others, view distant lands, and glimpse what may come to pass. That is our gift, my child, and by the dawn we shall possess it once more."

Vesper unwrapped himself from Indith's wings. "Why did the squirrels take it from us?" he asked.

"Jealously and fear," she replied, hopping back to the bowl of scarlet pigment. "Ever have the tree rats hated us and dreaded our birthright—lest one day we use it against them and their squalid lands."

"But we would never have done such a thing!" he protested. "Are all squirrels so mistrustful and full of malice?"

"Every one!" she affirmed. "Never trust the subjects of the Starwife, my son, nor any of the other branches of their unholy house. The only squirrel you can be sure of is the one dangling on the end of a gauntlet."

"Yet they must be very powerful, to cast the enchantment and to have made it last all these many years."

Indith gave the paint a severe stirring; it slopped over the edge of the bowl and drenched her toes. "Oh, yes!" she spat. "They have power—of a sort—but its origin is totally evil! That is how they have managed to keep their realm protected all these years, by weaving a wall of dark magic around it to keep us out. But soon they'll learn; soon our agent will complete her work and the defenses will be no more. The land of Greenreach shall fall!"

Abruptly, the distant hymn came to an end, and they knew the pouch bombers were taking to the air. Indith uttered a small gasp of annoyance, gathered up as many bowls as she could carry, and hurried out of the chamber to deliver them to the other Moonriders who would still be waiting.

Alone, Vesper looked back at the screechmask and sniffed unhappily. The greatest night in all their history, and he was too young to take part. It really wasn't fair—if only there was some way.

BLOOD ON THE OAK

It was a dark time, a time of magic and menace. Great forests covered the land, and the world was still wild and dangerous. In the ancient woods, spirits of stone and stream lingered, and fearsome beasts prowled through the gloomy leaf shade.

The folk who dwelt in the tiny hamlets at the forest's fringe feared what lurked in the frightening realm of root and branch.

The serfs and villains who waited upon the knights and tilled the fields trembled when the sun set behind the surrounding forests. In their fancy, the powers of the dark were abroad. Only a fool would venture from hearth and home after dusk, when demons stalked through the unlit land and in midnight woods all manner of terrors shrieked and hunted for prey. Everyone believed that dragons crept stealthily between the trees, blowing poison from their immense jaws, and the humble folk feared these imaginary creatures far more than the real dangers they had to endure.

Yet, if only they knew what was truly awakening, deep within the medieval forests. If they had but the slightest notion of the real evil that was taking shape and growing more powerful with each passing moonrise.

For all things it was a deadly time, yet in some isolated places, the light of reason and understanding continued to shine. Age after age, back to the dawn of dawns, when the first oak sprang from the soil and the hawthorn bloomed, the Starwives had ruled.

According to their legends, the black squirrels were the first to awaken, born among the branches of the new trees upon the green hill that reached down to the great river. There, in the Greenreach, they were divided into five royal houses, and they took for themselves lands to govern. Yet over all the Starwife reigned.

While the proud princes departed to seek new realms, the Handmaiden of Orion remained in Greenreach, for there was the source of her power, and there the spirits of growth and life wandered.

But as the years passed and the generations slid by, the royal houses were separated; their lands dwindled as the forests grew dark and their borders shrank until they were like islands struggling to repel a black tide, and the woods that surrounded them became filled with horror.

Yet, in the land of Greenreach, the flowers continued to bud. No frost nor breath of winter touched the sacred hill, and there at least the spirit of the Green still walked, blessing the groves and trees with His presence.

At the summit of the holy place, a mighty oak stood, its branches spread far and high, and within its vast trunk the Starwife dwelt, watching the darkening world and grieving for it.

For six hundred years the Hallowed Oak had towered over the blessed land, and its roots reached deep into the earth, delving down into the caverns and dark grottoes that twisted beneath the world. And there, moving silently through a dank, dripping tunnel, a cloaked figure moved with stealth.

It was a tall, black squirrel who, with furtive steps, crept along the slimy path. A long staff was clenched tightly in her grasp, at the top of which a candle dimly burned.

The frail yellow light guttered in the stale airs that moved through the underground passageways, and the squirrel's shadow swelled vast behind her.

Her face was gaunt, and her hair was scraped back over her bony head. The large eyes that glared at the treacherous ground were set deep behind a wedge-shaped nose, and heavy lids drooped over them. Upon her brow she wore a circlet of silver, and the brooch that fastened her black cloak was fashioned into the shape of an oak leaf.

It was an unpleasant face, and the candlelight fled before it as though it, too, shivered at such a grim visage.

The Lady Morwenna cursed the mud that oozed over the path. It was undignified to have to venture down here–but soon all humiliations would be over.

"Where is that wretched door?" she hissed to herself. Only she had ever dared to descend beneath the Hallowed Oak. No other squirrel, red or black, had ever had the courage to explore these ghastly caverns. A sinister smile split Morwenna's face. "Well, if they have," she muttered in a voice as sharp as her features, "none have ever returned."

The tunnel began to wind and she breathed a sigh of relief; for a moment she thought she had taken a wrong turn–even she was not completely sure of the way.

Holding the candle before her, she strode confidently forward, and there, appearing out of the darkness, was a small wooden door.

Leaning the staff against the rough wall, Morwenna fumbled for the keys that jangled at her waist. They were attached to a large iron ring and were of many different sizes and designs. Squinting in the flickering light, she selected a small, rusted specimen and slid it into the lock.

The door opened a chink; it was very heavy, and she had to push with all her strength before entry was possible.

The chamber beyond was loftier than the passageway, and she could straighten her back at last, but the place stank. The foul reek of stagnant water and rank mold invaded her nostrils and the squirrel spluttered for a second, mirroring the action of the candle.

Then she mastered herself and looked about her, holding the flame above her head.

She was standing upon a muddy shore that fell away into turgid water, the surface of which was covered by green scum. It was impossible to tell just how great the chamber was, for the light did not penetrate far into the blackness, yet judging by the resounding echoes, it must have been immense.

Morwenna pulled the folds of her thick cloak about her, keeping out the pervading chill, and cast her glance upon the shore.

The mud was churned with many, frenzied footprints. Here and there a splayed claw could clearly be discerned, and Morwenna noted with satisfaction that there were no signs of the last meal to be found.

She raised her sharp face once more and stared blindly into the dark. "Dear ones," she crooned, "come see what dainty I have for you. Come to me, my lovelies—where are you?"

From the invisible distance there came a sudden *plop!* as a bubble erupted on the surface of the water. Morwenna grinned and took from a pocket in her cloak some shreds of raw meat.

Another bubble burst from the foul water, and a vile, belching croak echoed around the cavern.

The squirrel threw the scraps upon the shore and waited, her paw resting upon the hilt of a dagger at her side.

Now the chamber was filled with horrible gurglings, the water seethed, and bestial grunts roared toward her.

Into the candlelight, floating on the surface and cutting through the scum, sailed a pair of round, golden eyes. They blinked when they came close to the shore, wincing at the harsh flame. Then the eyes rose from the water.

The head on which they sat was one of the ugliest nature had ever created. Clusters of warts peppered the snout and blistered down the ridged spine. The creature's mouth was misshapen, being repulsively gnarled, and webbed claws thrust forward, squelching through the mud as a vast toad hauled itself from the mire.

It was an odious, bloated abomination. Two narrow nostrils snorted the bad air, questing for the scent of fresh meat. Onto the slippery shore it lumbered, heaving its pale, sagging belly over the mud to where the squirrel was waiting.

"There," Morwenna purred, "see what I bring you."

The globular eyes roved in their bulging sockets, looking from the squirrel to the scraps that had been thrown on the floor.

Morwenna raised her paw, and her hideous pet waited for the signal. From the murky water beyond, other sounds were bubbling nearer, but the toad's brothers would have to go hungry this time.

Quickly, she made a sign and the creature dived at the morsels upon the ground. Black mud flew everywhere as the vile beast slobbered and swallowed its way through the meal.

"There's my beauty," Morwenna lovingly murmured, "there's my fine jewel." As she said this, and while the toad's attention was fixed solely upon the raw meat, the squirrel deftly drew her dagger from its sheath. Carefully, she stole behind the guzzling horror and slowly raised the blade.

Without warning, she leaped forward, bringing her foot violently down upon the back of the toad's head. The beast let out an outraged squeal as its face was forced into the mud, and, squirm though it may, it could not escape.

"Fret you not, my darling," Morwenna assured it, "there's naught to fear—'twill not take long."

The dagger flashed in the candlelight as she brought it close to the monster's putrid skin. After a moment's consideration she found the largest of the pustules that clustered over the slimy back and pricked it with the blade. At once, a watery, dark-green liquid squirted from the wound, but Morwenna was ready and collected all that she could in a tiny vial of blue glass.

The toad wriggled beneath her and gargled huge mud bubbles in protest, but Morwenna had got what she came for.

"'Tis over now, my emerald," she said soothingly. "What a fuss, pretty one." She tucked the dagger back in the sheath and placed the precious vial in her cloak pocket. As she rose and stood back from her pet, the creature thrashed its stumpy arms and the head reared angrily out of the ooze.

The squirrel jumped backward as the wide mouth lunged for her, snapping its bloodless lips.

"How dare you!" she screamed, reaching for the candle staff. "Get you back into the water—I'll teach you to snarl at me!" Furious at this unspeakable rebellion, Morwenna struck the toad with the end of the staff, clouting it round the offending jaws until the golden eyes squeezed shut and the beast shambled a hasty retreat to the water's edge, where it plunged silently into the blackness and sank from view.

The Lady Morwenna waited until she was sure the thing had gone before returning to the doorway. From the dark pool, several new pairs of eyes gazed morosely across at her, and she gave a cruel little laugh.

"Have patience, my other loves," she called. "Shortly, your rancid bellies will be full of the sweetest meat you have ever tasted." And with that she closed the door behind her.

With grim determination, she made her way back through the winding tunnels. Up she strode, passing under curtains of fibrous roots and narrow caves of cold stone. Her work this night was not yet over; there were still some matters she had to attend to—and now she was prepared.

"One final measure, and the deed will be done," she told herself. "Then will all those years of fawning and wearing a servile mask be at an end."

Up she climbed, up out of the dank grottoes, up to where the mud no longer flowed over the path, but where the earth was dry and the soil fragrant and wholesome.

Wiping the sticky grime from her feet, Morwenna paused before a plain wooden door and unlocked it swiftly. This led into the Hallowed Oak, and she hesitated before entering. Was there anything that would betray her evil intentions? Taking a moment to groom herself and adjust the circlet upon her brow, she opened the door and walked inside.

Within the ancient tree, all was quiet. Silver lamps were suspended from the carved ceiling, and they cast deep shadows over Morwenna's hooded eyes. A flight of stairs cut into the living timber rose before her, and she quickly blew out the candle she was carrying before ascending.

Over the centuries, the craftworkers of Greenreach had wrought many intricate and beautiful designs into the stairway and about its walls. There were images of the thirteen important trees that formed the squirrel calendar, and the emblems of all the royal houses were repeated in an endlessly twisting border. On the ceiling, arranged about the lamps, were the patterns of stars, and these were inlaid with burnished gold that threw back the silver light until it glittered and danced over the steps.

Morwenna paid the elaborate decoration no heed. She had been climbing these stairs for most of her life, and she never noticed nor appreciated the labor that had gone into creating them. Now her mind was focused on one goal only, and nothing could have distracted her from it.

The stairway was long and winding, spiraling as it did within the trunk of the great oak tree. The doors that she passed led only to storerooms and the chambers where the serfs slept. These were mostly red squirrels, for their wisdom was not as great as their black cousins and they indulged in too much laughter to be considered useful for anything else.

As she passed one of the dormitories, Morwenna allowed herself a sneering smile—yes, only one of the older race, such as she, could contemplate the ultimate, treacherous act.

"M'lady."

The voice startled her and wrenched Morwenna from her reverie. A guard was standing before her, a spear in his grasp.

She eyed him for a second. He was a black squirrel like herself. A tunic of green, edged with gold, showed that his duties were confined to the Hallowed Oak and the protection of the Starwife.

Morwenna gave him a syrupy smile and spoke the passwords. The guard bowed and stood aside.

She had reached the grand hall, and here, too, the artistry of those long dead proudly showed itself. Intertwining leaves in perfect detail rippled over the curving walls, seeming to grow up to the vaulted ceiling, where blossoms of every kind were suspended by golden wires.

The hall was filled with sentries and guards. Red squirrels laughed together as they hurried about their duties, and Morwenna gazed at them dispassionately. The merry voices failed to touch the black heart in her breast. Not a soul would be spared; she had decided this long ago.

From the crowd, a squirrel maiden came running toward her. "My Lady Morwenna!" she cried. "Stay a moment. Would you not tarry a while? We are all anxious for word of Her."

Morwenna turned. It was Fearn—one of the royal princesses, those maidens who dwelt in the sacred groves. She also wore a circlet about her brow, and in its center sparkled a finely cut stone. About her shoulders she wore a mantle of purest white, and a belt of silver was fastened about her waist.

"Have you marked any change?" the princess asked. "My sisters have sent me to discover what news I could."

The sharp-featured squirrel managed a frosty smile, and the wedge-shaped face took on the aspect of one burdened with care and concern. "As yet there is none," she replied in a hushed voice. "Alas, my mistress still lies abed and grows weaker, I fear."

"Then she is failing," Fearn uttered sorrowfully. "What unhappy tidings I have to tell my sisters. Tell her that we have prayed, and may the hours that remain be peaceful."

"I shall indeed."

The young princess waited for Morwenna to curtsy before leaving to break the sad news to the others.

She was hardly out of sight when Morwenna's expression transformed into one so ghastly that a red squirrel scampering nearby dropped the tray he was carrying and gaped at her dumbly.

"Run to your sisters," Morwenna spat. "Let them outwardly mourn; they don't deceive me. I know that their hearts shall secretly beat the quicker, hoping they will be chosen."

She spun on her heel, and the black cloak swirled around her. On she went, crossing the main hall and taking the royal stairway, that slender flight that few in the realm had ever climbed. This led directly to the chambers of the Starwife, and Morwenna had one final appointment to keep with her lifelong mistress.

A wide and impressive doorway opened before her. Within was the throne of the Starwives, and Morwenna was sorely tempted to deviate from her path for a few minutes—but such indulgences could be enjoyed to the full later on. Leaving this place behind her, she climbed another stair and came to her mistress's bedchamber.

Two sentries barred the way, but they stood aside as she approached, and she opened an ornate door as silently and as gently as she could.

Like a thief, she crept into the room.

One small lamp flickered in the far corner, filling the chamber with warm, cozy shadows. Rich tapestries adorned the round walls, and by a large, shuttered window was a beautiful bed that appeared to grow out of the floor, having been carved—like the walls—from the growing tree. Vines and berries twirled about the posts that reared at each corner, vanishing into the fringes of a sumptuously embroidered canopy.

Morwenna craned her neck, but the bed was empty. Then she saw her.

Almost hidden behind one of the bed curtains, a small and shrunken form sat slumped in a chair. The figure was silent and still, betraying no signs of life. Morwenna raised her eyebrows—perhaps her venture underground had been in vain.

She closed the door behind her, and at once a faint gasp issued from the chair.

"Who is it?" whispered a frail voice.

"'Tis I, madam."

"Oh, Morwenna—where did you go? I called to you, but there was none to hear me."

"I slipped out for the briefest of moments, madam," Morwenna lied. "I think perhaps you slept and wandered in a dream."

"There may be truth in that," the cracked voice admitted, "and yet I could swear it does feel like many hours have passed. Come here, let me look on you."

Morwenna drew close to the chair and smiled woodenly at her mistress.

The Starwife rolled back the blanket that she had tucked beneath her whiskered chin and wrapped it around her knees. She was an ancient squirrel whose black fur had long since turned white with age; the muscles of her body were wasted to nothing, and her bones were dry and brittle. Her face was so emaciated that the skull was clearly visible beneath the shriveled and withered flesh. She seemed more dead than alive, yet there was about her an air of majesty that the advancing decay could not hide.

Long, untold years she had reigned, governing her subjects with wisdom and compassion. But now the Starwife was dying.

For many days now, the present Handmaiden of Orion had been too weak to leave her bedchamber. She had felt Death creeping upon her many times over the recent years, yet always she had managed to shrug him off to continue her work. It was she who, in the late flowering of her youth, had woven the barriers about Greenreach to keep out the attacking bats, and there was so much still to be done. Eventually, however, that sinister visitor had come for her and would be put off no more. She had never felt so close to his malignant influence before. Her very insides seemed consumed with the grave, and it took all her powers to remain awake.

The ghost of a smile tugged the crabbed corners of her mouth. "I haven't left you yet," she gasped, "oh, but this fever plagues me like nothing I have known." Raising a crippled, arthritic paw, she pointed at the window and asked for it to be opened. "There is no air in here," she explained, "and my breaths are labored enough."

Morwenna pulled the shutters open and stared out at the Blessed Hill. The sacred groves were in full bloom, and everything was at peace. Here and there, warm glows shone from the four surrounding trees as folk made their way to their own beds. Soon they would snuggle down, fearing nothing, for no one could assail Greenreach while the magical defenses kept their enemies away.

"What is the morrow?" the weary voice of the Starwife asked. "Is the day of the alder already upon us?" She slid back against the pillow that supported her head and tutted huskily. "Then it will be the first I have missed. Have the maidens cut the alder wands? Great were the celebrations in my youth." She turned her head toward her handmaiden, but Morwenna was still staring out of the window and seemed not to have heard a word she had said.

"Morwenna," the old squirrel called, "what ails you? There is turmoil behind your eyes."

The other pulled away from the sill and gazed coldly at her mistress. "You are mistaken, madam," she muttered. "I am quite well. It is you who are stricken."

The Starwife frowned, but there were too many important decisions to be made, and her troubled mind did not detect the malice in Morwenna's voice. Her withered paws closed about the silver pendant that hung around her neck, and her eyes closed as she collected her thoughts.

"There must be no more delays," the Starwife said. "A successor must be announced."

Morwenna walked over to a shelf and took down a jug that contained a sweet-smelling, honey-colored liquid. Pouring a quantity into a bowl, she glanced slyly back to her mistress to make sure she was not watching, then took the blue vial from her cloak. Holding her breath, she let three dark drops fall into the bowl before slipping the vial back to her pocket.

"Drink of this," she said, offering the bowl to the frail form in the chair.

The Starwife received it gladly and took small sips, her trusting eyes turned upon her faithful handmaiden. Morwenna stood back, watching the poison slowly disappearing from the bowl. Strange that it had taken so long to take effect. For a whole week now, she had plied her mistress with the deadly mixture, yet this would most certainly be the final dose. Why, the old hag barely had the strength to lift the bowl.

"Yes," the ancient one continued once the vessel had been drained. "I have made my choice. Morwenna, I want you to summon the royal princesses. Tomorrow, the heralds shall announce the accession. What better–" she paused to cough, "what better occasion than–than Alder–Alder Day?"

A choking fit prevented her saying any more, and Morwenna watched with a cruel smile curling over her angular face.

"I think not," she hissed. "The princesses can stay in their groves. Let them hide there while they may."

The Starwife ceased her coughing and stared at her handmaiden as though she had gone mad. "What–what say you?" she stammered, and for the first time she beheld her servant's true nature.

"This night, the old regime of twig and leaf will end," Morwenna snarled. "No more shall the land of Greenreach be isolated from the world. A most glorious new power shall emerge to seize control, and its mighty reign shall stretch unto eternity."

The old squirrel's eyes grew wide with horror. "What moon-kissed fancy is this?" she cried. "Hearken to what you say." But the poison had done its deadly work, and a vicious spasm seared through her.

Morwenna unclasped the brooch at her throat and removed the cloak from her shoulders. "Long have I toiled over this," she declared turning the garment about to display what was hidden within.

The Starwife fell back against her pillow, racked in the most severe agony. Blood was in her mouth, yet as she stared at her handmaiden she forgot all pain and knew only fear.

The inside of the cloak was a black tapestry, and the scenes it depicted were vile and repugnant. A malevolent light burned in Morwenna's heavily lidded eyes. "Many were the nights I labored," she whispered, "and into the very fibers I did weave spells of smothering and silence, charms that will never yield and enchantments so great that no other power can penetrate them."

"I–I do not understand!" the Starwife cried in her anguish. "For what purpose have you done this?"

Morwenna emitted a strange high laugh and whirled the cloak around her. "Why, to cover the Starglass!" she hooted. "Then will its strength fail and its might withdraw from our borders. The barriers that you raised shall be cast down by me!"

"No!" the Starwife wailed, but even as she tried to call the guards, the pain in her chest grew too great, and her voice died in her throat.

Morwenna stared at the dying squirrel, who was gasping and choking like a stranded fish. "Now you have drunk from the cup of my ambition," she spat venomously. "To me it seems sweet, but I fear you have not found it so. Speed to the Green!" And with that, she strode to the door.

"Quickly," she called to the guards outside, "my mistress is most unwell. Run to the herbmaster and bring him hither. Hurry you both!"

The guards glanced fearfully at her and peered beyond to where the ancient squirrel sat stricken and contorted upon the chair. Dropping their spears, the pair went scurrying down the stairs as fast as their legs could take them.

The treacherous handmaiden chuckled darkly. "Let the herbmaster come—it will be too late," but now to make use of the time and the unguarded way that had been left open to her.

A narrower flight of steps rose to the right, and she wasted not a moment. This was the sacred stair, and, at its end, in the very crown of the Hallowed Oak, was the Chamber of the Starglass.

The room was a perfect circle, yet it was dark—no lamp burned with silver flame, and no window let in the moonlight. But from the center of the chamber, something shimmered and pulsed. Here was the heart of Greenreach and the secret power behind the might of the Starwives—the Starglass.

It was a disc of smooth black glass set within a wooden frame into which mysterious signs and devices had been crudely inscribed long, long ago. Inside was locked the wisdom of the heavens, and only the one who held the Starwifeship could command and wield it.

Morwenna entered the dim chamber, her vile heart pounding. Slowly, she crept toward the center of the room, where the Starglass rested upon an elaborate table. It was as wide as she was high, and for a moment she doubted if her cloak would cover it. But, no, she had made certain that the measurements were precise, many years ago when first she plotted and schemed.

Breathlessly, she stood beside the great disc and gazed upon its glimmering surface.

Although there were no windows in the chamber, the whole of Greenreach was reflected in the Starglass. In the center was the hill, and there were the groves and the ring of lesser trees. There the green sward stretched down to the great river and here, the borders of the great forest began.

Morwenna steeled herself and unfurled the cloak she had spent so long devising. Then, with a sweep of her arm, she cast it over the Starglass and a horrible blackness filled the chamber.

At once the peace of the night was disturbed. The enchantments were failing, melting and dispersing from the unguarded borders. Strange noises filled the air, and the doom of Greenreach was assured.

In her chair, the Starwife wept, sensing the downfall of her realm. A cold wind now tore through the groves, plucking the blossom from the boughs–all was ending.

Sobbing, she clutched at her throat, where her palm touched something cold. With a frail cry, the dying squirrel's heart dared to beat with hope. Morwenna had made a mistake.

Grasping the chair arms, she urgently dragged herself forward and tumbled to the floor. Desperate seconds flew by as she gathered whatever strength remained. The blood thumped in her temples and the poison blistered through her, devouring her insides and consuming her soul like a rapacious cancer.

But the Starwife was not done yet. Inch by inch, she crawled across the floor, hauling herself to the open window, where she clutched at the sill and her wasted arm raised her body until she leaned against the wall and stared at the world outside.

A dark cloud had covered the moon, and the hill was steeped in shadow. Terrible voices clamored in the night, screaming throughout the sky and striking terror into those on the ground. An unspeakable evil was brewing, and, as the Starwife gazed about her realm, she knew it was too late.

With a deafening rush of wings, the huge cloud began to disperse. A vast swarm of bats came swooping down in a gigantic phalanx, and their bloodcurdling cries tore through the tormented darkness.

"No," the Starwife wept. "Morwenna–why have you done this? You have betrayed us all!"

In a great, triangular formation, the pouch bombers came. Spiraling out of the sky, they dived swift and deadly. Each wore a leather harness, attached to which were six pouches containing the terrible fire eggs. Only the most agile and steadfast of Moonriders were selected to carry these lethal weapons of war– for one ill-considered move would prove fatal.

Upon their wings, two ovals were painted, encased in flame. For in the pouches they carried were two small eggs, and each contained a different but volatile powder. When the shells were broken and the compounds mingled, the result was catastrophic.

"The flame of victory is with us!" the bats shrieked as they plunged expertly between the branches of the trees.

The arms of the Starwife buckled, and she collapsed on the sill of the window as she saw the first of the pouches being torn from the harness.

Down it plummeted, whizzing through the air until it hit the ground.

An almighty explosion rocked the green hill, and a ball of crimson flame blasted upward.

A single tear rolled down the Starwife's wrinkled face as she witnessed the end of her blissful realm.

Another fiery tumult split the darkness, and hundreds of panic-stricken voices shrieked in alarm.

One after another the fire eggs erupted, and their dazzling flames blossomed like deadly flowers about the Hallowed Oak. The birch tree of the outer ring caught fire, and the glare of the blaze made it seem as though a vengeful and bloody morning had dawned. From the main entrance of the oak tree, a stream of guards and sentries came running, bearing spears and shields. Out of the lesser trees, other folk fled. Homes were burning, and a number of the terrified squirrels swooned in the heat and were trapped by the eager blaze.

"The bats!" they shrieked. "The bats have come!"

Confusion and panic were the squirrels' undoing. Too long had they trusted in the strength of their queen and the barriers she had woven. In their darkest dreams, they had never feared assault—but now it was happening all around, and nobody was ready or knew what to do.

The pouch bombers soared in a wide circle before coming in for a second attack.

Squirrel guards hurled their spears, but every weapon missed its mark as the bats swerved and dodged aside. Another volley of the fire eggs was released, and on the ground the chaos was absolute.

Two pouch bombs exploded in one of the sacred groves, and a thunderous storm of flame ripped through the trees as though they were parchment. A fierce orange glow lit the heavens as the hilltop blazed and palls of dense black smoke flooded into the sky.

"Stand and face them!" cried the royal guards to the others who ran blindly by. But a madness had seized the folk of Greenreach, and their wits had left them. Everything was burning now, and red flames dripped from ancient boughs, singeing the earth and shriveling the grasses. Only the Hallowed Oak remained untouched, a pinnacle of sanity amid the crackling uproar that raged around it.

From the inferno that roared uncontrollably within the groves, seven smoldering figures came staggering. Through plumes of billowing smoke and clouds of hot ash, the surviving royal princesses stumbled—their parched mouths unable to cry for the five sisters they had left behind. On scorched knees they fell as the fires consumed the glades and bowers where once the spirit of the Green had walked.

The pouch bombers glided over the devastation. Their part was done, and they laughed, cheering and applauding each other's efforts. Then, in one graceful movement, the formation veered away, up to where the others were waiting.

Resplendent in their screechmasks, the Knights of the Moon had seen it all. Their shielded eyes had witnessed the destruction of the Blessed Hill, and their hearts were nearly bursting with excitement. Impatiently, they hovered in the air, biting back the urge to fall upon their enemies. But now the time had come. As the triumphant pouch bombers flew by, their brethren threw back their armored heads and gave a fearsome shout.

Down swooped the ferocious generals, and the captains screamed after them. As one immense shadow, the bat host dived upon the burning realm with the talons of their gauntlets stretched wide and ready. The lethal blades sliced through the choking fumes, glittering from the fierce heats, and the bright arcs of light scored the sky.

The squirrels who saw them quailed; now all hope was lost. Terrible screams drowned the noise of the blazing trees as the first of the generals came hurtling among them.

Rohgar, with Slaughtermaw upon his head, fanned out his wings and hurtled over the shrieking squirrels. The talons of his gauntlets raked through four of the filthy vermin, and his bellowing laughter boomed out over the sloping lawns. A guard with an upraised spear challenged the huge noctule as he raced between two crackling trees, but Rohgar's gauntlets flashed out, and the foul creature fell dead to the ground.

Everywhere, the captains and their winged armies were slaying the abominable tree rats. Screechmasks turned blood red as the slaughter increased, and gore rained down from the vicious talons.

The squirrels were powerless to resist. Already vanquished by the nightmare of the fire eggs, they were no match for this more savage onslaught. The flying demons were unstoppable–nothing escaped their vigilance. The shields of the guards were slashed in two, and any who tried to fight were cruelly dealt with. Several bats would attack a fleeing victim, plucking him from the hill and bearing him into the sky, only to let him fall to a grisly death.

From her bedchamber, the Starwife's eyes drank in the monstrous spectacle. More deadly than the poison was this to her, yet she could not wrench her gaze from what was unfolding below her window. The heat from the blazing groves was unbearable, and the fur on her face was scorched.

"So it is over," she muttered slowly. No tears glistened in her eyes, for the night was beyond emotion now. There was but one meager chance left, one last way to cheat her enemies.

Clasping the amulet around her neck, the ancient squirrel closed her eyes and poured out her waning strength.

About the Blessed Hill, the carnage continued and death screams echoed across the great river.

*   *   *

In the distance, London slept. The barons snored in their solars, and the pages slumbered in the halls. In the kitchens the serfs sweltered by the hearth, and the dogs twitched and dreamed in the courtyards.

The horses dozed in the stables, their hot breath steaming in the sharp air. Nearby, the groom buried his face deeper into the hay and murmured grumpily to himself. Miles from Greenreach, the city was calm and still—but not all were lost in peaceful drowse.

The mews was warm and dark. A slant of moonlight slid through the poorly secured shutter, but none of the birds of prey who rested upon their perches within could see it.

Each wore a hood over its eyes, and their feet were tied to the perch by ribbons of leather. With their covered heads tucked under their wings, two merlins stood silent. Nearby, upon a lower stand, the squire's hobby shifted from one leg to the other. He was an impudent young fellow whose hooked bill always cheeked his elders and betters, but he had naught to fear, for no one could rebuke or punish him while the hoods were in place.

In the driest corner, upon a perch raised higher than the others, a handsome peregrine falcon slept fitfully.

He was the pride of the lord who had trained him, and his equal had never been seen in the city. Nothing could match the falcon's swiftness, and he was justly respected by all, except perhaps the boisterous hobby. Only today that insolent peasant had been boastful about his own plumage and rude about everyone else's. But the peregrine had shown great dignity then, not deigning to engage in vulgar jibes and insults. One day, that upstart would bitterly atone for the looseness of his tongue.

From the merlins, however, the peregrine commanded the greatest fealty, and when they spoke to him, it was in humble and devoted tones. It was a pleasant and comfortable life, flying for fat wood pigeons in the day and roosting in the warm darkness of the mews at night. It had never entered the raptor's head that anything would ever change, and he was not like the hobby, who longed for his freedom and cried for the heathlands when he thought no one was looking.

But this night, the falcon trembled. The black bars of his plumage quivered as a sickening shudder traveled all the way from head to tail. As he startled out of sleep, gorgeous visions of plump rabbits melted into the hood and he swayed giddily upon the perch.

The peregrine cocked his head and listened. Everything seemed quiet, and he wondered what could have awakened him. Probably that irreverent hobby, he thought to himself. Something really must be done about that wretch—it simply wasn't done to flout authority the way he did.

Moving from side to side in agitation, the bird of prey determined to settle the matter tomorrow when they were both being flown. Just a little scare would suffice to do the trick—plucking the nauseating pest from the air and throttling him would be most beneficial to them both. With this happy prospect in mind the falcon settled himself, and little by little his head drooped on to his chest once more.

Suddenly, he was bolt upright. Unfurling his powerful wings and shaking his primary feathers, he squawked his annoyance.

At once, the other birds blinked inside their hoods and were awake.

A terrible feeling of urgency and fear had overwhelmed their leader's heart–summoning and compelling him to act. Somewhere, he was needed; somewhere, a desperate struggle was taking place. The bird cried in dismay, beating his wings and straining at the jesses that held him.

"What ails our lord?" the merlins chirruped, blindly twisting their heads in surprise.

"Poor old stripeypants!" tittered the hobby. "Perhaps he'd like a lullaby to soothe him?"

"Be still!" the merlins cried. "Repent thy insolent words, knave!"

The hobby jiggled and preened himself. "Pooh!" he muttered outrageously.

The merlins recoiled and began gabbling in the direction of the peregrine.

But the great bird was oblivious to all that was said, so anxious was he to escape. His expansive wings thrust at the air, and the perch rocked alarmingly. And then, something strange began to happen. The tethers that held the falcon's feet moved as if invisible hands had clutched them. Slowly at first, the knots began to slip and were gradually untied by this unseen force.

With a tremendous, shrill yell, the peregrine rejoiced. His feet were free, and he immediately tore the hood from his head.

The other birds squealed and trilled in fright. What was happening?

"Our lord is loose!" the merlins wailed. "Our sovereign is at liberty!"

At this the hobby nearly fainted. "Clemency!" he beseeched.

"Have pity on a poor chick with no sense in its skull. Wound me not! Or if you must, make it quick!"

But the falcon was not listening. His bright yellow eyes gleamed in the moonlight and fixed upon the locked shutters. Then, with one sweep of his wings, he left the perch and flew around the mews in a frustrated temper.

The other birds ducked and cowered as he whirled over their heads; they thought he had gone mad, and all began pleading for their lives.

And then, by the same unseen power, the bolt was drawn back, and with a resounding slam the shutters of the mews were thrown open. The peregrine gave a grim screech, the sound of which made the other raptors quail, and shot out into the night– free at last.

*   *   *

Morwenna hastened from the Chamber of the Starglass and swept down the narrow stairway. All she had ever craved was coming to pass, and her pinched face was wreathed in ghastly mirth. The clamor of battle sang in her ears, and she reveled in the sounds of the dying. None would be left to oppose her suc-cession to the Oaken Throne, and she would be able to take up the Silver Acorn without fear of reprisal. How well the bats did their work, yet once they had served their purpose, they, too, would know the meaning of betrayal. Morwenna had other allies, and no one could have guessed where her true allegiance lay.

A dark and glorious future was opening before the faithless handmaiden, and, as she came to her mistress's bedchamber, she thrilled at what would come to pass.

Morwenna barged inside–but at once her dreams were snatched away. There, upon the sill of the window, a great falcon sat, and, standing before him–swaying and nearly spent–the Starwife held up the symbol of her high office and entrusted it into the bird's massive talons.

Morwenna screamed in rage and leaped forward, her paws reaching for the silver amulet that dangled from the peregrine's claws.

"Fly!" the Starwife commanded. "Bear it to safety. Let no other claim it!"

There was a beating of powerful wings. Morwenna dragged the ancient squirrel out of her way and lurched at the Acorn, but too late. The falcon left the window, and in seconds he was out of sight, leaving Greenreach far behind.

In her fingers, Morwenna clutched only feathers. Without the amulet she was nothing, and she stared at the scenes of burning and slaughter that still raged below and appeared as one turned to stone.

"Drink deep of this cup," the Starwife's cracked voice mocked her. "All your treachery has been in vain. At the very end, the Acorn has eluded you, and your victory is an empty one."

Morwenna's head twisted from the window, and her countenance was terrible to behold. Her thin lips parted, and a bitter voice came rasping from her throat.

"Too many years have I humbled myself before you!" she hissed. "Too long have I toiled for my own ends to have you cheat me now. This is but the beginning for me. The Acorn will be found, and I shall rule. But for you, vile old hag, it is indeed the end."

Quickly, she drew the dagger from her belt and took a step toward the ancient squirrel. "Now, pay the price!" she cried, and, shrieking with evil laughter, she put her mistress cruelly to death.

Rushing back to the window, Morwenna shouted at the top of her voice. "Rohgar!" she yelled. "Rohgar! Quickly–I command you!"

Taking a step back, she waited a moment, and presently a ferocious screechmask appeared over the sill, followed by the large noctule. With a rush of his leathery wings, he alighted upon the ledge, but the eyes that glared through the slits of Slaughtermaw seethed with hostility and anger.

"Curb thy tongue," he snarled. "The legions of Hrethel are commanded by none but he and the council. It would be tragic indeed should I forget what part thou played this night and give you over to my armies."

But Morwenna was not afraid, and she replied with haughty authority. "Be silent!" she snapped. "Your triumph is not yet assured, and your lord would be most displeased should you fail. Remember, I am in communion with him and have his complete trust."

Rohgar growled at her insolence and shook his wings to show displeasure. This tree rat had an inflated opinion of her own worth; it would be most pleasant to let his gauntlets close about her scrawny neck.

"Hear me!" the squirrel continued before he had the chance to threaten her again. "The Silver Acorn has escaped us! The harridan despatched it before she died—it must be retrieved at all costs!"

A hollow laugh rang within the screechmask. "So!" the bat cried. "The perfidious one has been robbed of her shining bauble. What care I for the loss of your heathen trinkets?"

Morwenna leaned forward, her voice rising to a shriek. "Idiot!" she screamed. "Without the amulet I cannot accede to the Starwifeship, nor can I wield the might of the forces locked in the Starglass. Only with the Acorn about my neck can I undo the spell laid upon your kind and restore your birthright!" She spat the last sentence, and her words had a remarkable effect upon Rohgar.

"What say you?" he bawled. "Tell me where this trinket may be found!"

"Your legions let it slip by," Morwenna snapped back. "Even now a peregrine bears it to some distant place of safety—I know not where. Go find this powerful talisman, Rohgar. Take a host of your brethren and return the prize to me–then shall prophecy and insight be given back to you."

The bat lashed his wings and circled over the hill. Furiously, he called to his captains and yelled his commands. Like a black mist, the bats rose from Greenreach, leaving behind their wounded and dying victims and, in an enormous sweep across the smoke-filled sky, the desperate chase began.

Morwenna moved toward the doorway, glancing with contempt at the body of her late mistress. The stairs outside the bedchamber were deserted, and not a sound issued up from the main hall. All the guards were dead, barbarically slain upon the hillside, and only a few terrified serfs remained huddled under tables or lay trembling in storerooms.

Descending the narrow steps, Morwenna rubbed her paws together, and her tail flicked with agitation. If Rohgar thought she would place all her trust in him, then he was a greater fool than she had anticipated. Her alliance with the legions of Hrethel was only temporary, and, with a wicked grin glowering over her face, Morwenna determined to send her own, more sinister, messenger to retrieve the Silver Acorn.

ALDERTIDE

Far away, amid the trackless and dangerous forests, a bright dawn gently edged into the pale, clear sky. It was a beautiful spring morning and surprisingly warm for the alder month. Here, the unruly tangle of the wild wood became ordered and the grass grew thick and green, free of scrub and nettles. Within the borders of this oasis of calm, the trees flourished straight and tall, attended and cared for by those who dwelt there.

Here then, the second noble house of black squirrels had long ago made their home. Coll Regalis–the Hazel Realm–it was called, for the hazel was regarded as the fount of all knowledge, and the one who ruled that land wore a bronze fruit of that tree about her neck.

Ninnia was her name, and her subjects loved her, for she was wise beyond mortal minds, and by her counsel and guidance the colony had protected its borders for many years. No magic defended the Hazel Realm, for only their cousins in Greenreach possessed such power. This land was kept free from harm by a constant vigil. Many sentries were posted near the untamed forest's edge, and the watch was never neglected.

Today, however, all thoughts of the dark were banished. It was Alder Day, a date high in the squirrel calendar, and wonderful festivities had been planned.

The warm rays of the morning sun gilded the avenue of trees that led to the circle of nine hazels. Upon the green lawns an excited and merry crowd had begun to gather. The celebrations were to begin early, and already those entertainers who still dared to travel were arriving.

Striding through the dewy grass came all manner of outlandish folk, and the children of Coll Regalis rushed to greet them, dancing around each newcomer as he strode into the central clearing.

Stalls were swiftly erected, with colorfully striped canopies and ribbons flying in the fragrant breeze. The merchants arranged their wares in pretty displays and called to old friends as they waited for the festivities to officially commence.

Three jolly red squirrels sat down and began lacing themselves onto tall stilts. It was not long before they were tottering loftily through the crowds, giggling and pushing one another, while those below tried to leap up and catch their tails. A fire-eating weasel cursed his luck when he discovered that his torches were damp and refused to light, while a traveling band of acrobatic voles were practicing the Daredevil Pyramid and getting it hopelessly wrong.

Through the thronging multitude, a strange figure slowly wound his way. It was a tall stoat. A jester's red-and-yellow headdress was pulled snugly over his ears, and the bells that hung from the three dropping points jingled sweetly as he went. Behind him the stoat pulled a garishly painted cart that contained all his tricks and props, and as he approached the clearing, he hummed humorous ditties to himself.

High above, from the branches of the central oak, a young squirrel maiden looked down, intoxicated with the glamour and delight of it all. She was a lovely creature with ebony fur and large brown eyes, and her dark hair fell in long tresses about her shoulders. She scampered from bough to bough to see what new joys she could discover.

This was Ysabelle, daughter of the Lady Ninnia and the Lord

44

Cyllinus, and never had the forest been graced by such beauty as she possessed.

The strains of a happy tune drifted up from below as the musicians practiced. A flute piped the loudest, and Ysabelle found her feet tapping to the melody, then began dancing over the branches.

"M'lady!" squeaked a nervous voice. "M'lady, come away from there! Oooh, it's so dangerous! You might break your neck– I can't bear to look!"

A mouse had peered out from a curtained window in the trunk of the tree, and her small paws were thrown over her face.

"Don't be silly, Griselda!" Ysabelle laughed as she pirouetted on a slender branch. "I'm in no danger. I have nothing to fear– the height does not scare me."

"Well it do me, M'lady," the mouse complained, her eyes stealing a peek at the clearing below them. She winced and drew back inside. "'Tain't right for one such as I to be so far up–and 'tain't seemly for you to be cavorting so."

Griselda had looked after Ysabelle since the day she was born and fussed a great deal over her charge. Red squirrels were the usual choice for nursemaids, but, in her wisdom, the Lady Ninnia had chosen a mouse instead to care for her daughter. Griselda was a worried little body, prone to fretting about the smallest detail.

She was a plump field mouse, and her chestnut hair was always hidden in a large cap of white linen. The frills of this shaded her eyes and tickled her whiskers, so she was continually blowing at the irksome thing from the corners of her mouth, but it never entered her head to change the cap. She was a stickler for tradition, and although those of the black squirrels were not her own, she zealously defended and adhered to them. This was the cap of a nursemaid, and it was her duty and privilege to wear it, so wear it she jolly well would, however inconvenient.

45

Ysabelle traced out a dainty little dance in time to the brisk music, and the mousemaid stamped her foot in irritation.

"You stop that at once!" she demanded. "Why, with your hair all loose and askew, what will folk think? That I'm not fit to wait on you—that's what! Is it your intent to shame me, M'lady?"

The young squirrel stopped dancing and laughed. "Oh, Griselda!" she said with a grin. "You win. I've no wish to cause you shame. You do worry so; I'm quite sure no one thinks you are a bad nurse."

"That's as may be, but you never can tell what nastiness some folk's tongues is capable of." Griselda glanced at the ground again and nearly wilted with fright. "Ooh, do come in, M'lady," she implored, puffing at the brim of her cap. "Makes my head all squiggly, it do, looking down there."

Ysabelle capered over the branches and climbed in at the window. "It's such a marvelous day—to think that this year I join the alder maids."

The mouse pulled her charge away from the hazardous opening and into the room. It was a cozy place containing two beds, the smaller being Griselda's. Fine tapestries were draped over the walls, some of them worked by Ysabelle herself in those tedious winter evenings that had passed, and clean rushes were strewn over the floor.

The maid extracted a twig from the squirrel's bush tail. "You won't be going nowhere, M'lady," she clucked, "not till you've braided your locks and made yourself decent. In front of all them folk, I ask you, and most of them strangers, too!"

Quickly, Ysabelle twined her long hair in nimble fingers until two braids hung down her back. Then, with a little help from Griselda, she coiled these upon her head and sprinkled some water over her face.

The mouse scrutinized her critically, smoothing and patting with her small pink paws before she would let Ysabelle go.

"Did you see the stilt walkers?" her charge asked. "They really are so clever."

"Tomfools, the lot!" Griselda tartly replied. "If they wanted to be so tall, they should have got themselves born saplings. There, you're presentable now, M'lady. Get you on down."

Ysabelle rushed for the door, then halted, came running back, gave the mouse a grateful kiss, and dashed down the stairs.

"Don't you forget any of your steps, mind!" Griselda called after her. "I'll be along shortly!"

Outside, the dew had melted from the grass, and the early spring flowers had thrown back their heads to release their perfume to the air.

A merrytotter, or seesaw, had been set up under the shade of one of the nine hazels, and children were lining up for a ride on it.

Beneath a fluttering canopy, two large chairs had been arranged, and around them many courtiers scurried, preparing for the arrival of their lord and lady. Some were busy raising banners and hoisting the standard of the Hazel Realm to the top of the central oak, while others made certain that everything was ready for the all-important dance.

By now the voles had managed to perfect their act and, to the wonder of the crowds, were leaping about the lawns and flipping each other into the air to great applause.

Winter finally seemed to be over, and the subjects of the Lady Ninnia had determined not to miss a moment of the revels. From stall to stall they scampered, visiting each new entertainment with wonder and delight.

Only when a horn blew was their attention diverted from the amusements, for this was the signal for the main part of the morning to begin.

From the central oak, a procession of squirrels came, and those in the clearing parted to let them through. Out marched the counselors—the four advisers to the sovereign. All were old, black squirrels with somber expressions upon their proud faces. They

were led by the eldest and most learned of their number–
Godfrey Gelenos. One of his many duties was to teach the young
princess the histories and customs of the land, and he never went
anywhere without a book or manuscript tucked under his arm.
Nothing gave him greater pleasure than to spend long hours with
his nose pressed against the pages of some scholarly document,
and it was rumored that even the Lady Ninnia had bowed to his
judgment on more than one occasion.

Following the humorless-looking advisers came nine maidens who tried to be serious but kept breaking into fits of giggles.
Ysabelle was among them, and it was she who led the laughter.
Behind these came a red squirrel carrying a cushion of purple
velvet in his paws, upon which a number of alder wands were
laid, and the bearer positively strutted along to be so honored
this day. The crowd cheered when they saw him, and he winked
proudly at his friends.

Then the noise subsided to an expectant babble as many
guards paraded from the entrance, their swords brandished in
the air, heralding the arrival of their monarch.

So came the Lady Ninnia, with the Lord Cyllinus at her side.

She was an elegant squirrel whose serene face held a time-
less beauty that nothing could wither. Her features were delicate
as any bloom, and, covering her ears, she wore a veil of some fine
gossamerlike material that floated on the air as lightly as the
strands of a spider's web. Every step she took was gracefully
majestic, and all who saw her bowed or curtsied. Hanging
around the lady's neck, a bronze hazelnut gleamed in the early
sunshine, and upon her long, tapering fingers she wore rings of
silver and gold set with precious gems.

At the canopy, the procession came to a halt. The Lady
and her consort took their seats, and the counselors assumed
places beside them. Then the wand bearer came forward,
pointed his toe, and made a perfect bow, offering the cushion
up to her.

The Lady Ninnia gave a warm smile and took the nine alder wands in her hand.

"My thanks," she said to the red squirrel. "'Twas expertly done."

The bearer blushed to the ears and burbled something inaudible before stepping aside.

The lady's gaze lingered on him for a moment before turning to the maidens who were impatiently waiting nearby. "Aldertide has worked its charm once again," she observed, glancing at each. "In my youth, I, too, was an alder maid, and great was my excitement that morning when first I danced. Rejoice in the ceremony, thrill to every note that the fiddlers play, for the dance shall lead you into adulthood. Every step guides you to a new life; just as the trees that you waken begin the year afresh, so, too, shall you bloom." With that her eyes rested tenderly upon her daughter.

Then Ninnia addressed the rest of her subjects. "The life of the trees is sacred to us," she declared, "and by them we measure our seasons and years. Few occasions can rival the joy that Alder Day brings–for with it comes the rebirth. Let us all now celebrate another dawning. Begin the music!"

At once, the fiddlers struck up the alder tune, and the pipers followed their lead. This was the cue for the maidens to step up to the thrones and receive their wands. When this was done, they all curtsied then proceeded to dance in a line toward the avenue of trees.

The first tree that the maidens reached was the birch, and, with laughter in their voices, they raised their wands and shouted to the indwelling spirit. "Awake! Awake!" they sang. "Thy sleep is ended."

Then, just to make sure, they danced round the trunk and beat the bark with the wands, crying, "Have no fear, for Spring is come! Put out thy leaves, oh sleepy one!"

After that, they danced to the next tree, which was the mountain ash, and repeated the performance.

49

Everybody came to watch this age-old ritual; even the trades-folk left their stalls, and it was the entertainers' turn to be enthralled. Only the voles appeared to continue their act, but they were actually balancing on each other's shoulders to obtain a better view.

The dancers visited each tree in the avenue before returning to the nine hazels, where a small fire had been lit, and into this they threw their wands. A great clamor of cheering and applause burst out, hats were thrown into the blue sky, and the air was shrill with whistles as the other festivities resumed.

Breathlessly, Ysabelle ran back to her parents, and they both held their arms out to her.

"My dearest," the Lady Ninnia cried, "how proud you have made me this morning."

Ysabelle held on to her tightly before giving her father a hug.

The Lord Cyllinus stroked his daughter's hair and kissed her forehead lovingly. He was a quiet, thoughtful squirrel, head of a house of princes, and he adored his child more than anything in the land.

"Did you see me, Father?" she asked. "How was my dancing? Did it compare to the others?"

With paw on heart, the lord had to admit that he had not even noticed that there had been any other dancers. "You were as the sun and they the stars." He told her. "You did outshine them all. Why, I doubt if there is a soul present who was able to take his eyes from you."

Ysabelle gurgled with pleasure. "I did stumble and falter on three occasions at least!" she chuckled. "But what a per-fect morning this is. Have you ever seen such a day before? Everyone is so happy—if I could, I would wish for it to last forever."

At this, the Lady Ninnia glanced at her husband and laid her paw lightly on his arm. "I think our daughter yearns to join the merrymaking," she said, "and at Aldertide a princess may do as she pleases. Let her roam among our subjects and enjoy the entertainments."

Cyllinus gave her a doubtful look, then relented when he saw the eagerness on his daughter's face. "Off with you, my Belle," he told her. "Go partake of the revels."

Ysabelle kissed him. "Do you think the stilt walkers would let me attempt to match their skill?" she asked.

Her father nodded. "Who could refuse you aught?" he smiled. "I know that I cannot—go child."

So into the joyful crowds Ysabelle disappeared. There was so much to see and to do; only a fraction had she spied from the branches of the oak, and her heart beat excitedly in her breast.

The delicious smells of the pie stalls now mingled with the scents of the flowers. All the fruits of last autumn's preserving jars were there: apple tarts, blackberry buns, pear sponges, plum pies, walnut scones, and a dozen varieties of seed cake. These sumptuous delicacies were all on display, and many squirrels munched contentedly, while others stood entranced at the antics of the entertainers.

A hedgehog had impaled hundreds of colored ribbons upon her spines and was flitting around a cleared space with the bright streamers billowing behind as she whirled and capered. It was not a very successful act, however, for the hedgehog was quite plump, and her steps rather ungainly, deteriorating at times into bizarre, ducklike waddles. The folk who watched were not sure whether they ought to laugh, and many politely covered their grins with their paws. One small squirrel was heartily tucking into a damson tartlet when the prickly performer tripped over one of the ribbons and tumbled head over heels into the audience. The poor squirrel nearly choked as fragments of damson and pastry exploded from his mouth when uncontrollable laughter consumed him.

Nearby, the troupe of voles were having more success. The Daredevil Pyramid had been completed twice already, and now they were encouraging some of the onlookers to take part in the act. Ysabelle admired them tremendously and wondered if she would be picked.

"Are there any among you kind and goodly people," cried one of the voles as he balanced upon a wooden ball, "just one who dares to attempt the simplest of our heroic feats?"

Before Ysabelle could raise her paw, someone grabbed her arm and tuttered crossly in her ear.

"What are you thinking of, M'lady?" squeaked Griselda at her side. "Think of your position—the royal houses can't partake of such frivolities. Why, one day—and may it be far off—you'll have to follow your mother and govern these folk. How would you command their respect if they remember you acting the fool? I never ever did hear of such a thing!"

"But 'tis only in fun," Ysabelle argued. "Surely there's no harm in merriment?"

The mousemaid brushed the floppy brim of her cap from her eyes and huffed coldly. "Such things aren't for you!" she reminded her. "Why, it might be one of your irresponsible red cousins I was talking to, instead of the future Lady of the Hazel. In truth, I am shocked."

The young squirrel knew it was pointless to continue. "Very well," she relented. "I will behave, and in the solemn, tedious way that befits my station."

Griselda brightened immediately. "Thank you, M'lady," she said. "Now, we'll have no more talk of joining the revels—observing only shall be enjoyment enough. Besides, I do think some rain is coming—then will this nonsense be washed away.

Ysabelle looked at the sky. The mouse was right: a great storm cloud was rolling over the forest roof toward them, but it still seemed many hours distant, and she pleaded to be allowed to enjoy the morning while she could.

"Oh, very well," the maid relented, "but remember thy

conduct, M'lady. I know! Come see the jester. I did hear he is most amusing."

Through the milling throng the mouse led her mistress, passing by many of the stalls Ysabelle had wanted to visit.

There, a trio of sparrows chirped, aided by the lilting voice of a speckled thrush; next to them, the fire-eating weasel had begun plying his second trade and was busily telling fortunes. Past the acorn toss Griselda bustled, squirming between the gathered folk until they came to where many creatures were laughing.

In the midst of them, the stoat jester had set up his pitch. Sitting upon his outlandish cart, he had been performing a comical play with the aid of humorous and insulting puppets.

A cruel caricature of a black squirrel was in his right paw, while in his left a red squirrel jiggled and twitched.

The assembled onlookers were applauding warmly as Griselda and Ysabelle squeezed in the front.

The puppets were put away, and the stoat took something else from his cart. It was an inflated rat's bladder tied to the end of a stick, and he leaped onto the grass with the ridiculous-looking object clutched in his paws.

"Who am I?" he cried, pulling a sour and serious expression.

"A jester!" one of the red squirrels piped up.

The stoat glared at him with feigned anger and began beating the unfortunate creature about the head with the bladder.

"Is there naught inside thy noggin?" he demanded. "What? Do they not teach thee thy lessons here?"

A gleeful murmur issued from the crowd as they recognized the impudent impression.

"Why, 'tis Master Godfrey!" they giggled. "He's Master Godfrey!"

The jester strode about the cleared space, bashing the noses of those who sniggered, while all the time the daylight grew dim as the storm cloud moved swiftly through the sky. "Verily, 'tis I," he announced, "Godfrey Gelenos—prime counselor of the Lady

Ninnia. Yet, why do you laugh so? Are all your wits so dull? Do you all have need of some sense? Shall I knock it into you?"

Someone blew a raspberry, and the stoat set about him at once, to the great amusement of everyone else—everyone except Griselda, that is.

"Scandalous," she said with pursed lips. "'Tis vulgarity of the lowest sort. Come, M'lady—I was wrong to bring you hither. The fellow's nothing but rude."

Unfortunately for the mouse, the stoat heard her, and he spun round to face the owner of this dissenting voice.

"What have we here?" he yelled, throwing the bladderstick behind him. "A mouseling, I believe. Come, my dearest little nibbler—let us dance a jig together."

Before Griselda could stop him, the stoat plucked her from Ysabelle's side and whirled her round in a mad dance. The mouse shrieked, and the laughter of the audience increased tenfold. Round and round the jester spun her, ignoring her pleas for mercy. There was nothing she could do except trot and caper as best she could, for her awful partner was strong and the jig so fast. Then her cap fell off and landed on the head of a cheeky youngster, who ran away and hurled it into the branches of a tree.

And then, when Griselda thought she would faint, the dreadful stoat stopped the dance and jumped to one side, leaving her lurching and lumbering in a wobbly circle, dazed like a drunken rat.

"Oh, my!" the mouse sobbed once the world had stopped spinning. "Oh, my! I feel terrible." She rounded on the jester, ignoring the laughter that thundered in her burning ears, and scolded him crossly. "How dare you!" she shrieked. "Never have I been so ill used!" But the insolent wretch only smiled, and poor Griselda had to salvage what little dignity she had left and escape as quickly as she could.

With her head in the air and her tail erect, the mousemaid stomped from the dreadful scene and went in search of her cap.

Ysabelle's ribs were aching. She felt sorry for Griselda, but it had been very funny. She looked back at the jester, and, to her surprise, found that his eyes were upon her. For a moment, Ysabelle feared she would be next in the crazy dance, but the stoat merely made a swift bow that set the bells of his headdress jingling.

"I crave your pardon," he said humbly. "Methinks I outraged your companion. 'Twas all in the name of mirth, I assure you—no harm was meant."

"I'll be glad to tell her that," Ysabelle replied. "But tell me, who shall I say apologized? What is your name?"

The jester raised both his arms, and suddenly there was a blue acorn in his left paw. With a wave of his right, a yellow and a red appeared beside it, and he began juggling them at once.

"Wendel, my mother did name me," he said. "Wendel Maculatum. A traveling duncefellow am I, and accomplished fool—never have I met such a simple gowk as the one who stands before you. From the pot of learning I did but take a sip, and found it so bitter to my taste that I did spit out what I supped. Beneath my tinkling hat, not an ounce of brains do I possess, and that I like full well. My life is a happy one, and for nothing would I exchange it."

No sooner had he spoken than one of the acorns dropped onto his head with a loud *crack*. The jester let out a strange cry, allowed the other acorns to fall to the ground, then did a spectacular backward somersault, landing on his knees with his arms outstretched.

"So I beg thee again, mistress," he called with a laugh, "tell thy companion that Wendel is awash with regret for the indignity he did cause her."

"I shall indeed," smiled Ysabelle, not believing his remorse for an instant. "And now I had better find her."

She gave the stoat one last smile, then made her way through the crowd.

Suddenly, a shrill blast echoed over the lawns. The music died on the piper's lips, and the dancers staggered to a standstill as the alarm trumpeted its warning.

All festivities ceased and everyone held their breath—only the direst emergency would cause the border guards to give such an alarm, and many hearts fluttered fearfully.

The face of every creature slowly turned heavenward, and there, in the middle of the bright clear sky, a vast black storm cloud blotted out the morning sun, and everywhere was plunged into an icy gloom.

Upon her throne, the Lady Ninnia stared at the immense blackness overhead, and its shade seemed to enter her spirit. It was a strange, dark mass—not like a real cloud at all. "Green spare us!" she whispered when she realized the truth.

"What manner of evil vapor is that?" asked her husband. "How can it move across the firmament so swiftly when only the slightest of breezes blow?"

But Ninnia had risen to her feet and spoke quickly to her counselors. "Hurry!" she commanded. "Find my daughter—take her to safety at once!"

Master Godfrey stared at her questioningly, then he, too, realized the peril that had come upon them. Without further hesitation, the prime counselor gave a yelp and barged into the silent and watchful crowd.

Worried murmurs now hissed from everyone's lips, and the Lady Ninnia called to her subjects in a voice filled with urgency and dread. "Beware!" she cried. "Run for cover! Save yourselves! That is no cloud—it is a host of bats! The forces of Hrethel are upon us!"

At that her people screamed, and panic seized them. In their haste to escape, families were separated, stalls were blundered into, and pies trampled underfoot. With frightened howls, the voles scurried to bolt holes, and the beribboned hedgehog dived under the flimsy shelter of a torn canopy.

Only the black squirrels remained upon the lawns, their eyes fixed upon the bats high above.

"Never have so many Knights of the Moon crossed our borders," the Lord Cyllinus muttered under his breath, "yet why do they not attack? Why remain up there? Are they waiting—toying with us to increase our fear?"

His wife touched the bronze amulet about her neck, as if searching for an answer. "I cannot tell," she answered, shaking her head, "but does it not appear to you that as yet the enemy is unaware of us? I doubt if they even know we are here. Remember that the sun confounds them; no bat goes to war in the daylight."

Cyllinus dragged his eyes from the great cloud and cast about the confusion that rampaged over the lawns. "Where is Gelenos with our Belle?" he asked. "I pray they are safe within the oak."

"Behold!" Ninnia cried. "See, my husband—the winged beasts are already engaged in battle."

Cyllinus glanced upward once more and, sure enough, it seemed that the bats were mobbing some other creature of the air. Now, the sounds of hideous voices were heard over the Hazel Realm, and tiny points of dazzling light flashed within that dark mass as countless steel talons executed their deadly work.

Alone, amid the rushing clamor of terrified squirrels and mice, Ysabelle stood. Her large brown eyes gazed intently at the horror above, and her ears caught the furious beating of many wings. She had heard hundreds of tales about bats, how wicked and cruel they were, but she never dreamed that she would see one. Now, thousands of the unclean nightmares were directly above her. A wintry cold seeped into her muscles as she faced this terrible spectacle, and the unnatural twilight grew deeper all around.

The immense host was gripped in a frenzy of hate and anger. They thrashed their wings and struck out wildly with their gauntlets—nothing was going to cheat them of their birthright, and though the sun bewildered and blinded them, they had pursued the quarry far and wide, and now he was theirs.

A feather drifted from the seething cloud, and the high voices of the Moonriders exulted in triumph—they had conquered, and it was beaten.

Upon the ground, Ysabelle saw a flurry of bloody feathers fall from the shadowy mass, and she shook her head in dismay. What vicious savages those creatures were!

At that moment, the boundary wardens came racing from the borders. Into the clearing they ran with longbows in their grasp.

"Green guide our arrows!" they called, stringing their bows and taking aim.

With a sharp hiss, fifty darts went singing through the sky, plunging deep into the bat swarm.

Ysabelle watched as a dozen Moonriders tumbled from the darkness and were dashed against the trees below.

Another torrent of arrows whistled upward, yet, even as the shafts shot into the vast cloud, something glinted and fell through the air like a glittering stone.

The squirrel maiden stepped forward in wonder as the shining missile came hurtling down, and, before she knew what she was doing, Ysabelle had caught it in her paws.

Trembling, she opened her fist and gazed at the wondrous thing in her palm. There, gleaming in the sunlight, was a Silver Acorn.

Ysabelle gasped, but there was no time to think. For as she raised her eyes from the symbol of the Starwives, the squirrel maiden screamed.

Ysabelle threw up her arms; a stream of crimson rained down, and spatters of hot blood showered upon her.

Shrieking, she leaped away—just as a great shredded mass of feathers came crashing to the ground.

Ysabelle was too horrified to speak; in ghastly tatters, the body of the peregrine lay still upon the blood-dewed grass.

The talons of the bats had been cruelly efficient, and the once proud lord of the air was dead.

Numb with terror, the squirrel maiden stared at it for a moment—then her ears heard—

The bat host was bellowing with rage. Out of the sky, the Knights of the Moon came, the jaws of their screechmasks open wide. Down they dived, their wings folded, plummeting after the body of the falcon, down to where a solitary squirrel stood with the amulet in her fingers.

Ysabelle saw them; she saw the dreadful face of the leader's barbaric helmet draw closer and watched as the blood dripped from the gauntlets that already reached for her.

"Guide our arrows!" cried the sentries as they fired into the rushing enemy.

"Get down!" a voice shouted to Ysabelle. "Get down!"

The squirrel wailed and threw herself upon the ground. Two pairs of talons sliced the empty space where she had stood, and she cold feel the draft of the bat's wings as it raced past.

"Stay there!" the voice shouted.

Ysabelle heard something clattering toward her, but she dared not look up.

Wendel Maculatum, traveling stoat and general ninny, pelted toward the maiden. With the handles of his cart in his paws, he sped to save her. The captains of the infernal swarm were almost upon them. Ysabelle covered her ears, and the jester let out a painful howl as a bitter blade raked through his shoulder.

Hurling his cart forward, Wendel launched himself after.

Ysabelle stared as two rickety wheels skidded to a halt on either side of her. Then, panting for breath and clutching his wound, the stoat dived under the cart.

"Hold on!" he yelled. "'Tis our only chance. They have us!"

The full fury of the bats fell on the jester's cart.

Ysabelle closed her eyes and clutched the underside of the little wagon for dear life. The noise was deafening as the ferocious might of the Moonriders ripped and tore at the painted wood above.

"Why doesn't someone do something?" Ysabelle wept. "Save us, please!"

"Don't you be afeared!" Wendel bawled, trying to sound brave. "Your archers are doing their best."

"Look out!" Ysabelle screamed.

One of the bats was crawling beneath the cart toward them. His screechmask removed, cruel black eyes glared at the pair of them, and he bared his fangs at the squirrel who held the Silver Acorn.

"Aaiiee!" Wendel shrieked. "Keep away, villain!" He kicked out with his feet, struck the bat's jaw, and sent him sprawling against a wheel, where his head cracked on a spoke. The creature slumped in a heap—but others were coming after.

The cart bucked and jolted, tearing the skin from Ysabelle's palms as she vainly tried to hold on.

"It's no use!" she sobbed. "We are lost!"

The stoat winced at the pain in his shoulder, but his eyes were on the bats who steadily crept nearer. "'Tis a sorry end for a jester!" he babbled. "No laughter to see me out!"

Roaring like a thunderstorm, the legions of Moonriders hurled themselves against the cart until it was totally obliterated. It was this that held their full attention, so desperate were they to retrieve the amulet. None paid any heed to the wardens of the Hazel Realm as they let loose volleys of arrows. Even when their brethren fell dead to the ground, they continued to vent their wrath upon the humble little wagon.

From a distance, the Lady Ninnia watched the terrible spectacle with her heart in her mouth. Tears were in both her and her husband's eyes. Their daughter was the focus for that boiling anger, and they were powerless to save her.

"Belle," Cyllinus murmured.

Then the guards of Coll Regalis drew their swords and, with grim faces, charged at the frightful enemy.

So blade and talon clashed. In the deadly combat that ensued, squirrels were slain by screechmask and gauntlet, but many bats were impaled upon spear and sword. The bows of the wardens continued to sing, and the toll of the dead mounted rapidly.

Faced with this unexpected challenge, the bats faltered. Already, the sun dazzled and bewildered them, and they were still weak from the chase. Now, bright swords glared from all sides, mirroring the fierce sunlight in a mesh of blazing steel, and they beheld how many of their number were already dead upon the grass of this strange land.

General Rohgar squinted about him, the talons of his gauntlets gouged deep into the cart, and he snarled within Slaughtermaw. One of his captains shrieked beside him as an arrow plunged deep into his chest. Another Moonrider was struck from behind and tumbled lifeless to the ground. With a furious beating of his wings, Rohgar took to the air and called his brethren to follow.

"Come," he bellowed, "this is not the time! The daystar confounds our senses. Let us withdraw to the darkness of the forest. These morsels can wait till nightfall."

He soared into the blue sky, and, like a plume of black smoke, the rest of his army reared up and followed.

But the boundary wardens continued to shoot, and a great number of retreating Moonriders failed to reach the safety of the dark woods.

The squirrels watched in silence as the host departed, flying in a straggly formation over the treetops until they were lost from sight.

"Ysabelle!" the Lady Ninnia shouted.

Running forward, she pushed through a sea of the wounded and dead to where the jester's cart stood splintered and broken.

Ninnia held her breath as she saw the damage that the Knights of the Moon had wrought—if their talons could do that to wood, she dared not think what horror awaited her.

"Mother?"

61

A meek voice spoke from beneath the wreckage. Ninnia's heart leaped, and she heaved at the cart to lift it.

A strong paw touched her own as Cyllinus joined her, and together they hurled the battered shelter aside.

There, trembling and huddled against the stoat, was Ysabelle.

The young maiden wept and threw her arms about her parents. "It was awful," she cried. "There were so many. Father, we couldn't have held them off any longer. They almost— they almost—"

Several moments passed as the three black squirrels held one another. Behind them, the guards lay down their weapons and offered prayers of thanks, while from the trees and countless bolt holes, other folk nervously ventured.

"Ooh, aah, eeh!" Wendel muttered as he gingerly staggered to his feet. "Never have I faced so unappreciative an audience. 'Tis the first time they truly were after my blood."

Ysabelle wiped her eyes and put out her paws to him. "Mother," she said, "this stoat did save my life. Without him, the bats would certainly have killed me."

Both Ninnia and Cyllinus turned to the jester. He was a sorry sight, and his wound was bleeding badly, yet even in this desperate hour, he looked comical. The red-and-yellow headdress was torn and hung sadly about his face like three drooping ears. He stared at the two squirrels and made a painful bow.

"Majesties," he spluttered.

"Good sir," Ninnia began, "you have saved our beloved daughter. For such a gallant deed, no reward would be enough, yet name what you will and it shall be thine."

"Whatever your heart desires we shall grant," Cyllinus added, "for our Belle is precious to us."

Wendel gaped at them for a second, then gave Ysabelle an impudent wink. "Gracious lady and noble lord," he said with a chuckle in his voice, "tell me—what would a fool do with such a reward? Nay, leave the jester be, let him continue his merry craft, and spoil him not."

"As you so wish," Cyllinus replied, "yet your wounds need attention, and our woodwrights can at least repair your cart. What say you–" He turned to his wife, but she was gazing at their daughter.

Ysabelle held up her paw, and there, shining in her fingers, was the Silver Acorn.

Ninnia touched the bronze hazelnut about her own neck, and the world grew chill once more.

Her husband frowned, and the crowd that had gathered about them gasped in wonder. "What does this mean?" he asked in a whisper. "What omen of disaster is this?"

The Lady Ninnia closed her eyes, and, when she answered, her voice was filled with grief. "Greenreach has fallen," she said.

FAREWELL TO THE HAZEL

Master Godfrey hurried along the corridor and tucked the scrolls he had been studying under his arm. Although the meeting was not due to start just yet, he was anxious to be one of the first there. For many years he had served the Lady Ninnia, but never had such a crisis occurred before–never again would Aldertide hold any joy for the folk of the Hazel Realm. The memory of the morning's events would remain long after he had sped to the Green.

The council chamber was a great room adorned only by the banners of the Five Houses. Two thrones dominated one wall, and before these a series of plain benches were formally arranged. Master Godfrey grunted at the guards outside the entrance and waved them aside as he strode within.

At once he drew himself up and stared about him. The chamber was full. The lord and lady were already seated, and all manner of folk were crammed onto the benches. Sitting on a smaller throne, the young princess sat with her maid, having bathed three times to be rid of the falcon's blood.

"Master Godfrey!" the Lady Ninnia called. "Come, we did delay the meeting for your arrival."

The squirrel cleared his throat and strutted pompously to his place beside the thrones, vexed that he had not been the first to arrive.

His fellow counselors nodded solemnly as he took his position–it was indeed a most grave and dreadful day.

"Did you discover what you sought?" Ninnia asked.

Godfrey patted the scrolls he carried and said that he had.

"Then we must make haste and begin," she said before directing her gaze at the multitude of troubled faces that were trained on her. "A grievous and ill-fated day has this become," she addressed them. "Who could have thought when the day of the alder dawned that its joy would be invaded and marred by our enemies?"

Everyone shook their heads and muttered angrily.

Ninnia held up her hand for silence. "Please," she told them, "this is not a time for vengeful words, nor talk of war. Let us consider what strange circumstances brought this disaster upon us." She signaled to the sentries who were standing at the back, and they hurried from the room, only to return a minute later, dragging something behind them.

The crowd caught their breath. Some of the black squirrels growled fiercely, and others leaped to their feet and drew what weapons they had. A red squirrel buried her face into her bushy tail, while another let out an accusing shriek and tried to clamber over his neighbors.

"Peace!" the lady commanded. "Bring him forward."

Bound in chains and surrounded by guards, the prisoner was dragged. He was a Knight of the Moon—one of Rohgar's many captains. His screechmask and gauntlets had been confiscated, but his pride was not so easily taken. A livid wound scarred the bat's chest, and a great rip had rendered his wings useless—yet his sharp eyes, which roved about the room, were filled with arrogance and hatred.

Into the center of the chamber the prisoner was thrust, right into the very heart of his enemies. If only he was free—then would they know true terror.

"Stop there!" one of the guards ordered. The squirrel yanked on a chain, and the bat fell awkwardly upon his face. The silence in the room seemed to press down as every eye fixed upon the bat and burned him with their loathing.

Ysabelle could not bear to look at the vile beast—what a specter of ugliness. She shuddered at the sight of him and was grateful that nothing so accursedly repellent roamed abroad in the daylight. By her side, Griselda did not disguise her own feelings, and she pulled an expression of pure disgust.

The clink of the chains was the only sound as the creature lumbered to its feet. He would not be subjugated by this filth—they would not see him grovel on his knees!

"What is thy name?"

The bat glowered at the squirrel queen and ached to kill her.

Ninnia asked him again. "I know that your kind understand our tongue. What is thy name?"

He spat on the floor, and his beady eyes grew narrow, sliding from one of his captors to another.

"Of the fallen," Ninnia continued, "thou are the only survivor—my archers are skilled in their art. The tally of thy dead has mounted to over seventy, but there are doubtless many more who were struck down outside our borders."

The prisoner snarled and lurched forward, but the guards held him, and, though he bared his fangs, Ninnia resumed the interrogation.

"Over seventy Knights of the Moon," she repeated. "Is that not a shameful waste of life? Even now, their bodies are being burned on a great pyre. Will you not tell me what mission brought your forces hither?"

The bat made no answer.

"Ysabelle," the lady said gently, "show to our guest that which you found this morning."

Slowly, Ysabelle rose from her chair, her eyes staring at the repulsive bat. Then she raised her paw for all to see and uncurled her fingers. The Silver Acorn gleamed in her palm, and everyone held their breath.

At once the prisoner squirmed and struggled, straining at his bonds to free himself. Griselda squealed, fearing that he would

66

succeed, and scampered round the back of the thrones. But the chains were strong, and the guards were not about to release him.

"Tell me," Ninnia commanded, and now her voice was cold and frightening, "what terrible fate has befallen the land of Greenreach? Why did the Starwife surrender her symbol of office to so strange a messenger as the one your kind savagely murdered?"

A mocking sneer crept over the bat's face. Why not tell them? Let them know the awesome might of Hrethel's forces—let them spend their remaining hours quaking in mortal dread.

"Heglyr is my name!" he declared in their speech. "Captain of the ninth colony—and may my words give thee no comfort."

He twisted his vile head and stared at the entire assembly, relishing the fear he saw on their faces. "Greenreach has indeed fallen," he hissed. "Our legions destroyed the stinking lair of the Starwife this past night—and she, too, has been deservedly put to death!"

Anger and astonishment rippled through the chamber; the Lord Cyllinus gripped the arms of the throne until his knuckles turned white, and Ysabelle gasped in disbelief. Only Ninnia seemed unmoved.

"Impossible," her voice rang out. "The power of the Starwife is unassailable—nothing can break through her defenses!"

Heglyr threw his head and guffawed. "Is that so?" he crowed. "Is that really the truth? Then know this: a traitor have we nurtured in the bosom of that squalid land. 'Twas our creature who opened the way, and the pouch bombers did wreathe the hiss with a crown of fire. Naught remains there now—only ash blooms upon the charred branches, and Death fills the air."

Ysabelle could bear it no more; she despised this stunted abomination, and to hear him gloating was too much. "You massacred them!" she cried. "You cowards! They did nothing to you—what right had you take their lives? May you and your wretched kind rot!"

"Return to your seat," Ninnia said firmly. "Do as I ask."

Her daughter obeyed, and Griselda came and took her paw. "That's telling the nasty devil, M'lady," she whispered.

"Tell me the name of this traitor," Ninnia demanded.

The bat merely sniggered. "I would fain cut out mine own tongue first!" he told her. "But this I shall willingly tell thee. None here is safe, for when the sun sets behind the world's rim, our forces shall return. All will be rested and ready for battle. I have no doubt that others of our kind have been mustered. Even as we bandy words, the legions are swelling. Come nightfall, they shall descend on thee, and with them they shall bring the dreaded fire eggs that nothing can withstand. Enjoy this day to the full, petty monarch, for verily it is thy last." And with that the bat chuckled, laughing at their scared and stupid faces.

There was a silence, which slowly slipped into a frightened babble of voices until the chamber was in uproar.

"Silence!" the Lady called, but no one heard her. So terrible was the prospect of the coming evening that they could think of nothing else.

"We will have order in here!" Master Godfrey had stepped forward and was clapping his paws for attention. "The Lady Ninnia has called for silence. Listen to what she has to say. You there, Mistress Toggle—shut up!"

"But if Greenreach has been destroyed," the squirrels protested, "what chance has our little realm? No magic defends our borders. If the bats don't get what they want, we shall all be murdered!"

"That's right!" laughed Heglyr. "Each and every one shall taste the steel. Surrender while you can; give up the pagan bauble. Let me take it to my kin."

A few of the red squirrels listened to his advice and thought it was the only solution. "Yes!" they yelled. "Give it back. Give the Acorn to the bats!"

68

At this, Ninnia strode from her throne. "Give it back!" she repeated. "The amulet belongs to no Moonrider! Only a Starwife may possess the Silver—what madness are you contemplating?"

"But the Starwife is dead!"

"Then a new one must be found!"

"But all the Greenreach maidens have perished!" they cried.

Ninnia paced before the thrones, fingering her own badge of office. Gradually, the outbursts were quelled as all looked to her to find the answer. Surely her renowned wisdom would find a way to save them. Finally silence reigned once more, with only the footsteps of the Lady to disturb it.

At length, she returned to the throne and breathed deeply. When she finally spoke, her voice was slow and deliberate, as if trying to control some deep and powerful emotion. "There is but one course we can take!" she declared, blinking away the tears that had sprung to her eyes.

"Whatever befalls us, the Acorn must be withheld from the forces of Hrethel. It is our duty now to restore a Starwife to Greenreach. To this purpose we must send an army to the holy land and rid it of the bat menace."

The squirrels stared at her, too stunned to speak. It was the prime counselor who eventually put their doubts into words. "But, forgive me," Godfrey muttered, "surely our strength, skilled though it may be, is no match for the might of the Moonriders and their fire eggs. It would take the combined forces of all the noble houses to vanquish and rout them from Greenreach."

Ninnia managed a faint smile. "The messengers have already been dispatched," she said softly. "In five days, the four armies shall meet on the borders of the holy land, and the battle for it will commence."

"Fools!" Heglyr yelled. "What pitiful schemes you plot! None of you will ever leave this place—my kind shall hunt you down. What chance have you against them? The armies of your cousins may meet in Greenreach, but you shall not join them. Tonight, the Acorn will be given to Rohgar, and all your designs shall be ended!"

Master Godfrey eyed the prisoner uncertainly; he did sound awfully confident. Leaning forward, he addressed his sovereign. "Madam," he began, "I presume this is why you asked me to find what maps of the outlying country I could. But tell me: just who is to take up the Silver? You know, of course, that as you already possess the bronze, you cannot accept another—unless, of course, you relinquish the Hazel?"

"Fear not, Master Godfrey," she assured him. "I have worn the bronze for far too long to surrender it now, and I know that my place is here."

"Then you must choose," he said solemnly. "An heir to the Silver must be found."

Ninnia glanced at her husband, and the guilt in her eyes betrayed her thoughts to him. "No," he breathed, "you cannot!"

But the Lady raised her paw. "The choice has already been made," she said flatly. "The new Starwife, the next Handmaiden of Orion, shall be the one who caught the Silver Acorn—my own daughter."

The assembly spluttered in surprise, and everyone turned to look at the young princess.

"M'lady!" Griselda squeaked, clutching her mistress's arm with one paw and her own heart with the other.

Ysabelle stared dumbly at Ninnia. She could not believe what was being said—she had no desire to be the Starwife, and her spirit quailed at the thought of it.

Cyllinus sprang to his feet. "Look at the child!" he cried. "See how she trembles at your words. Is this your wisdom, my lady? Would you send our beautiful daughter from this realm and into certain death?"

"It would be death for her to remain," his wife snapped back.

"Then let her die with us!"

"If she journeys to Greenreach, she may not perish—that way, there is hope."

The lord slammed his fist on the arm of her throne. "What hope?" he roared. "You know full well what dangers lie without our borders! Have we not heard the rumors? In the deep forests, the cult of Hobb is rising, growing stronger with every day. Would you send our Belle into their midst? Do you know what they do to those they catch? Would you inflict such horror upon your own child?"

Ninnia glared at her husband, and her gaze smoldered with such furious rage that for a moment it seemed she would strike him. Then the tension eased, and she quickly composed herself, but when she spoke, her tone was bitter and recriminating. "Is that the regard you hold for me?" she asked. "Do you truly believe I would spend my beloved's life so wantonly? Not easy is this for me, Cyllinus! The course I have chosen is perilous, yet there is no other."

Her eyes left him, and she turned to face her daughter. "Would that there were a different path," she said softly, "but often the most difficult is the only way. Gladly would I go in her stead—alas, that cannot be. If I could foresee no hope, then, yes, we should be together when the fire eggs begin to fall."

Ysabelle lowered her eyes and stared at the amulet in her fingers. She hated it and wished someone else had caught the wretched thing. It was hard for her to understand all that was being said. Why did her mother want to send her away?

The Lord Cyllinus gazed at her sadly. "Do you really think there is a chance?" he asked.

There was a pause as Ninnia hesitated. "Only the faintest glimmer," came the frightening reply.

Griselda could not bear this any longer. "M'lady," she blurted. "I know I'm only a field mouse and haven't your great wisdom, but what's all this talk of leaving? Why can't we just hide from the bats when they come? There's no need to go that long way to your holy land."

"Hah!" scoffed Heglyr. "See how the vermin squirm and squabble. Run where you may—our flames shall find you!"

"There is your answer, Griselda," Ninnia told the mouse. "And you, my husband, do you see now?"

Cyllinus stared at the repulsive bat, and he pictured the brutal scenes that would unfold that night. He shivered and returned to his seat. "So be it," he reluctantly agreed. "Into the forests the Acorn must go—back to Greenreach, and may the Green watch over it." Then he rested his chin on his fists and said no more.

"Then we can delay no longer," the lady said. "Ysabelle must leave as soon as possible. Before the afternoon comes, she must already be on her way."

At her side, Master Godfrey pressed his fingertips together and nibbled his bottom lip. "Who shall travel with the princess?" he asked. "The trackless woods are a peril; the entertainers who arrived this morning are the only ones who now dare to travel, and most of them journey together in great numbers. Already they have departed. We must send many guards and sentries with your daughter to protect her."

"My thanks, Master Godfrey; I do know that."

"Then how many shall accompany her?"

Ninnia glanced at the subjects who crowded the chamber. This was an evil day, and she cursed her tongue for the terror that it was about to speak. "All of them!" she answered.

"But—but my lady!" Godfrey stammered, and the room was filled with horrified murmurs. "That would leave our land defenseless. Surely we should retain some of our archers, at the very least?"

"They would be useless against the strength of our enemy!" she declared. "All hope now lies with my daughter. It is she who must be protected. Our guards shall escort her through the forests to the holy land."

"What about those of us left behind?" cried a red squirrel. "Are we to hurl stones at the Moonriders or hit them with sticks while you and your family escape?"

"You there!" Godfrey protested. "Show respect to the lady!"

Ninnia waved him into silence and smiled grimly at the insolent squirrel. "Each has a right to speak his mind," she told him. "As to arms, there are more than enough for all who remain. I do not think we shall resort to throwing stones—a sword and spear shall be in every fist." Then, taking hold of her husband's paw, she said, "And this night, I, too, shall bear weapons. For even though our warriors are gone, we must make it a glorious battle. With our lives, we shall buy time for my daughter and those that guard her. The Acorn must escape the vigilance of Hrethel's forces—that is the task set before us—and I shall not "escape," as you put it. This is my realm, and if it falls, then so do I."

"Be sure of that!" Heglyr hooted gleefully. "What folly you speak, and how easily you will fall victim to my brothers."

The lady stared at the prisoner. "A pity you shall not be here to witness it," she told him, "for you also shall journey to Greenreach."

"I?" Heglyr snorted. "For what purpose?"

"Along the way, I've no doubt, my guards will be able to extract much useful intelligence from you. They will need to know how your forces are deployed in the holy land. Perhaps you will also be persuaded to divulge the identity of your traitor there."

"Never!" the bat bawled. "Thou shalt learn nothing from me!"

"That remains to be seen!" Ninnia said, and Heglyr recoiled from the menace in her voice. "I have every faith in the honor of my subjects. I trust none of them would sink to the baseness of your kind, but who can tell? When they are far from here, and if their need is great, what means shall they employ to loosen your arrogant and defiant tongue? In the deep shadows of the dark forests, I fear for what may befall you, my fine, fallen warrior."

Her words filled Heglyr with fear. So all the stories were true: these tree rats were indeed monstrous and cruel.

Without warning, his head whirled to the side, and his fangs snapped at the guard holding his chains. The squirrel leaped back, and in a trice Heglyr was free!

"Hold him!" the lady commanded.

But the bat scurried from the guards, and the crowded chamber rang with shrieks and screams as he charged up to the thrones.

Cyllinus ran forward to protect his wife as Heglyr lunged at her. "Damn you into the darkness!" the prisoner screeched as rough paws seized him. "I'll not be made to betray my Lord Hrethel!"

Whirling round, he struck the guards with his damaged wing and, with a mad laugh bellowing in his throat, he rushed at one of the sentries.

Before the squirrel could move, the bat had thrown himself upon his spear and, with a hideous gurgle, the laughter ended.

At Ysabelle's feet, Heglyr slid silently to the floor. His upturned face seemed to stare up at her, but she knew that the wide eyes were unseeing.

Griselda covered her mouth, but a shrill scream still forced its way through. Her mistress, however, looked on the dead bat, feeling nothing but contempt.

"Good!" said Ysabelle coldly. "I'm glad it's dead. It was ugly and vile, and I hate all their kind!"

The Lady Ninnia said nothing. It was not like her daughter to be so cruel, and, for the first time in her life, she wondered if her wisdom had failed her.

*   *   *

The day that had begun so merrily, and that had held so much promise, was now transformed into a desperate time of grievous dread. All the boundary wardens had gathered within the avenue of trees, along with every royal guard and sentry, but midday had come and gone before the preparations were complete.

The great company resembled a vast, spiky caterpillar. A bristling array of spears and swords formed its spines, and the round shields of Coll Regalis were its hide. The host was ready, and though each of the squirrels, red and black, despised the fact that they had to leave their land defenseless, all knew their duty. On foot, Greenreach was far away, and they had prepared for a tiring march that would last for many days.

From the central oak, Ysabelle came. None of this seemed real to her. So awful was the nightmare that she almost expected to wake up at any moment. Moving in a daze, she crossed the clearing and made for the mighty rows of her guard.

Over her shoulder she carried a bag that Griselda had packed for her. The mousemaid had fussed a great deal about having to leave; the thought of the forests terrified her, and, even as she collected Ysabelle's belongings, she uttered distressed whimpers.

"M'lady!" she called, scurrying over the lawn after her mistress. "Stay a while; wait for me. Oh, what madness is this? Into the jaws of terror we're rushing!"

The mouse was burdened by many baggages: a bulging knapsack was strapped to her back, a satchel was slung over her shoulder, two fat wallets were fastened to a belt about her waist, and, as she ran, her mousebrass jiggled and swung madly about her neck.

"I'm sure to have forgot something," she scolded herself, running through the lists in her head. "Oh, well, it can't be helped now."

Catching up with her mistress, Griselda panted for breath and watched her curiously. Ysabelle looked awful–her face was drawn, and her eyes were glazed. She appeared to be on the point of collapse. The mouse's heart bled for the squirrel maiden. The poor mite–she was far too young to take on the terrible responsibility of the Starwifeship.

Griselda wondered if she ought to say something to cheer her, but her own feelings were so low that any attempt would fail dismally.

They came to the head of the army. A large crowd had formed about the rows of guards, and the sight was painful to witness. The entire population of the Hazel Realm was once more upon the lawns, although this time, the only sounds were wretched, and the tears that flowed innumerable.

Wives clung to husbands, children wailed, confused and forlorn because their fathers were going away, and their plaintive cries tormented the doughtiest of soldiers that day. The grief of mothers was also to be heard; to see their sons arrayed for war and the certainty that they would never meet in this world again was too much to bear. Coll Regalis was already a land in mourning.

Standing at the forefront of the lamenting crowd, Ninnia and Cyllinus waited for their daughter to approach.

"Belle!" the Lord cried. "My precious darling." He threw his arms about her, and the two remained locked in a desperate embrace.

Ninnia stood apart. A bleakness overwhelmed her; she wanted to reach out and never let go of Ysabelle.

Her soul screamed within her, but she must not falter–not now. The mask must stay in place a little while longer. It would be the undoing of everything if she succumbed to her feelings.

"Remember us, Belle," Cyllinus wept, "when the dangers are past and you sit upon the throne in Greenreach. Think of us. Do not forget me, little one."

"Oh, Father!" Ysabelle sobbed. "I don't want to leave. Please do not make me!"

Cyllinus glanced at his wife, but her face was like stone.

"You know you must," the lady said. "Come, daughter, make haste to be gone. You shall have to put much distance between yourself and this land before night falls. The litter is prepared for you."

Taking Ysabelle lightly by the paw, she led her to where a group of eight guards saluted and came to attention. A large, gilded couch stood at their side; upon this the princess and her maid would be carried to the holy land, protected on all sides by her mighty escort. A pale green canopy was draped over the litter, and soft cushions had been arranged to make the journey as comfortable as possible.

"This will bear you to Greenreach," Ninnia told her. "Griselda shall accompany you, and Master Godfrey will be your guide. Only he knows the route you must take, for only he has studied the charts and maps of the land. I know many of my subjects deride him, but Godfrey Gelenos is a most learned scholar. Do not hesitate in taking his advice. When you are the Starwife, you shall have need of his counsel."

"I don't want to be the Starwife!" Ysabelle protested. "It isn't fair!"

Her mother wavered; even now, it was not too late.

"You must fulfill your destiny," she said at last. "The Starwifeship is already yours. All that remains is for you to bring the amulet and the Starglass together. Once that is done, the power of the heavens will be yours to command. Use it wisely, for the forces locked within the Silver Acorn may be used for good or ill. On your journey, never be parted from it; always wear it about your neck."

"I wish I could use it now to protect us all!" Ysabelle snapped. "When I get to Greenreach, the first thing I'll do will be to use the magic against the bats. I'll set a terror in each and every one. They shall not live long to rue what they have done!"

Ninnia stepped back from her. "The day grows old," she said quickly. "Master Godfrey is coming, and you must leave now."

"Ooh, M'lady," Griselda cooed, "look at the prime counselor– see who's walking with him. Well, I never did!"

Down the avenue of trees the eldest of the queens' advisers came, and at his side walked Wendel the jester. The two seemed to be involved in a most heated discussion, punctuated by vehement shakes of the head from Master Godfrey and feverish hops from the stoat.

"Most certainly not!" Godfrey cried, unfurling a chart and trying to ignore his unwanted companion. "This is a most serious undertaking. There is no room for your base levity here!"

"Oh kind, most benevolent squirrel!" Wendel implored. "Most noble and clever scourer of books, let me tag along–I beseech thee, assuredly I do!"

Here, the jester fell to his knees and began hobbling over the grass with his paws clenched before him in supplication. As one of his arms was in a sling, this proved to be very distressing, and he whined at the pain between speaking.

"There!" Godfrey squawked, greatly flustered at this embarrassing show. "That's precisely the kind of foolery I mean. Now, get away with you!"

"You won't even know I'm there–I vow!" begged the jester. "For a few days only–oooch, my poor shoulder! Was it my fault I missed the others? I would have joined them but–eeeh, how it pains me!–but they left so quickly!"

Godfrey abandoned all hope of trying to ignore him and tucked the scroll he had been studying firmly into one of the satchels that he carried. "Am I to blame for that?" he said tersely. "I do know the voles came looking for you, but you were nowhere to be found."

"I was with the woodwright! My cart needed mending! I can do naught without it."

"Well, they obviously thought you weren't worth waiting for. Now, do get up off the ground. You're getting under my feet!"

He quickened his pace and approached the head of the company, leaving the stoat behind. When he reached the Lady

Ninnia, Master Godfrey bowed low and announced that all was ready–the route had been planned.

"Remember," Ninnia said, "the bats must not guess the way you have taken. The obvious paths must be avoided."

"Fear not," he replied somberly. "It will be difficult, but we shall not be marked by our enemies."

The lady nodded, then looked to where Wendel sat in the grass, his face miserable and forlorn. "Tell me, Master Godfrey," she began, "what were you and the stoat talking about?"

The counselor assumed a haughty and disparaging air. "Would you believe it, madam?" he replied. "That nauseating and vulgar personage was asking to join this noble company. Such unrivaled impudence I cannot remember."

"The other entertainers have left without him?"

"Indeed, and in truth I am not surprised–his constant banal babbling has given me an ache in my head."

Ninnia looked from the stoat to her daughter and wasted no more time. "Tell the jester he may join you," she said firmly.

Godfrey gasped and mumbled under his breath, but his sovereign had decided.

"The forest is too dangerous for him to traverse alone, and we cannot expect a stranger to remain here to defend our realm. Let him journey with you as far as he wishes–a small reward for the valor he showed this morning. Remember, Godfrey, that without him we should all be mourning the loss of my daughter. Go to him; tell him to collect his belongings. Perhaps you will learn to find his ways amusing."

"Who can say, madam?" Godfrey muttered before stomping off to tell the jester the news. In a moment, Wendel Maculatum had leaped to his feet, whistled his thanks to the Lady Ninnia, and sped to the woodwright's to retrieve his cart.

"Now is the time," Ninnia said gravely. "Come, Ysabelle; you must depart."

Ysabelle gave her father one final hug, and his tears mingled with hers. Neither of them spoke, for the agony of this parting was beyond words. He crushed her against his chest and carried the raw pain of that moment into eternity.

"Farewell, child," the lady said, and how magnificently she controlled her voice—not a tremor of emotion betrayed her anguish. "May the Green watch over you, and may he guide you safely to the holy land."

With that, she walked away and gave the signal for the company to leave.

Ysabelle stared after her mother and sorrowfully climbed into the litter. Griselda had already clambered in, and the mouse squeezed her paw tightly. "This is it, M'lady," she muttered. "Into the deadly forest we go."

The heralds blew their trumpets, but the sound echoed hollowly about the avenue like a funeral dirge. In one movement, the eight guards took hold of the bier and lifted it off the ground. Then, with the wailing of those left behind still ringing in their ears, the great host marched for the border, with the waddling form of the jester and his cart taking up the rear. None of them ever saw the Hazel Realm again.

As the somber procession moved away, the Lady Ninnia moved to her husband's side.

"Green be with you, my little Belle," Cyllinus whispered as he watched the last of the company disappear into the distant trees. "I will pray for your safekeeping, and may you come at last to the holy land and be victorious against our enemies."

Ninnia stared intently at the blank stretch of trees into which the host of Coll Regalis had marched. Desperately, she clutched at the bronze hazelnut about her neck, and the desolation that she had so valiantly been mastering now consumed her. The grief into which her spirit was plunged was too terrible to bear. Shaking, she fell into her husband's arms.

"What have I done?" she wept. "Our child is gone. She is lost to us!"

Cyllinus held her grimly; his heart was too injured to feel anything. "You did what your wisdom demanded," he said flatly. "You did what you had to do, for the good of all."

"But I never held her!" she sobbed bitterly. "I never even said good-bye!"

Cyllinus trembled as all the pain his wife had concealed erupted in great, racking bursts of emotion. But all his thoughts were for their daughter, and he could not comfort the Lady Ninnia. Awkwardly, he stepped back and looked about the avenue, where similar scenes of grief were being enacted. "There is no time to mourn," he muttered gruffly. "If we are to be ready for the assault that will befall us this coming night, then there is much to do."

Ninnia stared at him; now, more than ever, she needed him, but Cyllinus had grown cold toward her. She wiped the tears from her face and nodded. "We must prepare to fight a battle we have no hope of winning," she said.

A dark gleam shone in her husband's eye—win or not, he would take many Moonriders with him. "For our daughter's sake," he said, "we must fight well. A fine Starwife she will be— the greatest that ever there was."

With that, he strode to the center of the avenue and began rallying his subjects, spurring them to take up arms and give all in defense of their land.

Alone, her soul destroyed and her heart bereft and empty, the Lady Ninnia touched her amulet and closed her eyes. "No," she breathed, "I was wrong. This time, my wisdom has failed me. Our daughter is not ready. To become the Handmaiden of Orion, one must know terrible grief in order to learn compassion." She gazed after her husband and shook her head sorrowfully. "Even the deaths of us, her parents, are not, I fear, enough. May she find what she needs upon that dark and deadly road upon which I have sent her. My poor, poor child—farewell."

THROUGH GORSE AND BRAMBLE

The woods that flanked the Hazel Realm were calm and tranquil glades. Many creatures dwelt there in peace, safe in the knowledge that no harm could befall them while the boundary wardens kept vigil in the branches of the trees high above. But now the watchdreys were empty; every squirrel had joined the company of Ysabelle, and an uneasy silence possessed the once tame woodland. In the grassy, flower-speckled banks, the entrances to burrows and holes gaped blindly—for each inhabitant was away preparing for the coming battle.

No eyes saw the great army of Coll Regalis march deeper toward the shadowy forest; there was no one to hear the rattle of shield against spear as the host departed from Ninnia's land. On they marched, and the tramp of their many feet was the only voice heard beneath the blossoming trees.

Upon her couch of gold, Ysabelle drew back the curtain and let the sunlight of the warm afternoon play over her features, while upon its fine chain, the Silver Acorn burned with a cold white fire.

Griselda sat beside her; the mouse had brought some needlework along in an effort to keep her mind off things, but this proved to be an exceedingly vain hope. In the space of only half an hour, she had pricked nearly all her fingers at least twice, and the delicate embroidery she had been working on was spotted with red dots.

"Blether!" she said, throwing the fabric among the cushions and sucking her sore fingers.

Ysabelle glanced down at the embroidery, and the scarlet spots seemed to dance before her eyes. Silently, she wondered how long it would be until the blood of her parents spilled over the Hazel Realm.

Feeling sick, she turned away and took a deep breath of the spring air.

At the vanguard of the company, Master Godfrey finished instructing the royal marshals on the route he had devised and stood to one side. As the countless wardens, sentries, and guards marched by, he rolled up the maps he had been studying and went in search of the princess's litter.

"We make good time, my lady," he told her. "When evening falls we should have put a fair distance between us and our home."

Ysabelle nodded as Godfrey trotted alongside but did not know what to say. For as long as she had known him, Master Godfrey Gelenos had been her tutor—and a decidedly stuffy one at that. Most of her short life had been spent inventing ways to avoid his boring lessons and thinking up excuses as to why she had not been able to complete a task he had set her.

Now everything had changed; Godfrey was treating her with a respect and deference he had not shown before. Gone was the weary voice of the impatient tutor, and Ysabelle found it difficult to adjust to this different attitude.

The prime counselor cleared his throat. "The straight path to the holy land lies, of course, due north," he told her, "but we cannot go that way. Once the forces of Hrethel discover our flight, they shall naturally assume that to be our route. This is why I have chosen a large detour into the west that will hopefully confuse our enemies."

He held out the map for Ysabelle's inspection and approval, but the squirrel maiden barely glanced at it. "Forgive me, Master Godfrey," she said, "but mine head is too full of grief to think of aught else. Later, perhaps, I will be able to give it my full attention."

"There now M'lady," Griselda clucked, patting her mistress's paws. "This is no time for book learning. Why not try to get some sleep?"

"Come, come," pressed Master Godfrey, with some of his tutorial authority creeping back into his voice, "I really do think you should take a look."

Ysabelle sighed and stared for a moment at the chart he held out to her. In the center of the parchment was a detailed drawing of the Hazel Realm, but once outside its borders, the pictures became rather vague. The dense forest was everywhere, of course, and fine red and blue lines indicated where the main paths and sacred streams criss-crossed the country. Here and there, green symbols showed where holy shrines stood, but apart from a hesitant depiction of a wide river at the top of the scroll, there was very little else.

"Is this the best map we have?" Ysabelle asked. "I cannot see where Greenreach lies. Can it be that curious expanse there?"

"No, my Lady," Godfrey replied. "That appears to be an area of swamp and marsh. The Blessed Hill of the Starwife is up here, near the bend of the great river."

"But it looks smaller than our own land!"

The prime counselor coughed and muttered apologetically. "A regrettable trait of our chart makers and illuminators, I fear," he sorrowfully admitted. "Alas, these parchments are very old, and, in those simple days, our folk were wont to feature Coll Regalis most prominently. Remember that there was very little call for anyone to journey so far. No one ever traveled to Greenreach from our small realm—not in my lifetime, anyway."

Ysabelle frowned. "Forgive me," she began, "but it seems to me a very small distance between the two. I would deem it to be a day's ramble at most."

"Ah, there again, I fear the chart is deceiving. A good many days shall it be."

Ysabelle shook her head. "Then I pray we do not lose ourselves in the fastness of the trackless woods," she said.

"There is no chance of that," he confidently assured her.

The squirrel maiden breathed deeply. "What madness do we pursue?" she whispered. "Here are we, hurling ourselves deeper into danger, putting our trust in ancient maps and desperate hopes."

Ever more frequently, the sunlight grew dim as the ceiling of branch and twig became tangled and knotted overhead. Here was the beginning of the wild world, and a sensation of dread and apprehension coursed throughout the entire company as they left the safe woods far behind.

"I'm afraid our progress will be slower henceforth," Godfrey informed Ysabelle. "In places the undergrowth will hinder us and must needs be cut down. If you will excuse me, I shall have a word with the marshals."

"Ooh, I don't like this, M'lady," Griselda miserably whimpered. "If'n we have to constantly hack through weeds and brambles, we shall never get to your holy place, and those filthy bats will find us!"

Ysabelle leaned out of the litter and looked to where Godfrey was telling the marshals to unsheathe their swords and begin cutting through any obstacles in their path. "Fear not," she told the mouse, "for the undergrowth that slows us down will also screen us from the eyes of Hrethel's army."

But Griselda was not so easily comforted. "Well, if they don't get us, the Hobbers will!" she yelped. "You remember the stories I used to tell you, M'lady?"

Her mistress threw the mouse a reproachful look that was born mostly of fear. "Be quiet!" she snapped. "Are we not in peril enough without you wishing to add to it? Keep the ogres of the nursery under your cap, Griselda—I don't want to hear of them again!"

The mousemaid folded her arms and stared dismally at her needlework.

Very softly, a voice began to chant. Griselda looked up in surprise, for Ysabelle was repeating the lines of a rhyme she had taught her long, long ago.

Thread not into the fearsome night
But pull the covers high,
Step not into the wild dark wood
For the Hobbers are dancing nigh.

"Oh M'lady," the mouse spluttered, "I marvel you can recall that—why, you were only a babe in arms!"

Ysabelle did not hear her; for a brief moment, she was back in the nursery. It was a grim winter's evening, and a biting gale howled around the central oak. As a child, the young squirrel had been very afraid—the wind seemed to shriek with evil voices, and she imagined that they called her name.

"Who is out there?" her own meek voice had asked.

A much younger Griselda swept the squirreling into her maternal arms and kissed her forehead. "Don't you listen to them now, my little duck," the mouse had said. "'Tis but the Hobbers, wanting to lure you out. But they can't get us in here, can they, now? We'm all snug and cozy—and your mammy's soldiers would never let them near. No, so long as we're here, nothing shall trouble us—not even the Sleep Visitor shall haunt your dreams. Fret no more; you are safe from the Infernal Three."

The memory of the fear she had felt in her childhood now returned to Ysabelle, and for some time she felt cold and scared. Then its hold was broken, and the mood scattered in tiny ripples as a familiar clattering sound dragged her back to the present. Into the leaf-dappled afternoon, her childish fears melted, and once more she felt the warmth of the sun upon her face.

Twisting about, she peered back to where the company

stretched far behind, and the shadow of a smile flickered over her lips.

"Ho, Mistress!" came a voice above the clattering of the cart's wheels. "What can be the delay? I did bump into one of thy guards, so sudden was the halt. Not popular is Wendel back there; I fear mine prop wagon did shed some of its splinters into a soldier's behind."

Ysabelle's face broke into a full grin as the jester came hurrying alongside, pushing his repaired wagon before him. A loud "Tut!" issued from the litter as Griselda showed her disapproval of the stoat's familiarity, but neither he nor her mistress took any notice.

Wendel made a comical bow that set all the bells of his hat ringing madly. "A most peculiar road we have taken thus far," he observed, utterly bemused. "Surely little can be gained by trudging through every nettle patch and ditch? Or is this some new game devised by Gloomy Gelenos over yonder? If so, I find its merit and wit exceeding rare."

"Master Maculatum," Ysabelle began.

"Please, good lady!" he interrupted, holding up an objecting paw. "Address this tomfool as either Wendel or Squire Ticklerib, or perhaps simply Jester Long Body, but no "Master"–that is a title fit only for the glums and brainpans of the world, not I."

"Wendel, then," Ysabelle continued, "now that you are here, stay by my side. I need diverting from the dark roads ahead."

"Then here shall I remain," the stoat replied. He bowed once more, but, just as he was about to straighten, Wendel's expression changed drastically.

"What is it?" asked Ysabelle, disturbed by his staring eyes and shocked look.

"Thine ear, madam!" the stoat declared.

Ysabelle's paws went to her ears, but she could feel nothing wrong with them. Beside her, Griselda frowned and wondered what the impudent jester was up to now.

"Allow me!" Wendel begged, and he leaned forward, cupping her right ear in both his paws. "There!" he cried. "I have it!"

With an extravagant flourish, he appeared to pull a length of brightly colored cloth from the squirrel's ear. Ysabelle laughed in spite of her worries, and the stoat leaped in the air, whirling the material about him.

"I've seen that trick before," muttered an unimpressed Griselda, "and done better—why, 'tis older than I!"

Wendel pulled a small wooden chest from his cart and stuffed the cloth inside it before spinning round and staring at the mousemaid with a curious look on his face. "Is this not my dancing partner?" he chuckled.

"You keep your distance!" squeaked Griselda as he leaned under the canopy and reached for her. "M'lady! M'lady!"

The jester ran his fingers over the mouse's lips, and suddenly the litter was filled with the flutter of many wings as countless painted moths seemed to escape from her mouth.

"Eeeek!" she wailed as the insects issued forth and tickled her face. "Oh, you wretch!"

Ysabelle batted the moths away with her paw and giggled as they flew from the canopy.

"Dear jester," she laughed, "if you have any more tricks, you had best leave them in your cart. I fear my maid does not approve."

"Be not so certain, ma'am," the stoat replied with a wink. "I do believe thy nibbler has warmed to me already."

"I have not!" spluttered Griselda, fiercely throwing a cushion at the insolent fellow. "Why, I have never seen such disgraceful behavior! Keep away, you knave, before I tell the guards to see you off and leave you to the mercy of the Hobbers!"

For an instant, the stoat's face lost all trace of humor, as though the mere mention of the dreaded cult had terrified him. Quickly, he recovered and said hastily, "Why, here comes another of my many admirers—Master Godfrey of the gloomy disposition and humorless aspect."

The prime counselor blustered toward them. With a sniff for the stoat and a nod for Ysabelle, he briefly explained that all was now well and they could set off again; a group of wardens were clearing the way ahead.

"You may return to the rear of the company," Godfrey dismissed Wendel. "We don't want the ragtag cluttering things up here—now, run along."

Griselda's snort of approval was swiftly curtailed as Ysabelle spoke up. "The jester will remain where he is," she told Godfrey. "His presence pleases me."

The old squirrel scrunched up his face and clenched his teeth as the jester stuck out a pink tongue to him. "Whatever you wish," he said from behind a forced smile.

*   *   *

Through gorse and thorn, the army of the Hazel Realm cut its way. The day wore on, and the afternoon shadows grew long. Above them the sky was growing dim, and the hour that all of them had been dreading crept slowly closer.

As the shadows increased, Wendel tried to amuse the squirrel maiden, and at first she was grateful to him, but, eventually, nothing could turn her thoughts from the horror they had left behind. As the jester related riddles and nonsense stories, Ysabelle could think only of her parents, and his words washed over her like babbling water over an immovable stone.

At the forefront of the company, the wardens hacked and sliced through the thick undergrowth. Their palms were blistered, and the blades of their swords were notched where they struck hidden roots. It was tough work, and the squirrels strained and sweated over it.

Samuel Muin hewed at a stubborn thicket of holly. He had been in the service of the boundary wardens for nearly five years, and, behind him, he had left a wife and three young children. It enraged him to think what would befall his family, and his furious resentment was spent upon the vines and branches that barred the way. Every bough of thorn and bramble was, to him, one of Hrethel's bats, and his sword sang through the undergrowth more violently than any other.

He hated this place; it was nothing like the well-ordered woods of his home. Here, the leaves had been left to rot upon the ground, and at times he had to wade up to his middle to push through the moldering drifts. The sickly smell of leaf decay was everywhere, and he hoped that the long journey to Greenreach would not always be so arduous.

Suddenly, his sword ceased hissing through the air. Samuel held his breath and motioned for those about him to do the same.

"What is it?" wheezed his neighbor.

"There's something over there!" Samuel whispered. "I'm sure of it!"

Everyone stared in the direction the warden pointed. It was a dark hollow in the undergrowth where two ragged thorn bushes met and twisted together.

"I see naught!" someone grumbled uncertainly.

"Look there!" growled Samuel. "Small footprints lead into that gap, and—see! For an instant a pair of eyes did gleam in the shadow!"

That was enough for the others. With a shout, twenty of them ran forward, brandishing swords and spears. From within the thorn bush there came a terrified howl, and a small figure tried to scurry through a narrow opening in the brambles.

"A bat!" the wardens shrieked. "It is a bat we have cornered. Take him! Take him!"

Vesper squirmed between the sharp thorns as fast as he could. His heart thumped in his chest, and panic flooded his mind. He had been listening to the approach of the company for some time but had been unable to move for fear of discovery. Now it was too late; as tears of fright ran down his cheeks, he left his cover and anxiously pelted through the leaf piles beyond.

It was no good. The young bat's left wing was damaged, and he was unable to fly. He cursed himself for ever being so stupid. Why had he disobeyed his mother? Why had he put on his father's armor and followed the Moonriders to Greenreach? Now that armor was gone: Terrorgrin, which his father had worn with so much honor, he had lost, and the gauntlets with it.

They had been right—all of them. He had been too young to wear the screechmask. He hadn't even made it to Greenreach in time; the war gear was so heavy that all the fighting was over when he arrived. All he saw was the fierce flames that surrounded the hill, and, for a few desperate moments, he wondered where the other bats had gone. Fortunately, or so he had thought then, he saw the dark mass of the great host in the far distance of the southern sky and immediately set off after them. But how weary Vesper soon became, how the armor pulled him down, and how his muscles ached trying to keep him airborne.

Eventually, Vespertilio had plummeted from the heavens even as the sun began to rise. Down he fell, the gauntlets slipping from his feet and Terrorgrin spinning from his head. That was all he could remember, for the bat had struck the branch of a tree and fallen senseless to the forest floor.

When he awoke, he found that his wing was hanging limply at his side, and the pain of it caused him to cry out. And now his mortal enemies had caught him.

Floundering through the rotting leaves, Vesper dragged his wing behind, but all efforts were in vain. The squirrels had surrounded him, and their faces were vicious and cruel.

"Get him!" one of the tree rats cried.

Vesper shrieked as they launched themselves at him and their strong paws seized him roughly. For a terrible second he thought he would be torn to pieces right there, but one of the squirrels pushed the others away and lifted the bat off the ground.

"Maggot fodder!" screamed Samuel Muin into Vesper's face. "You'll pay for what you've done! Say a quick prayer to your vile lord for, by the Almighty Green, this is the last you'll see of this world!" He hurled Vesper down and swiftly drew his sword.

The young bat wept and scuttled backward, scattering the dead leaves about him. But Samuel raised the sword, and it came scything down.

"Hold!" cried a stern voice. Samuel Muin whirled round, and there was Godfrey Gelenos.

"Keep out of this, counselor!" the warden snarled.

"I will not!" Master Godfrey firmly replied. He pushed through the ranks of the other wardens that had gathered behind Samuel until he stood beside him and glared at the warden threateningly.

"The worm is mine!" Samuel growled, and the murmurs that issued from those around him agreed totally.

"Look again!" Godfrey told him. "What terrible warrior is it you have caught? What mighty general have you captured, Warden Muin?"

Samuel glanced back at the terrified Vesper, and his stomach heaved within him. "'Tis–'tis naught but a child!" he stammered. "Why–why, my own son Bergil can be no older!" He dropped his sword and staggered back, aghast at what he had been about to do.

Godfrey turned to the others; they, too, were sickened. "Does anyone else have a quarrel with this child?" the prime counselor asked. No one answered. "Then bring him to where the Lady Ysabelle waits. He must be questioned."

Once more, Vesper felt squirrel paws take hold of him, but this time it was different–the creatures were almost gentle. He winced when they took hold of his wing, and, when they saw this, they treated him all the more tenderly. Perhaps they were cowards, he thought to himself as they led him through the rows of sentries and guards. Why else would they have spared his life?

But Vesper soon had other things on his mind, for now he realized how great a host this was. Surely this must be the sum

total of all squirrels—never had he believed there were so many—
and all bore armor and deadly weapons. He blinked at the lethal
array of blade and spear and wondered what this portended for
the rest of his kind.

Every face was turned on him as he stumbled past, and he
wondered how long he would stay unharmed, for here, too,
anger and hatred smoldered at the sight of him. Vesper tried not
to meet the eyes of his captors, for his spirit quailed, and whatever courage he once thought he possessed had fled far away.

A strange frame covered by green material rose behind the
armored heads of the guards in front, and the bat found himself
even more frightened than ever before. He was going to have
to face the leader of his enemies. Vesper felt faint as he tried to
guess what the canopy was for—perhaps the squirrel lord was
so ugly that he had to be covered at all times.

Godfrey led the bat to where a stoat in a strange headdress
gawped at him stupidly, and beads of perspiration prickled over
Vesper's brow. This was it—the old black squirrel drew the green
material aside, and the young bat saw . . .

Vesper nearly choked; seated upon a golden couch was a
squirrel maiden and a ridiculous-looking mouse—it was so unexpected and peculiar that he almost laughed at them both.

"Master Godfrey," the maiden began, "is this the cause of the
disturbance we heard?"

"It is indeed, madam," came the solemn reply.

Ysabelle stared at the bat and shuddered. "It's as ugly as the
one who killed itself," she grimaced. "Are there more ahead?"

"I think not, madam," said Godfrey. "You will see that his
wing is damaged. The fellow must have been separated from the
main host."

Ysabelle leaned back as though the bat offended her sense of
smell, and she waved a paw in front of her face. "Take it away,"
she declared. "Give it to the guards—let them kill it!"

At that, Vesper's cowed spirit rallied a little. "Here, Miss High and Mighty!" he cried. "Who do you think you are? Turn thy nose up at me, would you? Well, hear this: no sweet flower art thou! Prettier dung heaps I've seen—but few with such low manners as thine!"

"Oh, the devil!" yelped Griselda. "Why, he's ruder than the jester!"

"And who art thou, Mistress Plumpmouse? Why do you recline upon a cushioned bed? Are thy legs too weak to bear thee?"

"Take this creature away!" Ysabelle commanded. "Execute it immediately—I want the foul beast dead!"

Godfrey gave the bat a cautionary look and whispered in Ysabelle's ear. "Remember the use your mother thought to make of Heglyr," he said. "Perhaps this servant of Hrethel can be persuaded to aid us in his stead."

Ysabelle listened to his advice, her eyes brimming with loathing for the prisoner. "Very well," she said when her anger had cooled a little. "Bind him and bring the creature with us. I shall question him later."

So Vesper was bound with ropes and made to march with the company.

Wendel Maculatum watched the guards bundle the young bat out of earshot, and he scratched his head thoughtfully. "Methinks you shall come to rue the advice of Master Godfrey," he told Ysabelle, "for are not all bats instruments of death and despair? Surely we both know that better than he? What viper have we taken into our bosom? Only evil will come of this, I fear."

For the few hours of daylight that remained, the company plunged deeper into the forest. Dusk was near, and every step brought them closer to nightfall. Slowly, the light failed, and the rays of the sun dwindled behind distant treetops. All talk ceased as they waited and strained to hear what they knew they must. And then it came.

Great pools of shadow now covered the forest floor, and the trees rose, dark and threatening, on every side.

As if controlled by a single instinct, the entire host of squirrels halted.

Far away, a dull explosion boomed into the night, and a red glare shone in the heavens. The battle had begun.

No one moved. All were as still as the trees that surrounded them, while the distant explosions continued to balefully light the sky.

"It is the end," Ysabelle whispered. "Coll Regalis is falling—the fire eggs have come to them."

The roaring resounded in all their ears, and they lowered their eyes so that they might not witness the awful glare any longer. Ysabelle's paw took hold of Griselda's, and the two gripped each other grimly. The world they had known was burning, and they both knew that, even now, the Moonriders were attacking.

Only Vesper's face was raised to the radiance of the mighty blaze, and a wonderful rejoicing filled his heart. The forces of Hrethel were victorious once more. He almost felt like cheering, but one quick glance at those around him soon quashed that idea. It would not be long before his kindred found this dreadful army, and then he would be set free. The bat gazed long at the crackling glow that illuminated the darkness, then he, too, had to hang his head, but that was because a broad grin had split his face, and he did not want the others to see.

The eight squirrels who were carrying the litter placed their burden upon the ground, and, beneath the canopy, Ysabelle wept.

Suddenly she gasped, clutching her breast as though a knife had been plunged between her ribs. Then she screamed, and a violent shuddering seized her. "Mother!" she cried. "Father!"

"M'lady!" howled Griselda, frightened by her mistress's behavior.

"They're gone!" Ysabelle whispered. "They're dead! I know it—I sensed their pain!"

She sobbed into the mouse's shoulder, then the host of squirrels lay down their weapons and knelt in prayer and sorrow upon the ground.

"Majesty," said Godfrey at Ysabelle's side, "now thou art our sovereign queen."

The maiden raised her head and drew her palm over her eyes. Godfrey was right—he was telling her that, henceforth, she must be like her mother and govern them. Trembling slightly, she took hold of the Silver Acorn and steadied herself.

Her old tutor nodded faintly, and his gaze held her for many minutes. "The time is come," he spoke quietly. "Now, when lesser folk would wither, thou must be true to the blood of thine ancestors. Much greatness is bred in thee; accept now this terrible mantle and take a step nearer thy destiny."

Ysabelle closed her eyes, and his words seemed to reach deep within her, awakening some ancient power that had long lain dormant.

When next she looked up, her glance was keen and clear. She knew now why her mother had forced her upon this road, and she was determined that the sacrifice of the Hazel Realm would not be in vain.

In a firm and level voice, she addressed her counselor and gave her first instructions as queen. "We cannot remain here," she told him. "Greenreach is still many leagues distant. We must press on."

And so the journey continued, while behind the silent company, the ruddy night reflected the blood that was being spilled in the land they had left.

For another hour the army marched, until Ysabelle decreed that the time had come to rest.

Beneath the shelter of a dense row of holly trees, where the dead leaves were dry upon the ground, the squirrels made their camp. Blankets were cast onto the soft, musty heaps, and a circular tent was erected for the new queen and her maid.

The many guards who were lucky enough not to be in the first watch ate a frugal and morose meal, then threw themselves upon the makeshift beds. But the slumber into which they quickly sank was filled with horror and the ghosts of those they had left behind.

Griselda patted the cushions she had taken from the litter and arranged them inside the tent. "Most unsuitable!" she observed, nibbling the last few crumbs of the oat biscuits that had formed her supper. "A bed of the softest down she ought to be sleeping upon."

Outside, Ysabelle was speaking to Master Godfrey. So far, his strategy had been successful, for the bats had not come hunting for them. No doubt they were searching along the main paths that led to Greenreach, but they would still have to be careful.

"We must travel only in the daytime," he counseled her, "for then are the eyes of our enemy the weakest. By tomorrow's night, we should already be encamped in a manner like to this. No fires must we light to cheer us or cook our food, for the slightest sign will betray our presence. No doubt the hunt shall travel farther afield the second night, and the spies of Hrethel can cover great distances.

"Now do we become truly wary—even if we have to creep through the forest like common thieves and footpads, that we must do."

Ysabelle pressed her paws together and rested her chin upon the tips of her fingers. "I pray the messengers my mother sent to our kindred arrive safe," she said. "Without the aid of the other houses, we shall be of little use in the holy land."

Godfrey smiled. "Let such worries concern you when we reach our goal," he said. "For my part, I fear there will be many dangers between here and that final battle."

The maiden cast her gaze about the hundreds of squirrels who lay upon the forest floor. The sound of their slumber filtered softly into the night air, and she shook her head sadly. "A terrible price have we already paid for the deliverance of the holy land," she said. "Look at them. How many fathers and sons are present here? All have lost someone this day."

Godfrey stared at her with some surprise. "How different you have become, my lady," he breathed. "Where has the giggling pupil gone to? Most certainly, she set off with us—but now she has changed much."

Ysabelle nodded and let loose a faint, butter laugh. "Have you forgotten?" she murmured. "'Tis Aldertide still, and this morning I danced with the wand. A lifetime ago that now seems, when I was a child without care or want. Curious how even a little time can alter so much."

"Very proud your parents would be of their daughter."

She sighed and rubbed her eyes wearily. "Strange," she said, stifling a yawn. "Even after all that has occurred, I feel that I could sleep. Where are the guards you sent to fetch the prisoner? Let us be done with him quickly, for I don't know how long mine eyes will stay open."

Even as she finished speaking, two black squirrels emerged from the shadows ahead, and between them hopped Vesper, his legs still tied together.

The young bat eyed the queen uncertainly; was he to be executed after all?

Ysabelle glanced at Godfrey, and her old tutor gave her an encouraging smile. "Trust in your own powers," he said gently.

The maiden turned to the prisoner and assumed a regal and superior air. "Tell me," she began, "how many legions of your kind now guard the Blessed Hill of Greenreach? What manner of defenses have you employed there?"

The bat pursed his lips resolutely and made no reply.

"Very well," she said, "then reveal unto me the name of the traitor who helped you massacre our kindred."

Vesper nibbled his wispy beard and ignored her absolutely. The fact that he didn't know the answers to her questions was neither here nor there—he wasn't going to let these pox-ridden squirrels know that. He didn't even know why Rohgar had led the bat host to the Hazel Realm in the first place.

The more she interrogated him, the more he raised his eyebrows and rolled his small black eyes.

Ysabelle strode forward until she was face to face with the ugly winged creature. "Too many have perished this night," she spat. "How dare you stand there and say nothing!"

"There's naught to say," Vesper shrugged. "I shall not betray my brethren unto thee—whatever you might threaten. Your paltry forces hold no fear for me," he lied. "'Tis thou who shouldst worry."

"What do you mean?" she snapped.

The bat shrugged once more. "My folk will find you," he said in a matter-of-fact way, "simple as that. You might have deceived them this one night, but you can never hope to succeed a second time. In utter silence can a Knight of the Moon skim the wind. The first you'll know of the attack will be when the talons come glinting for your throat."

Ysabelle lost control, and she slapped the bat across his furry face. Vesper reeled backward and was caught by one of the guards.

"Remove it from my sight!" she cried. "I don't want to see the creature ever again!"

The guards led Vesper away, and Ysabelle turned desperately to Godfrey.

"How can we ever hope for victory over such a race?" she asked.

"Your mother thought there was a chance," came his soothing reply.

But Ysabelle had had enough that night. "Has Wendel already bedded down?" she asked.

Godfrey sniffed at the mention of the jester's name. "He took his cart over yonder," he said, waving vaguely into the darkness. "I believe he wanted to try and entertain our red cousins, but I doubt if even they are in any mood for his fatuous antics. A more tiresome and unwanted fellow I never did meet."

Ysabelle smiled. "Yet he makes me forget," she murmured. "No, do not go find him. I fear that I am too fatigued for his stories and rhymes after all." The maiden stretched and nodded to her counselor. "Wake me at first light," she said. "I must retire to bed. If I could only forget everything for a few hours, it would be a great blessing."

"Good night, my lady," Godfrey said, bowing low.

Ysabelle disappeared inside the tent and cast herself upon the bed Griselda had prepared. The mousemaid pattered round her, tucking the blankets in and making sure her mistress was comfortable, before she lay on the smaller bed nearby.

"My poor lady," Griselda cooed, stroking the squirrel's raven hair, "may your dreams be untroubled."

Presently, they were both drifting into dark oblivion.

Outside the tent, the night was black and impenetrable.

For the sentries on duty, it was a weird, unsettling time. None of them had ever set foot outside their home before, and the sounds of the wild world were unfamiliar and startling.

The forest was strange, and seemed to press in on all sides. A strange scent floated on the still air–a putrid, cloying sweetness that grew stronger as the minutes passed. It tickled the nostrils of those on guard and disturbed the dreams of those asleep. It was as if the seal on some ancient tomb had broken and the moldering reek of stale centuries had escaped into the night.

Gradually, the fetid smell faded; then, one by one, each of the squirrels on watch became aware of a tingling between their shoulder blades. It was as though something was spying upon them–as if each tree had eyes to see and ears to hear.

Shaking themselves, they turned their faces heavenward and strained their eyes, searching for any signs of the forces of Hrethel. But the night was deep and absolute. No star shone, and no chink of moonlight crept through the thick, blanketing clouds above.

Not a hint of danger could be seen, yet every sentry gripped his spear and clutched his longbow in readiness for he knew not what. A terrible tension thrilled the air, charging the atmosphere with its tremendous power, and all found themselves breathing hard, their hearts pounding.

Wave upon wave of unreasoning fear flowed out from the darkness and wrapped itself around the encampment. It was as if a terrifying evil was gathering about them, and the paws that held the spears and longbows soon began to tremble before the malevolent and overwhelming force.

"Ulric!" one of the squirrels hissed to another. "What is it out there?"

The other wiped a nervous hand over his sweating brow. "Then you sense it, too, Ornus?" he replied in a hushed whisper. "I did think it was my own imaginings."

"Not that," returned the first, "for why do I quake so? Also, I find myself glancing over mine shoulder, expecting to see some frightful horror lurking behind. Something monstrous is abroad this night, or my nerves are no judge. Did you mark its stink afore?"

"How could I not? Mine nose still burns from the stench of it. Let us hope whatever is out there will pass us by."

But his friend made no answer, and when Ulric stared into the darkness where he had been standing, it was empty. Quickly, the sentry hurried across, and there, lying upon the ground with one arrow in his chest and another in his throat, was Ornus.

Ulric gave a fearful shout and called to the others. Then an arrow hit him in the back and he fell across his dead friend's body.

"What is it?" the other sentries cried, "Ulric! Ornus! Where are you?"

Suddenly, and without warning, the blackness beyond the encampment began to seethe and boil as a horde of dark

101

shapes slithered from the shadows and leaped among the startled squirrels.

"AWAKE!" one of the sentries shrieked, then a dagger silenced him forever.

Before any of the sleeping host had time to stir and reach for their weapons, the sinister figures were upon them.

With hollow shouts that struck terror into the squirrels' hearts, the raiders attacked.

In her tent, Ysabelle awoke from troubled dreams and shook Griselda from hers.

"M'lady!" the mouse squeaked when she heard the uproar raging outside. "What is happening? Are the bats attacking?" but Ysabelle had sprung from her bed and hurried from the tent. "Wait for me!" Griselda howled, pulling on her cap and gibbering with fright as she followed.

All was confusion. Dark figures charged from the shadows, and hideous struggles were taking place all around. Evil knives glinted in the night, and ghastly laughter echoed under the holly trees. Taken so completely by surprise, the squirrels were powerless, and many of the royal guards died in those first, bewildering moments.

Griselda rushed to Ysabelle's side and clung to her in terror. "Aaaiiyyeee!" she screamed. "The forces of darkness are with us!"

"Godfrey!" Ysabelle called. "Are you there? Godfrey!"

Only the sounds of battle answered, and the maiden looked desperately about her.

She scurried over to where one of her guards lay dead and pulled the bow from his grasp.

"Aaaaaiiiyyeeeee!" screeched Griselda again. "M'lady! Save me!"

The mouse covered her face as, from the darkness, a tall, hooded figure came lurching. It had huge claws, and beneath its deep cowl two eyes burned greedily. Cackling, it snatched

102

Griselda, plucked her from the ground, and threw her over its powerful shoulders.

The mouse screamed again as the monster carried her off into the dark, but Ysabelle was ready.

Swiftly, she had strung an arrow to the dead guard's bow, and, calling on all her strength, she pulled the bowstring back.

The arrow flew into the massive brute's leg, and it howled with rage and pain. Snarling, it threw the mouse upon the ground and advanced menacingly toward the squirrel.

Hurriedly, she fumbled for a second arrow, but even as she took up the feathered shaft, the beast towered over her.

Raising its immense claws, it brought an iron fist swinging down, and the longbow was knocked from Ysabelle's grasp.

"My LADY!" Griselda bawled, scrabbling to her feet.

Ysabelle stumbled backward as the figure gave a blood-freezing shout and threw back its head. At once, the hood fell around the creature's shoulders, and the squirrel screamed. Standing over her was an immense and repulsive rat.

There was no time to run, for the claws were raised again, and the same fist came smashing down.

The last thing Ysabelle remembered was the terrified screams of Griselda, and then the night closed over her, and she was lost.

ELDERFIRE

All was blackness; yet in the empty void, a small thought floated through the dark sea, carried along without consciousness and unaware of the voice that desperately called its name.

"Lady Ysabelle!" came the muffled cry. "Lady Ysabelle!"

Gradually, in the black expanse, the faintest glimmer of light pricked its way. A tiny red star edged into the vast night, and that distant voice slowly became clearer.

"My Lady!" it urged. "You must awaken!"

Then the star exploded, and the thought snapped back into its host.

"Uuhh," Ysabelle groaned as her temples pounded and her cheek stung.

"Thank the Green!" the voice declared at her side.

The maiden whimpered as she became aware of a biting agony in her wrists.

"Father," she mumbled dizzily, "what–what has happened? Griselda–"

"Hush," came the voice, "hush now."

For a moment, Ysabelle remained still as she tried to collect her jangled thoughts. Her eyes were closed, and she had not the strength to open them. Silently, she tried to remember what had happened and where she was.

The image of the monstrous rat reared in her mind, and she instinctively shrank away. But something held her paws, and the sharp pain in her wrists increased till she heard her own voice cry out.

"Try to stand," said the other. "See if you can."

Ysabelle swallowed—her mouth was parched and her tongue stuck to the roof of her mouth. "Who—who is that?" she asked timidly.

"'Tis I, 'tis Godfrey. Oh, my lady—we have been so anxious for you."

A meager ounce of strength began to seep back into the muscles of Ysabelle's legs. Awkwardly, she staggered to her feet and waited until her eyes were ready to flicker open.

The lids fluttered, and she wearily blinked away the sleep.

It was still dark, but fuzzy shapes slowly swam into view—then she saw Godfrey's careworn face gazing intently at her.

The counselor cried with relief and, from all around, similar gasps could be heard.

"Our prayers are answered," Godfrey exclaimed. "She is back with us."

Ysabelle stared at him, for her vision was still a little blurred, then it cleared and she drew her breath sharply. "Your lip!" she cried. "Godfrey, it is swollen and bleeding!"

Her old tutor put out his tongue and gingerly dabbed at the blood that ran down his whiskered chin.

Ysabelle tried to move toward him but found that she could not. Then she looked around her and beheld for the first time where they were.

It was an underground chamber: a dank, loathsome dungeon—a crudely dug burrow where not even a rat would live. The walls were roughly lined with stone, down which foul-smelling slime trickled and oozed over the earthen floor. A great wooden door sealed the dismal place, and flickering pitifully in a small bowl was a puny candle.

By the feeble light of this, Ysabelle could see that, set into the uneven walls, heavy chains of iron had been bolted, and attached to these were many sets of manacles and shackles.

Ysabelle tugged fiercely at her fetters, but the metal bands bit into the raw flesh that they had exposed at her wrists and the chains rattled, mocking her efforts with their cold clanking.

"Be still," Master Godfrey told her. "We have all struggled, but the restraints are strong and do not yield."

The maiden slumped against the wall and stared at the others. Apart from herself and Godfrey, she could see only six more prisoners, and each was chained and manacled. She knew all their faces, for they were black squirrels from her escort. Sorrowfully, they stared back at her. Some of them looked close to fainting and bore many wounds from the attack upon the camp.

"A glad sight it is to see you awake, my Queen," one of them uttered. "Master Godfrey has tried to wake you for many hours now."

"Hours?" Ysabelle asked.

Godfrey pulled on his shackles and edged closer to his sovereign. "Indeed," he said gravely, "by my reckoning we have been locked in here for the better part of the night. No doubt the sun has already risen above us."

"But I don't understand," Ysabelle spluttered. "What happened? Why are we here?"

Godfrey looked across at the others and they nodded—she had to be told. Clearing his throat and sucking the air through his teeth so that it whistled, he began.

"I am very much afraid that the rumors we had been hearing for these few years past are true!" he declared in a hurried and frightened rush. "The cult of Hobb has indeed grown again—oh, my lady, would that you had never lived to hear such awful tidings. And from mine own lips as well!"

"The Hobb cult!" Ysabelle breathed in horror. "Then it was they who attacked us?"

Godfrey waggled his head in confirmation. "Most assuredly," he cried. "The followers of the Infernal Triad have captured us."

Ysabelle's knees buckled a little, but she propped herself against the wall as the terror of the situation impressed itself upon her.

Many years ago, the three gods of the rats were worshipped in the depths of the dark forests. It was a pagan heathenism that all thought had finally died out. This hellish triad was called the Raith Sidhe, and they reveled in death and bloodshed.

According to the legends, the greatest of the three was the Lord Hobb, a hideous demon in rat shape. It was to him that the high priests of the cult made evil sacrifices and slaughtered any who would not join their dreadful congregations. The consort of Hobb was Mabb, a frightful apparition who plagued the dreams of the unwary and inspired them to murder. The Sleep Visitor, she was called, and in the past, those in her service had been responsible for innumerable wars. Finally, there was Bauchan—the Artful One, whose name was a byword for villainy and mischief. It was said that he could wear any shape he desired and, in disguise, stalked the waking world unnoticed.

At one time, they had been worshipped in great numbers, but they were now only a dim memory—and to many had become merely bogeys to frighten and bribe children with.

Ysabelle could hardly believe it. "Are you certain of this?" she asked.

Godfrey bowed, despising himself for being the one to tell her. "I am," he muttered. "While you have been unconscious, one of our jailers has visited us."

"He's right, ma'am," piped up one of the other squirrels. "Right nasty piece of work that villain is, too. Been pinching and squeezing us, as if seeing how ripe we are."

"Silence, Felago!" Godfrey sternly shouted.

"I was only saying!"

"Yes, well don't! I really do not think we should dwell on so unpleasant a thought as that," Godfrey said quickly. "Soon, the rest of our forces shall come looking for us. I'll wager we will not be kept locked up for much longer."

"So you think the rest of the company survived?" Ysabelle asked in great relief. "I thought we were the only ones left."

Another of the squirrels lifted his head and shook it grimly. It was Samuel Muin; a deep cut ran across his forehead, and the fur on his face was matted by his own blood. "Not that kind of attack," he said. "More of a dash-and-grab tactic. Nah, them stinking Hobbers don't have the guts for a real fight. Sneak up in the dark is all they had in mind: just charge in, do some throt-tling, then bear the booty away."

"And are we that booty?" asked Ysabelle.

"'Fraid so–begging your lady's pardon."

"So the rats have us," the maiden uttered miserably.

Godfrey sucked his teeth and raised his eyebrows. "Well not quite," he said. "It's not just rats. You see, my lady, the followers of Hobb are not restricted to those stupid creatures any longer. Now, other animals have become enamored of the darkness; if I had only listened to those rumors. No wonder the entertainers traveled in large numbers. They did say that the forests were being swallowed by an evil tide of hellish disciples, only I did not believe them–theatrical hysterics, I put it down to."

"It isn't your fault," she assured him. "No one could have pre-dicted the attack. I hope Griselda is safe. All we can do is try to plan our escape."

"Hah!" cried a voice from the deep shadows in a dark corner. "Listen to her now–what's it like, princess?"

Ysabelle stared in surprise as a small figure shuffled to its feet and edged into the gloom.

"You!" she cried.

Vespertilio dragged the chains that had been fastened about his ankles and moved forward as far as they allowed. "Oh, what a pretty show this is!" he chuckled grimly. "Glad am I to be here and see thee brought so low. Now, taste the bitterness of captivity thyself, O royal one."

"Keep your snout shut!" growled the sentry nearest to him.

"Tut, tut!" Vesper cried in mock indignation. "We cannot have that–all are equal now. Are we not prisoners together? Surely that makes us kinsfolk of a sort?"

"No bat is kin of mine!" shouted Samuel Muin.

Another squirrel strained at his manacles and snarled fiercely, "Did I not tell thee to keep silent, you stunted devil?"

"No," said Ysabelle firmly, "let the winged one speak. He does not frighten me. As Godfrey has said, we will not be prisoners for long. Our army shall come, and then all will be well."

"Hoo, hoo," chortled Vesper, "don't be too sure. What army would seek beneath the ground? A whole night they have no doubt been searching. I'll warrant they have already passed overhead and are gone far away." His words echoed around the dreary chamber, and the squirrels wondered if he was right.

"You seem very at ease," said Ysabelle. "What makes you so lighthearted? You are in the same predicament. You should hope our forces do find us!"

Vesper clicked his tongue, then ambled back into the darkness of the corner. "My position is the same as before," his voice drifted out to her. "All I have done is swap my captors and gain some companions."

"But these are Hobb worshippers!"

"So you say, but I see little difference–they have at least untied the bonds you set upon me. Now my wings are free."

Ysabelle shook her head, exasperated at the conversation. It was then that she noticed.

"The Acorn!" she cried. "Where is it? Godfrey, the amulet is missing!"

Her adviser sobbed woefully. "Alas," he wept, "I know–when they brought you in, it was gone from about your neck. Perhaps

109

it fell when you were taken, and even now your maid is keeping it safe. Oh, my lady, I pray that is the case."

Great tears ran down Ysabelle's face. Everything that had happened had been for that Silver Acorn, and she had lost it. Wretchedly, she closed her eyes—a fine Starwife she had proved herself to be.

From the shadows, Vesper laughed softly.

*   *   *

The pathetic candle had burned very low by the time footsteps were heard outside the stout wooden door.

Ysabelle pulled herself up and glanced questioningly at Godfrey.

"Our jailer," he declared, "come to taunt us once more, no doubt."

In the passage beyond the dungeon, the shambling footsteps halted. Ysabelle turned her head and listened, for out there a horrible voice was giggling and tittering to itself.

"Oooh, not long," it trilled excitedly, "then it'll be time, oh, yes—oh, yes." A key turned in the lock, and the heavy door was pushed open.

Ysabelle's eyes grew wide with astonishment; she had expected the voice to belong to a rat, but that was not what entered the chamber.

A large hedgehog came pattering inside. It was a foul creature with squinting little eyes that were too close together. A wet, snuffling nose drooled at the end of a long snout, and filthy bristles sprouted over its podgy cheeks, meeting the main sweep of its spines behind its tiny ears. The body of the jailer was fat, and it breathed with difficulty as glutinous rolls of flab quivered and wobbled when it moved. Its limbs, however, were exceptionally small and weedy; in fact, its feet were so dainty that it was impossible to see how the animal managed to walk on them.

Twirling a bunch of keys in its claws, it teetered into the center of the chamber and clapped its palms together in delight.

"Oh," it panted, "what a fine feast! Nine of the prettiest little darlings ever to have graced my cells! A pleasure to care for them—it truly is."

He tiptoed round to where Ysabelle was chained and cooed ecstatically. "What a pearl!" he squeaked. "How lovely to have you with us at last. Why, you naughty, naughty fellows!" he scolded the others. "You ought to have told Pigwiggen the fair one had stirred."

The hedgehog tottered closer, and Ysabelle balked before his horrendous breath. "Aw," he exclaimed, "she's so shy. Well, don't you fret none, my dove. Pigwiggen will take very good care of you." He reached out with his claws and gave Ysabelle's cheek a hard tweak.

"Unhand me!" she demanded, and around her all the squirrels bawled at the hedgehog and threatened him fiercely.

Pigwiggen threw his arms in the air and tripped daintily backward. "Now, now," he cackled, "I didn't harm the little treasure—I was just testing." He shook his spines, and a cloud of dust and soil gathered about his fat body. Then he went up to each of them in turn and laughed.

"How's your leg now?" he asked the first of his prisoners. "Ooh, it is healing well. Not nearly as messy as when you first arrived."

The squirrel, a sentry called Gwydion, merely gazed right back at the odious creature and said nothing. This was the third time the hedgehog had visited the dungeon since they had been taken. He loved taunting the captives and could not bear to see them without measuring the flesh upon their bones.

Slobbering, he poked Gwydion in the stomach and crowed with glee in anticipation of things to come. Then he scurried to the next squirrel. From one to another, the foul hedgehog danced, wrinkling his nose a little when he squeezed Godfrey's

111

stringy arms. Finally, he came to Vesper and pulled the bat from his dark corner.

"Should be very tasty when fried," Pigwiggen muttered, stretching one of Vesper's wings. "I do hope there'll be enough left for me to sample."

"Go sit on yourself!" the young bat yelled, for the inspected wing was the damaged one, and his eyes watered when the hedgehog pulled at it.

Pigwiggen laughed indulgently, then twirled about and drummed his fingers on his glistening lips. "Oh, what a divine selection," he cried passionately, "so many fancies and toothsome beauties to relish and savor. Of course, you'll be wasted on most of them—they don't have such a refined palate as do I. What a gathering it will be this night. How I am looking forward to it." He put his claw upon his brow as if the glamour and excitement of it all was just too much. Then his horrible little eyes swiveled slyly toward Ysabelle, and he giggled in a most vile manner that made the maiden shudder.

"Oh, it will be so extra special," Pigwiggen cooed, smacking his lips, "for never have I tasted royalty before. Does blue blood taste any sweeter than the common variety, I ask myself?"

With that, he waltzed over to the door and, with a final squeal of giddy delight, locked it behind him.

Ysabelle turned a frightened face to Godfrey. "What do you think that meant?" she asked in a faint whisper.

But Master Godfrey could not bear to answer and only hung his head.

"It means what it says," came the reply from the corner where Vesper sat. "Have you never heard what the worshippers of Hobb do to their victims?"

"Yes," she said quickly.

Vesper snorted, then told her anyway. "We're going to be peeled, my fine Lady—old Pigwiggen's going to make a bloody-bones of us all!"

*   *   *

For what seemed an age, Ysabelle, Vesper and the others remained in the dismal chamber. Presently, the candle burned itself out, and they were plunged into darkness, but no one came to renew it, and for a long time they were without any light whatsoever. Occasionally, the young bat clicked his tongue to see what they were doing, but he was more concerned with his poor wing–that foul brute had made it worse, and he nursed it in doleful silence.

Ysabelle was never sure if she slept at any time during that period of grim darkness. Occasionally, she would feel her head nodding but could not tell if she had indeed fallen asleep, for the waking world was as black as her dreams, and she drifted between the two, not knowing which was which.

"My lady!" Godfrey eventually woke her. "Listen, the time has come."

The sounds of footsteps once more echoed along the passage beyond the door, but this time there were many feet tramping toward them. Ysabelle and the others held their breath as the key rattled in the lock and the door swung open.

At once, the dungeon was filled with light, for many torches blazed in the passage, and Vesper and the squirrels shielded their eyes from the sudden brightness.

"Unchain 'em!" came a gruff and growling voice.

Ysabelle blinked and stared at the entrance.

Framed in the doorway was Pigwiggen, but behind him was a large group of ferocious-looking rats.

"Be quick about it!" one of the vermin barked.

The hedgehog skipped delicately into the chamber and began to unfasten the manacles of Gwydion, the squirrel nearest the door. Then he proceeded to free each and every one of the others. "Come, my chicks," he cried, "your time is come–the night is beginning!"

When she was released, Ysabelle carefully blew on her wrists and slid her paw into that of Godfrey, who stood beside her.

"What will happen?" she asked. "Where are they taking us?"

"I dare not ask myself that," he answered.

"Hoy!" shouted the largest rat. "Pipe down there! I don't want to hear any of your mewling!" He raised his fist, and in his claw he brandished a large cudgel.

One by one, the prisoners were led out, gripped and prodded by many sharp fingers. The passage beyond the dungeon was just wide enough for them to traipse three abreast, and, surrounded by their captors, Vesper and the squirrels stumbled miserably along it.

The tunnel rose in a gentle incline, and soon those at the front felt a breath of cold night air upon their faces.

A curtain of weed and grass covered the entrance, and the large rat swept it briskly aside before leading the others out.

From the damp underground, the prisoners filed into the open, then each stopped and stared in disbelief.

They were on the brink of a large basin-shaped dell that was ringed with trees whose misshapen roots had broken from the earth and wound about the edge like gnarled and twisting snakes. Down in the center of this great hollow, a group of three standing stones reared from the short grass, and before them a tall bonfire of elder wood burned brightly.

But what made the squirrels gape and gaze in fright was the sight of those gathered there.

About the stones, many thousand worshippers of Hobb yammered and shouted. Ysabelle and Vesper had never seen such a hideous collection of creatures. The rats who waited there were the most evil specimens of their kind, and alongside them countless other races cackled and roared. There were rabbits, hedgehogs, voles, and weasels. Even some mice could be seen slinking between the jostling bodies of their foul brothers. Also mingled among this dreadful company were rooks and gore crows whose sleek feathers shone in the firelight and whose sharpened beaks cawed with black merriment. High in the trees, lesser birds perched, huddled beside rats and shrews with torches in their grasp and malice in their glance.

A tumultuous cheer went up as all eyes turned to where the prisoners staggered from the tunnel entrance.

Ysabelle pressed herself against Master Godfrey, and her tail drooped. "What nightmare is this?" she gasped. "Where have all these vile abominations come from?"

Godfrey shivered as he held here. "I don't know, madam," he said nervously. "It's as if the foulest scrapings of the forest are assembled here. Oh, what an accursed time this is."

"Ho, my jewels," gibbered Pigwiggen as he came puffing from the passageway, heaving his blubbery bulk into the chill night air. "What a fine celebration we shall have. Is it not a magnificent congregation—did I not tell you it was to be exceedingly special?"

The rat who had led them spat on the grass and glared impatiently about him. "Hedgepig!" he shouted. "Tie these up and watch them till they are needed."

Pigwiggen tugged at a bunch of prickles on his forehead and smiled ingratiatingly. "Of course, brother; it shall be attended to at once."

The rat spat again, then he leaped down the slope to join the terrible gathering below.

Five other rats remained, and Pigwiggen handed each a length of rope and told them what to do.

A large claw grasped Ysabelle's shoulder and dragged her over to one of the twisting roots. Quickly, she was tied to it with her paws stretched behind her back. The others were attended to in the same way, except Vesper, whose wings were wrapped about an almost vertical piece of root and tethered to his feet.

"Now we can wait," tittered the hedgehog, strutting before his row of trussed-up appetizers, his eyes mirroring the blaze of the bonfire. "We shall wait, and we shall see."

Ysabelle trembled. Below her, a thousand wicked faces stared up, and she knew they were devouring her in their dark and malignant minds. "Help us, someone!" she wailed despairingly. "Save me, please!"

"Fear not, my lady!" Godfrey called over from where he was bound. "Have faith in the Green! We may yet be saved!"

"I pray it is so!" she answered. "But I'm so afraid—so terribly afraid. Look at them. They're just waiting to kill us—I cannot bear it!"

"Try not to let your spirits sink," he cried, forcing a hearty tone into his voice. "Think of something else—keep your thoughts off the devils down there." He looked about them and, in his finest tutorial manner, shouted, "Remember the alder dance that you performed yesterday. Think only of safe, happier times. Remember that even in the midst of the darkest night, a dawn must come."

She tried to do as he said, but it was impossible with the clamor of all those repulsive and eager Hobbers resounding in her ears. "I cannot!" she wept. "I simply cannot!"

"You must, you *must!* Think, what were the words you sang to the trees in the avenue?"

Ysabelle dragged her eyes from the seething masses and tried to concentrate. "Awake!" she managed to cry at last. "Awake! Thy sleep is ended!"

"That's right, my most excellent student and fairest lady!" Godfrey sang encouragingly.

"Have no fear, for Spring is come!" Ysabelle continued between her desperate sobs. "Put out thy leaves, O sleepy one!"

"Well done!" Godfrey cried.

But Ysabelle sank to her knees. "It's no good," she wept. "Even the tree we are tied to is the yew—Idho, the Tree of Death! Am I to awaken that? Are we not compassed round with

116

death already? Tread not into the fearsome night," she stammered unhappily. "Step not into the wild dark wood—"

Godfrey's heart bled to see her so distressed; he glanced at the others, and they, too, were crying for her—even Vesper seemed moved by the maiden's suffering.

"Let us all beseech the Green for our deliverance," the counselor suggested.

Each of the squirrels bowed their head—then, suddenly, the sound of a shrill horn split the night. Ysabelle craned her head; perhaps her army had arrived to rescue them. She cast her eyes wildly around the madness that raged before her, but not a sign of her host could she see. Then her spirit dwindled inside as she saw the source of the echoing sound.

On the far side of the dell, from the trunk of a dead yew tree, a spindly rat came marching with a horn raised to his lips. With deliberate slowness, he strode about the rim of the dell to where a large barrel stood. From somewhere in the vast crowd below, a slow, discordant dirge began as another rat started beating a horrid tune upon two grinning skulls. Hearing this, the former blew the horn one last time, then bowed and stepped aside.

An earsplitting shout erupted from the assembled Hobbers, and in their claws they all flourished what looked like sticks. Then they charged up the slope and plunged the sticks into the barrel. It was a chaotic scramble as those barging upward met those hurrying down.

Godfrey narrowed his eyes at the confusing spectacle; the ones who had dipped their sticks were now making for the bonfire. A flash of understanding illuminated his mind as the first of the creatures held the stick into the fire and lit it—they were Hobb lanterns, and the barrel must contain some kind of pitch, judging by the way the flames spluttered so readily into life.

Vile and raucous songs now resounded from the dell as more and more of the lanterns were lit. They were made of baked clay, having a short handle below a bulbous depiction of a rat's head.

This was hollow and open at the top; holes for the eyes and mouth had been cut into the rest of the frightening face, and flames dripped from the gaping jaws. Now, all the Hobbers' lanterns were ablaze, and the countless round eyes shone horribly.

Pigwiggen capered on the brink, giving excited little hops. It was all so beautiful to him.

Then a grim and grisly dance began about the bonfire and the standing stones. The worshippers of Hobb waved the lanterns above their heads, weaving patterns of flame in the smoky air.

Ysabelle watched in morbid fascination. The lanterns seemed to float above the Hobbers like demons of fire, and her eyelids grew heavy as the lurid symbols woven below mesmerized and entranced her.

"Hobb," the creatures chanted. "Hobb, Hobb, Hobb."

The rats whirled round and the rooks circled over the stones, calling the deadly name in cracked and ugly voices. The chanting continued, the dancing became faster, and the cries grew louder. Ysabelle found that beads of sweat had broken over her brow despite the cold of the night. Then, with one last, bloodthirsty shriek to their god, the creatures fell to their knees, facing the standing stones.

To Vesper and Ysabelle's horror, there came a flash of purple smoke—shot through with fiery sparks—and when it cleared, the tallest stone was no longer empty.

"Bless me!" yelped Vesper in terror.

"Godfrey!" Ysabelle howled. "It's him! Hobb has come!"

Upon the stone a terrifying apparition stood with its arms outstretched—the raw head and bloody-bones in which guise the leader of the Raith Sidhe was rumored to appear to his followers.

Ysabelle screamed as the peeled cadaver turned slowly round to view the infernal congregation.

"No," Godfrey called to the squirrel maiden, "that isn't

Hobb—look! Do you see? No magic animates that corpse—it is but a costume! The thing that they worship was banished from this world many ages ago."

Ysabelle stared at the awful figure and was reassured. It was indeed false—the shreds of sinew were only ribbons of colored material, and the shape of the peeled flesh was but cunning needlecraft that Griselda might have admired if the subject had not been so macabre.

"That must be the high priest of this region," Godfrey told her. "I have read that they dress up to impersonate their evil deity, mimicking him in their foolish adoration. Yet he is still just as deadly, nevertheless."

Upon the stone, the alarming figure abruptly leaped into the air and threw himself into the crowd. Snatching up a Hobb lantern, the figure ran three times around the bonfire, then returned to its lofty position.

A frightened gasp issued from Godfrey's throat as the high priest sprang back upon the stone. For there, hanging about the neck of the ghastly fiend and gleaming in the harsh light of the lantern, was the Silver Acorn.

Ysabelle saw it, too, and she shook her head in disbelief.

"The amulet!" she cried. "He must have stolen it from me!"

"Mercy," gibbered Godfrey as a dreadful suspicion began to form at the back of his mind. "What madness are they about?"

But now something new was happening. The high priest held up his lantern, and the frantic yammering of his followers ebbed and died. An unearthly quiet fell about the crowded basin as they all strained to catch his words.

"Children of the Raith Sidhe!" the costumed figure declared, throwing its head back and flinging its arms open wide. "Welcome! Once more are we assembled in the Ring of Banbha to do homage!" it grandly proclaimed. "In this sanctified place do we honor and revere the Mighty Three. Praise their unholy names and do obeisance—Hobb, Mabb, and Bauchan!"

119

The crowd roared fanatically and stretched their claws toward their leader in complete devotion.

The high priest basked in their adoration before continuing. "But this night," he announced, "our celebrations are special indeed, for no ordinary sacrifices have we captured, but noble beasts from Coll Regalis, and among their number is one born of the royal line itself."

Ysabelle cringed; the voice of the high priest rang coldly and seemed to cut right into her. She watched as the crowd eagerly spun round to stare, but when the bloody-bones figure pointed straight at her, she squirmed and looked away.

The mouths of the thousands that filled the dell lolled open, and their tongues slid greedily from their jaws.

"Now, let the Lord Hobb be worshipped!" the high priest demanded.

Countless lanterns bobbed in the air, and the shouting resumed.

"Here we go," gurgled Pigwiggen. "This is the moment." He teetered forward and clapped his claws with joy. "Well, well, my succulent berries," he addressed the prisoners, "which shall be first?"

He hopped a little jig that brought him close to Vesper and pulled at the bat's large ears. "Shall it be you, O cuckoo in my delicious nest?" The young bat glared back at him, and the hedgehog hummed happily to himself. "No," he announced, "not thee, not yet!" Turning aside, he considered Vesper's neighbor and nodded with satisfaction. "Of course," he said brightly, "what better way to begin than with something strong and probably full of flavor."

He motioned to the rats who stood nearby, and two of them came forward to untie the selected squirrel.

"No!" bawled Gwydion as the ropes were cut from his paws and the rats led him down the slope. "For pity's sake!"

Pigwiggen chuckled. "Well, at least his leg won't be hurting for much longer," he mused. "A fine tail that one had, though;

p'raps if I asked I could have it afterward? Keep the winter drafts out lovely, that would, and my poor neck do ache so."

"Stop this!" Godfrey yelled. "You must!"

But the hedgehog took no notice, wondering only why his food was always so loud and fond of shouting.

In horror, Vesper stared after Gwydion as the rats dragged him through the crowds to the stones. The young bat shook with fear; he had never seen anything so terrifying as the grisly scene that now unfolded before his eyes.

Ysabelle cried out and quickly looked away as Gwydion was pinned down upon the flattest stone and the peeling knife was raised.

"No!" murmured Godfrey as a triumphant cheer roared from the loathsome Hobbers.

"Heathen scum!" cried Samuel Muin.

Warden Felago clenched his teeth and kept his eyes tight shut, and the other three squirrels yelled in anguish as the evil work was done and the screams of their comrade were finally stilled.

Only Godfrey forced himself to watch the actions of the high priest. The heathen devil was holding the Silver Acorn aloft for all to see, then it plunged down, and when Godfrey saw it next, the amulet was covered in blood.

"Come, Hobb!" the figure called out. "Join us here!"

"What's happening?" Ysabelle cried. "What is he doing?"

The high priest steeped the Acorn twice more, and with every sweep of his arm he called to his master.

Godfrey shook all over. "Invoking the Lord of the Raith Sidhe himself," he answered.

"But you said that was impossible!"

"That was before I saw the Acorn about that villain's neck!" the tutor exclaimed. "That amulet holds tremendous powers. Until it is joined with the stabilizing forces of the Starglass, it is a perilous device. I dread to think what may befall the world if it is used for evil! There is every chance that Hobb may indeed appear!"

"Bring another victim!" the high priest called.

Pigwiggen hurriedly untied another squirrel, and the rats led the unfortunate fellow down to his awful fate.

"Ooh," Pigwiggen wistfully sighed when he was alone with the remaining prisoners, "hearken to those sounds. An expert peeler is our leader—nothing goes to waste. He's not one of those ham-fisted hackers who just want to have a go. Real nice job that one does—proper art, it is—a pleasure to watch him at work."

The hedgehog leaned forward and stood on his toes to get a better view. They were enjoying themselves down there; he glowered at the other Hobbers enviously, and his mouth slobbered to see them.

"Coo," he muttered, "how they go at it, look at them a-carousing—they'd best not forget me. They'd best put some giblets by!"

He jumped up and down in agitation, wringing his claws distractedly.

Godfrey eyed him, and he tutted sympathetically. "Poor, poor Piggywiggy!" he said. "It isn't fair, is it?"

The hedgehog spun round, a confused and hungry expression fixed upon his ugly face.

"Just look at all your friends down there," Godfrey continued. "Well, you cannot in truth call them friends, can you? They won't save you anything, and after all your hard work guarding us so well. Just listen to them guzzling and stuffing their filthy faces—not a drop, not a shred, shall you get."

Pigwiggen was beside himself with despair. He had looked forward to this all day. It had been a long time since he had eaten fresh meat and drunk warm blood, and these dainties were all so violently desirable.

"Quiet!" he told Godfrey with a stamp of his foot. "They won't forget me."

Godfrey laughed, and his fellow prisoners stared at him in amazement—what was he doing?

"Well, even if they do remember," he told the slavering hedge-hog, "there won't be much. Just look how many of them there are and how few of us to be shared round. I know what will happen, my prickly friend: those at the front shall scoff the most, and those at the back won't even get a lick. Up here, you have no chance."

"Ooooh!" moaned Pigwiggen, tearing at his spines. "'Tain't fair–that's downright selfish and greedy."

"Bring another to the altar!" the high priest's voice rang from the stones.

Pigwiggen whimpered and reluctantly untied another of his precious lovelies.

When two rats came to take him, the squirrel called Felago did not cry out but gazed back at Ysabelle. "For the Hazel Realm," he said simply before they hauled him to his doom.

Godfrey winced at this new torment, but he had to resume what he had started.

"Oh, deary me!" he shouted above the horrendous cheers that met this fresh victim. "Not many of us left, are there? Only six– soon it will be only one, and when the one has gone, what shall you do then, Pigwiggen?"

The hedgehog was biting his claws in dismay. "Not one juicy drop for me," he lamented. "Not a morsel to be had; no marrow to slurp, and no bone to chew."

"Of course," Godfrey persisted, "there is a way to cheat them."

"Cheat?" snapped Pigwiggen crossly.

"Only of what you deserve," Godfrey goaded him.

The hedgehog scratched himself, then pattered closer to the tutor. "How could I do such a thing?" he asked in a conspir-ing whisper.

"You could always slip away with one of us," the squirrel replied, "go to some dark retreat and have a quiet munch of your own, with none to disturb you."

Pigwiggen's eyes sparkled at the thought, and he moistened his lips as his beady eyes roved toward Ysabelle.

Godfrey saw it, and an approving smile lit his face. "If I might proffer a suggestion, may I nominate my mistress? See how tender her young flesh is."

Pigwiggen squealed in rapture. "Yes, yes!" he vigorously agreed. "I shall take her!"

Godfrey shook his head. "Not yet," he whispered so none of the others could hear. "She won't go with you. Untie me first; the maiden trusts me. I can persuade her to follow you to your table."

"Hoo, hoo," the hedgehog wickedly cackled as he untied Godfrey's paws, "a fine feast I shall have, and nothing will I spare for the others—"

But that was the last they heard him utter, for Godfrey's fists punched the stupid hedgehog with all their might and he stumbled backward, rolling into a bristling ball.

"Well done, Master Godfrey!" Ysabelle cried.

The tutor rubbed his knuckles and hastily set the others free.

"Hey!" shouted Vesper. "What about me?"

But the squirrels did not have time to release a wretched bat, for they might be spotted at any moment.

"Let us run!" Ysabelle urged them. "We must escape this nightmare!"

But Godfrey shook his head. "Not yet," he said. "They would catch us at once. No, I think I see a way to even the balance."

He scurried along the edge of the dell, keeping well out of the crowd's sight. Up to the pitch barrel he hurried, and, with the help of Samuel Muin and the other two squirrel guards, he heaved the vessel on to its side.

Oily black goo went splashing and rushing down the slope, and when it reached the bottom, it spread over the ground, seeping between the feet of the infernal congregation. But the Hobbers did not notice the sticky pitch that oozed over their toes, for the third sacrifice was over and the body was flung among them. In the mad frenzy that followed, nothing would have diverted them.

"Please," Ysabelle insisted, "let us go now!"

124

"No, my lady," Godfrey said, "the Silver Acorn must be retrieved at all costs."

Ysabelle stared at him incredulously—had he gone mad? How could they possibly hope to take the amulet from the high priest?

Godfrey whispered a few words to the other squirrels, and, after a moment's hesitation, they all consented. "Very well," the tutor whispered before turning back to address his sovereign. "My lady, we must do all we can—but you stay here. If we do not succeed, then run for your life."

"But—but, Godfrey!" she stammered. "The risk is—"

Too late—the four squirrels were already creeping down the slope.

Over the pitch-soaked grass they slithered, keeping well out of the circle of firelight. Toward the standing stones, they stealthily made their way, at times running back into the shadows to escape the sight of the hellish revelers.

Godfrey kept his gaze fixed upon the high priest, who towered over his disciples. The Silver Acorn still gleamed about his neck, and the old counselor hoped that his hastily conceived plan would work.

But the third sacrifice had already been devoured by the terrible followers of Hobb, and some were now wiping their mouths and turning to where the remaining prisoners were held.

"Ahh!" they screamed. "They are gone—only one is left!"

"Find them!" snarled the high priest.

"Look!" shrieked a vicious little mouse. "They're over there!"

Everyone glared at the dark area behind the standing stones, where four shapes crept through the gloom.

"Kill them!" screeched the high priest. "Kill them all!"

"Godfrey!" Ysabelle called from the top of the dell.

Thousands of Hobbers surged forward through the tarry mire, streaming past the altar like a foul and deadly tide.

Ysabelle watched helplessly as the seething masses rushed for Godfrey and the guards, yammering for their blood. "Run," she told herself. "It's hopeless now—he wanted you to run! Escape while you can!" But instead of hurrying away from the horrendous spectacle, the squirrel maiden tore down the slope to where Godfrey and the others were cornered.

A short, skinny rat, whose eyes shone with a ruby light, came charging at the forefront of the infernal crowd. With a long sword in his claws, he let loose a blood-curdling yell and plunged the weapon into the first of the squirrels.

Samuel Muin sprang at the beast and ripped the sword from its grasp. "Maggot!" he bawled. "Go serve thy master in the Underworld!" And in a moment the rat was dead.

Yet more of the congregation took its place, and they had many daggers, knives, and spears. Samuel swept the sword through the front rows, cutting them down like reeds, and the foul enemies squealed as they fell to the ground.

From the ferocious mob, a huge rat came lumbering. A great pike was in its fist, and with a hollow chuckle, it ran at Samuel Muin and slew him cruelly.

"Samuel!" cried Godfrey as the hellish horde advanced. Only two squirrels now remained, and the last boundary warden ran in front of the counselor to protect him. But a black feathered arrow came singing from the shrieking mass, and he collapsed with it buried deep within his breast.

Alone before the pagan crowd, Godfrey eyed them fearfully. Another arrow was aimed, and countless daggers glinted thirstily as the Hobbers came slowly toward him.

Then a foul-looking rabbit, whose teeth had been sharpened into fangs, chanced to look behind the solitary squirrel, and its grimy ears quivered with evil joy. "Look!" it shouted. "Another of them!"

They all stared past Godfrey to where Ysabelle came hurrying to her tutor's side.

The counselor wailed to see her, then darted forward and snatched a Hobb lantern from a startled vole.

"Kill them!" commanded the high priest upon the stone nearby.

Godfrey dragged Ysabelle behind him and threw the lantern into the midst of the murderous children of Hobb.

With a rush, the pitch-covered ground burst into flame, and the worshippers screamed in panic. Sheets of fire rippled outward, and many were roasted alive. The Hobbers howled in dismay and ran wildly from the crackling blaze, for the dell had become a frightful cauldron of swirling flame. Fur was smoking, whiskers frazzled, and no one had time to deal with the prisoners—to flee the terrible fire was all they could think of. With flames licking about their feet, they rampaged over the sides of the dell, abandoning those who could not escape.

The foul-looking rabbit bounded from the scene with an insane shriek screeching from his lips. The beast's tail was burning, and its long ears smoldered, leaving two threads of black smoke trailing behind him. Somewhere amid the furnace, a badger screamed, his huge bulk rearing above the flames that blasted upward to swallow him. With a tremendous crash, the writhing creature fell, overcome with flame and smoke, and in the ruin of his fall, many other animals perished.

A carrion crow furiously beat its wings to flee, but the flames caught it and the bird plummeted into the lethal heat. Streams of rats and squealing mice poured up the grassy banks with white-hot sparks fizzing after them and leaping into their fur.

Upon the stone, the high priest shrieked with fury. A sea of flame raged about the altar, and in his boiling anger he threw down his own lantern, which exploded amid the fires.

"Now, my lady!" Godfrey cried, pulling Ysabelle after him. Together they braved the scorching flames and quickly scrabbled onto the stones.

The bloody-bones figure glared down at them—they were responsible for this. Most of Hobb's children were engulfed in the fiery tumult, and his magnificent celebration had been defiled.

A long knife flashed in the high priest's claw as Godfrey clambered up to him.

"Prepare to meet thine end!" his evil voice rang out. "No agony is too great for thee!" He lunged forward, and Godfrey scurried to one side before leaping onto the top of the stone.

The high priest whirled round and stabbed at the air between them.

"First you," the tall, masked creature growled, "then the fair one below."

Standing on the smallest stone, Ysabelle clasped her paws and stared up at them intently. "Be careful, Godfrey!" She breathed.

"A tasty brace of skins you shall make," the high priest taunted the tutor. "Thy blood I shall sip, and on her flesh shall I dine."

With a swift movement, he sprang at the squirrel, and the knife shone cold and deadly. But Godfrey leaped aside and, as the blade came slicing down, caught hold of the high priest's arm.

The bloody-bones snarled and struggled to wrench himself free.

"No, you don't!" Godfrey wailed, trying to shake the weapon from his opponent's claw.

Frantically, the two figures wrangled, yet the high priest was stronger, for Godfrey was old, and too long had he been absorbed in the study of books. His experience of combat was limited, and at last the claw that held the knife was free.

"Now die!" laughed the bloody-bones, and he plunged the knife into the squirrel's chest.

Godfrey gasped, and his face turned toward his beloved sovereign. "My lady!" he choked.

"Godfrey!" Ysabelle screamed.

The high priest crowed in triumph as his enemy sank to his knees—but it was not over yet.

With the darkness welling up around him, Godfrey clutched at the scarlet material of the bloody-bones costume. A surprised cry issued from the high priest as the squirrel tore at him.

The world was slipping from beneath the counselor, and he toppled from the standing stone.

Yet his paws were still gripped about the garish disguise, and the high priest lost his balance. With a startled yell, he followed Godfrey through the air, tumbling and somersaulting toward the ground below.

It was the bloody-bones who landed first and, with a thud, Godfrey fell on top of him.

Ysabelle gaped at them in despair, for neither moved. The high priest was stunned, and behind the crimson mask his eyes were shut. Godfrey lay across the prostrate body, his own blood staining the ghoulish costume.

Slowly, the old squirrel lifted his head and, in a rasping whisper, called to Ysabelle.

"My—my lady—" he muttered.

Ysabelle rushed forward and knelt beside him. Around them the fire still raged, but neither was aware of the fierce, baking heat. "Do not worry," she sobbed, cradling her old tutor's head in her paws. "You will recover. 'Tis but a scratch, no more. You will get well, Master Godfrey—you must."

A great sigh wheezed from Godfrey's lips, and he feebly shook his head. "No," he said, "my time is done." He raised a shaking paw and clasped his fingers about the neck of the high priest. "Take it," he gasped, pulling the Acorn free and passing it to the maiden. "Bear the Silver unto Greenreach. Make me proud, my little student. May the Green—may the—" And with that, Master Godfrey Gelenos breathed his last and his eyelids closed forever.

"Godfrey!" she called. "Don't leave me, Godfrey!"

But only the crackle of the flames answered her, and she bowed her head to kiss his brow.

Suddenly, a savage claw flashed out and seized the maiden's wrist.

Ysabelle screamed. Behind the mask, the high priest's eyes glared up at her.

"Give it back!" he demanded. "The amulet is mine!"

The maiden leaped away, and the claw lost its grip. Clasping the Silver Acorn to her breast, Ysabelle spun around and ran as fast as she could.

"Garr!" bellowed the high priest. Contemptuously, he flung Godfrey's body to one side and jumped to his feet. Through the narrow eye slits of the bloody-bones costume, the loathsome creature watched Ysabelle hare up the bank of the dell.

Still tied to the tree root, Vesper wriggled and squirmed, but the ropes were firmly tied. From this vantage point, he had seen everything, and when the pitch caught fire, he had feared that the escaping Hobbers would slay him in their anger. But though many smoldering and singed worshippers raced past, none had paid him any heed.

In silence, the young bat witnessed the final struggle between Godfrey and the high priest, and through the billowing curtains of smoke and flame, he had seen the old squirrel die.

Now, Ysabelle clambered over the edge of the burning basin, and Vesper cried in amazement as she hurried over and hastily untied his bonds.

"You're coming with me!" she told him in a rush of words.

"What–" he began, but the squirrel maiden roughly shoved him forward.

"Hurry!" she commanded.

Vesper turned on her angrily–this tree rat wasn't going to order him around any more. His mouth opened to tell Ysabelle exactly what he thought of her, but then his eyes saw that the altar stone, where the high priest had stood, was now empty.

"Come on!" the bat shouted, hopping quickly through the undergrowth. "Run!"

Ysabelle hurtled after him, and the pair of them raced beneath the yew trees and vanished into the darkness of the wild, midnight forest beyond.

OUT OF THE MISTY HAWTHORN

Ysabelle had never run so desperately in all her life. She and the young bat were level now. Vesper scooted through the long grass, not once daring to glance behind. Twice he stumbled, tripping over hidden roots, then he trod on his own wing and tumbled head over heels into a heap of rotting leaves. Quickly, he recovered, grumbling fretfully about his broken wing, then set off once more.

Ysabelle almost stopped to help him, for the bat was her only chance now. She wavered a moment as Vesper picked himself up, then bounded forward again.

Suddenly, she ran headlong into a thick cobweb that spanned two trees. The sticky nets clung to her face in a suffocating mist and, spluttering in disgust, she wildly tore it away.

"Hurry!" cried Vesper as he raced by.

Ysabelle spat the last strands of spider's web from her mouth and hastened after him.

The forest was a grim and frightening place. Hideously shaped trees loomed out of the darkness, and even they seemed intent on stopping the escaping prisoners. Spindly twigs reached down toward them, raking through their fur, scratching their faces, and tangling in Ysabelle's long, unbraided hair.

Further into the unlit wildness they ran, until their hearts hammered against their ribs and the air they breathed wheezed into their lungs in great gulps. A desperate weariness overtook the unlikely pair, and, increasingly, their steps faltered.

131

Ysabelle knew she could run no more. The muscles in her legs burned with fatigue, and all she wanted to do was throw herself into the long grass to rest. Gradually, the squirrel maiden slowed her pace, and the distance between Vesper and herself quickly widened.

"Wait!" she called, trying to catch her breath. "I must . . . sit for a moment."

The bat continued running. "No time!" he shouted back. "If you want the Hobbers to catch you, it doesn't worry me. Tarry here all you wish."

Bent double and panting hard, Ysabelle fumed to hear him. She would show that miserable, small-eyed villain! Straightening, she watched as Vesper disappeared from sight, then she tore after.

With enormous strides, she swiftly caught up with him. The bat had stopped, and was staring at the ground. Ysabelle reached out and seized him by the scruff of his neck.

"How dare you not wait!" She cried. "How dare you run away! I'll–" Then she realized why the bat had stopped–but it was too late for her.

Vesper had been standing on the edge of a ditch, where the ground fell sharply away. Even as Ysabelle grabbed the bat's furry neck, she felt the loose soil crumble beneath her feet. Emitting a cry of surprise, the squirrel maiden slipped, let go of Vesper, and slithered down the sheer bank.

"Heeeeelp!" came her startled wail as she tumbled down.

But Vesper was also in difficulties. Ysabelle had thrown him off balance, and the young bat frantically flapped his wings to save himself. But it was no good, and down he went.

With a squelch and a splash, Ysabelle landed in the soft mud below and rolled into a trickling stream.

For a second, she sat in a most undignified position amid the swirling, freezing water, drenched and dazed. Then Vesper came crashing beside her, but the bat fell headfirst into the ditch, and when he raised his head, his face was covered in sticky black mud.

"You stupid, brainless, idiotic, clumsy blunderer!" he stormed, spluttering mud and ditch water. "For the Moon's sake! What made you charge into me like that and pull me down? Did you not see why I had halted?"

Ysabelle assumed some of her shattered dignity and glared at the bat angrily. "Hold your tongue!" she scolded. "Choose you words more carefully when you address Ysabelle, daughter of the Lady Ninnia and the Lord Cyllinus!"

Vesper floundered in the mud; the pain of his wing was almost unbearable. "Oh, go eat a wormy apple!" he snapped. "You're nothing but an uppity tree worshipper."

The squirrel picked herself up and stared down at him icily. "Foolish of me," she snorted.

"You're not wrong there!"

"I meant," she hurriedly put in, "that it was foolish of me to expect anything more from a baseborn creature like yourself."

Vesper made a rude gesture to her, then wiped the mud from his face.

"Peasant," Ysabelle muttered. "Your kind are no better than those disgusting Hobbers back there. Vermin with wings—that's what you are!"

"Keep your poxy insults to yourself!" Vesper protested. "It's you who are called tree rats—we Moonriders aren't related to them villains. Why, it's a sore pity you weren't peeled back there!"

"Listen to how hotly you deny it!" she said with a scornful laugh. "Verily I must have touched upon the truth—vermin."

Vesper splashed to his feet. "Tree rat! Tree rat!" he yelled.

The squirrel put her paws on her hips. "You're no Moonrider," she sneered. "You're not old enough."

Her words stung the bat, and, with his good wing, he scooped up a great quantity of the cold water and hurled it at her.

"Aaggghhh!" Ysabelle shrieked, dripping from head to toe.

"How dare you! I am of the royal house!" She could do nothing but gape and stare as the bat pointed at her and hooted with derisive laughter.

"I can see this is going to be extremely difficult for me," she managed to utter at last. "It would be better if we said nothing more to one another until the journey is completed. There would be no benefit to either–much wiser to assume a distinct and agreeable silence."

Vesper stared at her, perplexed. "What are you chattering on about now?" he asked.

"Greenreach," Ysabelle told him. "I still have to get there. Why else do you think I saved you? I would gladly have left you for the Hobbers, but alas I am ignorant of the way to the holy land. I should have been more attentive to poor Godfrey when he was showing me the maps. You, however, have already been there, so now you shall be my guide."

The bat threw back his head and roared. "Oho!" he scoffed. "Never have I encountered such a wooden head before! What fancy has made thee think that I would be willing to lead you to that place? Oh, no, my fine, bush-tailed madam, if you want to go there, you shall have to find it on your own. Vespertilio had had enough of thy company to last him well into old age, so–"

Suddenly, his voice failed as, high above them, they both heard soft, sinister laughter.

Standing upon the edge of the ditch, the tall figure of the bloody-bones was glaring down at them.

Fearfully, Vesper sprang back, and Ysabelle stared up in dread.

"So," the high priest spat, "finally, the two lost lambs are found. What a frightful noise they did make, yet it was their very bleating that led me to them."

In his claw he held the knife that had killed Master Godfrey, and he lifted it high above his head so that the dull night shone over the steel. The blade was still covered in blood, and Ysabelle murmured in horror, stumbling backward, where she splashed into the stream once more.

The grim blade flashed a cold light over the hideous bloody-bones mask. "Now," the figure said in a murderous voice, "it is time for you to return to the fold."

Tensing his muscles, the high priest slashed at the air and prepared to spring. Ysabelle covered her face, knowing that this was the end—this time, she was too tired to escape. Beside her, Vesper's eyes snapped shut as the terrifying bloody-bones leaped from the bank.

Down the evil creature dived, his infernal gloating filling the ditch with fear and despair. But even as his malevolent form rushed to kill Vesper and Ysabelle, something strange occurred.

The trickle of water that wound between the muddy shores abruptly began to glow. Veins of emerald light streaked through the stream, welling up until the entire forest seemed to blaze with its eerie brilliance.

The high priest's laughter died in his throat as powerful forces gripped his body, catching him in midair, leaving him dangling like an abandoned puppet.

Ysabelle took her paws from her face and gasped in wonder around her. The water was dazzling; it shone like a ribbon of pure sunlight. All shadows were driven far away, and, above her, the high priest flailed his arms and legs, unable to move in any direction.

"It's a miracle!" Vesper whispered in disbelief.

The squirrel maiden dipped her paw in the shining stream. "Praise to the Green!" she cried as the liquid dripped from her fingers like sparkling jewels. "Do you not see? By some happy chance, we have stumbled upon one of the scared streams that traverse the forest and connect His holy shrines!"

A furious shout made her glance back up to where the bloody-bones figure helplessly writhed.

The water around her increased in brilliance, and above,

with a shriek of rage and fright, the high priest was hurled upward, back to the edge of the ditch. As he went flying through the air, the knife was torn from his grasp and fell, spinning harmlessly down into the mud below.

At once the figure scrambled to his feet and attempted to lunge down the bank once more. But each time he tried, the forces that were channeled through the stream drove him back.

"I–I don't understand!" Vesper stammered, gaping up at the infuriated high priest. "What is happening?"

"The villain is powerless!" Ysabelle laughed. "There is naught he can do to us now. While we remain in this hallowed water, we are under the protection of the Green."

At last the bloody-bones ceased his struggles and stood upon the ditch's brink, trembling with anger and shaking his fists. His fury burned hotter than any fire, and he stretched out a quivering claw that pointed at his unreachable victims.

"Rue this you shall!" he snarled in a voice taut with rage. "If a contest of strength is what thou desirest, then so be it! Soon you shall both wish I had dispatched your lives swiftly this night, for now the sport is ended." He lifted up his arms and called upon his infernal master. "Hobb!" he yelled. "Lord of the Underworld and greatest of the Raith Sidhe, hear now the words of thy servant! Give strength to the curses that I utter in thy unholy names–imbue them with thy might. Let all enemies of thy children perish, and let me be the instrument of their destruction." As he spoke, the finger seemed to grow, becoming a terrible towering shape that was wreathed in awful magic.

Below, Ysabelle and Vesper held their breath; the high priest was calling a terrible doom upon them, and, though the power of the Green still coursed through the stream, they both felt afraid. A curse had strength to maim or kill, and nothing could save them once the pronouncement had been made. Ysabelle shivered as the bloody-bones glared down and delivered the dreadful words.

"Both shall die!" he roared. "Yet, even as they look Death full in the face, they shall beg mercy of me—but all to no avail. This, now, is the doom my Lord shall visit upon them." Reaching his claw toward Vesper, the high priest snorted with loathing. "For his part in allowing the royal maiden Ysabelle to flee," he declared, "the winged one has chosen his own time of death and is henceforth cursed by that name."

Behind the mask, the creature's eyes narrowed as he continued. "Beware the sound of bells, O Moonrider!" he warned in a hollow voice. "For when thou art surrounded by their clamor, thy death will surely come."

Vesper swallowed nervously and wrapped his wings about him as this dreadful doom was proclaimed. Then the high priest turned to Ysabelle.

"As for thee," he hissed, "last of the Hazel line, thy weird shall seek thee out, and the terror of it will haunt thy dreams. The amulet that you now wear has thrice been steeped in the blood of thy subjects. On the very stones sacred to Hobb was the sacrifice made, and thrice did I call his terrible name."

The high priest crouched down and put his claw to the raw ears of his costume. "Listen," he said in a cracked whisper, "already my Lord stirs. Ages past was he banished from the waking world—now he is free. The Silver Acorn has released him, and, even as I speak, he stretches and begins the journey upward. From the unfathomable reaches of the Pit, the Lord of the Raith Sidhe comes, and when he does, Ysabelle, daughter of Ninnia and Cyllinus, shall serve him for eternity in Hell's dungeons!"

The figure flung its arms wide and gave a horrible laugh. "Now, my lambs," it shrieked, "do you not wish the peeling knife had done its work? To the terror of thy fortunes I leave thee— farewell!" And, with that, the high priest turned and vanished into the night.

Quickly, the green light faded from the stream and the forest was dark once more. Ysabelle stared at the ditch's edge, where now only shadows mocked her, and shook herself. Lowering her eyes, she looked at the young bat by her side, and he gazed back in fear.

"Did you hear that?" she asked. "Did you hear what he said?"

"He said I would die, surrounded by the sound of bells!" Vesper muttered. "I'm going to die!"

"What does that matter?" she cried. "Did you not hear him say that Hobb is coming? Godfrey feared this would happen—he said the amulet had the power. What am I to do?"

Vesper stared at her, and anger overcame his present fright. "This is all thy fault!" he shouted. "By thy name was I cursed—and by the stupid rogue's misunderstanding! 'Twas not I who helped you to escape; it was thee who untied me! By what unjust ruling am I now doomed? It isn't fair—it never, never is! Would that I could roll back the days and prevent myself flying after the others. Then would I have been spared the sight of thy foul and ugly countenance."

"And I thine!" she snapped back. "Wait, where are you going?"

Vesper kicked at the water around him and stomped through it crossly. "'Tis enough!" he bawled. "I'm away and shall take my leave whether you will or no. Many leagues would I like to put between us."

"Your curse won't be lifted that way!" she called after him.

The bat said nothing but waded miserably upstream, hanging his head sorrowfully, the thought of his approaching death bearing down upon his spirits.

Ysabelle stamped her feet angrily. She needed him to show her the way to Greenreach; if she could only find some way to persuade him. She gazed down at the amulet that hung about her neck and shivered. The silver was tarnished, covered as it was by dried blood. Hastily, she unfastened the fine chain and tried to clean it in the stream. But the blood would not wash off, and the Acorn remained dulled by the brown-red stains.

The squirrel maiden looked up and watched helplessly as

Vesper barged farther away. Fastening the amulet around her neck once more, she cast her gaze desperately about the ditch, and then she saw the high priest's knife embedded in the soft mud. Quickly, she ran over and pulled it free.

It was an evil-looking weapon; mysterious and ghastly symbols had been scratched into the steel, inscribing charms of death and destruction. Ysabelle shuddered in disgust as she held it, but there was nothing else she could do.

Hurriedly, she clasped it tightly in her paw, then set off after Vesper.

"Halt!" the squirrel shouted as she splashed upstream.

Vesper ignored her and plodded farther on. He could hear her crashing toward him, but there was nothing she could do to change his mind—or so he thought.

"Now!" Ysabelle cried, catching up with him. "You are going to obey my commands!"

The bat was about to blow a raspberry when he felt a sharp pain in his back as Ysabelle pressed the point of the knife against his spine. Twisting his head, Vesper saw the blade glitter, and he swore under his breath.

"Craven scum!" he muttered. "Are you so base you would use the weapons of that Hobber fiend—the same one that slew your adviser?"

Ysabelle's paw shook; she hated doing this, but she had to get to Greenreach. "Be silent!" she told Vesper. "If you don't want to die here, then be my guide."

The bat sighed wearily; he was extremely tired of hearing that squirrel's voice. "Very well," he grumbled. "I will show thee the way."

He lifted his head and sniffed at the air. Even on a dark night like this one, a bat could sense where he was. A hundred and more scents thrilled through his nostrils; the smell of blood and burning was strong on the breeze, but mingled with it were other fragrances: the numbing chill of the forest's icy heart, the dankness of stagnant water, the distant echo of a great river—and there, the faint rumor of the city.

Vesper nodded, satisfied with the evidence of his nose, and turned slowly, not wanting to alarm the squirrel into causing an accident with the knife. Then he began retracing his steps downstream.

"Are you sure it lies in this direction?" Ysabelle asked.

"As certain as Hrethel is my lord," he flatly replied.

So the pair of them waded farther along the ditch until the shadows of the tangled forest engulfed them.

*   *   *

Oily black smoke issued from the countless cracks and fissures that split the charred ground. Here and there, among the rubble of ash and glowing embers, the roasted body of some unrecognizable creature lay twisted and scorched amid the soot. It was a terrible scene—even the standing stones had fractured under the fierce heat of the blaze—but now the fires had died.

In the choking cloud of floating ash and smoke that hung above the dell, the high priest came. Through the eye slits of his mask he looked on the devastation, and his temper boiled inside—yet he had paid back his enemies with fates more terrible than this, and that knowledge soothed him a little.

Carefully, he stepped over charcoal roots, to where the cindered earth sloped down into the Ring of Banbha. But the bloody-bones did not venture any farther, for already the ground scalded his feet and the fumes of burnt fur and feather made him reel backward. The sound of lamentation was everywhere as the singed survivors licked their wounds and whimpered in shock.

The mournful cries rang piteously in the high priest's ears, but he was oblivious to them all. His eyes glinted like two diamonds—and his heart was just as hard.

"Many have fallen this night," his bitter voice hissed through his teeth. "Many of the Children of Hobb have perished in the

140

flames. Yet they were but a fraction—the forest is filled with many more believers."

He whirled around and strode purposefully to one of the smoldering yew trees. As the figure swept aside a withered curtain of flaking ash, it looked at the blackened dell one last time and hurried down a steep flight of steps. "Soon, all shall know what has occurred here," he vowed, "and every corner of the wild woods will know who is to blame."

Deep below the blistered earth, the high priest descended. The heat had reached even here, and the walls of the passages were baked dry and hard. Quickly, he made for an arched doorway and passed inside.

The chamber beyond was large, and the two Hobb lanterns fixed to the walls were not enough to illuminate the whole of it.

The place was bare except for that which dominated the far wall.

It was a hideous carving, crudely done in wood and clay; the subject, however, was unmistakable. Towering in the darkness, the image of an enormous rat head leered, its face contorted into a repulsive scream.

The bloody-bones closed the door behind him and walked briskly over to where the immense jaws gaped and the fangs spiked down.

The light of the lanterns played over the frozen features, giving them a semblance of life, and for a moment the high priest stared about him doubtfully. Then he made a humble bow and gazed into the great mouth of the terrible carving.

Upon the wooden tongue, two bright golden discs stared back at him.

"I wish to speak with her!" the bloody-bones commanded.

The discs blinked, and the creature they belonged to prepared itself.

It was a small, yellow toad who sat before the high priest. Warts covered its fat body, and slime glistened down its potbelly.

141

With its large, bulbous eyes, it considered the figure for a moment, then shifted its weight upon the carved tongue and gave a slow nod.

The high priest took from his costume a pouch containing incense and cast a quantity of it into the Hobb lanterns nearby.

As the chamber filled with a sickly-sweet smell, the toad's head waggled and its jowls quivered like jelly. Slowly, the bulging eyes closed until only the merest slivers of gold shone in the flickering gloom.

The bloody-bones bowed once more and looked intently at the squat creature. "Is everything ready?" he asked.

No reply came, for the toad had successfully put itself into a trance. Then the wide mouth of the beast gaped open and the high priest knew it was time, and he removed his mask.

"Mistress of the distant land," he called, "priestess to Mabb and destroyer of our enemies—hear me."

The sleeping toad gave a little shudder, and all its loose flesh wobbled and squelched. Then, from its open mouth, a cruel voice issued—yet it was not the toad's own.

"Quickly," it cried, "tell me—did you find the amulet? Is all well?"

The high priest glanced nervously at the floor. "Alas!" he began. "The Acorn was indeed in my grasp—"

"You did not let it slip from you?" the voice shrieked. "Fool! Have you lost it? You know why we need its power! Without it, all our designs shall go astray. Hrethel grows suspicious—I need that amulet. Where is it?"

"Mistress," the bloody-bones tried to explain, "the squirrels were more cunning than I anticipated. They did steal the Acorn from me."

"Idiot!" came the screeching reply. "Must I attend to everything? Can I not put my trust in anyone? Who has the device now?"

"A maiden," he spluttered, "the daughter of the royal house."

There was a pause, and, during the silence, the high priest fidgeted awkwardly. When the voice spoke again, it was filled with doubt and concern.

"This maiden must not become the Starwife," it hissed. "Find this princess—prove that I have not trusted you in vain."

"It shall be done," the high priest assured her. "Already, I have lain curses upon her."

"I am not interested in your curses!" it screamed. "Seek out this maiden and destroy her with your own hand. The Acorn must come to me—nothing must get in the way. Do you comprehend that?"

The high priest bowed. "I do," he said, "and I vow that I shall personally lead the hunt for our enemies—they will not get far."

"Just see to it that none of your vile followers decide to steal the amulet for themselves!" the voice warned.

"As you command," the bloody-bones promised. "I shall obey. The Acorn will be found."

"It had better be," the voice threatened, "or you shall suffer."

The conversation was at an end, and the toad shuddered, and only gargled belches now issued from its mouth. Slowly, it opened its eyes and watched timidly as the high priest replaced his mask and stormed from the chamber.

Far away, in the land of Greenreach, the Lady Morwenna stepped back from an identical carving, situated in the middle of a marshy island deep beneath the Hallowed Oak. As her toad began to stir, she pulled a sour expression and spat upon the floor.

"The Silver Acorn must come to me," she breathed, "it must be mine!"

*   *   *

Vesper trudged wearily through the ditch, the high priest's knife still pressed into his back.

143

For nearly an hour, he and Ysabelle had followed the course of the stream, and both were extremely tired and hungry.

The lids of Ysabelle's eyes fluttered shut as she stumbled along, and she had to pinch herself to remain awake. She couldn't fall asleep now—not while the bat could snatch the knife away and use it against her. The only way she had discovered to remain alert was to keep talking, and, as they waded through the cold water, she chattered incessantly.

"Godfrey used to tell me about the sacred streams," she prattled. "In the old time, the forest was filled with them. They linked the sacred shrines with one another, and it was a great honor to tend them, making sure no weeds clogged the banks or halted the flow."

"Really," Vesper mumbled without enthusiasm.

"Yes, and those who lived at the shrines were all members of royal houses. It was they who guarded the holy wells and hallowed orchards and kept the evil at bay."

The bat groaned. How much longer could the squirrel go on squawking? "What happened to them then?" he asked sarcastically. "Someone should tell them they are not doing such a good job."

"I suppose the Hobbers came," Ysabelle answered. "We never really believed the rumors, though. One by one, the shrines are being defiled and their wardens murdered. Soon, there won't be any left."

"You and your precious Green spirit!" Vesper scoffed. "A barrel-load lot of use He is!"

"It was His power that saved you before!" she cried. "You were glad of it then!"

Vesper snorted. "He didn't stop the Hobbers ruining His shrines, though, did He?" he scoffed.

The squirrel frowned. "They must have attacked in winter!" she declared, not liking the bat's disrespectful tone. "That's when His power is weakest. Has your kind never heard of Him?"

"We don't care for the barbarities of you tree worshippers," he replied. "We venerate the Lady of the Moon and have no need of false gods."

"False!" she cried. "It's you who are deluded—and we do not worship trees! It's the spirit of spring and new life we honor. You'd soon miss it if the Green vanished from the world—and if the Hobbers get their way, that might just happen. If all the holy places are destroyed, the land will be a darker, uglier place where the only growing things are molds and fungus. That's why I have to get to Greenreach; the lights of hope must not be extinguished."

Vesper scowled, and her words echoed in his mind. Strange that a squirrel should be so concerned for the future of the world. He fell silent, and his thoughts were fixed upon reaching his own home, where his mother would be waiting.

After another hour's walk, the water of the ditch began to dry up. The trickling stream grew even narrower, and the thick mud spread more thickly about the banks. Eventually, the trickle became solitary puddles and then disappeared completely as the ditch was clogged with dense tangles of weed.

"That's the end of it," Vesper said. "Do you want me to push through those nettles, or do we scramble out of this gully and continue the march up there?"

Ysabelle looked about them. "I don't like this," she said. "Away from the stream, the power of the Green no longer protects us."

"But there is no more stream!" he argued. "Not unless we start walking back along it. Is that what you want to do—spend the rest of your days tramping up and down the course of this wretched brook?"

"Of course not," she replied, "but neither do I wish to be caught by the Children of Hobb." She pointed the dagger up the bank and told the bat to start climbing. "For the remainder of the night, we shall rest," she told him. "I will feel a lot safer with the sun in the sky."

145

"I shan't!" Vesper countered. "The daylight confounds me. How will I guide you then?"

"You'll find a way," she said, pressing the knifepoint into his fur. That quelled any more argument, and the bat began to clamber up the side of the ditch, swiftly followed by Ysabelle.

When they stood upon the forest floor, the squirrel immediately set about looking for shelter. "We need a place to hide," she muttered, "away from the trackways."

Vesper pointed to the dark bulk of a fallen tree. "What about there?" he suggested. "It may be hollow."

The squirrel shook her head, "No, I think we ought to stay in the open–I do not wish to be trapped in such a confined place."

Through a carpet of ground ivy, she led him over to where the shaggy silhouette of a large bramble bush stretched above them.

"This will suit our needs," she nodded. "From under there we can see any enemies before they see us."

"Didn't do me much good when your sentries found me," Vesper piped up.

Ysabelle ignored him. It was the best the forest had to offer, and she wanted to rest.

Waving the knife before her, she made Vesper step under the brambles first, then, after gathering up some ivy, followed him in.

Once beneath the thorny boughs, the bat sat down and tried to make himself comfortable. Curiously, he eyed Ysabelle as she came up to him, carrying lengths of vine.

"Turn around," she instructed, "and hold your wings out behind you."

"Hoy!" the bat cried as she used the ivy to bind him. "Not so tight–even the Hobbers weren't that cruel. Oooch! Mind my sore wing."

"There," she said brightly, tying the Moonrider against a large, solid branch. "I'll feel a lot safer knowing you can't take the knife from me and slit my throat while I sleep."

"As if I would," Vesper protested.

"Oh, you would," she answered, "and well you know it. I've kept you alive because you're useful, but I know you have no use for me. Our kind are sworn enemies; I don't trust you any more than you do me."

"How your words wound me," he chuckled grimly.

The squirrel made sure the vines were secure, then settled down a little distance away.

"You won't succeed, you know," Vesper told her. "You won't be able to keep me a prisoner all the way to Greenreach. Something will happen; your vigilance will falter, and then the tables will be turned."

"Oh, be quiet," she said. "I'm tired and hungry, and I just want to get some sleep."

Vesper said nothing, and his ears twitched excitedly.

"What is it?" Ysabelle asked, straining to catch what he had heard.

The bat seemed flustered for a moment, then coughed loudly and remarked in a voice that was almost a shout. "Oh, nothing! There's absolutely nothing the matter with me, my dearest squirrel!"

Ysabelle stared at him and wondered what he was up to. He was making the most dreadful noise, as though he wanted to be heard by every creature in the forest.

"Hold your tongue!" she whispered. The bat started to whistle, so Ysabelle hurried forward and pressed the knife against his throat. The whistling ceased, and Vesper made no more noise.

Then Ysabelle heard. High above, there was a rush of wings, and many high-pitched voices called across the sky in a language she did not understand. A legion of bats were flying overhead, and she knew they were searching for her.

She turned an anxious face to Vesper. "If you do anything to signal them," she warned, "you'll be sorry."

Vesper nibbled his straggly beard. He longed to call to his brethren high above, to tell them he was here so they might save him from this hated enemy, but the blade she held was sharp, and he felt it nick his skin. Eventually, the bat host passed them by, and the night was still once more.

Ysabelle gasped, and her breath rushed from her lungs, for she had been holding it fearfully for some minutes.

"They're gone," she sighed in relief. Vesper said nothing but glared at the squirrel. His kind would return; they would find him.

Ysabelle went back to her leafy bed and spent some time dragging her fingers through the knots that had tangled her long hair. "It will be a long march tomorrow," she informed the bat. "You had best get some sleep yourself. I want your wits refreshed in the morning."

Vesper's eyes only gleamed at her from the place he was tied. The squirrel smiled, wrapped herself in her tail, then lay her head upon the dry leaves and drifted off to sleep with one paw clenched about the knife and the other touching the blood-stained Acorn around her neck. Soon, her gentle snores floated on the calm breeze, and the young bat smiled to himself.

Gently at first, Vesper began to wriggle. He kept his eyes fixed on the sleeping form of the squirrel maiden, just to be sure, while his tethered feet pushed against the branch. Then, very slowly, he started to draw the vines that bound his wings over the thorns. The first of them snapped, then a second, until Vesper's wings were free and he hurriedly untied his feet.

"Now," he whispered, glowering at Ysabelle, "'tis time I repaid your kindness and hospitality."

Carefully, he crept forward, not making a sound to disturb the squirrel's slumber.

Vesper reached across and eased the knife from her paw, then put it to her throat.

"So do all tree rats perish!" he hissed. "In the name of Hrethel I kill thee!"

The bat drew the blade back and prepared to plunge it deep

into her neck. But Vesper was trembling, the knife quivered in his grasp, and furrows creased his brow—he had never killed anything before, and though he had fought many mock battles with the other weanlings, when it came to it, he couldn't bring himself to such a horrendous deed.

Ysabelle looked so peaceful sleeping there, with her large eyes lightly closed and her raven hair flowing like smoke over her shoulders, Vesper felt that if he murdered the squirrel, then he would be accursed forever. Gingerly, he lay the knife at the maiden's side and stumbled away, sweating with fear. For an instant, he had been so close to becoming nothing more than one of the followers of Hobb, and he felt ill and confused.

"I must leave," he told himself. "Hurry from this strange squirrel, whose very existence now mocks you, Vesper. What Knight of the Moon are you to let her live?"

He feebly flapped his wings and whimpered the answer, "I know not—yet what else could I do?"

"Slay her, and take the amulet she bears to your Lord—then would thy name be trumpeted and sung forevermore. 'Vesper, hero of the colonies—he who put an end to the Hazel Realm once and for all!'"

"Stop it!" the bat wailed. "I will have no part in her murder. What honor can there be in such a cowardly act? None, so let that be an end. Oh, Vesper, leave the maiden's side before you change your mind and despair for the rest of your days!"

Staggering from the bramble bush, the bat fled from the sleeping Ysabelle and tore through the ground ivy, not knowing what to do.

Only a few hours remained before the dawn, and a low-lying mist had risen from the forest floor, curling about the trees, filling the hollows, and covering the paths.

Vesper cut a swath through the chill gray vapor, leaving a swirling wake behind him. Then, as he floundered toward a neglected trackway, he stopped, and his blood froze.

A desolate and mournful sound filled the young bat's ears—it was the sound of a solitary bell.

"No," he breathed in dismay as he remembered the high priest's curse.

The dismal sound was muffled by the mist, and Vesper stared with wide eyes in the direction it came from. Farther up the path, where the stark branches of the hawthorns formed a tunnel over the track, a wall of fog clung to the trees, and from the depths of this, the bell continued to coldly toll.

With his panic rising, Vesper heard the lonely sound growing louder, and he wished he was far away.

"Oh, why did I not bring the knife?" he reproached himself. "Everything I do goes awry!"

The dull clanging drew nearer, and Vesper thought he saw strange shapes within the dense mist.

Frightened, he spun around and scrambled back the way he had come.

A dark figure loomed before him, and Vesper fell on his face in terror as the ringing seemed to surround his prostrate form.

"Please!" he blurted. "Spare me!"

Ysabelle stared down at him in surprise. She had awoken to find the bat gone, and, to her surprise, she was still alive. Vesper had obviously removed the knife from her grasp yet had refrained from using it. Not knowing what had happened, she took up the weapon and hurried to find him.

"What are you doing?" she cried as Vesper gaped up at her. "Are you mad?"

The bat almost wept to find that it was only the squirrel he had blundered into. "Listen," he murmured, lumbering to his feet.

The melancholy bell rang throughout the fading night, and Ysabelle shivered to hear it.

"Do you recall what the bloody-bones said to me?" Vesper asked.

Ysabelle nodded, and she gazed fearfully down the mist-enshrouded path. "What manner of creature approaches?" she breathed.

Vesper hid behind a tree and pulled her after him. "There!" he said. "The nightmare appears!"

From the thick fog that filled the tunnel of hawthorn, a peculiar figure emerged.

Into the low-lying mist, a small shrew came hobbling. Its long snout snuffled the damp air, and its bright, brown eyes stared fixedly ahead in an attempt to penetrate the flowing layers of smoke that, at times, covered him entirely. The shrew was lame; a dirty bandage was wrapped tightly about its right leg, and it leaned upon a wooden crutch. Over its shoulder, a heavy-looking satchel had been slung, and about its waist it wore a belt of string.

"Forward, forward," the small animal chirped to itself, "all clear, all clear."

Ysabelle folded her arms and looked at Vesper crossly. "There's your great peril!" she chortled. "My, oh, my, I can see why you were so afraid–I've never seen such a bloodthirsty-looking rogue!"

Vesper took no notice of her scorn but stared down at the stranger and tapped the squirrel on the arm. "Behold," he observed, "I fear our diminutive friend is not alone."

Ysabelle followed his gaze and leaned forward. Strange–from the shrew's belt of string, another length stretched back into the mist. "What is it?" she asked, but he could only shake his head.

"Forward, forward," the little shrew said again, "path twisting, left two paces at this point."

From the dense fog, a deeper, more resonant voice boomed out. "I have it, Tysle," it declared. "Two to the left, four summer worms away."

Both Vesper and Ysabelle watched in fear as the owner of

151

that voice sailed from the mist, attached to the other end of the string.

At first they could only see a large, hooded shape, wreathed in wisps of vapor. Then, as it lumbered farther onto the path, the squirrel maiden squealed in horror.

The large figure halted and gave the string a brisk yank. "Wait," it called to the shrew. "I do believe—wait a moment."

The newcomer raised its face and pulled the pointed hood from its head. Two blind eyes squinted upward to the place where Vesper and Ysabelle hid. It was a stout mole who stood there, waiting and listening with its fat head cocked to one side. Tendrils of mist floated about the mole's middle, while his sensitive ears tried to catch what he thought he had heard. At the top of the long, knobbly staff that he leaned upon, a bronze bell dangled and clinked.

"Is there aught amiss?" called the shrew, whose ears were the only things visible as he pattered back through the fog to where the mole stood.

"Humm," considered his large companion. "I feel there are others nearby."

At this, the shrew pulled a short dagger from his satchel and hopped about in a frenzy of excitement.

"Is it Hobbers?" he squeaked, raking the tiny blade through the mist. "Is it Hobbers? Let me at them—fourteen rain worms, Master, that should do it!"

"Peace," the mole instructed, laying a huge, spade-like paw upon his friend's shoulder. "No children of the Raith Sidhe I believe—and yet—" Seeming to stare straight at Vesper and Ysabelle, the mole raised his paw and beckoned. "Who watches my guide and me?" he called. "If you be enemies, then begone—but if you be friendly, will you not join us?"

Vesper looked sheepishly at Ysabelle; it seemed he was wrong after all. "Come on," he told her as he left their cover, "there is nothing to be frightened of—they won't eat us."

Ysabelle had been staring at the second newcomer in fear, but now she roused herself and put a restraining paw on the young bat's wing.

"Wait," she urged, "don't you see?"

Below them, the mole took the satchel from his companion and dangled it enticingly. "Most willing would I be to share our breakfast," his voice rumbled.

"'Tis not lordly fare but serves our humble wants."

That settled it for Vesper; he shook himself free of the squirrel's paw and trotted down to meet the two strangers.

"Vespertilio!" Ysabelle desperately cried. "Don't you see? The bell—it is the warning sign of the leper!"

IN THE ORCHARD OF DUIR

Vesper skidded to a standstill and the mole advanced, tapping his staff upon the stony ground before him.

"What have we here?" the creature asked, reaching out with its paws. "Tysle, what manner of being is it?"

The shrew limped up to Vesper and studied him keenly. "Bat," he said at last.

"A Knight of the Moon?" remarked the mole with some surprise. "Have we not espied many of their kind these past few nights?"

"Indeed we have, Master," the shrew eagerly replied. "Hosts and hosts of them—all a-swooping and a-scouring. You remarked upon it then, did you not? 'Tysle,' says you, 'there's more to this than we know of,' and you're right, of course—as ever."

The mole smiled benignly and brought his wet nose close to Vesper's face.

The young bat cringed away. Ysabelle was right—the creature was leprous. In irregular patches, the velvet of his skin had turned white and in some places had fallen out completely. Strips of cloth bound the mole's wrists and toes, and around his jaws and lips, painful-looking cracks marred the threadbare flesh. It took all of Vesper's courage not to turn and run, but he could not stop an expression of pity and revulsion stealing over his own face.

The shrew saw this and shook his crutch angrily. "What be

154

the matter with you, winged one?" he squeaked. "Don't ye pout so, or I shall knock the scorn from your big-eared noggin!"

"Tysle, Tysle," the mole said in a calming tone, "let the poor fellow be. No doubt he has met few travelers like myself on the roads he journeys along."

Vesper began to stutter an apology, but the leper waved him into silence.

"Not another word," he said, "until your friend comes down and joins us."

"M—my friend?"

"I may be near completely blind," the mole explained, "but mine ears are as sharp as ever they were."

"Sharper than thine, I'll wager!" put in the shrew.

The mole cuffed his companion about the head. "Mention not the vice of gambling!" he admonished. "Where was I? Ah, yes— why not call to the one who conceals himself up yonder?"

Vesper glanced back to the tree where Ysabelle was still hiding. "Come out!" he called.

The shrew ambled forward and peered into the misty darkness. "Ooh!" he exclaimed as Ysabelle came into view. "'tis a fair beauty, my Master."

"A damsel?" the mole inquired. "How pleasant, a batling and his lady—"

"No, Master—begging your pardon, 'tis a squirrel who approaches."

The mole struck his staff on the ground in wonderment. "By the Green's whiskers!" he declared incredulously. "A Knight of the Moon and a squirrel? This is a most unusual spectacle!"

"She do have a knife," Tysle observed, "and a grit long one it is, too."

Ysabelle now stood at Vesper's side, and she looked on the two strangers much as he had done.

"There," the mole said, "it's been a long time since I was 'in society,' and I may be a trifle rusty, but now I believe the correct etiquette is an exchange of names." He blinked and stared expectantly in the squirrel's direction.

The maiden eyed him uncertainly—it would be foolish to say too much. "I am Ysabelle," she told him, giving Vesper a kick to introduce himself.

"Vespertilio," he blurted, rubbing his ankle.

"Ysabelle, Vespertilio," the mole repeated, committing them to memory. He pulled on the string that joined him to the shrew and looped the excess around a hook on the wide belt fastened about his own portly middle.

Then he cleared his throat and stood with his feet apart as though about to deliver a speech. "Now let it be known," he announced. "that under the warm hills of a land not too distant, I was dubbed Giraldus. A fine appellation, and one that I am more than content with."

He made a slight bow and gave a flourish of his paw. "Alas," he sorrowfully added, "I recall that at this juncture, 'twould be seeming for me to kiss the fair damsel's fingers and shake Vespertilio by the wing."

Ysabelle recoiled, but the mole was quick to put her at ease. "Fear not," he hastily assured, "there is no danger of that—I am not insensitive to your revulsion. No, my vision may be of little use, but I am not, I trust, feeble headed. The pretty—and I use the word for its irony—the pretty sight that by now you must have seen and been at pains to overlook—no doubt you are both polite creatures—is being ravaged by a woeful disfiguring disease."

He held up one of his massive paws for their inspection. "Only three claws are left to me this side," he intoned, "for it is the way with this ailment for the extremities to shrivel—I do hope you are not squeamish—to shrivel and fall clean off the body."

"I'm sorry," Ysabelle murmured.

Giraldus leaned heavily upon his staff and sniffed glumly. "You cannot understand," he uttered. "What is a mole without his paws to shovel away the earth and dig for him? A pitiful figure am I now."

"I know what it's like," Vesper broke in. "My wing is damaged."

The mole blinked, and the blind eyes squeezed shut for a moment. When they reopened, Giraldus had decided to change the subject.

"A seat!" he cried. "Let us not stand in the cold like gibbering rats too witless to notice the icicles dripping from their snouts! Tysle—find something suitable." He let out the string once more, and the shrew went scouting into the mist.

"Over here!" his high voice soon called. "Nice arrangement of logs—not too damp, and cushioned with moss. Four spring worms straight ahead, then a summer one left."

Following his directions, Giraldus led Ysabelle and Vesper over to his companion. "There," he said in a cozy sort of way. "Is that not much better? Now, what point in my life had I reached?"

Abruptly, the mole slapped his forehead. "I am forgetting!" he gasped, heaving on the string. "Enough of my history; let me introduce my most faithful servant, Tysle Symkyn. He is my eyes in this unhappy world, and without him I should trip over every root and stumble into every tree the forest had to offer."

The shrew scuttled closer to Ysabelle and grinned at her. "How do," he chuckled.

"And greetings to you, sir," she returned with a smile. "But, tell me, why are you both abroad in the forest at this time of night?"

Giraldus squinted down and patted his servant's head. "If that isn't the very question I was going to ask of you," he said, "but pry I won't. Yet we have no reason to hide our aim. Tysle and I are on a pilgrimage and are wont to begin our days before the sunrise."

"That's right!" the shrew cried, hopping around on his crutch. "A tidy way we've traveled—have we not, Master?"

"Oh, yes," Giraldus continued, drawing in more of the string to stop Tysle jigging around so much. "And the route we have chosen demands that we must visit each shrine along the way, whether they still stand or no."

"A pilgrimage?" Vesper asked, trying not to smirk. "But to where?"

"Why, to Greenreach!" came the instant reply from both of them.

Vesper bit his tongue and said no more.

It was Ysabelle who spoke next. "Why there?" she asked.

The mole chortled, and the many pouches and bottles that hung from the leather belt around his waist all rattled. "Surely a squirrel has no need to ask that!" he laughed. "More than any, you must know what powers are contained in that holy place. For is it not written that about the blessed hill and in the sacred groves of Grinuvicia–to give it its ancient name–the Green Himself does walk?" He clapped Tysle heartily on the back, and the shrew's legs buckled beneath the mighty blow.

"Once we are there," Giraldus confidently declared, "my servant and I shall both be cured of our ills–he of his lameness, and I of this accursed leprosy."

Vesper hung his head and stared at the ground.

Ysabelle glanced at him coldly, then told the unfortunate pilgrims all that had happened. When she came to the end of her tale, Giraldus gripped the shrew tightly for support, and Tysle gazed up at his master with tears streaking down his long nose.

"Then there is naught left?" the mole asked in disbelief. "You say the groves are destroyed and the Starwife killed?"

"A wounded survivor of the attack on my mother's realm told us."

Giraldus whipped round to where Vesper sat. "Why?" he murmured despondently. "What for did your forces destroy all my hopes? Is it too much to ask for a fair green place in this dismal world?"

Vesper said nothing; for the first time, he had heard the full story, and he felt ashamed for what his kind had done. He had not realized the amount of slaughter that had taken place, and though he had not taken part in the countless murders, he felt just as guilty.

"No," Ysabelle told the mole, "it was not this bat I spoke of, but another–I don't think this one was even there when Greenreach was attacked." She looked at Vesper and remembered that he had spared her life this night. "No blood stains the wings of this Moonrider," she said.

Giraldus still frowned, however, and Tysle pulled on the string until he was able to waddle over to the young bat and growl at him.

With a forlorn groan, the large mole slid from the log, sank to his knees, then slumped upon the path. "All is lost," he mumbled. "All our efforts have been in vain; we have journeyed for naught–for now no end can I envisage. Giraldus will gradually fall into pieces. Have I not noticed the disease stealing over me more each day? Now, there are no chances left." He lay his staff across his lap and sobbed as huge tears sprang from his tiny eyes.

Tysle hopped with agitation and dismay to see his master so stricken. "Now, now," he said brightly, "'tain't no use a-moping and a-wailing! A goodly way have we traveled, and a merry old time of it have we had so far–the pilgrimage is just as much about getting there as arriving, Master. 'Twould be a poorly shame to turn back now; why, I do believe it's downright wrong to even think it!"

Giraldus sniffed a little as he contemplated the shrew's words. "Yes," he agreed at last, "I see that now–'twas the Evil One trying to subdue me and afflict my faith. Help me up, lad."

The shrew grunted and puffed as he heaved the bulky mole back to his feet. Then, leaning upon his staff once more, Giraldus affectionately tweaked the end of Tysle's nose.

"Two staffs do I possess," he told Ysabelle. "The wooden one I require for my infirm body, but Tysle is my soul's support. "'Tis he who props my sinking spirits and sets them spinning with his unfailing optimism."

"Are you still going to Greenreach?" Ysabelle asked.

The mole pulled the pointed hood back over his head. "That was our destination when first we set out," he answered," and it has not altered, though what we may find when we arrive might not be to our liking. That is where we are bound."

The squirrel maiden wrung her paws together. "Let me go with you!" she asked abruptly.

Both Tysle and Giraldus stared at her, and a gasp came from Vesper.

"But you can't go with them!" the young bat hissed.

"Why not?" she cried. "That is where I'm headed, after all, and if our paths lie together—"

"But—but—"

Giraldus gave an understanding smile. "I believe your friend fears for your safety," he said gently, "and I must admit that I, too, am amazed at your suggestion. Mark me well, Lady, I am a leper, and as such not a fitting companion for anyone."

"Excepting me, o' course!" trilled Tysle.

Ysabelle shook her head. "Nonsense," she protested. "From all I have seen and heard, I do not believe I could have met two more trustworthy creatures than yourselves. It would be an honor to me if you would let me accompany you."

Giraldus bowed his head. "You do me and my servant much kindness," he breathed, "and such a stout heart will not go unrewarded. The Green will watch over you, Mistress."

Vesper was astonished at Ysabelle's compassion for these strangers, and the doubts that had only just begun to surface in his mind about the holy wars took root.

"What about me?" he asked suddenly.

Ysabelle stared at him. "You are free to go," she said dismissively. "I have two guides now; you are a captive no longer."

160

"Glad am I to hear it!" he cried. "Yet what of me? My way also lies with you–for a great part at least."

"Then come with us," she said.

Vesper eyed her uncertainly. He had no desire to brave the vast forest on his own; it would be much wiser to be a member of a larger group. And yet, there was something about the mole he did not trust. That warning bell rang whenever the staff moved, and the young bat had not forgotten the curse laid on him.

"Very well," he replied. "I'll join you also."

"My heart is lifted," Giraldus proclaimed, "but, before we depart, let us offer up a prayer to He who has brought us together." Lacing his remaining fingers, the mole muttered a Green Psalm.

"Now," he said cheerfully, "let us be off–three summer worms, Tysle!"

A faint pinkish light was rising over the towering treetops as the dawn broke over the world. The mists that covered the path were tinted a delicate orange and seemed to glow as the sun climbed into the sky. Bathed in the golden morning, the forest looked a much safer place, and the clean scent of the dew refreshed each of the strange party who wandered through the fragrant carpet of leaves.

It was not long before Ysabelle remembered that the last time she had eaten was two days ago. On hearing this, Giraldus pulled on the string and sent Tysle off in search of mushrooms. It was here that he explained the method of measuring the shrew's lead. Each particular length related to a memorable worm the mole had once had the pleasure of eating. Spring worms were the shortest, and the longest allowance of string was accounted in autumn-rain worms.

Given a lead of twenty of the latter, Tysle hurried off, only to reappear some minutes later with a quantity of freshly harvested mushrooms. Together with some bread and cheese the shrew carried in his satchel–or scrip, as he called it–they formed an excellent start to the day, and both Ysabelle and Vesper tucked into the meal with much enthusiasm.

"No, no," Giraldus refused, when Ysabelle offered him some. "If you would excuse me, I think I shall break my fast over yonder." And with that, the mole wandered several summer worms away and sat down with his back to the rest of them.

Vesper chewed a mushroom, absently wondering why the mole had declined to join them.

"'Tis a penance, you see," Tysle explained, "for his doubt afore–bad news ever takes him like that, and he's always sorry for it. Lack of faith, he says, so he takes it upon himself to do this penance."

"And what form does it take?" Ysabelle inquired.

The shrew put down the lump of cheese he had been nibbling and lowered his voice in case his master overheard. "'Tis his food," he whispered. "You might have noticed the fine girth my Lord has about his middle. Well, he didn't get that not liking his victuals–mighty good appetite he has, that's why he does it."

"But what does he do?"

"Caterpillars!" Tysle hissed. "When he feels he's doubted, he forces himself to eat caterpillars."

"Yuck!" said Vesper, pulling a face.

"Just as you says," the shrew agreed. "Terrible bitter them furry wigglers are, and how he despises them–but that's the penance he feels he has to do for being found wanting, so to speak."

"But why must he eat them over there?" asked Ysabelle, still puzzled.

"Done that to spare your stomachs, I reckon," the shrew said. "'Tain't no pretty sight seeing them caterpillars go down, and watching his screwed-up face ain't no better. Poor Master, he ain't had a real juicy worm for weeks now–the road's been a mighty tough one thus far."

After that, neither the squirrel nor the bat felt very hungry, but they finished the mushrooms Tysle offered them so as not to hurt his feelings.

When Giraldus came back, he was wiping his cracked lips and airing his stinging tongue. The aftertaste was most unpleasant, but he told himself that it would serve as a reminder not to lose faith so readily in the future.

For the rest of the morning, Tysle was put on a three-winter-worm string, and they made excellent time along the paths.

At first Ysabelle had been shocked at Giraldus's treatment of the little shrew, at times thinking that he was a bully and a tyrant, but now her opinion had changed. It was true that the mole depended upon Tysle for practically everything, but the same was also true of Tysle. Both were reliant on each other, and, as the sun rose to its highest point, the squirrel maiden and Vesper learned how the two pilgrims came to meet.

Nearly four years ago, Tysle and the rest of his family had been living in a peaceful riverside hamlet. By the banks of this sleepy backwater, they led a contented and happy life; then word began to spread about the growth of the Hobb cult. It was said that the Hobbers were rampaging through the woodlands in search of new recruits to be initiated into their infernal brotherhood.

But in their idyllic world, beneath the shade of the willow leaves, no one had paid much attention to the hushed whispers. When they should have been securing their homes and furnishing themselves with weapons, the shrews and their neighbors continued to engage in the relaxing pastimes the river afforded them. Then, one dark night, their peace was shattered forever. Without warning, a raiding party of Hobbers attacked the hamlet, dragging out its inhabitants and forcing them to join their foul legions. Many refused, yet a great number accepted through sheer fright and were never seen again.

As he recounted the tale, Tysle's face clouded with anger, and his normally cheerful self sank beneath his hatred for the children of the Raith Sidhe. "When it came to my turn to be hauled from my home," he said in a wavering voice, "I saw what them villains had already done to most of our folk. Those who wouldn't follow them had been strung up as an example to the rest. 'Twas an evil sight, and I shan't never forget it." He paused for a moment as his heart became filled with the horror of that night once more.

Ambling behind him, Giraldus gave the string a gentle tug– just to remind his friend that he was there–and Tysle drew strength from this gesture but fell silent, as though to continue would be too much for him to bear.

"It was the next morning when I chanced upon the river bank," the mole told the other, "and I thanked the Green then, and I do so now, that mine eyes were too weak to see the full and terrible nature of the violence that had been visited upon those goodly folk. 'Twas a chilling discovery nonetheless, and I set about doing what services I could."

"You tended to the wounded?" asked Vesper.

Giraldus glowered, and his usually thunderous voice was soft and murmuring. "Wounded?" he said. "Weren't no wounded there, young batling. No, the only services I in my small way could perform were the rites of burial. None were left alive, you see, and many were the graves I had to dig. I might add that in those times my affliction was not so advanced, and my paws were still of use."

At this, Tysle stirred from his brooding and interrupted. "Don't you believe it, my sweet lady," he put in, giving Ysabelle a nudge. "Master'd do it all over, even today."

The mole flicked the back of his servant's head and resumed his tale. "There I was," he told them, "with the morning gone and still a sorrowful quantity of the deceased to inhume, when I hear a small voice gasping beneath the mound of mortal remains–and what do you think I did find in the midst of that ghoulish heap?"

"It was me!" Tysle cried.

"I know that!" the other declared. "I was just coming to it, you hasty, long-nosed river dweller!"

"Beggin' your pardon," the shrew uttered meekly.

Giraldus sniffed authoritatively and continued, ignoring any further interruptions. "Then did I find this self-same shrew," he told Ysabelle and Vesper, "Tysle Symkyn, but the poor little fellow was in a dreadful way. The Hobbers had left him for dead, you see, having delivered unto him grievous injuries."

"Worst of it were my leg, though," added the shrew forlornly.

"I am no leech master," admitted Giraldus, "but did what I could to heal my find, and together we saw to it that my original task was finished there."

"And you have traveled with each other ever since?" marveled Ysabelle.

"That we have, Mistress," said Tysle, "and a most high honor it is for me to be in my Master's service. Why, there aren't many as pious and venerable as he! Grateful I was at first and followed him round like a real dafthead, until one day I sees how I might be of real use to him. 'Why, you could be that great personage's guide, Tysle Symkyn!' declared the thought which just popped clean into my head—and a true and respectable vocation it is, to be sure."

Ysabelle smiled and thought that it was strange how something good had actually come out of one of the Hobb cult's raids.

Walking beside her, Vesper was lost in his own thoughts—the attack of the Hobbers sounded very much like the way his race had destroyed Greenreach. Was the squirrel maiden right—were the Knights of the Moon no better than rats? He blinked in the strong spring sunshine and contributed very little to the subsequent conversations.

As the afternoon wore on, the talk ranged among many things, and all learned something abut each of their traveling companions. Giraldus, at Tysle's invitation, gladly showed everyone his collection of items brought from the shrines he had

165

visited. There were bottles of holy water from the sacred wells and springs and bunches of dried leaves that hailed from blessed groves, and in one special purse he reverently carried a relic of the Green Himself—a preserved grain of wheat said to have fallen from the spirit's woven crown.

It was a most pleasant time, and Ysabelle nearly forgot the nightmarish few days that had gone before. With the warm sunlight shining upon her, it was difficult to believe that anything as evil as the followers of the Raith Sidhe could exist. Yet she knew that as soon as night fell, the forest would be full of fear once more.

Eventually, the sun began to sink in the heavens, and the clear daylight was tinged with the somber colors of the encroaching evening.

"We ought to find shelter," Ysabelle said nervously as the shadows deepened about her.

"Fear not," Giraldus rumbled, "for we are very close to the next shrine that we must visit—are we not, Tysle?"

The shrew nodded, slipping a rolled-up map from a pocket in the satchel. "Before the night closes round us," he said jovially, "I reckon we'll be there. Be careful of this hollow—two summer worms ahead!"

"The Orchard of Duir," Giraldus muttered to himself, "where the seven trees were planted by the Green in the time before the winter came to kill the year. Much would I give for mine eyes to see that blessed sight."

Tysle chuckled and gave Ysabelle a secret wink. "Master says that every time," he whispered.

Presently, the trees that they passed grew very close together, and Tysle was kept busy shouting his directions to Giraldus, warning him to avoid fallen branches and treacherous roots.

From then on, the party's progress slowed considerably as the obstacles in the pilgrims' way steadily increased. Once, the mole stumbled and fell to the ground. In a trice, Tysle had bounded over to him to see if he was injured, but his master pushed him away and hauled himself up with the aid of his staff, mouthing a rainbow of oaths that he instantly regretted.

"That means caterpillars for his supper," the shrew mumbled to himself.

"It's getting very dark," Ysabelle said at length. "Should we not be sighting your next shrine?"

"I can't see any orchard," commented Vesper.

"We shall not miss it," stated Giraldus, "a beauteous arboreal collection marked out by its divinity."

But as the darkness deepened about them, no sign of this orchard could they see. Tysle was put on a twenty-autumn-wormer to scout the way ahead, and, as the moon began to shine over the uppermost branches, his excited voice called to them.

"Master!" he cried. "The marker—I've found the marker!"

Giraldus pounded his staff in delight. "The marker of Duir!" he boomed. "The entrance to the hallowed orchard—what an occasion for rejoicing!"

With Tysle shouting eager directions, the mole bowled over the ground, leaving Ysabelle and Vesper to hurry along behind.

When they found Tysle, the little shrew was sitting upon a square, gray rock, swinging his legs in time to a tune he hummed to himself. The marker was surrounded by weeds, and a low wall made up of smaller stones curved away on either side, forming an immense circle in the forest.

But the wall was overgrown with ivy, and the ever-advancing roots of the surrounding trees had plowed beneath it, breaching and scattering the stones over the earth for creepers to smother.

Giraldus tapped the staff before him until it struck the marker stone, then reached out with his fingers and stroked the weathered surface with a rapturous expression upon his face.

"To think," he breathed enchantedly, "that once He placed this very boundary here, girdling His orchard in a last attempt to keep the ice and snow of the winter at bay. What a wondrous sight it must be for you lucky youngsters—does the blessed place not fill you with awe?"

Vesper stared beyond the tumbledown wall and grimaced at Ysabelle.

It was a sad, shabby place. Within the ruined circle, a chaotic tangle of wildness met his eyes. Of the seven fruit trees mentioned in the old legends, and that had been planted when the world was young, only three remained, and they were so ancient that Vesper was amazed they were still standing. Both the pear and the cherry tree were beyond bearing anything except ragged leaves, not managing a spray of blossom between them. The apple that had once grown in the exact center of the orchard, and whose fruit had inspired bards to compose the first songs, had withered and died long ago, being now fenced inside a mesh of knotted beech and spindle trees.

Everywhere, the lesser trees of the forest had sprung up, usurping their position and strangling any scions that the original inhabitants of the orchard had attempted to put out. Now the area inside the broken wall was more overcrowded than anywhere else in the forest, as if the rich soil that had once nourished the divine fruit now fed more than was natural.

The moonlight filtered through the matted branches, and Ysabelle looked sorrowfully at Giraldus, knowing how disappointed he must feel.

But the mole could not see the overcrowded mesh of bough and twig—to his dim-sighted eyes, the place was perfect.

"Tysle," he murmured, "is it just as we thought?"

The shrew glanced quickly at the squirrel and Vesper and gave a broad grin. "Why, 'tis a comely vision, Master," he blithely lied. "Never did I see such a lovely orchard. There's plum trees, apples, cherries, pear, chestnut, rowan, and hazel—magnificent, all of them."

Giraldus clapped his paws together in delight and sniffed expectantly. "I cannot smell the blossom!" he said uncertainly.

"Ah, well," Tysle quickly put in, "none of the trees are in flower as yet, but there's a goodly array of buds just a-waiting to burst."

"Oh, yes," the mole conceded, "in the heart of the forest, winter does tend to linger—though I should have dearly liked to inhale the heady mingling of scents. Perhaps on our return journey, Tysle. Once we are cured of our ills, we shall abide here a while."

The shrew gazed at the near-impenetrable thickets within the circle and raised his eyebrows. "Nothing sweeter," he replied.

Ysabelle and Vesper stared at the shrew—how could he deceive Giraldus so unashamedly? Tysle returned their stares unabashed and jumped from the marker stone. "'Tis better this way," he mouthed as he took hold of his master's paw.

"Lead me in," Giraldus instructed. "Let me touch each of the hallowed trees so that I might offer up a prayer to Him."

The shrew twitched his whiskers and gave a doubtful cough. "That be a good idea," he said, "but what about finding a place to put our heads down for the night? These young folks must fancy a bite to eat—been a long march since we munched last."

Giraldus nodded. "Forgive me," he said, turning to where he thought Ysabelle and Vesper stood. "In my excitement, I did forget myself. Tysle, fourteen spring worms, seek out a suitable bower for us to spend the night. I must confess that, yea, by the Green's whiskers, I am weary of the road myself."

Before limping away, the shrew gave the others a look that warned them not to tell his master the truth, then hurried around the circle obediently.

Giraldus leaned his staff against the stone and carefully felt the roughly shaped sides with his fingertips. "Here they are," his deep voice said eagerly, "the inscriptions the Duir carved into the rock—can you read them, child?"

Ysabelle realized that he was talking to her, and she stared at the marker stone intently. Just visible were a series of grooves and swirls carved into the rock. But the long years of neglect had filled the ancient symbols with grime and mold, and centuries of hard winters had worn them smooth in places. The squirrel maiden glanced from this to the mole's expectant face, but she could not lie to him as Tysle had done.

"No," she said slowly, "I cannot; the writing is too weathered."

Giraldus looked disappointed, but he groped for his staff and smiled. "A pity," he sighed. "I should have liked to know what words Duir put into the stone—the histories do not tell us that."

Vesper frowned at Ysabelle; he saw no harm in humoring the mole—she might have made something up. "Never mind," he said brightly, "at least you are here, and a wondrous sight it is."

The squirrel maiden turned away, exasperated, but Giraldus grinned and was happy.

When Tysle returned, the mole had shuffled forward a few paces and was squinting at the orchard with his head on one side, as if forming a picture of its beauty in his mind.

"Well, Master," the shrew declared, "at twelve spring worms, there's a fine old oak tree whose low branches would make as fair a place to spend the night as is possible to think of."

"An oak?" cried Giraldus. "Surely that must be the selfsame tree that the Green finally took shelter in when the ice overcame His defenses!"

"I reckon so," said Tysle indulgently. "Why, it does seem awful ancient to mine eyes."

"And in those I trust," the mole answered solemnly. "Lead me there, my faithful servant."

Ysabelle took a deep breath and reproachfully shook her head at Tysle as he guided his master over the broken wall.

"It is not right," she told Vesper. "The shrew is not being fair to him."

"I have found that there is little fairness in this world," the bat replied as he followed them.

When Ysabelle caught up with them, they were already settling down for the rest of the night.

The oak tree Tysle had found was indeed ancient, and the squirrel could almost believe that it was the one in the legend. It was a squat, snarled creation whose roots radiated from it in fat, twisting spokes. The bole of the oak was swollen, and horrid bulges sagged beneath the crumbling, moss-covered bark. The weirdly shaped branches wove a jagged web overhead, yet no new leaves adorned them—only the dried-up relics of ages past that had never fallen.

Not too far from the ground, two of these unshapely branches forked from the trunk, and it was upon these that Vesper and the others were sitting.

The many unsightly lumps and ulcerous growths that ruptured and blistered about the oak tree made climbing extremely easy, and Ysabelle was soon sitting on a branch, not too far from Tysle and his master.

The shrew foraged inside his scrip and shared the remaining bread and cheese while Giraldus contemplated another meal of caterpillars. In the end, the mole decided to do without altogether and begged pardon for any growls that his stomach might make.

With his eyes reflecting the silver moonlight, Vesper scanned the surrounding woodland and clicked his tongue. Nothing. They were alone in that part of the forest—no other creature stirred, and for that he was grateful. Perhaps this night he could sleep soundly, knowing that the disciples of the Hobb cult were nowhere near. He thought it might still be prudent to keep a watch, but when he suggested this, Giraldus vehemently shook his head.

"What for should we fear?" he cried. "Within this place we are protected by the Green. He shall not let any harm befall us. No, my winged friend, lay thy head down and rest, for tomorrow's march shall be long also. Tysle and I hope to find the last of the shrines upon our journey before we reach the holy land."

"We shall, Master," assured the shrew in a drowsy voice, "we shall."

"Goodnight then," Vesper said to them. "And may you get more sleep than you did yesterday, princess," he told Ysabelle.

But the squirrel was already fast sleep, and Vesper shrugged, then leaned against the tree trunk, where he fell into a deep and much-needed slumber.

"In the arms of the Green," Giraldus muttered to himself, "once more we consign our spirits into Thy care for Thou to guard this night. Bless our humble company, Lord, and see us safe till the morning." The mole closed his blind eyes and joined his paws over his stout and solid stomach, then began to snore.

The moon-filled night closed over them, and the long-dead leaves of the oak tree rustled in the whispering airs above.

Empty hours rolled by; not even the voice of an owl disturbed the deep hollowness of the dark, and all the forest was still.

A warmth beat upon Ysabelle's cheek. Groaning in her sleep, the squirrel turned over, burying her face deeper into her tail to escape the dawn.

"Child," a voice spoke in her ear.

Ysabelle squirmed lazily; surely, it wasn't time to get up yet? She tried to sink back into the delicious realm of her sleep, but the voice spoke again—only this time, it seemed to be right inside her head.

"Awaken, child," it said gently.

Gradually, the maiden surfaced from her dreams and rubbed her bleary eyes.

Suddenly, Ysabelle sat bolt upright and stared wildly round.

A glorious light, like nothing she had ever seen before, now blazed all about her. Gold and green it burned, edging her fur with glittering stars and dancing in her astonished eyes. Yet that was not all: the oak tree was different—it was young again.

No longer was it a misshapen ogre; its bark was smooth, having a lustrous, silken sheen that threw back the sumptuous gold of the light. New leaves were opening, and they, too, were fringed with the delicious flame. The acorns that budded and swelled in their cups were of pure gold, and they shone like tiny

172

lamps. It was a bewitching vision, and she could only gape as it unfolded before her.

Heavenly fragrances filled the warm air, perfumes so exquisite that the squirrel almost wept from sheer joy. For now, the whole orchard had changed. Gone were the unruly tangles of the lesser trees—now, only the original seven grew there, and all were magically in bloom. The heart of each blossom brimmed with a glimmering dew, and the petals fluttered in a pink-and-white snowfall to the verdant grass below. The boughs of the trees were laden with burgeoning fruit, yet the blossoms continued to bud and burst open.

Ysabelle closed her eyes and swayed unsteadily, giddy from the spectacular celebration of life and growth that overwhelmed her senses.

"Giraldus!" she called. "Tysle, Vespertilio!"

"Your friends cannot hear you!" the voice said in her mind.

Ysabelle whirled round. "Who's there?" she demanded. "Who is it?"

"Do you not know, child of the Hazel Realm?"

The squirrel felt herself tremble as she finally guessed, and she humbly lowered her eyes.

"Forgive me," she implored, "I–I–"

Kindly laughter shook the brilliant foliage that surrounded her. "Naught is there to forgive," came the tender reply. "Raise thy head, Handmaiden of Orion, thou hast borne thyself well thus far. Look on me now and take heart."

Ysabelle lifted her gaze and let out a cry of fear. There, amid the shining leaves of the flourishing oak tree, two great green eyes stared at her.

Within their emerald depths, the fires of spring flashed and sparkled, kindling all things into vibrant life.

"Have no fear," the voice told her, "for in thee lies the hope of all. Only thou can deliver the land from darkness."

"How can I?" she asked. "I am just one against so many."

The eyes gleamed behind the dappling leaves. "Yet the smallest acorn may become the tallest oak," came the answer. "Despair no more, child, for help is near to thee. Know now that thine army is safe and but a little distance away."

"Then the Hobbers didn't destroy them!"

"They did not—and now thy forces are continuing their march to the land thou knowest as Greenreach."

"I must find them!" she cried. "How far away are they?"

"Not far; if thou adhere to the straight paths and are swift, all will be well. Yet if thou falter and go astray, then all shall be lost. My power will protect thee for as long as it may—but shouldst thou wander away from my streams and the places where my will still flows through the forest, then thou art beyond my help."

Ysabelle promised that she would not let anything stop or mislead her. Then her gaze fell upon the sleeping form of Vesper, and she touched the Silver Acorn about her neck.

"What of the Moonriders?" she asked. "Are we to destroy them all?"

"The Knights of the Moon are not wholly at fault," the voice told her.

"But they murdered everyone in the holy land!" she said. "Then they attacked my home!"

"Not all perished in the first onslaught," came the swift reply, "and the bats were but tools of the true enemies of light and reason. Thy friend's people were misguided, and I do forgive them. Thou must learn to do the same, or thou shalt never ascend to the Oaken Throne."

Ysabelle thought of all the misery and terror that the forces of Hrethel had caused her subjects. "I—I do not know if I can," she said honestly.

"Time will heal," the voice assured. "Your hatred shall melt. Already, thou hast forgiven this Moonrider."

"He spared my life when he could easily have killed me," she hastily explained.

"Then be not overquick to judge the rest of his kind, for other forces are at work and strive to confound thee with anger."

The squirrel maiden looked doubtful, then she asked about Tysle and Giraldus. "What of these stout-hearted pilgrims? Is it possible for them to be cured?"

"When thou bringest the Silver to the Starglass, all things will be possible, child."

Then the light of the eyes dimmed and the voice was filled with warning. "Yet have a care, for my heart forewarns that one of thy companions shall betray thee. Beware thy trust of them, for assuredly one of their number will stop at naught to bring all our designs unto ruin."

Ysabelle stared at the sleeping figures nearby—a shocked and stricken expression frozen on her face. "Which one?" she asked. "Which is it to be? Who will betray me?"

But around her the light was growing dim, and the eyes were fading from sight. "My time with you is at an end," said the ever-diminishing voice. "Remember—trust only in thine own self and judgment, and fare thee well."

"Wait!" Ysabelle cried. "I must know!"

Only a chill breeze answered her, and the world was dark once more. The bleak silhouettes of the overgrown orchard crowded round, and the cold moonlight shone starkly upon Ysabelle's face.

"Which one?" she asked herself, gazing at her fellow travelers. "Who among them is thinking of betraying me—and to whom?"

Even as she tried to concentrate on this disturbing thought, an overpowering drowsiness crept over her. Perhaps it was a lingering gift of the Almighty Green, bestowing a deep, restful sleep upon the squirrel maiden to refresh her for the times ahead. Within moments, Ysabelle was sleeping soundly.

So it was that she failed to hear the sound that disturbed the eerie peace of the orchard. From the fathomless molten reaches beneath the earth, there came a tremendous bellowing. In the Pit, something was stirring and making its terrible way upward—up to where the squirrel slept, her paws clasped about the blood-stained amulet that had summoned it back to the waking world.

THE TIME OF THE ROWAN

A dull, insistent clanging jolted Vesper from his sleep, and he unfurled his wings, momentarily panic stricken. The young bat's dreams had been haunted by the image of the dreaded high priest, and the bloody-bones costume had flitted before him, repeating the curse and reveling in Vesper's approaching doom.

The bell continued to ring, yet, to his relief, the bat discovered that it was only Giraldus taking up his staff and shaking it at Tysle.

It was a pleasant, warm morning. Ysabelle was already awake and occupied in braiding her hair. The dazzling memory of her visions the previous night made her paws shake, and her mind reeled at the recollection. She had actually spoken with the Almighty Green and wanted to shout the fact out loud. But the warning she had been given weighed heavily upon her, and the squirrel said nothing to the others about it.

Tysle had some trouble preventing his master exploring the orchard, but Vesper came to the shrew's aid and insisted that they could not dawdle, and ought to set off immediately.

"That's right!" Tysle broke in. "And Greenreach be a mighty long way still. Why, this day we must put a goodly distance 'tween us and this place if we're to make the last shrine before the night—and that be in the most deadly heart of the wild forest."

"Remember," Vesper added, "that thus far we have been extremely fortunate, having seen no sign of the Hobbers. Our luck may not last for much longer."

Reluctantly, Giraldus consented to be led away—but he made Tysle promise him that they would return to this beautiful place when they had both been cured of their ills.

So the four travelers left the Orchard of Duir behind them and pressed deeper into the forest. Bright sunlight sparkled through the naked branches overhead and shone upon the ground in ripples of bright gold.

Giraldus was in a fine mood; it was good to feel the sun on his diseased skin, and a benign smile split his face.

"By this evening we should reach the last holy place on the road to Grinuvicia," he said. "It is a holy well, and tomorrow you youngsters ought to be able to espy the hallowed hill itself in the distance."

Vesper laughed. "There's glad tidings," he said. "Why, I shall be able to return home. You'll be happy to see the back of me won't you, princess?"

"I shall not be happy until the Acorn is brought to the Starglass," she said curtly, "and your kind is driven from Greenreach."

Vesper chuckled and gave several quick hops to catch up with Tysle.

The morning passed slowly, and the group penetrated deeper into the forest's heart. Knowing that he would soon be able to see the familiar towers of his home, Vesper's spirits were high, and he regaled them with amusing stories of his life and those that he knew. His wing was less painful today than it had been, and though it was still not strong enough for flight, the encouraging signs that it was on the mend kept his toothy smile forever on his lips.

Through dense stretches of tall ferns they pushed. Once, in a damp clearing, they came upon a slimy gathering of snails. Hundreds upon hundreds of curly shells and glistening bodies had to be carefully stepped over, and, as Tysle diligently guided him, Giraldus brought the shrew sharply to a standstill. After a few moments searching with his fingers, the leprous mole popped dozens of snails into his food bag, muttering that his supply of furry wigglers would not last for much longer.

Once the clearing was left behind, the travelers were compelled to journey in a gathering gloom. No ivy crept over the ground and no weeds clogged the track, for now the trees grew so closely together that only pale shadows covered the forest floor. In their perpetual competition for light and space, the trees seemed to jostle one another, and through the matted ceiling of branches that they had created, nothing could penetrate.

It was a dreary wilderness, bereft of color, and the melancholy of their surroundings soon entered the spirits of the four companions, and they all yearned to walk in the warm sunlight once more.

Then the cold began.

Vesper was the first to notice it; the sensitive membrane of his wings caught the chill airs, and he let out a startled gasp.

"What is the matter with the batling?" Giraldus called.

"Uuggh!" the bat replied with a shiver. "'Twas as if icy breath did blow upon me."

The mole quested the air with his snout. "I can detect naught amiss," he said.

As if in answer, another icy blast blew upon them, colder and with more force than before.

Everyone shuddered, and Ysabelle rubbed her arms where goose pimples had suddenly appeared.

"As I feared," Giraldus commented, "in the forest's heart the winter lingers. No doubt we shall become increasingly aware of its ghastly presence."

The mole was right, and, by midday, it was as if the alder month had not yet arrived and the world was still locked within the time of the rowan.

Frosty cobwebs gleamed white and sparkled like strands of spun diamonds over the trees and branches. The leaves

179

that the pilgrims walked upon were laced with ice, and the muddy pools they came across were covered by an intricate lattice of cold.

The air they breathed steamed from their mouths in great clouds, and Giraldus pulled his pointed hood down over his face to keep out the chill drafts.

As she trod on the brittle leaves, keeping her tail close about her, a disturbing thought occurred to Ysabelle. In this wintry place, the power of the Green was dormant, and she urged the others to hurry.

Long, thin icicles dripped from sagging boughs in huge, glittering curtains that tinkled ever so faintly before the glacial airs, and the still, blanketing quiet that oppressed the frozen forest echoed to these bleak and tuneless chimes.

A hoary rime now covered everything, and the ground was almost too cold to walk over. Threads of icy white mist clung to the trees, throttling them with the numbing death of winter.

Vesper flapped his wings several times in an effort to keep warm, and his wispy beard had become clotted with a frosty dew.

Tysle's teeth chattered uncontrollably, and his directions to his master were halting and broken as he tried to control his shivering speech.

No one could believe the ice-bound world that bit and pinched at them, and Giraldus uttered psalm after psalm to keep himself going. Leading the way, some distance in front, Tysle gave a shout, and they all stopped in their tracks.

The shrew help up a paw that trembled with more than mere cold, and Ysabelle and Vesper stared at what he had found.

"Bless us!" the young bat whispered.

Ysabelle clutched her amulet, but the silver was frozen, and she had to tear her paws away in shock.

"What is it?" Giraldus boomed, peering from beneath his hood. "Tysle, what have you discovered?"

The shrew leaned heavily upon his crutch and turned toward his master. "Hobb posts," he breathed.

Impaled upon sharpened twigs were the bodies of five sparrows, and, next to them, the picked-clean skulls of three weasels grinned and gaped.

"So," Giraldus murmured once Tysle had explained, "the cult of the Raith Sidhe is strong hereabouts. This no doubt is a warning to travelers such as we."

Tysle looked down from the macabre totems and spat on the freezing ground. "If'n I sees one o' them foul villains, they'll be sorry!" he promised.

"Ssshhh!" hissed Vesper suddenly.

Swiftly, he pulled Tysle from the path and herded Ysabelle and Giraldus behind the bole of a tree.

"Listen," he told them.

Everyone held their breath, and then they heard–something was approaching.

Crunching footsteps were coming toward them along the path, and Ysabelle looked at Vesper in horror.

"Who is it?" Giraldus murmured, muffling the bell on his staff with his paw.

"Can't tell yet," said Tysle, whipping out his tiny knife and jabbing it in readiness.

As the footsteps drew closer, Ysabelle took hold of her own blade, and the bitter steel that had once belonged to the bloody-bones shone grimly.

"How many are there?" she asked.

"More than one," Vesper answered, "though I can't quite–"

From behind the screen of silvery twigs and the ragged shreds of icy mist, two figures emerged.

Tysle lowered his knife in disappointment, Vesper laughed, and Ysabelle put her paw to her brow–sighing in relief.

"What is it?" asked Giraldus.

"Nothing to worry about," Vesper chortled, "only a couple of mice collecting firewood."

Standing on the path, two strangers squinted at the tree that seemed to be speaking with many voices. Both mice were plump creatures, with knitted scarves wound about their mouths and necks and swaddles inside long woolen tunics that came down to their knees. Bundles of twigs were stacked precariously upon their backs, and they looked at each other nervously.

One of them pulled the scarf away from his mouth and asked cautiously, "Did 'ee hear that, Mahtild?"

The second mouse nodded. "That I did, Pountfrey," she returned, adjusting the teetering pile of fuel she bore.

"Tha doesn't think it's—"

"Nay, 'tis too early for they to be out yet."

The first mouse mulled this over and agreed with her. "Right," he said sternly. "Then whoever it is skulking yonder had best show their faces!"

Vesper and Ysabelle stepped from behind the tree, followed by Tysle. The two mice squeaked in surprise, then their mouths fell open and their eyes bulged as Giraldus came ambling after.

"'Tis a leper!" the one called Pountfrey yelled.

"Stay back!" squawked the other. "Fancy a-coming across a band of roguish disease carriers virtually on our doorstep!"

Giraldus roared for silence and told the mice that he would not harm them. They looked at him and the others doubtfully for a moment, and their whiskers twitched furiously, then they relaxed and gruffly introduced themselves.

"Name's Pountfrey, and this be my good lady Mahtild. "'Scuse the nerves, but you done give us a bit of a start, you did. Don't meet many folk on the road these days."

"Not like it was, is it?" his wife sadly reflected. "Oh, the comings and goings then when I was a teeny wee lass."

Pountfrey waited until she finished, then continued. "Got to know who is what if'n you live in these parts," he explained. "You gets a smell for it, you might say—there's been fairer than 'ee traipsing these woods that I would'na trust."

"Ooh, a frighty bad set of vagabonds and cutpurses, the lot," Mahtild put in.

"Hobbers?" asked Tysle excitedly.

The mice looked uncomfortable and fidgeted with their bundles of firewood. "Aye," Pountfrey finally admitted, "them do have a hold here, yet we have nowt to do with the likes of they. Keep usselves to usselves and bolt the door when the evening comes."

"We not ones for upping sticks like all else!" his wife blurted.

"Tush, dear!" he told her. "Not now."

"Been here all these years!" she ranted. "Why, my brass was given to me 'neath yon beech tree—and they 'spect me to go off all calm like? Shan't do it, I says!"

"And we won't!"

"Don't 'ee get any notions, Pountfrey Gromyn—I still says what I said then!"

"I knowed that!"

"Good an' well—no ones to uproot us! Adhere, we will!"

Giraldus jiggled his staff, and the bell clanged the bickering mice into silence.

"Forgive me," he begged, "yet my fellows and me are bewildered. What do you mean? Who wanted you to leave—was it the Hobb cult?"

"Pooh!" said Mahtild scornfully. "'Tweren't they. No, 'twas them other woodlanders all deciding to band together."

"We weren't for joining them!"

"Not quitting our snug wee home."

"Let them go and fight if they can—we didn't want aught to do with it!"

"Still don't!"

"We're not saying as we likes having foul brigands as neighbors, though. We hates 'em as much as the others, but if'n we keep the door locked, us doesn't see the purpose in grouping together and playing at soldiers."

Ysabelle's head spun trying to keep up with what the mice were saying. "Do you mean some of you actually formed an army to fight against the Hobbers?"

"Not us!" Mahtild smartly replied. "'Twere others. They upped and went, abandoned thems homes, and started waving swords and knives and the like—I ask you."

"Should have known better, the lot of them."

"I told them, didn't I?"

"That you did."

"Plain crazy notion, I said. Them'll all be sorry for it, mark you."

"If they're still alive."

"Well that'd be a lesson to them to go off and not adhering."

Taking advantage of a rare pause, Vesper interrupted. "Where, exactly, did they go?" he asked. "Was it far away?"

The mice sniffed and pursed their lips truculently. "Don't know, don't care," Pountfrey declared. "Good riddance—we doesn't need their company, does we, missus?"

"Certainly not," she tartly replied. "Only accidents ever come of playing with sharp blades, I told 'em."

"That you did."

"I knowed I did. Anyways, we're still here and happy."

"Though cold; 'tas been awful nippy like this fer too long, to my thinking."

"Well, let's not stand here any longer catching our deaths," she scolded him. "A nice, crackling fire we can have now, and there's a bit of broth to put on it—soon be toasty and warm."

"Pleasant talking with you folks," Pountfrey waved as they turned to leave.

"Wait," Giraldus cried. "There is much you do not know. There is much we have to tell."

Mahtild wrinkled her nose at him and shook her head. "Not today," she said. "No time for chatter—lots to do, haven't we, my chuck?"

"Plenty," he replied.

"But the land of Greenreach!" the mole called out. "That blessed place has been destroyed, and it is our beholden duty to restore a Starwife to the throne! Rejoice that you, too, can play a part in this most honorable quest. This is a time of destiny, when great deeds must be done!"

"Which broth will that be, then?" Pountfrey inquired mildly.

"The chestnut and maple."

"Not the rose hip?"

"Away with you, Mister Gromyn! We haven't set eyes on a rose hip for nigh on six month!"

Giraldus thumped his staff angrily. "Cast aside thy worldly goods!" he shouted. "Let fall those burdens that trammel thy journey to the blessed Green!"

"Master," Tysle chirped, "'tain't no use—they've gone."

"Join us upon our noble quest!"

"Didn't even invite us back to have some of that broth," Tysle grumbled.

Giraldus let out a weary sigh. "Ah, well," he said at length, "the way of the pilgrim is not for all."

"I wish those mice had told us where those woodlanders had gone to," said Vesper. "If they really have formed some kind of fighting force against the Hobbers, we might need their help if we haven't come across your shrine by tonight."

"Have faith," the mole told him.

"Oh, I have faith all right," commented the bat. "Faith in those who skewered them poor birds and weasels—I believe in them absolutely."

As they set off along the path once more, Ysabelle glanced behind, and the grinning skulls seemed to watch them depart.

For the rest of the afternoon, they tramped through the frozen forest, and at every turn of the track there was some new sign to remind them in whose country they walked.

The severed heads of those who would not join the infernal congregations became a common sight, and Ysabelle was astonished and appalled at herself that she could grow accustomed to such horrific and grisly objects. Alongside the mutilated remains, which the gore crows had picked and pecked at, vicious and crude drawings were daubed on the tree trunks—depictions of the Raith Sidhe, scenes of murder, and evil-looking symbols whose meaning they were all relieved not to be able to interpret.

They met only one other creature, and that was a gaunt rabbit out foraging for food. When Giraldus asked him to lay down his possessions and follow them to Greenreach, the rabbit swore and rudely clicked his fingers at the mole.

"Clear the way," the buck-toothed stranger said crossly. "The evening comes, and I've a mind to get away from this place before then."

Giraldus spread his arms wide and tried to prevent the creature passing, determined this time to finish his sermon.

The rabbit bounced in front of him for several moments, glaring at each of the company until he stopped and stared at Ysabelle.

"What's this? What's this?" the rabbit cried skittishly. "A maiden? What are you doing, dear lady? Leave these benighted woods—escape while you may! Art thou ignorant of the horror that haunts the forest? A tithe of flesh does that pagan crew pay to their evil master!" He tugged at the squirrel's arm and glowered at the others for leading her into such peril.

Ysabelle pulled away. "My road lies this way!" she told him. "I cannot turn back now; though my death might be around the next corner, I am bound to press on."

"Then seek shelter!" the rabbit told her. "Go to the woodlanders who resist the hellish brethren. Find them and be safe! For mercy's sake!"

"Do you know where they are?" Vesper asked. "We should be very grate–"

The young bat faltered, for a dramatic change had come over the rabbit. The creature's long ears pricked up suddenly, and his mouth fell open as a look of sheer terror spread over his face.

"Too late!" the rabbit shrieked. "Too late! No more time! They are coming–out of my way, Scabface!" With a terrific leap, he jumped over Giraldus and scooted away. "Fools!" his fading voice cried as he vanished into the distance. "You'll never leave these woods alive!"

Vesper stroked his frosty beard, deep in troubled thought. "I wonder what he heard?" he muttered after listening to the sounds of the wintry forest and finding nothing unusual.

"Probably just the poor thing's nerves," said Ysabelle. "It's growing dark, and he was frightened, that is all."

"Well, I have no wish to be abroad in this terrible place after nightfall, either," said Vesper. "Let us resume the march."

They set off once more, and, after a short time, Ysabelle shook her head. "I wish that fellow had told us where we might find the woodlanders," she said regretfully.

Vesper looked at her, and his brow creased into many furrows. The gathering gloom was making him nervous also, and he snapped at Ysabelle before he knew what he was doing. "If it wasn't for your kind," he told her, "I would be able to find them myself."

"How?" she asked, taken aback.

"Insight," he said promptly. "That is the birthright of the Moonriders."

"Well, why put the blame on us?"

"It was the old Starwife who denied it to my people!" he told her. "It was she who started the holy war!"

Ysabelle threw back her head and laughed. "Nonsense!" she hooted, but the sound of her own voice startled her, and it was then she realized that she and the bat had been hissing at one another in whispers.

"I don't like this," Vesper murmured. "I may not have insight, but I can feel that all is not well. The rabbit was right—something is out there."

The squirrel maiden looked around them. The dismal light of the wintry day was already beginning to fail, yet there was something else—something that made the hair on the back of her neck prickle and stand on end.

Even Giraldus noticed the growing atmosphere of unease, and he tugged at Tysle's string to hurry the shrew along.

Presently, they were all walking hastily over the path, their pace quickening as the shadows grew longer.

It was as if the forest was aware of them, listening to everything they said and following their movements with hostile interest.

"Is it just my imaginings," Ysabelle asked Vesper, "or are we being watched?"

The bat gazed about the stark, frost-covered trees. "If that is so, then whoever it is, their sight is better than mine," he answered. "I see nothing!"

As their disquiet increased, only Tysle seemed unafraid. With his knife in his paw, the shrew was ready for anything, and greatly looked forward to encountering any Hobbers. "If they want a fight," he said with an expectant grin lighting up his face, "then let them come—I'll give 'em a bashing they never bargained for. I'll teach the filth not to tackle the Sickens twice!"

"Now, now," Giraldus scolded, cuffing the shrew's head, "you know how I deplore violence of any kind."

Vesper had gone pale. "If it comes to a fight," he said, remembering the hellish throng around the standing stones, "we shan't last very long."

"Please!" Ysabelle begged. "We're only frightening each other. 'Tis all the fault of that long-toothed rabbit. He started this. Why, here we are, walking as fast as we can for no reason at all. None have seen or heard anything out of the ordinary—'tis only our fancy—"

Suddenly, a high, mocking sound rang through the trees. "YIP–YIP–YIP!"

"What was that?" Ysabelle cried, whirling around.

Giraldus twisted his head to listen. "Some kind of bird, no doubt," he suggested, but his strides had widened, and he almost trod on Tysle's bandaged heel.

"That was no bird I know of," muttered Vesper. "That was a call of some kind."

"Hobbers," Ysabelle gasped fretfully. "They're here, aren't they?"

Tysle jumped up and down. "Why don't they show themselves?" he chirped. "Why do they hide?"

"They're watching us," Vesper replied, "probably waiting for the right moment."

"What shall we do?" asked the squirrel. "Should we run?"

"No," he said quickly. "Without a doubt, that is what they want—send us dashing off, scared and witless, and right into their midst."

"We must continue along the path," Giraldus agreed. "Do not let them affright us."

So they continued on their way, but from deep within the shadows of the trees that surrounded and pressed in on every side, they began to hear strange voices and rustlings.

"They are moving with us," Vesper whispered.

Ysabelle bit her lip to stop from crying out. The tension was unbearable. "They don't care that we can hear them now," she wept. "They no longer try to disguise their presence."

"I wonder when they will show themselves," said Giraldus, and he, too, sounded afraid.

Out of the corner of her eye, Ysabelle thought she saw something dart between the trees, but when she looked there was nothing.

"I–I could have sworn I saw a movement," she stammered.

The sounds were louder now: twigs were breaking beneath eager feet, and tree trunks slapped impatiently. An excited babble of wicked voices murmured to one another. From some dark place, two sticks were struck together, beating out a horrible rhythm that gave a pulse to the seething woodland. Ysabelle could not stand much more; she felt like screaming and tearing off down the path. Her breath came in short gasps, and her eyes flicked from side to side, dreading the moment when she would catch a glimpse of the unseen enemies.

It was Vesper who saw them first.

"Look!" the bat cried. "Up there, in the treetops."

Ysabelle and Tysle stared upward. In the high branches of an elm tree, a large, black carrion crow sat hunched and ready. With red-rimmed eyes, it returned the anxious looks of the travelers and gave a croaking cackle.

"'Tis only a bird," Tysle murmured. "Master did say the first call were a bird."

"No," Vesper told him. "By Hrethel's name, that creature is a servant of Hobb. See how it regards us!"

"I pray that is all it does!" said Ysabelle.

Giraldus tutted and told them not to fear. "For the shrine cannot be far–the holy well is almost within our reach!"

"It had better be," said Vesper, "for there are two crows up there now."

Sure enough, another of the ugly carrion birds had joined the first, and it, too, let out a chilling, ghastly caw.

Ysabelle shivered and turned away, but her eyes saw a furry shape leap through the darkness, and she took hold of Vesper's wing in fear.

"They're going to jump out at us!" she cried. "Any moment now, we shall be overwhelmed and cut to pieces!"

Vesper said nothing, for his own eyes had seen a figure skulking in the shadows. It was a monstrous rat with a glittering sword in its claw, and, for an instant, it bared its fangs before stepping back into the gloom.

"Cast your eyes upward," said Tysle slowly.

Above them, dozens more crows had alighted. With greedy eyes, they watched those passing beneath, and a number sharpened their beaks upon the frozen bark. The trees were smothered with them now; it was as though a vile black foliage had burst into life upon the previously bare branches.

Hundreds of eyes were shining within the dense forest—cruel, narrow slits that burned with savagery and hunger.

Then a chant began; soft at first, it gradually spread until the whole world seemed filled by the raucous and discordant sound.

Ysabelle no longer dared to look around her. Now she kept her eyes fixed on the path at her feet, yet the evil words that the children of the Raith Sidhe endlessly recited made her feel sick and faint.

Four fine morsels, see how they run,
Rip out their hearts until their lives are done.
Peck out their eyes and do a good job,
Peel off their skins and give them to Hobb.

"Hobb!" they hissed. "Hobb! Hobb! Hobb!"

Vesper saw the strain on Ysabelle's face as the squirrel gritted her teeth and tried not to break into a run. "Don't," he told her. "Try not to listen—think of something else."

Behind him, Giraldus uttered Green psalms to try to block out the hideous chorus, but his voice wavered as the foul mouths of the Hobbers shouted all the more loudly.

On corpse flesh shall we dine,
Hot blood shall be our wine.

Ysabelle tried to do as Vesper said. She tried to remember the vision she had seen the night before, and fill her mind with those

191

emerald eyes, but that seemed so long ago now, and her strength began to fail her.

From out of the ranks of the trees a hunchbacked rat poked its snout and tittered at her. The squirrel took hold of the Silver Acorn and repeated over and over to herself, "I am not afraid. I am not afraid!"

A disgusting gurgle issued from the shadows, and Vesper pulled Ysabelle back as a large missile was hurled onto the path.

Ysabelle stared at it fearfully, and the terrible voices of the Hobb cult grew silent.

At the squirrel's feet was a round bundle. It seemed to have been knitted from wool, and for a moment none of them recognized it.

The shrew blinked at the thing, then ventured forward. There appeared to be something inside.

Using the end of his crutch, Tysle gave the large, lumpy ball a nudge, and a part of the knitting fell away.

Blood oozed over the icy ground, staining the frost pink in an ever-widening circle.

A ghastly laugh was sent up throughout the forest, and Vesper squeezed his eyes shut to blot out the grisly sight.

"Pountfrey," he breathed.

"Filthy Hobbers!" Tysle shrieked.

Terror and panic finally overcame Ysabelle. Screaming, she tore down the path.

"No!" Vesper called after her. "We mustn't separate! That's what they want!" He turned quickly to the others and told them to follow and run as best they could.

As the bat set off, Tysle yanked on the string, and Giraldus scurried over the ground behind him.

But the game was over now; the children of Hobb had had their sport.

A wild howl screeched above the din of the sniggering laughter, and, in the trees, the carrion crows flapped their great wings and swooped downward like some terrible dark swirl of autumn leaves.

"Tysle!" Giraldus cried. "What is happening? Tysle?" The mole hurried along as best he could, but the noises disoriented him. He fumbled at his belt where the lead string should have been looped, but the hook had fallen, and, for the first time in many years, he was alone and without guidance. "Ysabelle!" he bellowed as the shrieking cries grew closer.

"Forward, forward!" the shrew called. "Mind the root at two summer worms. Forward, forward—left now!"

Tysle skidded to a halt. Something was wrong—no answering tug yanked on the string, and he spun round desperately. The string was slack, and his master was not attached to the end of it.

"Aaaiiyeee!" he squealed, limping back the way he had come. "Master! Master!"

There was Giraldus, thrashing his staff over his head as a sea of carrion crows plucked and tormented him.

"Leave me!" he howled in a high, frightened voice. "Leave me!"

The crows mocked him and pecked at the sores on his face, scratching his mottled velvet with their claws.

"Warm red blood to drip from our beaks!" They croaked eagerly. "Rich ruby honey to slake our thirsts!"

Giraldus was floundering; the staff whirled less intensely now, and his pitiful cries were drowned by the furious beating of the ebony wings.

Down he dropped, onto his knees, and the carrion birds tore at him.

Suddenly, into the frenzied mass of feather and claw, a bitter little blade flashed and stabbed.

"Master!" roared Tysle in a voice larger than himself. "Don't worry—I'm here! I'll rip out their quills and stuff them up their parson's noses!"

Brandishing his tiny knife, the shrew lunged at those who pecked at Giraldus, and so furious was his temper that the birds fell back, dismayed.

"Get you up!" Tysle said to the mole. "Take the end of my string and fear no more–we'll be no crow bait!"

A cloud of bloody feathers flew about the shrew as he rampaged around his master, seeing off any who dared approach. Then he gave a tug on the string, and the pair of them hastened down the path. But the maddened crows came after them, and, with wings outstretched, they screeched for the pair's deaths.

Ysabelle was too afraid to stop. She could hear Vesper calling to her, but the fiendish cries of the Hobbers filled her with despair, and she raced beneath the crowded trees as fast as she could.

The rats and other evil worshippers of the Unholy Triad were chasing her, leaving the crows to finish off the leper and his guide.

With cudgels in their grasp, they beat the trees as they pursued her, reaching out with their twisted claws, saliva dribbling from their open jaws.

"Fly!" their deadly voices coldly rang. "Run to your doom! Speed to your death! A necklace shall we make of your entrails, and down our gullets shall your torn flesh slip."

The squirrel maiden ran blindly on, the trampling feet of her enemies gaining on her with every anxious stride.

From the darkness ahead, an enormous badger loomed, rearing up directly in front of her.

In the creature's wide and vicious mouth, the tail of a mouse dangled, and, sucking it in, it then licked the blood from the knife it clutched in its claws.

Ysabelle covered her face and swerved to one side, bounding wildly through the forest away from the path.

An outstretched wing wrapped itself around her waist, and she screamed in terror.

"It's me!" cried Vesper as he fended off her fists. "Stop it, you stupid squirrel!"

Ysabelle wept, but Vesper grabbed her wrist and dragged her farther into the trees. "This way!" he shouted.

As they ran, black-feathered arrows sang past their heads, and a dagger spiraled through the air, just missing the bat's right ear.

"We shan't make it!" Ysabelle sobbed. "Those devils will hound us until we drop!"

"Stop squawking and run!" Vesper yelled. "I'll be no meal for the likes of them!"

Plunging farther from the path, they came to where a thick hedge covered the ground and barred the way in all directions.

"Trapped!" Ysabelle cried.

"Not yet!" Vesper said, bundling her through a narrow gap and leaping after.

But Ysabelle had stopped just beyond the opening, and the bat crashed into her and fell on his face.

"What are you doing?" he cried. "Are you mad? Hurry!"

Ysabelle could only gaze at the sight that lay before them.

"Vespertilio!" she whispered. "We are here!"

Brushing flakes of ice from his wings, Vesper looked up in surprise. "The holy well!" he uttered in astonishment. Then he, like Ysabelle, could only stand and gape.

Behind them there came a frantic series of cries and howls as the others found them.

"Here we come!" squealed Tysle, dashing through the hedge. "Forward, forward—squeeze in!"

Giraldus came lumbering after, his large girth barely managing the narrow way.

"Burn in the eternal fires of damnation, scavengers of the underworld!" he trumpeted, brandishing his staff once more. "Tysle, where are they? Are the corbies regrouping for another assault?"

The shrew peered into the sky, but it was clear. He pattered back to the gap in the hedge and stared at the way they had come.

Not a sign of the carrion crows could he see; neither were the rats following them, and suddenly the forest was quiet.

"They've plumb vanished!" he cried in amazement. "Why do you think they left us like that? I did think we was done for, good and proper!"

"Who can fathom the wiles of the heathen hordes?" Giraldus muttered. "Let us be grateful for the present—yet I fear the respite will be all too brief."

Tysle opened his mouth to answer; then he saw where they were.

"The last shrine!" he squeaked. "Master—we reached it!"

The mole let out a joyous yell and clapped his paws together. "Then the Green has protected us!" he bellowed. "That is why the vermin of the skies could no longer hound us and the loathsome wights of the woods have abandoned their chase."

Tysle swallowed doubtfully and wandered over to Ysabelle and Vesper, who stood speechless and aghast.

"Tysle?" Giraldus called. "Lead me to the holy water."

The shrew gazed up at Ysabelle, and the squirrel shook her head at him. "You cannot lie this time," she said.

Tysle knew she was right, and he stared at the vile scene one last time before returning to his master to explain.

In a small clearing, fringed by twelve elder trees and the rambling hedge, the Well of Ruis had remained for centuries. It was square, its sides being cut by the cunning craft of those who had lived long ago. In this place, it was said, the entire forest was first born, and many were the streams that owed their sources to this enchanted, crystal water.

The virtues of the well were legendary: heroes had gained great strength after drinking there, wishes had been granted, and many wounds had been magically healed after bathing in it. At one time, a warden had tended the site, but, like so many other of the sacred shrines, it had been deserted for untold years.

Ysabelle looked at the sorrowful sight, and a tear streaked down her cheek.

The holy well had become a hideous place, for the children of the Raith Sidhe had come and left their infernal marks there.

Locked in the grip of the pervading winter, the divine power of the holy well was weak, and the spirit of the Green had not been able to defend it. Now, the place was a repellent parody of its former glory. Black ice sealed the well head, yet the trapped water within was dark and foul. The Hobbers had defiled it with their filth, and the once pure water was polluted beyond redemption.

Nothing had escaped the evil vigilance of the hellish brethren. Once the well had been poisoned, they had turned their dastardly attentions to the surrounding area. Many of the elder trees had been cruelly hacked at; some still bore the scorch marks where wicked fires had burned them, and others were no more than a miserable collection of pathetic stumps, but everywhere was covered by obscene scrawls.

The nightmare images that the travelers had seen earlier by the wayside were nothing compared to this devilish work. On all sides, depraved scratches had been gouged into the wounded trees, indecent charcoal scribbles and base messages defaced the broken stone that had once covered the well, and the most disgusting drawings filled any spare space.

Beside the blackened, frozen well, a great heap of charred branches and lopped boughs had been assembled, and Vesper guessed that here was another meeting place for the unholy worshippers of Hobb.

Giraldus gripped his staff tightly when Tysle described the scene to him. "Is there to be no haven?" he asked hoarsely. "Are the powers of the dark to conquer all?"

Vesper lifted his face to the darkening sky and scowled. "I do not understand," he said. "The power of the Green no longer defends this place, so why did the Hobbers abandon their attack?"

"Maybe they still think of it as a place of dread to be avoided," suggested Ysabelle.

The bat dismissed that idea. "No," he said. "Look at that pile of branches. It's just like the fire in the dell where we were their prisoners. The Hobb cult have been congregating here for a long time, by the looks of things."

He took several hesitant steps toward the burned wood, then he quickly turned away and buried his face in his wings.

"What is it?" Ysabelle asked fearfully.

The young bat parted his wings, and the look in his eyes shocked her into silence.

It was Tysle who went to discover what Vesper had found. Unraveling plenty of string, the shrew hobbled over to where Vesper was standing and stared behind the blackened heap.

The shrew staggered backward, and it was some time before he could speak. "'Tis—'tis the worst mine eyes ever behold," he said at last. "No, don't you come over here, sweet mistress. You'll never sleep peaceably again."

Ysabelle glanced at Vesper, and the bat shuddered. "It's the remains of a stag," he told her in a wavering voice. "Just the head, of course. The Hobbers seem to have a special liking for them. First Pountfrey, and now this."

Tysle felt faint. "How could they?" he whimpered. "The poor beast's antlers all sawn off—and—and—"

Giraldus pulled on the string, and the shrew quickly came back to him.

"What are we to do?" Ysabelle asked.

"We cannot remain here!" Vesper told her. "It has become an evil, accursed place. I can think of nowhere more dangerous."

Giraldus had been listening to all this with a grave look upon his face. Now he raised his immense paw and said softly, "Hush. We are not alone."

Everyone stared at him; then, from somewhere behind the mutilated elders, they heard a voice, and it was sobbing.

"O woe," it blubbered, "what a sorry pickle you have landed thyself in. Why, oh, why could He who doled out brains not have bestowed any upon thee, unhappy dolt?"

Ysabelle caught her breath—she knew that voice!

"It cannot—it cannot be," she stuttered, "and yet—"

Without a word to the others, she hurried in the direction of the self-pitying voice and let out a delighted cry.

There, in the dreary shade of the broken trees, sitting upon his cart and with his head in his paws, was Wendel Maculatum.

BY THE MOURNFUL
WILLOWS

At the sound of the squirrel's voice, the jester leaped to his feet and backed away in terror.

"Oh!" he yowled. "A phantom! A phantom is come to haunt me! Avaunt, dreaded specter—begone!"

Ysabelle smiled. "Wendel!" she cried. "I am no ghost. 'Tis I, Ysabelle, the daughter of Ninnia."

The stoat wrung his paws before him. "Alas, wretched shade," he said, nodding gloomily, "only too well do I know thine countenance, and how it was taken from this world."

"I am not dead," Ysabelle insisted. "The Hobbers carried me off to one of their dungeons, but I am most certainly alive." To prove this, she stepped up to the jester and took his paw in hers.

At first, Wendel flinched and tried to wriggle away; then his eyes grew round as he realized she was indeed flesh and blood. "Mistress!" he cried, falling to his knees. "Then 'tis true. Oh, I did fear all was lost when those figures attacked the camp."

"So did we all," she said, "but it is so wonderful to find you. How did you come to be here?"

The jester put his fingers to his lips and spoke in a hushed tone, as if the mention of those events would bring some terrible calamity upon them. "'Twas all confusion," he told her. "There was I, ready for the snoozing, when out those villains sprang, and madness was everywhere. I recall that thy nibbler screamed that they had taken you, and everyone lamented. But in the chaos

200

that followed, when thy guards did give chase to the midnight hordes, I and my cart were left behind, and poor Wendel has not seen them since."

"But how did you get here?"

"For days have I wandered, lost in the wilds. In terror have I spent my nights listening to the shrill sounds of those who prowl in the dark. I had all but given up hope when I came upon this dismal place, and then those hideous noises began again. I thought they were finally coming to get me, and thus you found me a-quaking and sobbing. Oh, how mine heart does rejoice now!"

He kissed the squirrel's paw and laughed rather hysterically.

Standing a little way behind, Vesper peered at the stoat and frowned. "It does appear to me," he said, "that you have been extremely fortunate so far."

For the first time, Wendel seemed to notice him. "Why, 'tis the Moonrider!" he declared. "Yet where are his bonds? Why is he not trussed and bound?"

Before anyone could answer, he then saw Giraldus and Tysle.

"Don't worry," Ysabelle said hastily when she saw the look of horror steal over the jester's face. "These are all my friends, and the bat has saved my life more than once since last I saw you."

"Is that so?" the stoat mumbled, staring aghast at the leprous mole and his lame guide. "I'll own that your roads have been darker than mine if this company seems fair to thee. What have we here? A runty shrew with a game leg, and the most ill-favored knave I have ever bruised mine eyes to look on—no ornaments are they."

"Here!" growled Tysle. "Who is this bad-mannered rogue? I'll not have him looking down his nose at us!"

Wendel looked startled at the shrew's retaliation, then made a comical bow. "Forgive me, goodly sirs," he apologized. "In the sudden shock of finding this jewel of the Hazel Realm alive, I did forget myself, but am now recovered. Take not the slightest notice of aught I prattle. I am what the Green made me, a simpleton who knows no better. Wendel Maculatum, forever stupid, a dotard before his time."

"Ah, well," Tysle grunted, "can't say fairer than that–just so long as you don't go calling us names again."

"May the Green wash out my mouth if I do," he replied humbly.

Giraldus sniffed while Tysle introduced himself and his master. He was not sure if he approved of the stoat's irreverent tone, and the mole assumed a stiff-necked piety that none of Wendel's jokes could thaw.

"I should dearly like to know why the Hobbers stopped chasing us," said Vesper, glancing back at the defiled well. "They could have killed us easily."

The jester raised a paw to silence him. "Be glad that they did not," he said. "Why question such a happy occurrence?"

"Because it doesn't make any sense," the bat replied.

"To those odious malefactors it does!" Wendel exclaimed. "It seems to me that they revel in teasing and taunting their victims. Have I not heard them night after night, calling to me and making my flesh creep? To toy with our fears is their delight."

Vesper was still doubtful; why did he have the feeling that they had been purposely driven to this place? He tried to put his thoughts into words, but the simple stoat was so ecstatic at finding Ysabelle that he was now capering madly around her. The three bells upon the jester's headdress tinkled sweetly, and Vesper recalled the curse laid on him and said nothing. Now there were two sources to constantly remind him of his doom.

In spite of herself, Ysabelle could not stop laughing. It was as though all the emotions she had been forced to keep under control would not be bottled up any longer, and burst to the surface, released in one insane fit of giggles.

Then the tears flowed, and she gasped for breath between the mingling of sobs and mirth.

During this time, Wendel pranced around, somersaulting and juggling three acorns that he snatched from his cart. Tysle gazed at him admiringly; the life of a pilgrim allowed for no frivolity such as this, and he marveled at the jester's antics.

Giraldus listened to all this and was most unimpressed–the stoat seemed to have infected them with inane silliness. He gave a slight tug on the string, but Tysle was so busy chortling that he failed to notice.

Vesper was not pleased by the effect the jester had on Ysabelle. Had she forgotten that a few minutes ago, they had barely escaped with their lives? The darkness was complete now, and he feared what the dead of night would bring.

"We ought to be moving on," the bat said brusquely. "We dare not stay here."

Ysabelle and Tysle broke off from their merriment and stared at him for a second, then they collapsed into more giggles.

"Your face," the squirrel cried. "It's so serious!"

Wendel put his paws to the side of his head, pretending they were Vesper's ears, and a morose expression dragged his mouth into a make-believe frown.

"We Knights of the Moon have no time for laughter," the jester said dolefully. "There is no honor in a titter."

Vesper ignored him and stomped back to the well area. "You may do as you wish," he said flatly, "but I'm going to leave now."

Giraldus turned his head toward him and agreed absolutely. "The batling speaks wisely," he rumbled. "Let us not linger here. We must put the ice and cold behind us this night." He gave the string another tug, only a little more sharply this time, and Tysle was nearly yanked off balance.

Wendel put the colored acorns into one of his prop chests and wheeled the cart into the clearing.

"I, too, have no desire to remain in this grim spot," he said. "Whither are you bound?"

"Greenreach," Ysabelle told him. "That plan has not changed."

"But without thine army?" the jester asked. "Surely that is not the course that one with so full a brain pan would contemplate. Is it not still swarming with thy winged friend's forces?"

Ysabelle looked uncomfortably at Vesper; she had not told them that she knew her army would be there when she arrived. "Master Jester," she answered with a smile, "let us not think so far ahead. Tonight is the present problem. What are we to do? Find the path again and risk another chase?"

"I know of no other way to Greenreach," said Vesper curtly.

The stoat gave a theatrical shiver, and the bells of his head-dress jangled loudly. "In the dark wilds!" he exclaimed. "I do fear it already."

"No one relishes the idea," Vesper told him, "but no other choice is open to us."

Tysle stuck out his bottom lip. "A sore shame it is that we never found them woodlanders."

"They were probably just so much rumor," the bat said.

Wendel pricked up his ears, and his paws fluttered in agitated excitement. "Woodlanders!" he cried. "Why, I, too, have heard of those valiant warriors. On one of my travels, the village was rife with the news. Oh, if only we could seek them out; then would we be safe for sure."

"Did you learn where they live?" asked Ysabelle quickly.

The stoat closed his eyes and slapped his forehead, trying to remember. "A long time ago it now seems," he groaned, "before the celebrations of Yule–oh, what was it I heard? Wendel Maculatum, thy mind is like unto a pickled onion! Aha! This much I recall. By the shore of a lake the place was!"

Giraldus blinked and snorted huffily. "How does that help us?"

"Why, if we could discover the whereabouts of this great pool, then surely their sentries would find us and take us to their hideaway!"

Vesper shook his head. "That's nonsense!" he said. "How are we to reach this lake? It might be anywhere. I would rather keep to the path; the danger would be exactly the same, and we do know where it leads."

"Be not so hasty, my damaged Moonrider," Wendel tutted. "This very afternoon, I did come across a stream. If we followed it, then most certainly it would guide us there."

"But it could lead either to or from the lake!" Vesper protested. "That's if it has anything to do with it at all, which I sincerely doubt!"

Ysabelle folded her arms and glared at the young bat. "What ails you?" she asked. "I think the plan has merit. We can see which of the courses we take seems the likely one. Perhaps when we find the woodland folk, we can persuade them to accompany us to Greenreach."

"I don't think they'll have a litter for you to sit on!" Vesper snapped back.

The squirrel turned to the others.

Giraldus stroked his chin and gave the matter long deliberation. "A stream might lend us protection," he finally consented, "providing it is not frozen."

Tysle readily agreed with his master. He liked the stoat already, and the brief glimpse he had had of the prop chest's contents tantalized him, and he longed to peek inside the others.

So, against Vesper's better judgment, it was decided to hurry to the stream and follow it to the lake. Taking the handles of his cart, Wendel led them farther away from where the path cut through the forest, and, reluctantly, Vesper trailed behind.

On a three-autumn-worm string, Tysle trotted alongside the jester and drank in all that he said, chuckling at the funny or downright ridiculous comments he made.

Ysabelle was overjoyed to have found him again. The stoat was a reminder of her home and the happy time before she was burdened with the Silver Acorn. For a brief moment, she felt as she had done when she was an alder maid, free from care, with nothing to trouble her.

Walking beside Vesper, Giraldus stumbled often, for Tysle had become so engrossed in the jester's humorous tales that he forgot to direct the mole properly, and so roots and stones were kicked and tripped over by the poor leper.

The way to the stream was longer than Wendel remembered, and for over an hour, they had to traipse through the chill darkness.

"Beware of a dip in the ground just here," said Vesper, clicking his tongue and guiding the mole in Tysle's stead.

"Thank you," Giraldus replied. "'Twould seem my erstwhile companion has found a more absorbing vocation."

When they eventually found the stream, it was frozen and choked with weeds.

"So the power of the Green is dead here also," the mole muttered.

But Ysabelle was determined to continue, and so they began following the stream to its source.

Under the oppressive blanket of night they journeyed, and Vesper soon tired of hearing the stoat's lighthearted and cheery voice. With the bell on Giraldus's staff clanging somberly and those on the jester's ludicrous headgear tinkling away, the bat felt surrounded by the incessant sound, and a shadow crept over his soul.

The forest was trackless here, and they were forced to pick their way over difficult terrain. The mole suffered the most and at one point fell headlong into some thorns. Tysle quickly came to the rescue and, after that, stayed with his master, feeling terribly ashamed to have neglected him for the sake of this newcomer. Giraldus patted the shrew on the head and said no more about it. The thorns had speared one of the leper's diseased fingers and torn it from his paw, yet he clenched his teeth and told no one, wrapping his bandages tightly about his fist so they could not see.

Eventually, the trees began to thin out, and patches of sky appeared through the thick canopy above. The frozen stream grew wider, the ground dipped in a gentle slope, and then they saw it–the lake.

It was a cheerless, dreary place. Dark water stretched before them in all directions, and though a slight breeze ruffled through their fur, the surface of the lake was still and unbroken; no rippling waves lapped against the shore. There was only a bleak meeting of turgid water and liver-colored mud, marred only by occasional webs of ice that spiked away from the land.

Great, sad willows wept over the dismal drink, and their drooping branches were untidily cluttered by the unfallen leaves of many summers.

Clouds of gnats hovered about the shore, and a stagnant reek poured out from the center of the silent lake. Ysabelle coughed into her paw, and Tysle pinched his long nose.

"'Tis a foul, stinking place that you have brought us to," Vesper told the jester. "Why, 'tis more a putrid mere than a lake. I'll warrant nothing lives in it."

"Verily, this drabness is not what I expected," a dejected Wendel admitted.

Ysabelle batted away the insects that buzzed about her face. "I cannot imagine anything wanting to live near this forbidding water," she said. "It is a hateful spot. This is worse than the holy well. At least that was beautiful once, but this has never been anything but ugly."

"It do give me the creeps, too," put in Tysle, "and what a whiff wafts over the horrid water–smells like something too long dead and not yet buried."

"I said we should have returned to the path," Vesper told them.

The jester rested his cart in the frozen mud and tried to salvage the situation. "A noxious malodor, to be sure," he said, trying to sound cheerful, "but no doubt we shall soon accustom our hooters to the staleness."

Giraldus could not believe his ears. "What did the juggins say?" he cried. "Tysle, tell me he does not intend for us to remain in this Green-forsaken spot."

"What else can we do?" Wendel answered. "I, for one, am too weary to march back the way we came, and I can tell that my lady is also in much need of sleep."

The mole cast the pointed hood from his head and grumbled under his breath. "I have no desire to tarry here—all mine senses tell me nay. Some devilment is brewing; this lonely mere holds nothing wholesome, I'll be bound."

Wendel sat on his cart and shrugged. "Be that as it may," he said, "it is still our only hope of finding shelter. If those gallant foes of the enemy do swell hereabouts, then, for the gracious lady's sake, should we not do our utmost to discover them?"

"And how do we do that?" Giraldus inquired. "Shout at the top of our voices, I suppose, and bring the forces of the Hobb cult down on our heads for our labors."

"Simpler than that, blueskin," said the stoat, rummaging inside one of his chests and bringing out a tinder box. "We light a fire."

"You must be crazed!" cried Vesper. "That will certainly bring the Hobbers running. Why do we not just go looking for them—or drown ourselves in this foul lake? 'Twill have the same outcome!"

Wendel gave the bat an indulgent look, then sighed. "I do not think the followers of Hobb are our main worry once the fire is burning," he said gravely. "No, 'tis the hunting parties of thy folk we ought to beware. On my midnight wanderings since I was left behind, I have seen many Moonriders coursing through the heavens, searching for my lady. We must pray that the woodland folk espy our campfire before they do."

He turned to Ysabelle, and the squirrel gave him permission to build the fire.

It was a matter of minutes for them to collect enough sticks and branches, and, presently, tongues of yellow flame crackled into life.

The fire did much to lift their spirits, for it dispelled the all-pervading gloom, and they toasted their palms gladly before the flames, waiting in hope for the band of woodlanders to show themselves.

Only Vesper sat apart from the group. Preferring not to sit around the hearty blaze, the bat crouched in the darkness near the water's edge and mulled things over in his mind.

After a short while, Wendel pattered away and began searching beneath the willows. There, he discovered a chunk of wood that he brought back to the campfire and began carving with a sharp little knife.

Tysle sat beside him, and he watched, entranced, while a rough shape slowly emerged from the whittled wood.

"What is it you do?" he asked at length. "Is it to be a figure of the Green or a stature of a blessed martyr?"

The jester laughed. "I sincerely hope not!" he chuckled. "What would I want with anything so dull and yawnsome?"

Giraldus shifted on the ground nearby and solemnly pressed his paws together.

"Then what can it be?" the shrew breathed.

"A puppet, of course!" Wendel replied, waggling the unfinished head at him. "Something to bring a smile to the lips of the miserable and raise a cackle to the dullards of this world." He gave Tysle a nudge and pointed the knife at his master. "Mind you," he added with a snigger, "'twould have to be one of extreme comicality to put even the shadow of a smirk upon that pompous face. How do you bear the ill-countenanced fellow?"

Tysle glanced hastily back at Giraldus, who was staring intently into the flames. He had never thought of the mole as being dull before, and his kind nature berated him for thinking it now. Compared with the colorful jester, however, the shrew saw that it was true. Tysle blinked sheepishly and wondered if Giraldus had heard what had been said, but the other made no sign that he had, and the shrew soon relaxed and resumed watching Wendel at work.

"What shall the puppet be of?" he asked.

The stoat winked at him. "Perhaps I'll fashion it into the likeness of a shrew," he said.

Tysle beamed from ear to ear. "Wouldst thou really?" he whispered eagerly.

Wendel laughed again. "Or perhaps a squirrel maiden," he teased. "What of that, Mistress? How should you like it if I carved this in thine image?"

Startled, Ysabelle looked round. She had not been listening; her attention was taken by the dark, silent lake, and she had been gazing at it for some time. "Pardon?" she said. "Oh, yes–do as you wish, Master Jester."

Rising, the squirrel stretched and added, "I think I shall take a walk before I close my eyes. Do not fear–I shan't go far, just along the shore a little way."

The stoat bowed his head. "You need only call if you require assistance," he told her. "Meanwhiles, I shall resume my work." And in a blur, his quick and clever paws moved over the wood.

Tysle was disappointed, but perhaps the jester could make another puppet–of him, next time. The little shrew was beguiled by Wendel's talents; already, the head was taking shape, and he watched, fascinated, as a squirrel's nose appeared through the shavings. Then his gaze wandered over to the stoat's cart.

His sparkling brown eyes traced the patterns of the garish paint work and lingered over the intriguing prop chests.

"You know, Master Jester," he sighed, "I reckon you must be the cleverest and most interesting fellow I ever did meet."

Wendel laughed and began relating a long and funny tale that tickled the shrew so much that he giggled and kicked his legs in the air.

Sitting on his own, Giraldus no longer felt the heat from the fire—all was cold, and though his eyes were dry, inwardly he wept.

*   *   *

The gloomy shore stretched dismally before her, and, with only the rustle of the mournful willows to break the unnatural quiet, the lake was an eerie place. As Ysabelle slowly walked over the cold mud, she found the strangest thoughts creeping into her head. It was as if every bitter tear that the world had shed had found its way to this secluded spot, making it a distillation of melancholy and despondence that was estranged from the living world.

"Vespertilio was right," she murmured. "I fear nothing dwells nigh to this forlorn lake. Surely someone would have seen our fire by now. We ought to have stayed to the path; then would the journey be nearer to its end."

She thought about what that meant for her. Even if she managed to reach the holy land, there was still much to be done and many dangers to face. The noble forces of Coll Regalis may have arrived at Greenreach already, yet her mother had told her that only the combined might of all the squirrel houses could drive the bats from the blessed hill and purge it of them forever. How it was to be achieved, Ysabelle had no idea, and she wished more than ever that the Silver Acorn had not come into her possession.

She stared across the mysterious black water. Here, too, the bat had spoken correctly: it was a putrid mere. The dark night made it impossible for her to see the far shore, and, in her fancy, she felt as if she was standing on the edge of the earth. It was as though, at this desolate place, everything ended, and only a cold void now stretched before her.

"I wish the skies were clear," she breathed. "Then at least would the stars be reflected in the lake and make it less forlorn."

The squirrel strolled on beside the dark, icy water, staring at times at her own distorted reflection. The Acorn about her neck gleamed in the stagnant mirror, and she touched it reverently. The rust-colored stains of Gwydion's blood still tarnished the amulet, and, as she turned it over in her fingers, she wondered if it would ever be cleansed.

Suddenly, she gasped and sharply pulled her paw away—the amulet had burned her fingers.

Ysabelle stared at it in fear. The dark bloodstains seemed to swirl over the surface of the silver, and veins of glowing crimson glittered faintly from its depths.

The squirrel almost tore the thing from her neck in terror, then she heard—

From many leagues beneath the earth, a dreadful roar thundered, making the shore tremble and quake. The willow trees nearby shook, and their agitated rustling disturbed the water in which their branches trailed. Great ripples fanned out toward the center of the enormous pool, churning the scum that covered the surface, and the nauseous smell grew stronger.

Ysabelle stood transfixed as she listened to the frightful shrieks that echoed deep below the groans. Some tremendous creature was bellowing, and the squirrel swallowed nervously as she felt the curse the high priest had damned her with descend upon her.

"Hobb!" she gasped. "It's him! He's coming for me."

The rumbling voice raged fiercely, but it was still a great distance away. Then, as suddenly as it had begun, the roaring ceased, and all was quiet once more. The tremulous ripples that marred the perfect calm vanished from the lake, and it was as if nothing had happened.

For several moments, Ysabelle could do nothing as the full horror of this sank in. Everything she had striven for would come to nothing: if Hobb were indeed to appear, then all her hopes would be in vain.

Shivering with fear, Ysabelle turned and fled.

"Hey!" cried Vesper as she ran blindly into him. "Watch out!"

He caught hold of her, then saw the terror graven in her face. "What is it? Are there Hobbers? Have they found us?"

The squirrel glared at him. "Did you not hear?" she asked. "You cannot have done otherwise–the mighty roar, the frightful voice–"

The bat looked puzzled, and it was obvious that he had heard nothing. "I did but follow you to talk," he told her mystified. "What was it frightened you?"

"Never mind," Ysabelle said, pushing past him impatiently. "It would matter nought to you anyway." She glanced back to where she had heard the awful sound, then stared down at her amulet.

The Silver Acorn was now dull and cold, and the bloodstains immovable as before.

"I–I must have been mistaken," she said, although her tone fooled no one. "Fatigue can play strange tricks on the mind. An illusion conjured up by my weary brain–nothing more."

Vesper decided that it would be wiser not to continue, so he quickly changed the subject.

"When I told you about the birthright of my race," he began, "I said that the Starwife had withheld it from we Moonriders, yet you laughed. What was the reason?"

"Exactly the one I gave," Ysabelle replied. "It was just so much nonsense. Why should a Handmaiden of Orion trouble to do such a thing? I doubt if she had even given thy kind much thought until you started attacking the outposts and laying waste to the smaller colonies!"

"But my Lord Hrethel has told us the blame lies with her!" Vesper insisted. "To regain our gifts of prophecy and insight, we would do battle till the end of all things. That is what started the holy wars."

Ysabelle shook her head. "Then they have been waged for nothing," she told him, "for I am certain we had no part in with-holding those things from you."

Vesper stroked his beard, confused.

A mild breeze stirred the willows that fringed the shore, and the young bat gazed at them with a faraway look on his face. "The osier is beloved of the Lady Moon," he murmured. "It is said that she owns it, and at whiles would come down to walk beneath the graceful boughs." He gave a regretful sigh and added, "There were no withy trees near my home, and when I was a-weanling, I would dream of finding one and spending the delicious hours of night there, hoping to catch a glimpse of her."

"I do not think your Lady would visit this dreary place," Ysabelle said. "Is it not strange? My folk call the willow, or saille, the tree of enchantment. Only witches know its virtues, I was told."

She looked at the bat and managed a smile. "But then, I was told many things," she said. "I have learned a great deal since first we met. Griselda used to tell me your kind were brutal and savage. She had many tales of squirrel children taken and devoured by bats and would repeat them time and again with much relish. I used to think you and the Hobbers were all in league with one another."

Vesper nodded. "My mother used to relate the exact tale of you!" he exclaimed. "Only, your folk would make sacrifices to the trees you worshipped and feed their roots with blood."

The squirrel smiled, then nibbled her lip thoughtfully. "How we have altered in this short time," she said. "Oh, I pray Griselda is safe. I have not dared to think what has become of her."

"Wendel seemed to think she was alive when he was parted from your army."

"I have been a fool," Ysabelle confided. "If it was not for me, we would not be here. Why did I listen to Wendel? His heart is full of good intentions, yet he is the first to agree that his brain is the weakest point about him. Coming here was a stupid mistake, yet I was too hard headed to realize. I ought to have listened to you."

"A princess of the royal house taking advice from a bat?" Vesper teased her.

214

"If I had, we should be well on our way still," she replied, "not forced to endure this foul place. Do you think we shall ever see sight or sign of those mythical woodland folk?"

"Not unless the jester carves them himself!"

They laughed, but it was a strained sound, and they could not sustain it.

Ysabelle gazed at the bat's furry face and lowered her eyes. "You do realize that when this journey is complete, we shall be enemies again. When I take up the Silver, it is laid upon me to rid the holy land of your kind."

"You are mistaken," Vesper said firmly. "There will be no more Starwives—their time is ended forever. You have not seen the full strength of our legions. If you had, then you would not be so confident. I tell you, if Rohgar wants that amulet you bear, it will eventually come to him. Would it not be best to give up this hopeless task that you are chasing? The only possible outcome will be your death—I promise you that."

He held back from saying any more and wondered why he had been so harsh. The words had fallen from his tongue before he could check them and had sounded threatening. Now he regretted what he had said, but Ysabelle had heard enough.

The squirrel moved away from him. "We shall see who will die," she said sadly. "It would appear that neither of us has changed after all. Now I shall return to the others. Good night to you, Vespertilio."

Quickly, she retraced her steps and left the bat gazing wistfully into the night.

The campfire was still burning when she arrived there, but only Wendel had remained awake. Giraldus was lying on his side, snoring loudly, and at his feet a guilt-ridden Tysle had crawled and curled into a snug ball.

The jester pressed a finger to his lips when he saw her, and Ysabelle came to sit next to him.

"How does the puppet progress?" she asked.

Wendel shaved off some irregular bumps before showing it to her. "Soon, I shall paint it," he said with a strange smile on his face, "then make the body from some cloth."

"I hope it will amuse those who see it," she said absently, "but for myself I am too tired."

She yawned and spread dry leaves and grasses over the ground where she would sleep.

Wendel watched her all the while until he finally put his work down.

"May those sprites who grant peaceful slumber visit you," he said, "and bear thee to a fairer place than this in thy dreams."

Ysabelle sat on the prepared ground and made herself as comfortable as she could.

"Tell me," Wendel began in a quiet voice, "now there are none to overhear us, may I speak openly with you, Mistress?"

The squirrel frowned. "Of course," she said. "What is it that troubles you?"

The stoat pointed at Giraldus and looked most disapproving. "I did ask you before," he said, "but now I ask again. Do you think it is fitting for one of thy rank and station to travel with such as he?"

"Why should I not?" Ysabelle answered in surprise. "The mole and his servant have shown me naught but kindness."

Wendel threw a stick into the fire and stared at the fury of sparks that flew out. "Nevertheless," he intoned, "the daughter of Ninnia, at such close quarters to a leper? His company is not to be borne—what would Gelenos say?"

"Godfrey is dead!" the squirrel replied. "And I'm sure he would be glad I was not alone. These pilgrims are my friends now."

"Are they?" the jester asked mildly. "In truth, how much dost thou really know of their intents and purposes? I do not wish to be a sower of such dark and doubting seeds, Mistress, yet is it prudent to trust them so readily?"

"Perhaps not," she replied. "'Tis true that all they have told us might be a pack of falsehoods—and yet they are so sincere."

Wendel drew patterns in the thawed mud with a twig. "Maybe I am wrong," he muttered, "yet I was most dismayed to find you freely conversing with that detestable Moonrider. Have you forgotten how your parents died?"

Ysabelle glared at him, but there was truth in his words. She remembered the warning given to her by the Green, and, instead of rebuking Wendel, thanked him for keeping her alert to the dangers.

"What else should I do?" came his simple answer. "Thou art the last one of a noble line—most high in the world. I would not see you betrayed and that majestic light snuffed out forever."

Ysabelle settled down for the night and wrapped her tail about her. Wendel looked at her with a smile on his lips, wandered over to his cart, and took a reed pipe from one of the chests. Then, sitting just beyond the circle of firelight so that the dancing glow illuminated only the tip of his nose, he put it to his lips.

A slow, drowsy tune floated from the instrument. It was a lulling melody that dragged Ysabelle's eyelids down and poured sleep into her ears.

Nearby, Giraldus snorted in his slumber, and a happy smile stole over Tysle's face as the lilting music permeated their dreams.

The jester's skillful fingers played languidly over the pipe, and the delicious refrain flowed out over the dark waters of the mere.

Suddenly, Ysabelle awoke.

"What was that?" she cried.

The stoat took the pipe from his mouth. "A lullaby, taught me by my grandmother," he answered.

Ysabelle stared at him, "Not that!" she said. "I did hear a cry!"

Wendel raised his eyebrows and looked at her oddly. "I did not hear anything," he said.

The squirrel gazed about her, then she heard it again. A high voice, shouting in panic and fear. She jumped to her feet and whirled round.

"That is Vespertilio!" she declared. "He is in danger!"

Taking up her long knife, she dashed forward, but, before she could run along the shore, Wendel raced over to her.

"Stay, Mistress!" he told her sternly. "Thou must not imperil thyself–think of thy mission. Thou art too precious to waste, and he is only a bat, when all is said."

Ysabelle scowled at him, then tore away.

Since the squirrel had left him there, Vesper had been sitting thoughtfully upon the shore. His heart was troubled, but when the strains of Wendel's melodious music reached him, he had forgotten his sorrows, and it had been a struggle to remain awake.

As his head nodded for the third time, the bat sat up with a jolt, rubbed his eyes, and realized that he was not alone.

Something was moving within the lake. Slow, turgid ripples broke against the frozen mud, and Vesper cautiously clicked his tongue to try and see what had caused them.

"Bless me!" the bat uttered. "What in Hrethel's name–"

In the middle of the loathsome mere, vile shapes writhed and twisted. Out of the stinking water they rose, dripping filth and slime as they reared. Up into the reeking airs the horrors floated, then they began to move swiftly toward the shore.

Over the surface of the lake, the specters of long-drowned creatures silently skimmed.

Vesper fell back in fear as they glided closer. He had never seen anything so hideous in all his young life.

The specters were revolting masses of bones, sticks, and clinging pond weed. Bound together by the malevolent spirits that animated them, they were ghastly imitations of life, a confused and gangling mess of tattered shreds. On one of them, a rotting fish tail slapped the water, and the bundle of twigs that served as legs galloped quickly up the muddy shore.

"Aaaaaarrrgghhh!" Vesper screamed as the apparition bore down.

The nightmare clattered after him, and long fingers of yellowing bone came snapping for the bat's throat.

Vesper turned, but another of the abominations was rising from the water's edge. Among the foul fronds of its shaggy mane, it had the putrefying head of a fish, and from the open mouth a hollow shriek issued.

This second specter lunged forward with crablike movements, scuttling over the mud and leaving a trail of stinking black slime behind it.

Vesper tried to run, but the vile phantoms were too quick. Fast as lightning they snaked after, and a mangled claw flashed out, grabbing him by the neck.

"Help!" Vesper cried. "Help me!"

The decaying head stared down, the empty sockets where its eyes should have been burning into him.

Vesper nearly swooned before the overpowering stench of death and corruption that flowed out from it, and he howled when cold fingers squeezed around his body.

Now, the rattling bundles of bone and scale swept their twigs over Vesper's squirming form covetously. The spirits of those unwary creatures that had drowned in the haunted mere resented anything that had life—life that they, too, had once owned, life that they had lost in that freezing darkness below the water.

Their malignant souls screeched for the warm blood that flowed through their victim's veins; they hated it with all their accursed strength. But most of all, they despised the breath that filled Vesper's lungs.

Long ago, these unclean spirits had been dragged down into the mire. Then they had been even as he—living, breathing animals who strayed too close to the forbidding waters and were lost. Deep under that lake their chests had burst, and bubbles had trapped their screams. The struggle for breath was the last they remembered, and now they were intent on bestowing that agony upon Vesper.

"*Deliver the hated life unto the deep!*" their empty voices shrieked. "*Drown it in the consuming dark!*"

Down to the water's edge they dragged the kicking and wailing bat. Into the sinister lake the two grisly apparitions hauled him, pulling the Moonrider into their freezing and unholy grave.

Vesper was powerless to stop them. The bones that gripped his throat and tore at his wings were as strong as Death itself, and though he flailed and struggled, it was all in vain.

The shroud rags of cadaverous flesh and rank weed clung to the bat's face, smothering and suffocating his gasping mouth as the specters dragged him down.

"*Join us in the deep,*" their icy voices rang. "*Walk no more under the sun. Come rot, let your flesh dissolve and take on other guises.*"

Vesper's wings beat against them in a last futile attempt, as many other creatures had done before him. But the blighted, moldering bones and twigs tightened, and he felt the last breath throttled from his body.

Stinking water filled the bat's mouth as they started to pull him under, and the unnatural claws tugged his head below the surface.

A numb darkness engulfed Vesper, and the shades of the cackling dead prepared to accept another life essence into their rotting number. The body of the bat went limp in their strangling grasp, and they began to drift away from the shore, their unholy work done. Yet their macabre appetite would never be quenched.

"*Another soul,*" they chanted horribly. "*Another wraith to hate the living. We must find more. There can never be enough. Let us find another.*"

"Vespertilio!" Ysabelle yelled "Come back!"

As she ran along the shore, following the bat's urgent screams, the squirrel maiden had seen the ghoulish apparitions drag him into the mire.

Without pausing to think, Ysabelle leaped from the edge and plunged into the lake. The touch of the foul water made her balk, but she splashed toward the sinking horrors, keeping an anxious eye on the motionless winged body tangled in their midst.

"Let go of him!" she bawled, holding the knife out before her. The water was up to her waist now, and she pushed through the waving, weed-filled mere, desperate to save Vesper.

The knife thrashed in the water as she hacked blindly. Through putrid fish skin and brittle bones it tore, cutting a path through to the stricken Moonrider.

The lake seethed as the specters turned their fury upon the squirrel, but Ysabelle's desperation had made her fearless. Against the tendrils and twigs that rose against her she lashed and thrust, valiantly parrying their outraged assaults.

Slime-covered finger bones snapped and fish spines buckled before her ferocious blade. Finally, the tenacious claws that clutched at Vesper released him and came reaching for her.

"*Another life*," the chilling voices rang. "*Come into the dark. Join us in the cold of death.*"

Ysabelle darted beneath the outstretched claws and grabbed at the bat, calling his name over and over.

But the ghostly fingers closed round her, tearing at the squirrel's tail and plucking at her hair.

"*Cast your life aside!*" the ghosts wailed. "*Slip beneath the waves and be free!*"

With a tremendous shout, Ysabelle spun round and brought the knife crashing down. Splinters of wood and fragments of diseased scale exploded about her as the hellish claws flew apart.

Swiftly, Ysabelle seized the moment and rushed toward the shore, trawling Vesper after her.

When she stood upon the muddy bank, the squirrel quickly threw the bat to the ground and pushed her paws against his chest.

221

At once, Vesper choked, and a fount of black water spouted from his mouth. For several minutes he retched and, turning on his side, spat out the poisonous filth of the mere.

"They wanted—wanted to drown me," he spluttered. "When they took me to the water, I knew what they wanted. I was to be like them—a stinking ghost delighting in murder!"

Ysabelle stared out to where the dark shapes of the specters regarded her from the lake, but the ordeal was not over yet.

"Vespertilio," she whispered. "Can you stand?"

"I—I think so," he coughed.

"Then do it," she hissed. "Those creatures are coming back!"

Gagging, Vesper raised his head. The tattered shapes were rising from the water once more and heading straight for them.

Ysabelle took hold of his wing and heaved him to his feet, but even as they headed back to the camp, they heard Tysle's voice squealing and the resounding tones of Giraldus raised in panic.

"There are more of the foul creatures!" Ysabelle cried. "They're attacking the others!"

The squirrel and bat sped along the shore, while behind them the specters came clattering over the mud.

"*Embrace the dark!*" they called. "*Let us take you! Come to us! Join us!*"

Around the campfire, three other phantoms had found their victims.

"Put me down!" Tysle squeaked. "Put me down!"

Two of the ghastly, spirit-enslaved jumbles had snatched the shrew and were now bearing him toward the lake.

"Master!" Tysle called. "Master!"

The string that joined them was taut, and, though Giraldus had not yet been caught by the third bundle of putrescence, he was nevertheless being hauled to his doom.

"What is happening?" the blind mole howled. "What madness is this?"

"Eeeeek!" squawked Tysle as the twigs and water-logged bones plucked him from the ground and carried him into the water.

Giraldus waved his staff in fear as the string drew him over the shore. He could not see that the third specter was stealing up behind him.

Cold laughter issued from dark gashes in the animated weed as it entered the lake once more.

"Master!" Tysle shrieked. "I'll be drownded!"

Giraldus drove the staff into the icy mud with all his might and clung to it desperately.

The string creaked, and the progress of the specters was halted.

Hissing, they heaved on their prize, and, at the other end of the lead, the mole gritted his teeth.

It was like some ghastly parody of a tug-of-war, but it did not last for long.

"*A life!*" came the echoing voice behind Giraldus as the third phantom claimed him.

The mole roared in fear as clammy, scaly claws wrapped about his neck and plucked his paws from around the anchoring staff.

"And the Green did bring light to the darkness!" he wailed. "The Green is my salvation—in Him am I redeemed!"

Into this horrible scene Ysabelle and Vesper came tearing.

"Get Tysle!" the bat called to her, and they both hurried to where the small shrew floundered, half submerged in the water.

Ysabelle stabbed the gristle and knotted twigs that clutched him, and Vesper tore the smothering black weed from Tysle's face.

As soon as the shrew's arms were freed, he struck at the specters with his fists.

"You keep your filthy claws off me!" he stormed.

But they were not about to let him go so easily, and they frantically wrapped more slimy strands about his body. Then the hideously decayed arms of some cruelly murdered animal whipped out and knocked the knife from Ysabelle's grasp.

"Into the dark," the spirits cackled, *"we will take your life! Follow us down—molder with us!"*

Ysabelle raked at the shrew's bonds with her bare paws, but it was no use. Without the knife, it was impossible to free him, nor could she find the blade in the stale, muddy water.

"Tysle," she cried. "I'm sorry!"

The eyes of the poor shrew were wide with terror as the water covered his nose and filled his ears. Ysabelle tried to pull him back, but the malevolent will of the dead was too strong for her.

"Vespertilio," she pleaded. "Help me! Tysle will drown!"

But Vesper was not there. She looked round wildly, fearing that he had been pulled into the lake—then she saw him.

With a burning branch plucked from the campfire in his grasp, the Moonrider charged back to the lakeside.

"Keep back!" he howled, thrusting the flames into the heart of the tangled bundles of death.

"Noooooooooo!" the hollow voices shrieked. *"Not the burning fires! Noooooooooo!"*

They fell back before the flames, their claws and tendrils snaking away from Tysle and leaving the shrew free to clamber back to shore.

Vesper waved the torch at them threateningly, and the phantoms cowered farther into the water, gibbering with woeful moans.

Tysle shook his fist at them, then he remembered his master and glanced round quickly.

Giraldus was surrounded; the wraiths that had first captured Vesper had joined forces with the remaining specter, and all clawed at the mole, herding him to the water's edge.

Tysle gave a yell and hobbled for the fire, but the string was not long enough, and he sped round in a wide circle before charging headfirst into one of the grisly apparitions and beginning to beat it with his crutch.

Then Vesper came to his aid, and Ysabelle followed, also carrying a burning torch. The ghosts slunk away, wailing and groaning.

Giraldus was left on the ground, and Tysle came hurrying up to see if he was harmed. The mole breathlessly told him that he was not hurt and was about to thank the Green when Tysle sprang away, running after the retreating specters.

Giraldus felt the string go taut as the shrew strained to reach them, but he pulled the little fellow back and then staggered to his feet.

Vesper and Ysabelle strode about the water's edge, making sure the unholy spirits sank below the surface. Then the grim lake was still and silent once more, but they were certain that hostile eyes still watched them.

"Do you think they will stay away?" Ysabelle asked.

"Not for long," Vesper told her. "Their hatred for us and the lives we own will soon conquer their fear of the fire. We must leave this terrible place at once!"

Ysabelle was only too glad to agree—then she remembered Wendel.

"Where is he?" she cried. "Oh, no, were we too late? Had those vile things already dragged him under before we returned? Wendel—Wendel!"

She ran up and down the shore to see if there was any sign, and, by Giraldus's side, Tysle was dismayed to hear her.

"Please, no," he whispered, "don't let the jolly jester have perished."

Vesper ran after the distraught Ysabelle and spun her round. "We haven't time to find him!" he told her. "If he's dead, then there's naught you can do!"

"But if he is not," she implored, "he might be unconscious somewhere, and if those things return—"

From out of the trees where the forest began, a tall figure bashfully stepped.

Tysle saw him first, and his face cracked into an enormous grin. "Wendel!" he shouted.

The stoat wrung his paws and padded down the shore, muttering wretchedly to himself. "How can you forgive me?" he blubbered. "What must you be thinking? Oh, a craven stoat am I! When the first of those slimy horrors rose from the dank water, I did squeal and hare into the trees, leaving my friends to their callous mercy. Oh, please! I know 'twas a cowardly and unspeakable action—no, don't tell me, I know it too well! A thousand curses would not repay me for such a yellow deed."

The others merely stared at him, not knowing what to say. The cowardly jester had left them to die, and nobody, not even Tysle, could find any words to say to him.

Vesper avoided the stoat's gaze and told Giraldus and the shrew to pack up their belongings so they could leave immediately.

"Dear friends!" Wendel whimpered. "Forgive me, I beseech thee! I know not what came over me, but I know I would have been of little use combating those frightful monsters."

He ran up to Ysabelle and trotted beside her, pleading for her understanding. "Mistress," he burbled, "think not too lowly of this, thy humble servant—was it my fault my nerves are as weak as mine brain?"

"I don't understand," the squirrel said. "You were not so craven when you saved me from the bats."

"Alas!" Wendel bemoaned. "That was before I had spent long nights alone in the forest; if I had not learned swiftly to conceal myself when danger came near, I should not be here now."

"You had best collect your cart," Ysabelle told him. "We are not staying here."

The jester scurried to his painted wagon and thrust his scattered knife and half-finished puppet into a chest.

"What of thee, little shrew?" he asked Tysle. "Art thou angry at this follysome idiot? I could not bear it if all were to scorn me."

Before Tysle could answer, Giraldus tugged the string, and he was compelled to begin leading the mole up the shore. But he gave the stoat a disappointed and mournful scowl.

"Pray don't bother to waste your breath," Vesper said when the jester caught his eye. "Just wheel your cart and keep quiet from now on."

Wendel whined miserably to himself. "Oh, my," he bleated, "was there ever one so reviled? I could punish myself—truly I could."

Vesper shook his head in disgust, then hurried to catch up with Ysabelle.

"Thank you," he told her. "You did save my life in that stink-some mere. You acted most bravely, and I am in thy debt."

"Call it a debt repaid," she said with a smile.

"Very well," he answered, "but let us march swiftly and find somewhere safe to rest for what remains of this night. I feel as though I could sleep for an entire week."

And so the five travelers passed once more into the forest, and the haunted mere was left far behind.

FROM THE SHADE OF THE BEECHES

It was fatigue that finally forced them to halt. The urgent and anxious steps that had carried them swiftly from the shore soon dwindled into faltering stumbles. Then, very softly, it began to rain.

At first it was no more than a gentle, refreshing drizzle that they all welcomed, and they lifted their faces so the fine, sprinkling drops might cleanse them of the mere's festering stink. But it was not long before it became a steady downpour that splashed over the frozen forest floor and turned the dead leaves into a slippery mulch, treacherous to the weary travelers.

Skidding and sliding through the now pelting storm, the five soaked figures sought shelter. The deluge fell in thick gray sheets that battered against their cheeks, stinging them with cold, and made it almost impossible to see where they were going. Then, finally, from out of the driving, drenching rain, reared the dark silhouette of a dead and hollow tree.

Through a hole in the trunk they scurried and cast themselves on the soft moss within. Soon the aches and fears of the past hours vanished as sleep gradually garnered them to its bosom.

The rest of the night belonged to the storm, and the unceasing rain drummed on the bark of the hollow tree like the din of ten thousand tiny hammers chiming on an anvil. High above, the gushing water trickled along the branches and came sluicing in swollen rivulets down the withered trunk. Over the sopping ground the surging rain flooded; old stream beds overflowed, and new pools filled the dips and dells. Then, when it seemed the torrent would never be stilled, the clouds scattered and the last hour before sunrise was silent. The uncovered stars glittered over newly washed forest, glinting in the brimming ponds and sparkling over the dripping branches.

A bleary dawn edged into the heavens, and, within the hollow tree, as the sun climbed higher, the travelers slept on.

Vesper nuzzled his face into his wing, lost in a deep slumber. That night, he had been too exhausted to dream, and no images of the high priest came to haunt him.

He rolled over, but from the hole in the trunk a bright beam of sunlight came slanting in, and he unwittingly brought his face directly into it.

The dazzling rays beat upon his eyelids and the bat groaned, opening them a chink.

Grudgingly, he sat up and gazed sleepily at the outside world. Then Vesper's ears twitched and he caught his breath—someone was out there.

"How much longer can this plaguey hunt continue?" complained a voice.

"Till the enemy is found and captured," said another.

"Then I crave that shall be soon. I tell thee, Leofa, if I have to cross this forsaken forest many more times, then I shall be driven crazed."

"For myself, I am at a loss to fathom how the wretched creature hath managed to evade us thus far. Have we not dispatched our brethren far and wide, and still no sign have they seen. Each day the captains return with naught to report—it maketh me think we chase after ghosts."

"I did believe the ashes of that fire by the side of that drearsome lake did hold a clue—a sore pity the rain washed all traces and foot marks away."

"Perfect fools, that is what our enemy has made of us!"

Vesper allowed a grin to cross his face, pleased that they had caused the Hobb cult so much trouble. Yet he hoped that neither of those unseen speakers decided to peer inside this hollow tree and was relieved that he had made Wendel cover his cart with fallen branches and twigs before retiring the previous night. Then the smile faded from his lips as he realized that the voices had not been speaking in the common tongue.

"Bah," the one called Leofa spat, "we ought not to be compelled to suffer this—Rohgar hath made a pretty mess of things."

"'Tis rumored that Hrethel hath withdrawn into his underground chamber and suffers no other to enter."

"Ah, he will not fail us."

Vesper uttered a startled cry—it was a couple of bats he had been sleepily listening to.

"What was that?" one of the bats hissed in Vesper's own language. "Didst thou mark that sound?"

The other paused to listen. "Nay," he replied, "'tis thine ears a-playing games with thee."

"Canst thou expect aught else under the garish scrutiny of the Daystar? How can other creatures bear it? 'Tis all I can do to keep from falling from this bough, mine senses are so bewildered."

"Another flaw in Rohgar's reckoning. How can he expect us to spy that hated tree worshipper in this dazzle?"

As their conversation continued, Vesper's mind reeled and whirled in a confusing clash of thoughts.

The first thing he wanted to do was rush out of the tree and declare his presence, overjoyed to see folk of his own kind.

"You get out there, Vespertilio!" he urged himself. "How shocked them Knights of the Moon will be to see thee—and just think of the honor that will be thine. The enemy they seek is here; you can deliver her to them and receive great praise and renown."

He ventured closer to the opening in the trunk but stopped himself just in time.

230

"Ha!" shrieked the bat above. "Was that not a fine night, when we were victorious over that stinking colony? How those tree rats fled before the fire eggs. Didst thou see that circle of hazel trees ablaze?"

"Mine gauntlets fair bathed in the vile blood of those heathens."

"Mine also, yet what puny sentries guarded the borders. A good thing it was that our enemies were only squirrels, otherwise I would have balked at killing children and womenfolk."

"'Twas no wonder the sport did not last long."

Vesper felt sick, and he looked guiltily across to where Ysabelle soundly slept.

The squirrel maiden was lying peacefully on a bed of dry leaves and spongy green moss, innocent of the exchange uttered above. Her large brown eyes were closed, and her raven-dark hair fell silkily over her shoulders, entwining with the tip of her bush tail. Ysabelle's breaths were soft as a butterfly's, and, as the sun's rays stole farther inside the hollow tree, her fur glinted and shimmered.

The young bat gazed at her lovely face and, knowing what would happen if his kind caught her, turned cold and looked away. He could never betray her—not now.

"I would dearly like to find that wicked creature," came the voice of Leofa. "Did you hear those reports of the great burning? 'Twould appear she set light to an entire village—scorched bodies everywhere! A sordid black heart that tree rat must have."

"But what of those poor unfortunates impaled hereabouts?" returned the other. "What manner of monster spears birds and the like of those we found upon sharpened twigs? No ordinary foe is she—not a shred of remorse must she have; no trace of right and wrong can beat in her barbaric breast."

"'Tis just as the old tales tell. Those savages are the most loathsome vermin ever to sully the world. Didst thou hear that our brothers found a mouse's head wrapped in a scarf?"

"She did that?"

"Aye! And no doubt 'twas she who poisoned that lake and caused the rain to wash away her trail–dreadful powers of enchantment are hers to command, they say. Pacts with demons has she signed, for no soul does she possess now, and all pure things shun her."

"Much would I give to run my talons through her throat."

"Or see her guts spill on to the ground," Leofa sighed wistfully. "Then would all our troubles be over and the birthright returned to us."

"Even now she keeps the mighty spell strong to deny the gift of the Lady. I could kill her over and over!"

Vesper shook his head; nothing the bats believed was true, and, more than ever, he knew that the holy war had been a terrible waste of life.

The bats continued to grumble to one another until they finally decided it was time to resume the search. With a beat of their leathery wings, the Moonriders rose from the branches of the dead tree and disappeared over the forest roof.

When all was quiet and he was sure they were gone, Vesper's eyes grew moist and a solitary tear rolled down his cheek.

A short while later, once he had composed himself, the young bat crawled from the hollow tree and stepped outside.

The morning was already growing late, but it was a heavenly day. It was as if the entire world had been cleansed and reborn. The air was sharp and clear, the glistening trees dripped diamonds, and the forest floor was free of frost.

Vesper breathed deeply and stretched–he felt completely refreshed. Lazily, he flapped his wings, and, to his astonishment and joy, he began to rise from the ground.

"My wing!" he cried. "It is healed!"

Cautiously, the bat beat his wings faster until he soared into the air. There was still a dull ache in his shoulder, but apart from that all seemed well, and he spent several happy minutes flitting about the trees, spiraling around them and swooping down in great, graceful arcs.

It was a glorious feeling to be master of the breeze and tear through the shafts of golden sunlight. Breathlessly, he lighted upon a high branch and let out a rejoicing shout.

"I CAN FLY!"

He was so happy that he did not know what to do. "I could leave now," he told himself, "fly back to my home. Wouldn't Mother be surprised to see me after all these days! I need not say anything of the squirrel maiden's whereabouts—I could feign ignorance, and none would be the wiser."

He was giddy with the possibilities—no more skulking about the forest, having to march with the others, no more running from the terrifying Hobbers, no more nightmares to hound him. In the air Vesper was free, and the dangerous paths he had been forced to tread were already forgotten.

Up he soared, up through the highest branches and out above the treetops, where the forest became a soft blur of rolling colors.

Up he sped, over the horse chestnuts and beeches below, his eyes squinting under the blinding sun.

Yet what did he care? Soon he would be safe at home, safe in the ruined tower, where no peril could reach him, where nothing ever happened and no squirrels ever ventured.

Vesper's laughter died in his throat, and his fiercely beating wings slowed to the merest flick to remain airborne. The young bat stared down. There was the withered tree, and, as a feeling he had never thought possible kindled in his heart, he knew that he could never leave.

A terrible sadness overwhelmed him, and all thoughts of home melted silently away as his winged form sank back to earth.

It was not until midday that the others stirred. First out of the hollow tree came Tysle, who blinked like an owl and yawned in the middle of guiding his master through the opening.

233

Giraldus emerged, sniffing the air and clutching his staff. "A wholesome day," he announced, then, feeling the warm sun on his face, tutted at the lateness of the hour. "Noon already," he said. "Perfidious shrew, why did you let me sleep so long?"

"Good morning!" Vesper greeted them.

The pair turned, and there was the bat, sitting on a low bough where he had been keeping a lookout.

"And to thee, batling," Giraldus hailed him. "Is it not a day of the Green's own making? All the fearful shadows of the night have fled, and we are left to bask in the bright sunlight."

With a sudden jingling of bells, the jester poked his head from the tree and gave a nervous grin.

"A merry morning, my friends," he said.

Only Tysle bothered to return the greeting, for the others had not forgotten the stoat's cowardly actions.

"How do," the shrew piped up.

Wendel gave him a grateful smile, then stepped out and padded over to his camouflaged cart.

Giraldus closed his ears to the jester's pathetic attempts at mirth and addressed himself to Vesper.

"If we are not misled this day," he rumbled with an obvious and scathing allusion to the previous night's diversion to the lake, "come evening, the blessed hill of Grinuvicia should be in view."

Vesper was only half listening to him, for at that moment Ysabelle left the hollow tree, and the young bat's face lit up with a wide and special smile.

As there was nothing to eat for breakfast, the company set off as soon as they were ready. With their stomachs growling, they found their bearings and followed the now-gurgling stream back to the holy well and from there returned to the path.

The day continued fine and warm, and it was heartening to see that spring seemed to have arrived in that part of the forest at last. Gone were the cascading icicles, and the ground was soft underfoot.

As they marched, Wendel fussed and made such a nuisance of himself, profusely begging their forgiveness for leaving them to the specters of the mere, that in the end they forgave him—if only to shut him up.

During this time, Vesper said nothing about his mended wing and contented himself with walking alongside them as before. He did not want to mention it—not just yet—and his twinkling eyes looked increasingly in Ysabelle's direction.

The scenery around them gradually changed; the densely growing trees began to thin, and, here and there, spring flowers were sprinkled beside the path. Wood anemones cheered them with their purplish-white petals, a clump of marsh marigolds toasted them with their golden cups raised to the sky, and blue periwinkles pricked through the grass like tiny stars in a heaven of green.

The woods they now traversed seemed friendlier than before and had a sleepy air about them. Many oaks grew stout and stately, with enough room to spread and flourish.

Ysabelle felt less uneasy than she had done for many days and, once Wendel had been forgiven, listened gladly to his rambling, idiotic talk.

Tysle listened, too, and his infectious chuckling filtered through the pleasant woods, much to Giraldus's irritation, and the pious mole was shocked and scandalized to hear Vesper's voice joining the laughter.

As the sunny afternoon beamed about him, the leper reflected sadly that his companions seemed to have forgotten the gravity of their situation. It was almost as if they were simply strolling through the woods at their leisure, having no fears to dampen their spirits. He walked on with his head lowered and wondered if they ought not to sample a caterpillar or two to bring them back to their senses.

Eventually, the path led them to a beautifully sunny glade, and Ysabelle clapped her paws in delight.

Growing there were hundreds of daffodils, and their golden trumpets mirrored the sunshine, casting buttery lights that danced about the clearing as the flowers gently nodded and swayed.

The squirrel maiden capered into their midst, and the glimmering reflections shone upon her twirling figure, transforming her ebony body into a moving statue of the richest gold—an idol that had sprung into jubilant life.

"Is it not a marvelous sight?" she cried. "What beauty the forest contains. May we rest here a while?"

The others agreed, and they trailed into the daffodil glade like merry children. Even Giraldus could sense the wonder of the blooms, and his nose thrilled with the delicate scents.

Where the ground rose slightly, they sat on the sweet grass and drank in the shimmering sea of yellow and gold around them.

Whistling a jaunty little ditty, Wendel took the carving from one of his prop chests and resumed his work on it.

Tysle beamed, intoxicated by the glamour of the flowers and the jester's skill. The wooden head was nearly finished—all it needed was careful painting.

"Then shall I make the body," said Wendel, still anxious to please everyone and atone for last night. "And, once that is done, shall I make one of us all? Wouldst thou like a puppet of thyself, Master Moonrider? I already have one of a bat that could easily be remodeled to resemble thee."

Before Vesper could answer, Tysle blurted out that he would dearly love to see himself carved in wood. "Whittle a likeness of me," he beseeched. "Oh, please do!"

"Tysle!" the mole's voice cut in abruptly. "These things are but vanities! Thy head should not be filled with the lust of them!"

The shrew meekly murmured an apology, but his eyes stole to where the brilliantly painted cart seemed to glow in the sunlight, and he longed to ask Wendel to perform some tricks.

Basking in the golden glory of the flowers, Ysabelle chatted with Vesper, encouraging him to speak of his life and the ways of the Moonriders.

"All our folk look to the five counselors for guidance," he began shyly. "Each is a venerable creature with a white beard and much wisdom. The first has the title of the Lord of the Twilight, the second is the Keeper of the Hidden Ways, then there is the Consort of the Lady."

"What of the other two?" she asked.

"Fourth comes the Guardian of Battle," he answered, "whose office is to ensure the legions are always ready for war."

Ysabelle looked away. "And the fifth?" she inquired.

"The final counselor is the Lord Hrethel, the Warden of the Great Book," he said. "He is the most learned of the five, for from the Book of Mystery he has gained much wisdom. All Knights of the Moon respect him and obey his every command."

"Did you not say that 'twas he who blamed the loss of your birthright upon the last Starwife?"

"Yes," answered Vesper. "Never has he been known to err before, and I marvel that he should make such a grievous blunder."

"'Marvel' is hardly the word I would choose," said Ysabelle.

"No," the bat replied, and they fell into an uncomfortable silence.

Around the golden glade, amid the pale shade of the tall oaks and beeches, a pair of curious eyes stared at the unsuspecting travelers. Then others appeared as many shadowy figures crept around the outskirts of the clearing. Stealthily, they surrounded the beautiful daffodils, and waited.

Giraldus cocked his head to one side, and a frown wrinkled his mottled brow. "'Tis time we set off," he said quickly. "Too long have we idled here already—come, Tysle!"

Just as the shrew rose to his feet, an arrow flew through the air and embedded itself in the ground where he had been sitting.

"Eeek!" he yelped. "Hobbers!"

Before anyone could move, there came an angry shout and from all sides leaped a ferocious host of armed creatures.

"Hold!" commanded their attackers. "Move, and you die!"

Bows were strung and swords slid from their sheaths as they hurried to where the travelers sat, amazed and afraid.

Tysle groped for his knife, but a leaf-shaped blade was pressed against his throat, and he pretended that he had only wanted to scratch his bandaged leg.

Two dozen fully armed and stern-looking animals formed a tight circle about them. There were mice and hedgehogs, rabbits and weasels, and all were robed in cloaks of dark green.

"Oh, woe!" wailed Wendel, his lip quivering in fright. "Don't let them hurt us!" He waggled the carved head at them in a pitifully feeble attempt to amuse, but one of the hedgehogs growled and knocked it from his grasp. "Oh, make it a swift ending!" the jester bleated. "No lingering agony, I beg thee!"

Vesper and Ysabelle moved closely together, and the bat spread one of his wings about the squirrel maiden's shoulders, baring his teeth at any who came too close.

"What have we here?" one of the mice snarled, leering at Giraldus. "A scab-riddled mole tied to a shrew! The children of the Raith Sidhe must be desperate indeed if they are recruiting from the infirm and diseased!"

Giraldus stiffened and stomped his staff on the ground. "How dare thee!" his booming voice blared. "No worshipper of that hellish triad am I, nor is mine servant!"

"Hobbers, the lot!" spat the hedgehog. "Only them and us walk the woods. I say kill 'em now!"

Vesper folded his wings, and he eyed the strangers keenly. "Then are you not in the service of Hobb?" he asked.

"Are we Hobbers!" another mouse exclaimed.

"Don't let them squirm out of it!" the hedgehog insisted. "You know how tricky they can be!"

Tysle's ears were purple with rage, and he suddenly exploded.

"Three generations of my family them devils murdered!" he roared. "My old granddam, my parents, and four sweet sisters were hauled out of our home and put to the peeler! So don't you ever call me a worshipper of that horned rat god, or I'll knock your blocks off—every one!"

His impassioned outburst amazed everyone, except Giraldus, who drew on the string and put his paw on the shrew's head. "Peace," he whispered. "Think not of that dark time. I am here; be still."

Tysle sniffed, but he continued to stare angrily at those around them.

Ysabelle looked from one member of the cloaked gang to another. "If you are not in that evil brotherhood, then who are you?" she asked.

They stared back at her; Tysle's protests had taken them all by surprise, and they mumbled to one another in bemusement.

"Now you looks at them," a short mouse admitted, "they doesn't look like Hobbers—none that I seen, anyhows."

"What'll us be doing with them then?" piped up the rabbit.

" 'Taint up to me!"

Then their talk ceased, for at the rear of the attacking party, a hedgehog hissed, "Fenny approaches."

"That'll sort it," they all murmured.

While Giraldus comforted Tysle and Wendel's knees knocked together, Ysabelle and Vesper waited for the one called Fenny to arrive.

From the surrounding trees strode the tallest mouse either of them had ever seen. Like the others, he wore a cloak of green, but, fastened about the neck, a silver badge in the shape of a leaping hare gleamed in the sunlight. The mouse was a dark brown color, and his face was grim and determined. A finely proportioned nose sat between two deep-set eyes that were steady and resolute and that, by the merest glance, could either inspire or instill fear. In a leather band tied about his head, three small

239

woodpecker feathers denoted his leadership, and he came forward with the easy motion of one who possesses natural authority. When he passed the others, they stood aside and put their paws to their breasts in salutation.

"Captain!" the hedgehog declared, "see what trespassers we have captured!"

The mouse looked at each of them in turn. Not a flicker in those deep eyes, nor a twitch at the corners of his mouth, betrayed his impressions.

Giraldus, Tysle, and Wendel he seemed to take little interest in, but when he saw Vesper and Ysabelle, the fixed expression changed, and they heard him speak for the first time.

"Now, here is a strange spectacle," he declared. "A bat and a squirrel traveling together! There are tales to tell here, or I am no judge. Tell me, from whence do you come? What are you doing here?"

Ysabelle folded her arms and gazed back at him haughtily. "I am the daughter of Ninnia!" she proclaimed. "Last of the royal house of the Hazel, and these are my companions. We mean you no harm, but are all foes of the Hobb cult, and if you wish to do them injury, then let us be about our business."

"Oho!" Fenny roared, and the rest of his host followed his lead, guffawing at the squirrel's impudence. "It is for me to decide whether you be enemy or no," he gruffly told her, "and remember this: none may pass our borders without our leave."

A slow smile spread over Vesper's face. "Are you the woodlanders we have heard rumor of?" he asked.

The mouse regarded him strangely for a moment, then nodded. "A small portion of their number are we," he curtly replied, "and we have all taken solemn oaths to rid the forest of the Hobb cult."

He swept his outstretched paws to encompass the woods around them and said, "Our forces are the gleanings of each tiny hamlet and small village that the black tide of Hobbers has ruthlessly swept aside. A motley collection, maybe, yet our quest is an honorable one, and though we hail from different quarters, we abide peaceably enough together."

Ysabelle abandoned her imperious tone and began entreating the captain to help them. "Please," she said, "our quest also is a noble one, and if we succeed, then the Raith Sidhe will be only a memory again, and the followers of that fiendish high priest will be vanquished forever." She would have said more, but Fenny hushed her into silence and looked warily about them.

"You know of the high priest?" he asked.

"The one who dresses like a bloody-bones? Yes, I have seen him. He–"

"This is not the place for such talk," the mouse said quickly. "I have decided! The strangers are to come back with us!"

"Back?" the other woodlanders cried. "What, after so brief an exchange?"

"I have seen enough to be satisfied of this squirrel's worth," Fenny said sternly. "Bring her and the bat–the other three may remain here under a guard of four."

"No!" said Ysabelle. "Our friends must accompany us. We have been through too much to be separated now!"

"I cannot agree to that," Fenny told her. "I do not like the looks of your fellow travelers, and the location of our stronghold is a secret that we guard above many things. Very dearly would the Hobbers like to learn where it lies, and that is a risk I am not prepared to take."

"Then I am going nowhere with you," she said flatly.

"All or none," added Vesper.

The mouse looked at them threateningly, then he glanced at his warriors and saw that they were watching him, waiting for him to decide. "All, then!" he declared. "Now, let us waste no more time!"

He gave a signal to the woodlanders, and, raising their weapons, they flanked the five travelers on either side.

Wedged between three mice and a rabbit, Wendel picked up his fallen puppet and took up the handles of his cart. Tysle was put on a short one-spring-wormer, and Giraldus muttered to himself. Then they set off, and the enchanting glade of daffodils was soon far behind.

On through the forest they were marched, and Vesper noted with dismay that they had left the path and were going in the wrong direction for Greenreach.

When he pointed this out to Ysabelle, the squirrel did not seem to mind; the detour was worth taking if it meant she could persuade these folk to assist her in her mission. Their strength would swell the forces of her own army, and that was a prospect she could ill afford to miss.

The route they were compelled to tread was a meandering zigzag, and Vesper guessed that this was to confound them if they ever tried to find their way back to this secret destination.

Eventually, the ground began to rise, and up a steep incline they all trudged, up to where a bare, grassy mound reared amid the encircling woods.

The entire time they had been marching, none of the wood-landers—not even their captain—had uttered a word. Now Fenny, who was at the front, turned and called for them to halt.

"Here is where the folk of the wood reside," he said. "From this secret place, our troops depart and raid the Hobbers, assaulting them when we may. Never have they discovered from whence their enemies come."

Ysabelle gazed about them and looked at the mouse questioningly. "But where do you live?" she asked.

Fenny tapped his nose and led them around the side of the great green mound to where a patch of dandelions grew.

"Open up!" the mouse called. "'Tis I, Fenny, returned!"

The dandelions shook and their stems parted to reveal a recess in the hillside, which ended at a stout wooden door peppered with studs of iron.

A small brown face peeped out from between the plants, and the sentry quickly saluted the captain.

"Pass inside," he said, stealing a look at the unusual party the mouse had brought back with him.

Fenny returned the salute and led his warriors and the five travelers up to the door, which he banged on with his fist.

Immediately, a small grilled window flew open and a bright, suspicious eye pressed against it.

"Who be that?" the voice squeaked behind the door.

"'Tis I, Fenny."

"What is the flower that blooms in the summer?" demanded the voice.

"The meadow sage," the mouse replied, using the appropriate password for the time of day.

The eye vanished from the grille and the window snapped shut. There came the sound of many bolts being drawn, and the now muffled voice grumbled at the rusted state of them.

"'Tis an amazement that I do not tear out mine arms dragging this stubborn–*oof!* There, 'tis done.

The door swung open, and the owner of both the voice and the eye bowed and waved them inside.

Ysabelle and Vesper followed their guards, and, once inside the mound, they lifted their heads and stared in disbelief.

It was a staggering spectacle; they had expected the doorway to lead only into a roughly hewn passage and had never dreamed or suspected the truth.

Beyond the entrance an enormous hall opened out, upheld by many strong beams and supporting pillars. Cut into the curving earthen walls, countless tunnels radiated in all directions, worming deeper into the great hill, and above each archway a small lantern or candle gently burned.

Arrayed on one wall was a deadly collection of weapons: spears, swords, longbows, clubs, daggers, maces, and pikes all gleamed in neat rows, and several mousewives were busily

243

making certain that everything in the armory was accounted for on the long tally sticks that they carried.

In the center of the capacious hall, about thirty warriors of differing races were practicing their skills on one another to tests of strength and agility. Among them, veterans of old campaigns observed and bawled their comments at appropriate intervals, at times grabbing the sword or knife from a bumbling youngster and demonstrating how it should be done.

At the far end, behind all the commotion and activity, was a small forge, and there a stout hedgehog hammered metal and tempered steel as a small vole heaved on a pair of bellows, keeping the fire glowing.

Both Vesper and Ysabelle breathed in wonder at the skill and toil that had gone into creating this fortress beneath the ground and looked at Fenny speechlessly.

"At all times are we ready to defend our stronghold," said the mouse proudly, "for we can never lie easy, not while those pagans sweep through the world."

Just then Giraldus stepped over the threshold and the mole lifted his head, snuffling the dry, musty air with glee while straining to hear the echoes that rang from the tunnels.

"Oh," he murmured with undisguised admiration, "what a blissful place. Never have I been in such a charming underground. Such a delicious sense of space, and can I not detect a vast network of extensive and labyrinthine passageways below us? A most splendid accomplishment is this."

Tysle chortled to see his master pleased, and he looked back to where Wendel stood. The jester's eyes were roving about the vaulted hall and shone with intense fascination. Unlike Giraldus, he was quite unable to find anything to say that would adequately express his wonder and stood gawping idiotically at the impressive scene before him.

"Entrancing," muttered Giraldus. "So many ravishing air currents—oh, yes, this is indeed a delving beyond any compare."

He turned to one of the guards and asked politely, "Badgers, was it? The original excavators, I mean. I feel their vigorous yet poetic approach to subterranean architecture. Of course, it has been much altered and improved on since."

He quested the air again and added critically, "Alas, one can never truly rid a place of fox scent, but that merely adds to the history and grandeur of this unsurpassed monument to tunneling endeavor. Do you know, I believe there is evidence of mole hereabouts also; dearly would I like to exchange my views with their better-acquainted knowledge."

"You're not exchanging anything with anybody!" Fenny said sharply. "This is the way you're bound."

Briskly, he led them across the great hall, and the dummy fights and mock battles were halted as all eyes turned to the newcomers, and many woodlanders stepped fearfully aside as the leper went by.

"A most rare opportunity for me to entertain," Wendel told himself. "What a grand audience!"

But the five travelers were marched into one of the smaller passageways, and, as the hall was lost from sight, the sounds of training and combat sprang up once more. The tunnel was low, and Giraldus had to stoop to walk down it. Many doorways lined the route, but when they came to a small chamber that was heavily barred, their progress was brought to a standstill.

"Inside," said Fenny. "Hurry, now."

Vesper gazed in puzzlement at the cramped, straw-strewn room and looked curiously at the mouse captain, whose face was set and stern.

"Get in," he repeated.

Reluctantly, they obeyed, first Wendel, pushing his cart before him, then Tysle, Giraldus, and Vesper.

Only Ysabelle hung back. She stared, bewildered, at Fenny and asked, "I do not understand. Why are you consigning us here? Have I not made it clear just how important is my mission?"

"Oh, aye!" the mouse replied archly. "The daughter of Ninnia, was it not?"

The squirrel nodded, but the captain was tired of playing games and shoved her roughly inside.

"What manner of simpleton do you reckon me?" he cried. "Cease this foolish pretense! Why would any of that noble house be abroad with so peculiar a retinue? Addled, you Hobbers are!" And, with a heave of his paws, he slammed the door shut and locked them inside.

The prisoners were dumbfounded. They had been tricked into this place; the woodlanders had not believed a word they had said.

Vesper gripped the bars and pushed his nose through them as far as he could. "Are you witless?" he yelled. "Release us at once!"

"Pipe down!" Fenny shouted, hitting the bars with a stick. "The reason I did bring you all here was for one purpose, and that alone."

"And what would that be?" rumbled Giraldus.

"I shall wring from you all knowledge of that infernal brood and their plans," came the answer. "But, most of all, you will tell me of that accursed high priest!"

Ysabelle shook her head. "We know nothing," she insisted. "The fiend tried to kill Vesper and me and has laid a curse upon us both, but we know naught else."

The mouse glared at her, his temper boiling, and he hit the bars a second time. "Then your time here shall be a long one," he snarled. "For from this locked room none of you shall ever leave. In here shall you be imprisoned for the rest of your days!"

"No!" Ysabelle shrieked. "You must let me go!"

Fenny threw back his head and laughed. "Listen to her," he told the guards. "Listen to the Hobber squeak!"

"You show her respect!" demanded Vesper hotly. "This lady is worth all you and your peasanty brigands combined!"

The woodlanders sniggered, and with a last look of contempt, their captain led them from the jail.

As their departing footsteps faded from earshot, Ysabelle looked desperately at Vesper, and, in the corner of the chamber, Wendel sniveled into his paws.

"Trapped," the stoat wept, "for the rest of our days . . ."

THE FURZE CAT

Giraldus sat down morosely. "A lamentable predicament," he observed.

Tysle nested beside him in the clean straw and tried to sound more cheerful. "Aw," he said, "them won't keep us here for long—not when they realize how downright daft they've been."

"Let us hope you are correct," Ysabelle commented. "If only they would trust me; if they could but see how I might help them."

Vesper kicked the bars of their prison, then leaned against them. "That Fenny won't ever listen to reason," he said. "His sort never do. I've seen the generals of my folk behave like him—too ready to suspect the worst, and not willing to pause and actually look beyond their own noses. That is how enmity breeds and wars begin."

For nearly an hour, they remained locked within the small cell, too despondent to talk and with only the unhappy sniffs of Wendel to break the oppressive silence.

Then Giraldus looked up. "Someone approaches," he whispered, and in a moment they all heard the sound of footsteps tramping down the tunnel toward them.

"A dismal quiet is this," said the voice of Captain Fenny as the mouse looked in at the bars. "Where are your protestations now, daughter of Ninnia?"

Ysabelle regarded him with disdain. "I shall not waste any more words on you," she said coldly. "Your mind is too closed to hear them. Show to me instead a higher authority to whom I might prove mine lineage."

"Tut, tut," Fenny scolded. "Still the play actor, aren't we? Well, my patience will not be everlasting; you will give me the intelligence I requested, whoever you pretend to be." He brought his grim face close to the bars and added with a hiss, "As for someone higher than myself, there is no one. The folk of the wood have no use for tyrants or princes."

"Yet they have a captain," put in Vesper.

Fenny eyed him crossly. "That they have," he answered, "and more beside, but only to keep the Hobbers out and purge the forest of them. Once that is achieved, then I shall return to my old life and have no more dealings with sword and spear."

At this, Giraldus was spurred to disagree and gravely muttered, "You can take the plow from the paw, but never can you remove the sword—so it is written. A warrior and leader shalt thou always be—and if there is a peaceful future beyond this dark time, then you will have no part in it."

The mouse scowled at him. "Very well," he spat. "If you persist in concealing your true intentions and denying your dealings with the Black Brotherhood, then no food shall be sent unto you until I decree otherwise."

He whirled around and was about to storm back along the passage when a small vole came rushing up to him, breathless and panting.

"Captain," the gasping creature wheezed, "I must speak with you."

"What is so urgent?" Fenny asked, his paw straying to the hilt of his sword.

The vole was quick to reassure him. "Oh," he cried, "there is no alarm, nothing of that kind. No, 'tis from the lower depths I have come."

The effect this statement had upon the mouse was remarkable. At once, his eyes widened and his tail thrashed wildly. "The lower depths," he breathed, stealing a glance at the prisoners and pulling the vole out of their hearing. "Then you must wait until we are removed from this unholy crew before you begin to relate your message."

Taking a great gulp of air, the vole violently shook his head. "I cannot!" he said. "For the message I am entrusted with concerns them."

Fenny glared at him. "How so?" he demanded.

The small creature trembled before his angry voice, but he remembered the urgency of his errand and closed his eyes to recall the precise wording of the message. "Of those you have recently captured and now hold prisoners," he began, "know now that two of their number must be sent down at once."

"Sent down?" Fenny muttered, and now his voice was filled with doubt and, it seemed to Giraldus, plainly tinged with fear. "Why?" the mouse asked.

The vole replied in a whisper. "The Ancient orders it," he said.

Fenny drew a sharp breath, and his fingers played anxiously about the neck of his cloak. "The Ancient?" he echoed in a reverent murmur. "Is this true?"

One look at the vole told him that it was.

"Then, which of the prisoners are to be sent?" he asked nervously. "Which pair does he wish?"

The vole peeped in through the bars. "The Moonrider and the squirrel maiden," he said.

Fenny nodded swiftly and brought out a key to unlock the door. "I shall send a company of guards with you," he said, "in case the prisoners attempt an escape."

"Oh, no," the vole replied, "did I not make it plain, Captain? You are to accompany them—the Ancient wishes to see you also."

The mouse dropped the key on the floor in surprise, and, with a prim bow, the vole raced back down the passageway. Fenny watched his small figure vanish round a corner, then

250

fumbled with the lock and ushered Vesper and Ysabelle from the chamber.

"Tysle!" Giraldus cried. "What is happening? Where are our friends being taken?"

"Oh, dear!" whimpered Wendel wretchedly. "So, this is how it shall be. Two by two are we led to our doom."

"My poor Mistress, will I never see your face again?"

"What do you want of us?" Vesper asked as the door was locked behind them. "Where are we being taken? Who is this Ancient you speak of?"

Fenny turned a drained and awe-stricken face to the young bat. "Him, by whose leave we are permitted to abide here," he said, and he seemed about to say more when he decided against it and led them up the tunnel. "You shall see soon enough," was all he would tell them.

Once again, Vesper and Ysabelle entered the great hall, but now the training had stopped, and an elderly weasel was standing before a seated group of very young woodlanders and instructing them in their lessons.

All the youngsters turned their heads as Fenny and the two strangers passed, and they nudged each other excitedly.

"Those are Hobbers!" one of them hissed in an audible whisper.

"She's too pretty!" piped up another.

The weasel tapped the floor impatiently until he had the attention of all of them and then resumed the lesson.

Across the expansive hall, the mouse captain led Vesper and Ysabelle, and when they came to a wide archway, he passed beneath and they followed closely behind.

"What do you think is waiting for us?" Vesper murmured to the squirrel.

"I know not," she answered, "but did you see how pale Fenny went at the mere mention of it? We had better prepare ourselves."

The passage they were now in began to slope downward before it joined another and then a third, till both Vesper and Ysabelle's heads swam in confusion. The interior of the hill was a maze of walkways and caves, and, after only a few minutes, they had totally lost all sense of direction. Even if they had tried to escape, neither of them would have known which was the way back to the hall and the entrance. The only course they could take was to follow Fenny—he seemed to know where he was going.

Then, at a crossroads, where four tunnels met, the mouse hesitated and looked uncertain.

"What is wrong?" asked Ysabelle. "Have you forgotten the way?"

The captain pulled his cloak about him. "How can I have forgotten that which I never knew?" came his reply. "For never have my errands or wants taken me down this far."

He spent a moment tentatively peering into each of the possible tunnels before deciding. "This one," he declared. "I feel sure it must be—it is the only way that smells old and moldering enough."

Vesper raised his eyebrows and glanced at Ysabelle. "What can that mean?" he wondered.

The tunnel that Fenny had chosen sloped downward more steeply than any they had yet been in and seemed to curve steadily round in an ever descending spiral. Deep below the mound they journeyed, their way lit by small lanterns suspended from the earthen ceiling at long intervals. These lanterns illuminated only a small area of the winding path, and the spaces between their glimmering boundaries were engulfed in pools of somber darkness.

The smell in that gloomy, twisting tunnel was like the stale, dry must of old hay. No other scents drifted on the still airs, only a centuries-old, muted aroma of great age and shabby neglect tingled like pepper in their nostrils. Ysabelle was reminded of her late tutor, Godfrey, whose room in the Hazel Realm was always filled with fusty-smelling scrolls and charts.

As they continued along this seldom-trod path, Vesper and Ysabelle saw that, occasionally, large fragments of stone protruded from the soil walls. The irregular pieces of rubble were covered in what had once been elaborate carvings, and the images could still be discerned. Even Fenny took time to slow down and look at them.

There were chiseled pictures of distant lands and strange vessels that crossed the rolling seas with many warlike creatures on board, all fierce looking and armed to the teeth. At one point a tall, reclining figure formed part of the passage wall, and they stepped alongside the sleeping effigy with their gaze trained upon the sculpted features.

Fenny narrowed his eyes as he examined these remnants of another age and nodded his head with understanding. "'Tis said this mound was a place where old kings were entombed," he muttered. "'Twould seem the tale is borne out."

As they pressed deeper, large, pointed flints began to litter the passage floor, and in the walls dull gleams were picked out by the lamps, for treasure had been interred with the forgotten dead, and the exposed gold threw back the light of the lanterns over the ground.

Eventually, however, they came to a flight of granite steps carved with many swirls and interlocking circles. Down this stair the mouse led them until they found themselves standing in an arched cave, the end of which was covered by a faded tapestry depicting the sickle moon. Vesper's eyes opened wide, and at the back of his mind some distant memory began to surface.

"This is the place," Fenny told them, and they could tell that he was just as excited and nervous as they were—more so, perhaps.

Striding up to the tapestry, he was about to draw it aside when the material twitched and a velvety snout emerged from behind its folds.

Into the cave a mole, shorter and with less bulk than Giraldus, trotted. He blinked several times, then bowed gravely and said, "The Ancient awaits thee." And with that he took hold of the tapestry and pulled it aside.

A dimly lit cavern lay beyond the faded curtain. Inside, tapering fires flickered within two basins of stone, and images of the moon, in all her phases, adorned the smooth stone floor.

Yet behind the flames all was shadow, and Ysabelle peered into the void, where small shapes were constantly moving.

"Welcome," said a voice from the darkness, and at that sound Fenny fell on one knee, humbly lowering his head.

"Welcome to thee, Captain Fenlyn Purfote," the rich voice hailed. "Rise. There is much worth in thee, most valiant of mice.

Fenny did as he was bid, and, as Ysabelle listened, she thought the voice sounded warm and kind–then she heard her own name called.

"Welcome to thee, Ysabelle," it said, "daughter of Ninnia and Cyllinus, fairest sapling of Coll Regalis. Valiant also art thou."

Fenny looked up when he heard this, amazed that the squirrel had been speaking the truth, but the voice continued.

"And finally," it purred, "welcome to thee, Vespertilio, a true Knight of the Moon, despite thy tender years."

Vesper nibbled his beard, and his wings opened as, at last, he guessed.

"I–I know you," he stammered, "or, at least, of you!"

Gentle laughter flowed from the shadows and a look of extreme wonder stole over the bat's face.

In the gloom, the small shapes moved toward the light, and three moles came to stand beside one of the stone basins. Then they took up a lamp and lit it in the flames before retreating to dispel the darkness beyond.

Then Ysabelle and Vesper saw him–the Ancient.

There, sitting in a shallow dip in the floor, brindled with extreme age, and with his eyes closed in meditation, was a great and wizened hare.

254

Ysabelle uttered a cry of surprise, and Fenny fell to his knees once again.

Upon its wrinkled and hoary brow, the creature wore a crown of dried leaves. The passage of time had etched many lines over the hare's face, and frosty whiskers stubbled its chin. For many ages the Ancient had dwelled here, long before the old kings had chosen to be buried above him. Dispensing his unbounded wisdom to those who would listen, he was the wisest sage that had ever breathed—a figure from the mythology of all cultures.

"The messenger of the Moon Goddess!" Vesper breathed in hushed respect. "He who took on earthly form with raiment of flesh—can it really be true?" With his eyes still closed, the Ancient smiled faintly and, when he next spoke, it was in a dry whisper. "Verily, 'tis I," he answered, "the purblind one, the dew hopper, the furze cat, the stag of the stubble, he with the leathery horns, the legs of the four winds—the Moon-Sent Angel."

Tears came unbidden to Vesper's eyes. All who venerated the Lady knew that the first creature to walk the earth was the hare—for in that form did her divine messenger descend and speak with the spirit of the Green. But that was many, many thousands of years ago, and that creature was thought to have perished from this world and his soul returned to the Goddess.

Now, Vesper had come face to face with a power far greater than he had ever imagined, and he, like Fenny, sank to his knees, then prostrated himself before this awesome creature.

Ysabelle was left standing alone before the Ancient, and she nervously put her paw to her mouth.

"What—what do you want of us?" she asked in a tremulous voice.

The Ancient raised his head a little, and the crown of leaves restless faintly. "Come forward, child of the Hazel," he said. "Mine old eyes would see the countenance of the new Starwife."

Ysabelle looked uncomfortably at Vesper, but he was weeping into his wings, so she took a step nearer to the great creature.

Then, very slowly, the Ancient's eyelids opened, and the squirrel maiden recoiled, almost crying out in fear. The eyes that the creature turned on her, and that stared so keenly in her direction, were of the brightest, purest silver.

"Be not afraid," the hare said soothingly, "for there is naught here to harm thee."

"Your—your eyes," Ysabelle stuttered.

A smile played about the Ancient's mouth. "Why dost thou fear them?" he asked. "Dost thou fear the moon when it shines above thee?"

"No."

"Then be not afraid now, for I look on you with the sight of one who has seen the Lady in the splendour of her youth, and in mine eyes that vision is forever mirrored. Step closer once more."

Ysabelle obeyed, and the silver eyes gazed long at her, fixing at last upon the Acorn around her neck.

"A dreadful burden is laid upon thee," he declared. "In thy paws are the fates of many held. Tell me, what is thine intent once thou arrivest at the place thou knowest as Greenreach?"

The squirrel glanced nervously back to where Vesper lay on the ground. "I must drive the Moonriders from the holy land," she told him.

"And how is this to be achieved by one lone daughter of the Hazel?"

"I shall not be alone," she said, "for there my army awaits me."

At this Vesper stirred and looked at her suspiciously. How could she know that?

The Ancient muttered to himself. His shining eyes seemed to look into Ysabelle's mind, and she knew he was aware of her conversation with the Green that night in the Orchard of Duir.

"And if thy forces can rid the land of the bats?" he asked.

"Then shall I take up the Starwifeship and rule as my predecessors before me. A wall of defense shall I weave about the blessed hill so no one may assail it ever again."

The silver eyes stared at her a moment longer, then the Ancient called for Vesper to approach.

Ysabelle stepped back as the young bat rose from his knees and awkwardly came forward.

"Vespertilio," the hare began, "why dost thou journey and keep company with a mortal enemy of thine own race?"

Vesper mumbled incoherently, but the Ancient spoke again.

"The war between the Knights of the Moon and the Five Houses of the squirrels has been waged for many years. What hast made thee turn traitor and betray thy mother's kindred?"

"I have not done such a black deed!" cried the bat, stung at last out of his fearful reverence. "I was taken captive by Ysabelle's guards, that is all—I have betrayed no one."

The Ancient laughed kindly. "That I know," he whispered. "Yours is a true heart, Vespertilio. Beware of it, for it is surely too large for thy chest to contain. Now, tell me of thine own legion's plans."

"I–I know nothing," Vesper replied, staring at the ground.

The hare muttered to himself again. "Didst thou learn naught from Leofa?" he mildly asked the young bat.

Vesper looked up quickly—how could he know of that? "Leofa?" he began.

"One of the two Moonriders thou didst hear speaking this morning," the Ancient reminded him.

This time, it was Ysabelle's turn to stir, and she listened keenly to what the bat had to say.

Vesper gazed into the silver eyes and folded his wings behind his back as he answered, while wondering all the time what Ysabelle was thinking.

"The two said that the search was still under way," he told the hare. "They and the forces of Hrethel are intent on finding Ysabelle and—and killing her."

"Dost thou know why that is?"

"Because they think she is evil and denies us our birthright."

"And what dost thou believe, Vesper?"

The bat shook his head. "I do not know any longer," he replied with a mounting anxiety rising in his voice. "Only that nothing Leofa and his companion said with such certainty had any foundation in truth, and—and—"

"Proceed."

"And I find that I am questioning many things now!" he exclaimed. "I do not know why the holy wars were begun, and, increasingly, they appear not holy at all, but bloody and savage! Ysabelle is not like any of the squirrels in the old tales. She is kind and brave and—"

The Ancient did not press him on this point, but his eyes seemed to burn into the young bat, studying and assessing, yet under their influence Vesper became calm and his anxieties faded.

"Vespertilio," the wizened hare said, "most proud should thy mother be of her offspring. Of all creatures, thou art the only one who has learned. Both sides canst thou see, and the truth is but a glimmer away. Now do I pronounce mine judgment. Fenlyn Purfote, rise and approach."

The mouse captain staggered to his feet and came to stand beside Vesper. "What is your will?" he asked meekly.

"Hear now the wisdom of the Moon-Sent Angel," the Ancient addressed them all. "Here you stand, three emissaries from differing lands. To each, the fortunes of their own house must come above all others, and blindly do they pursue their goals—and unto the ruin of all things would they go."

Here, the hare's voice became harsh, and the flames in the stone basins shot upward, roaring and boiling to the ceiling.

"Know this," the Ancient angrily told them. "Amid the petty wars of bat, squirrel, and woodlander, there will come a foe more terrifying than anything that has been, since first I danced under the newborn moon."

"You mean the Hobbers?" Ysabelle asked. "But once I bring the Acorn to the Starglass, I can cast an enchantment against them–"

"Against the seething tide that rises against thee now, nothing can stand!" the hare warned. "None in this time know of the terror that was before the rising of the moon and the budding of the first spring, when the Infernal Triad ruled the unholy night."

Now the flames dwindled and, except for the lamps that the attendant moles still held, all became dark.

"Those who do think themselves safe from the advancing hordes," murmured the Ancient, "shall be proved cruelly wrong when they strike. The armor of the Moonriders shall be no protection from the talons of the baseborn birds that are mustering. Carrion crows, jackdaws, rooks, and ravens now gather to feed on the battlefield flesh they have been promised. Soon, their mighty number shall strike at the very heart of the winged legions, and the forces of Hrethel shall fail before them.

"Then shall the paltry strength of the remaining houses be assailed, and all squirrels shall perish. The land shall flow with blood, and the Children of the Infernal Triad shall carouse in rivers of crimson. Then shall all fortresses be overthrown and the last strongholds be unearthed and conquered–not a life shall be spared that will not worship the horned rat god."

Ysabelle and Vesper said nothing, for, in their minds, the Ancient's words conjured ghastly images of a world plunged into chaos and madness. Darkness would smother all, and the land would be without order: murder and war would reign, and, in this nightmare, Hobb alone would rule.

Fenny lifted his face, and despair was ingrained upon it. "Then is there to be no hope?" he asked. "Are we all to fall?"

The silver eyes closed, and the Ancient sighed. "It need not be so," came his answer. "The vision of darkness I have shown unto you can still be averted—but in one circumstance only."

"Then how?" asked Ysabelle. "What is it we can do?"

"Only if all the enemies of the Infernal Triad unite and do battle together can this be done. Only then shall the land be cleansed and order restored."

"All the enemies?" repeated Ysabelle, glancing at Vesper.

"Then it cannot be!" the bat cried. "My folk would never join with the squirrels—their hatred of them is too deep!"

The eyes opened again, and their brightness pierced him. "Yet that hatred thou hast turned into a different passion, Vespertilio," the hare muttered.

Vesper looked shyly at Ysabelle. "But no other Knight of the Moon could be persuaded!" he mumbled.

"Vespertilio," the Ancient said, softly chanting his name, "hearken to me now and know the destiny that is mapped out for thee."

The bat flinched, but he could not tear his eyes from those that now blazed fiercely before him with a radiance all their own.

"Unto thee the task is given," the hare said. "Thy duty it shall be to bring the two opposing forces together—bat and squirrel. If only for a short time, they must act as one. And shouldst thou fail, then the world is doomed and condemned to the dark."

"But—but I cannot!" Vesper spluttered. "Such a thing is impossible! Who would listen? All Knights of the Moon believe the squirrels withhold their birthright—I might ask the sun to cease rising, for all the good it would do!"

To everyone's dismay, the brindled hare let out a horrible growl, and the moles scurried around him to placate and soothe.

"A time may come when the sun shall indeed rise no more if thou shouldst refuse the task!" he roared. "Yet know this, and let the knowledge be the instrument of thy success in this venture."

The Ancient lowered his voice, and the words he spoke left Vesper feeling empty and cheated beyond belief.

"The gifts of prophecy and insight can be bestowed or denied by no other creature than the one to whom they were given. Listen to me, Vespertilio: thy true enemy was never the Starwife, but none other than the Lord Hrethel himself!"

"That cannot be!" Vesper objected. "It cannot—"

"He it was who denied the birthright of his fellows," the hare said. "The gifts of the Lady were a danger to him, for with their aid thy kind would see into his black heart and the dark malice that simmered there would be revealed. Know now, Vespertilio, thy beloved and revered Warden of the Great Book hath become enamored of his charge and gloats jealously over the charmed pages, allowing no other sight nor touch of it. By the powers of the Great Book was he able to wrench away thy birthright, yet, dissembling his evil thoughts and intent, he did place the blame at the Starwife's door."

"No," Vesper gasped.

"Thou knowest it to be true; have thee not already suspected? Never was so terrible a treachery perpetrated, save in Greenreach alone; yet see in his vile lies the seeds that will bloom under the realm that is to come. Lies breed distrust, and distrust brings conflict."

Vesper was too stunned by this awful revelation to think. "But—but," he stammered, "What can I do? No one will believe me! Would you not come to persuade them? My fold would listen to you—but they won't even look at one small weanling!"

At that, one of the moles came up to Vesper carrying a leather bag and strapped it about the bat's shoulders.

"The herbs and powders that pouch contains," the Ancient said, "will summon all thy kind. Should thou cast it into a fire, then all Knights of the Moon will gather; they shall attend to thee then. Yet that is all; no virtue to persuade them does it have. That task is thine alone, for never shall I leave this place.

Such is thy destiny, Vespertilio—turn their hearts and unite against the common foe."

Vesper fell silent. He was no great orator; perhaps if the Ancient had given the mission to Giraldus, they might have stood a chance.

The eyes of the hare left him and were turned to blaze at Fenny. "Now is this discourse to an end," he said. "Guide these honored guests up to the great hall once more and treat them and their companions with the respect due to each. When they desire to leave, go with them. Now the time is come when this place must be left behind, for skulking and secrecy shall protect no longer."

The Ancient's gaze held the mouse for a moment, then, for the last time, it turned to Ysabelle.

"About thy neck the Acorn is stained with blood," he told her, "and by that blood was Hobb invoked. Thrice was it steeped, and thrice was he called, and by those very marks shall the monster be drawn from the Pit. Unto thee shall he come. Art thou prepared for this?"

"No," she admitted, "and when I heard him bellowing beneath the ground, I was very afraid."

The eyes narrowed. "Then already he has awoken," the hare said with a trace of alarm in his voice. "I did not expect it should be so soon. Mighty in strength must the magic of the amulet be, yet now it works for evil. How many times hast thou heard the unholy one?"

"Only once," Ysabelle said, "by the shore of the haunted mere last night."

"Then only one day remains," the hare muttered, "for assuredly tonight thou shalt hear him again, but on the third occasion, Hobb will come. From the depths of the underworld, the Lord of the Raith Sidhe shall emerge, and, unless the Acorn is brought to the Starglass before that time, no power on earth can stop him, and thou, daughter of Ninnia, shalt be his first victim."

The hare uttered a weary sigh, and his eyelids fluttered shut. "Now, all of you may go," he said, "and may my blessing go with each. Herein, my part in the story of the world is ended, and I will have no further dealings with mortal concerns. For the good of all, I pray thy missions succeed–fare thee well."

The moles came bearing their lamps, and the most ancient and magical creature that ever danced beneath the moon was lost in darkness once more.

In stricken silence, Fenny led the others back up the stairs and along the winding tunnels. Ysabelle clasped her amulet fearfully; there was so little time, and yet so much still had to be done.

But the squirrel maiden did not know that when she had heard Hobb bellowing beneath her, it was in truth the second night of his awakening. If she had realized, she would have abandoned all hope completely. Outside, the afternoon was already drawing to a close.

"Tysle!" Giraldus bawled. "Tell thy friend to stop his infernal prattling. I can stand it no more! Penance I will gladly suffer, yet the unceasing babble of his nonsense would make saints shriek and stop up their ears!"

Wendel pulled a rude face. Ever since Vesper and Ysabelle had been taken away, he had been hatching the most ludicrous escape plots and gabbling them to Tysle in the most confused manner, making wild gestures with his paws, attempting to make him comprehend. Now he was trying to get Giraldus to help him, but so far had met with no success—but the stoat was not deterred.

"Please!" he implored. "'Tis the only way left to us! Soon that felonious mouse will return, and we shall be the next ones sent to our deaths. Canst thou not see, most sagacious and doughty mole? Thou art our only chance."

"Tysle!" Giraldus rumbled.

The shrew turned to Wendel and tried to make him stop; he could see that his master was becoming more and more agitated.

"That's enough, Master Jester," he urged him, "'twon't work, I tell you! Best leave well alone!"

"Course it will!" Wendel replied. "What else are a mole's paws for, if not to dig? Such a perfect solution to our predicament, if thy friend would but listen. He alone can save us!"

"Silence!" roared Giraldus. "If you do not keep a hold on thy tongue, I shall tie it about one of those bars!"

The stoat opened his mouth to protest, but the mole snapped at him before he could utter a word.

"See these paws of mine!" Giraldus cried, tearing the bandages away. "What use do you think they would be?"

Wendel stared at the leper's diseased fists and looked away, sickened.

"All tunneling is denied to me!" ranted the mole. "Must you continually torment me? Be quiet, you absurd dolt!"

Carefully, he bound the strips of cloth back around his remaining fingers and sat in a brooding temper.

Tysle crept beside him and racked his brains to think of something to say. In the end, it was his stomach that spoke. A loud groan issued from it, and the shrew glumly reflected on how ravenous he was.

"I have only one caterpillar left," Giraldus offered. "I fear the snails have slithered out of my bag. If you wish, you are most welcome to have it."

Tysle was so hungry that he almost accepted, but then they all heard footsteps coming down the tunnel toward them.

"This is it!" Wendel howled. "Our time is up!"

Desperately, they waited as the sound came closer, then Tysle jumped for joy and cried, "Why, 'tis the fair damsel and the batling! Master, they are returned!"

"So, too, the mouse captain!" put in Wendel.

Giraldus hauled himself to his feet as the barred door was unlocked. "A most joyous event is this!" he thundered. "Our blackest fears are unfounded!"

Fenny smiled and held the door wide open. "Well," he said, "are you going to remain in there all night? Come, you are freed!"

"What new deception is this?" Wendel asked suspiciously. "Are we to cross that threshold, only to feel a knife in our backs? No trust do I have in thee, mousie, and it would take more than thy words to make me draw nigh."

Vesper pushed past Fenny. "'Tis true," he told the stoat. "The woodlanders no longer believe we are in league with the Hobbers."

Still Wendel doubted. "By what miracle didst thou manage that?" he asked. "I shall not leave this jail unless my Lady herself assures me all is well, for is she not strangely silent?"

Ysabelle stirred. "Have no fear," she said. "You have nothing to worry about. Fenny speaks the truth."

"Glad is my heart," said Giraldus. "Green be praised!"

Wendel looked curiously at Ysabelle, for the squirrel maiden really was unusually quiet and thoughtful.

"Mistress," he began, "why so melancholy? If we are indeed free to leave, then surely this is a time of celebration, not sad faces."

Ysabelle nodded, but she was troubled with dark thoughts and turned quickly to Fenny. "We must go at once," she said. "I must arrive at Greenreach before tomorrow's nightfall."

The mouse agreed but told her, "My folk require some time if they, too, are to leave this place. I fear we cannot depart till sunrise."

"But that may be too late."

The shadow of a smile flickered over Fenny's lips. "Follow me," he murmured.

To the great hall they went, and Giraldus was once more moved by the magnificence of the subterranean architecture. Excitedly tugging on Tysle's string, he drew the shrew aside.

"Let us remain here a while," he said. "We can follow the others later. For myself, I yearn to explore this wondrous warren to

265

my heart's content. Never would I have believed that such a marvelous place existed. Most fortunate of shrews, that you may behold its remarkable splendor."

Tysle smiled; although his master was strict and pious, he had one weakness. Ever since his affliction had denied Giraldus the true use of his paws, the mole had been haunted, and he continually ached to do that which was now impossible. He was only truly happy when a ceiling of soil reared over his head, and many were the times when he had compelled his guide to lead him into an earth or burrow. Tysle enjoyed indulging him, and, though he would have liked to go with the others, he understood that Giraldus's foibles and wants must be pandered to.

"Come, Tysle," the leper declared, "describe unto me the exact details of this glorious underground, and leave out not the slightest thing."

And so, as the mouse captain led Vesper, Ysabelle, and Wendel to the heavily studded doorway, the two pilgrims journeyed about the hall. The woodlanders they came across leaped in surprise when they saw the leper, and, before either Giraldus or Tysle had time to greet them, they fled in all directions.

The sun was low over the treetops, gilding the new spring leaves, when Fenny guided the others from the mound and through the clump of dandelions, and the whole world seemed calm and peaceful, bathed in the mellow radiance of dusk.

"Why have you brought us out here?" Ysabelle asked.

"Climb with me to the top of the hill," the mouse told her.

"All the way up there?" Wendel objected. "Why, mine poor legs do refuse to carry me up such a steepness."

"Then you stay here," Fenny told him.

The stoat put out his bottom lip sulkily and returned to the entrance, kicking the plant stems on his way.

"Strange companions you travel with," Fenny muttered with a sorry shake of his head, "yet it is not for me to question the daughter of Ninnia. Now, unless you or the Moonrider wish to follow him, we had best ascend before it grows dark."

Up the mound they climbed, and the forest sank around them. Through the lush, daisy-freckled grass they went, until at last they reached the top and, as they caught their breaths, a most unexpected and marvelous sight awaited.

"There she is," Fenny declared, unsheathing his sword and pointing it into the hazy distance.

Over the trees, Ysabelle gazed, and the heaviness of her heart lifted.

Rising above the forest roof, a large hill, far greater than the one on which they stood, reared into the dimming sky. There, unmistakable, was the land of Greenreach, where the Starwives had ruled since the time of the first stars, and, though Ysabelle had seen images of it only in old manuscripts, she recognized the blessed hill at once.

"The holy land," she breathed.

"Barely a day's march away," Fenny told her. "If we set out at first light, then by the evening we shall arrive there."

Vesper stared at the vast shape in astonishment. "I did not think we were so close," he remarked. "Yet if we are, then yonder must be my home." He turned his face toward the north and thought he could just make out the highest steeples and towers of the medieval city of London, shimmering in a pale blur.

Fenny sniffed the air and glanced at the fiery ball that was the dying sun. "Evening falls," he murmured. "We would do well to return inside the mound; no doubt the Hobbers will be abroad this night. They beset and besiege us with their heathen barbarity, and though we do what little we can, my folk fear the night and those that stalk in the darkness."

"I, too, have reason to fear the night," Vesper said regretfully. "Once I reveled in the rich nocturnal airs, yet now only horror and lurking menace do I see beneath the moon. I shall never regain that feeling for as long as I live. The once sumptuous night is forbidden me now, and I yearn for the day to break."

Ysabelle continued to gaze at the distant hill, for there her destiny or doom awaited her. "I should like to remain here a little while longer," she said. "There is much for me to think of."

The mouse captain bowed. "Then I shall take my leave of you," he said. "Yet do not tarry overlong. Aside from the danger, we woodlanders would deem it an honor for your party to be our guests this night. A feast we shall give, and, come the morning, if it is still your wish, with you shall we go."

"Thank you," she answered. "Now that I know the holy land is so close, to stay here is the best solution. Also, we have not eaten this day. We would be delighted to sit at your table."

"So be it," said Fenny, and he began to descend.

Ysabelle stared out over the forest; her fate lay upon that immense hill, and her mind was filled with nothing but dread.

"I wish I knew how to persuade my folk to join forces with thine," commented Vesper forlornly.

Ysabelle started, for she had forgotten the bat was still beside her.

"I can see no way of achieving this impossible task," he continued.

Ysabelle managed to tear her eyes from the horizon and frowned at him. "The Ancient thought it could be done," she reminded the young bat, "else he would not have suggested it. He must hold you in high regard.

"You think so?"

"Most certainly; you would not have been chosen otherwise."

"Maybe," sighed Vesper, only slightly encouraged.

The squirrel maiden's eyes returned to stare at the holy land. Already, the blessed hill was fading from view and merging with the shadows that surrounded it.

"This will be our last night as we are," she said, "for tomorrow our lives will change and be sundered forever. I must bring the Acorn to the Starglass, and you must return to the Knights of the Moon."

Vesper looked at the ground. "I know," he uttered sadly. "I wish it were not so."

Ysabelle furrowed her brow. "Why is that?" she asked. "Do you not wish to return to your home?"

"I don't know," he replied. "A small part of me does, but another–the most important–does not. Can you not tell why? Do you in truth not know?"

"You speak in riddles," she said, turning back to the near-invisible hill. "I doubt if I shall ever understand your kind."

Vesper bit his lip and looked away.

Ysabelle's paws reached up to the amulet, and, as the crown of the holy land disappeared into the deep shadows of evening, she felt the weight of the high priest's curse fall upon her.

"Hobb is coming for me," she whispered. "If I could throw this wretched Acorn away, I would! Yet without it there can be no Starwife. Oh, Vespertilio, what am I to do? I dare not think what will happen. How can I face such an evil force?"

She fell into weeping, and the bat stood awkwardly at her side, not knowing how to comfort her. He longed to stretch out and put his wings around the squirrel's shoulders and tell her that all would be well, yet how could he? She was a child of the Hazel Realm and he one of the reviled enemy of her race. His heart bled inside, and again he told himself that nothing was fair–the world was indeed a cruel, harsh place.

As Ysabelle sobbed, Vesper felt totally helpless; she might as well have been on the other side of the world for the good he could do. He reproached and scolded himself, but his wings remained by his side, and the squirrel was forced to cry alone, and the gulf between them seemed to widen.

Then, from the far-distant city of London, which was now hidden behind a dim veil of purple shadow, a church bell rang.

The lonely sound floated on the dusk out over the trees and to the mound where they stood.

Vesper trembled when he heard it, for now he felt his own doom draw tightly about him, and he closed his eyes in anguish.

Beside him, Ysabelle listened to the dismal ringing, and she alone in all the world knew how the bat was feeling. Instinctively, her paw reached out for him, and, as the sun blazed crimson beneath the treetops, Vesper took it into his wing.

Not far away, with a secret smile traced over his face, Wendel crouched out of sight, not wanting the couple to see him.

"Ah," he murmured, "so my Lady hath found him, and he her."

In his paws, the jester held two puppets–the now-finished one of Ysabelle, and that of a bat. Sniggering softly, he brought the two together, and the wooden heads kissed.

As the last rays of the setting sun shone faintly over the grassy mound, flickering over the closing daisies and turning all things a delicate rose, Vesper gazed deep into Ysabelle's eyes and brought her close.

Tittering mildly to himself, Wendel looked away.

The lips of the bat touched those of the squirrel maiden, and, for an instant, all their cares melted and were forgotten.

"Let us not think of tomorrow," Vesper said gently. "This night, let all thoughts of darkness and horror be forgotten."

The jester crawled down the mound as silently as he could and slunk over to a patch of weeds, where he took from a pouch around his belt a small cone of incense.

"Now," he whispered, "the time has come."

With his tinderbox, he lit the strange cone, and, as a thread of smoke curled into the air, the stoat backed away and hurriedly sought the iron-studded doorway to the mound once more.

WITHIN THE RUIS CHEST

That evening, in the great hall, the folk of the mound held a feast for their guests. It was partly to make up for the way the visitors had at first been treated, but it was also a farewell to that place that for so long had been the woodlanders' home and stronghold.

About the curving walls they hung small jars of patterned green glass in which small candles brightly burned. Between them, garlands of spring flowers were strung, and their honey-sweet fragrance quickly filled the cavernous vaulted chamber. Around the central, supporting pillars, and in a large circle, sixteen long tables had been arranged, and upon them the feast was being set out by the countless animals who dwelt beneath the guarded mound.

Each family brought their own specialty to the celebration and sat upon stools, benches, chairs, or piles of cushions around the splendid display. At the main table sat Fenny and the honored guests—except Giraldus, who, because of his disease, had been asked to sit by himself some distance away. Tysle had objected to this at first, but the mole had accepted the temporary banishment quite willingly.

"No one wishes to sit at table with a leper," he commented. "My gruesome visage would no doubt turn their stomachs and dispel their appetites. I shall be quite content to dine in solitude; be not upset, Tysle."

So, when the feasting began, the shrew made certain his master had plenty of everything before he sat down to enjoy his own meal and silence the growls of his stomach.

Tysle had never seen such food; the feast was a fabulous spread of toothsome delicacies. The different courses seemed to utilize nearly every plant and tree in the forest, and the shrew clapped his paws in excited glee, not knowing which to sample first.

There were herb soups, walnut and hazel pies, fennel and oak-apple pasties, twelve kinds of stew, a mash of vegetables, freshly baked bread still warm from the oven, all steaming with delicious scents that set Tysle drooling.

He was so famished and so eager to launch himself at the various dishes that by the time the puddings arrived, his stomach was already swollen and stretched to its utmost capacity. As he washed the meal down with a swig of dandelion mead, Tysle gazed at the sweet-smelling desserts and wished he had room for them.

Sitting by himself, Giraldus had been more patient and less enthusiastic over his food. His sense of taste seemed to have almost disappeared, and whatever he ate was as bland on the tongue as unsalted porridge.

"Too many furry wrigglers," he muttered despondently. "Their bitterness has jaded my palate. Never shall I enjoy a juicy worm again. This banquet may just as well have been gruel and mud."

As the evening progressed and the folk of the mound grew merry, some even came to him—at a safe distance, of course. The mole abstained from all drink, except elderflower water, and was horrified to discover the others were tasting the bramble wine.

"The fruit of that tree is the blood of the Green," he warned them. "Thou shalt not drink of it."

In response to that, Wendel defiantly swilled down a whole goblet full and hiccuped loudly.

Sitting next to Vesper, Ysabelle munched a small cake flavored with raspberries and the two spoke only of lighthearted matters, neither uttering a word about their cares and troubles.

When just about everyone had finished eating and was simply nibbling and picking at whatever was left over, Fenny stood up and addressed his people. The woodlanders listened gravely as he told them of the harsh struggle ahead.

By the time he sat down again, all faces were turned to Ysabelle, and it was apparent they expected her to say something, too. Nudged by Vesper, the squirrel rose and thanked the folk of the mound for their hospitality and for agreeing to join her in the fight to regain the holy land.

When she was done, they all cheered, yet the sound was hollow, and presently a still solemnity fell as all thoughts turned to the following day and what it might bring.

Tysle looked quickly at each pondering face, and his bright, brown eyes gleamed. Putting down a spiced bun he thought he might just be able to find a space for, the shrew hobbled over to where Wendel was patting his stomach contentedly and whispered in the stoat's ear.

"Aha!" the jester cried. "Indeed, my limping friend, this is the perfect occasion!"

Leaping to his feet, albeit rather drunkenly, Wendel waved his arms to gain everyone's attention and announced that he would be only too glad to entertain them if they so desired.

Amid great applause and banging of fists on tables, Wendel wheeled his cart into the center of the gathering and at once began to juggle while roaring scandalous jokes, to the delight of the audience.

Mice and hedgehogs rolled from their benches, too full to laugh without hurting their sides. The elderly weasel tutor guffawed at a particularly scandalous jest, then turned bright pink and hid his face behind a large pie dish. Wherever he saw boredom or pomposity, the jester scurried over and punctured

273

them with his needle-sharp wit. Wendel scampered about the assembly, mysteriously pulling objects from behind ears or out of mouths, to the astonishment of everyone.

As the merriment proceeded, Giraldus let out a deliberate yawn just as the stoat capered by. But Wendel had no wish to waste his time and talents trying to raise a smile on that one's lips; far better to ignore him and win this new audience over.

The mole sniffed disdainfully; he did not care for the fellow's irreverent humor, and it occurred to him that he might aid his digestion by having a little nap. There was nobody near him now; those woodlanders who had spoken with him seemed to have done so only out of curiosity, and now they were far too busy appreciating the jester's performance to take any notice of the secluded pilgrim.

"'Tis the illness that does affright them," he sadly observed. "Let us hope that the damsel can restore the fortunes of Grinuvicia and can heal both Tysle and me."

He pulled gently on the string and noticed with dismay that Tysle took longer than usual to respond, and, when he did arrive, it was with some reluctance.

"Do not worry thyself," Giraldus said in a dejected tone. "I shall not keep you from the silly antics of your friend. If you could but guide me to some out-of-the-way corner where I might rest a while and close mine eyes, I should be grateful."

Thus, Tysle directed his master over to a shallow cave just off the hall and made him comfortable on the small bed there.

"Thank you," the mole said. "What would I do without my trusty friend?"

Tysle smiled, then looked over his shoulder as tremendous squeals of laughter broke out around the jester.

"Ooh," cooed the shrew, "the fellow has brought out a bladder on a stick and is a-beating folk about the head. He do look funny. Why, he is pretending to be Captain Fenny!"

Giraldus shut his eyes. "Tysle," he began, "what will you do once you are cured of thy lameness and I of my ailment?"

"I–I don't know, and that's the truth," replied the shrew, taken aback by the question.

"If I am no longer blind," Giraldus continued, "then no need of a guide shall I have. You will be free to do as you wish–whatever life you choose to lead."

Tysle knelt beside his master and took a bandaged paw in his own. "What's this?" he asked in a quavering voice. "What are you a-saying?"

"Only that you need not feel duty bound to remain with me," the mole replied.

"But you did save my life," the shrew murmured, his eyes growing moist. "I could not leave you."

"You must not feel obliged simply for that," Giraldus said gently. "I–I know how fond you are of the jester. If you wanted to journey with him instead and see new lands, then I would understand. The life of the pilgrim is no happy vocation; I have no tricks or pranks with which to entertain."

At this, Tysle broke out crying. "Master!" he sobbed. "Don't say such things. I don't want to leave–not never! 'Twas you who gave me a purpose in life after the Hobbers destroyed my family. Oh, I grant the jester is mightily funny, but I ain't willin' to traipse round the country listening to the same old jokes day after day. You and me can't ever be split apart now–not after all we been through. Did we set out on the pilgrimage for it to end like that? I think not."

Giraldus sniffed and squeezed the tiny paws that gripped his bandaged fist. "Stout hearted and most loyal of friends," he said huskily. "What did I ever do to deserve a companion such as thee? Blessed in the eyes of the Green must I have been that day."

The mole wiped his own eyes hastily. "Go now," he said thickly. "Enjoy the stoat while I slumber."

So, on a lengthy, forty-three-autumn-rain-wormer, Tysle left his master and returned to the hall.

Wendel had been an enormous success, and the woodlanders demanded that he entertain them once more before the night was through, and, with a flamboyant bow, the jester agreed.

A group of mouse and vole musicians began playing their instruments, and the folk of the mound tidied away the remains of the feast. Gradually, the cleared floor became filled with couples dancing, their tails sweeping through the air as they cavorted and their voices raised in happy rejoicing.

Vesper looked at Ysabelle and raised his eyebrows. The squirrel stared back at him for a second, then giggled as she had done long ago, before the Silver had come to her. Taking his wing in her paw, the two capered into the twirling woodlanders, and, leaning against the wall, Wendel watched them with much amusement.

Tysle limped about the merry hall, chatting amiably to anyone he encountered. Everyone liked him, for he was so eager and willing to listen, and, in that brief time, the shrew made many friends and learned a great deal.

Every woodlander, it seemed, had the highest regard for their gallant captain, and they never tired of relating the brave deeds he had done. Many were the Hobbers Fenny had killed, and countless innocents had he saved through his unmatched valor. No equal had he; not in all the forest was there such a heroic leader, and unto the ends of the earth would they gladly follow him.

"Yet despite his vigor in dispatching the enemy," a plump mousewife told Tysle, "our captain has sworn that one day he will lead us from all dangers. To find a new land is his heart's desire, some place away from dark forests. Some fair meadow by a stream is his wish, and all would go with him."

Tysle beamed at her, though, when she asked him to dance, his worm string made it impossible, and he would not remove it in case Giraldus awoke and needed him. Shrugging, the mousewife found another partner and disappeared into the whirling throng, leaving the shrew standing alone.

He scratched his head and meandered about the edge of the dancers, exchanging pleasantries and answering whatever questions they put to him about the life of a pilgrim. Yet always his eyes returned to where Wendel's cart stood by the side of the blacksmith's forge, and eventually in that direction the shrew's feet slowly pattered.

No one was near the cart when Tysle approached, and he reached out a paw to touch the garish paint work. Bright flourishes and scrolls twisted over the boards, and his eyes gazed fixedly at the prop chests. Casually, Tysle glanced about him. Everyone was too wrapped up in the dancing to notice him—even Fenny had joined them now, and the mouse bounded from one lady to another as a brisk reel piped up.

"I suppose them chests is locked anyhow," the shrew mumbled to himself. He flicked at the catch on the one nearest to him, and the lid lifted a little.

Tysle guiltily looked around; still, no one was looking.

"What do you think you be doing, Tysle Symkyn?" he muttered. "You were brought up better than to peek at someone else's property."

"But I mightn't get to see it again," he countered. "Master Jester might go off soon, and I won't be stealing anything—I just wants a play, that's all."

"A play? What age are you? Too old to get excited over such vain fripperies! Think of thy master!"

Gingerly, he touched the string that linked him to Giraldus, and his gaze turned in the direction of the sleeping chamber, where at the moment the mole was snoring contentedly.

It was reassuring to be moored to such a solid and noble anchor, for the pilgrim could always be relied upon to support and save him from any trouble. The shrew looked back at the cart. "I just need the teeniest of glimpses," he mumbled. "Just a teeny, eeny one."

"No," his conscience scolded him. "You just get away from here right away. Wendel won't thank you for meddling with his tricks!"

Tysle frowned. "Very well," he consented, "I shall go and find some other thing to do."

But his fingers had closed about the cart's handles, and, before he knew what was happening, the shrew had wheeled it into an empty passage, away from the noise and any curious eyes.

"My!" he breathed, his paws stroking one of the intriguing and beguiling boxes. "'Tis such a lovely thing, all them whorls of color, and how bright Wendel do keep them biddy brass hinges."

Carefully, he opened the lid, and his shining eyes looked inside. At once, two painted moths flew out, and Tysle uttered a woeful cry of dismay as he leaped up and down, trying to catch them.

"Oh, dear!" he yelped. "I'll get what for if Master Jester finds them missing!" After a few desperate moments, he finally managed to recapture the bedaubed insects and stuffed them hastily back into the box, slamming the lid down shut and sitting on it just to make sure.

"That were a near thing," he told himself. "You just mind to take this back now before you does some real damage."

Tysle sucked his teeth and studied the other prop chests thoughtfully. "'Twould be a pity to miss out now," he admitted. "P'raps if I just peep at one more."

The shrew took up another and shook it cautiously before looking inside.

This one contained the jester's colored acorns, and Tysle spent several unsuccessful minutes attempting to juggle them. When they had fallen to the ground over a dozen times, he gave up and peered to see what else the chest contained. There seemed to be a square of silk at the bottom. Tysle reached in and pulled it out, but the material was tied to another, and that to another. Presently, he was up to his knees in festoons of colored silk, and after he had thrown them into the air and fluttered them in pretty patterns abut his head, he pushed them untidily back into the box.

Tysle was enjoying himself immensely and lifted a third chest. This was smaller then the others, made of elderwood; it was painted black, with a ruis, or elder, leaf daubed in scarlet upon the lid.

From this, the shrew brought out four wooden hoops he had seen Wendel twirl about his arms and legs. The little fellow tried to imitate what he had seen, but he ended up spinning round more than the hoops themselves until one went whizzing through the air and clattered over the floor.

Scampering after, he retrieved the mutinously wayward circle and checked that it was not damaged, then he looked once more into the chest. There he discovered more material, and the shrew unrolled it to see what manner of trick this was.

The scarlet cloth unfurled, and he held it at arm's length in order to see better.

"Funny," he muttered. "'Tis a sort of garment–a costume with peculiar stitching running all across–"

His voice evaporated into nothing as a vivid memory flooded before his eyes. It was the night of the Hobbers' attack; his sisters' screams were deafening his ears, and vicious claws dragged him from their riverside home. Tysle's heart thumped in his ribs as he remembered the awful figure striding up to him, the long knife in its grasp still dripping with his family's blood.

Here, held in his shaking paws, was the very costume that evil fiend had worn–a ghastly representation of a bloody-bones!

Tysle wailed and threw the foul material away from him in terror. Yet in the chest there was one more object–the undeniable shape of a Hobb lantern.

Tysle pushed the ruis box from the cart, and it fell with a crash. The shrew was in a frightful state, and he realized, with a knot tightening in his stomach, what this all meant.

"We–Wen–Wendel!" he spluttered. "It's–it's him! Master–I must tell my master!"

But before he could take up his crutch and leap from the cart, his string gave a sharp tug–Giraldus needed him.

Tysle whirled round, but there, framed within the gloomy passage, was Wendel himself, and in his fist he was holding the string. "Tut, tut," came the soft, hissing voice as he teasingly pulled the lead a second time, "I can't have you toddling off to tell anyone, now can I?"

"You're the one!" the shrew exclaimed.

The lips of the stoat parted, and he bared his sharp teeth unpleasantly as a cold chuckle gargled from his throat. "Yea," he snarled, "'tis I: the duncefellow, the gowk, the simpleton–the dark deceiver." He cackled and stole nearer, his deep shadow falling across Tysle's frightened face.

"I am the loyal servant of the Lord Hobb, and though I was forced to endure thy contemptible company, I should do it a thousand times over to return Him to this world. When the time is ripe, all shall know, and the despised pretense will be done with, but that is not yet upon us. I fear, little hobbling one, that I must still your squealing tongue–forever.

He lunged at Tysle, but the shrew jumped from the cart and tried to dodge past him. Yet Wendel still held the string, and, with a vicious yank, he dragged Tysle backward.

"No!" Tysle screamed, desperately trying to untie the lead. "No!"

Wendel Maculatum, high priest of the Raith Sidhe, laughed wickedly as he lifted the wildly squirming shrew off the ground and drew a knife from his belt.

"Now, join the rest of thy family, halt-footed one!" he growled.

The knife glittered. Tysle screamed once more, then his voice was silenced.

*   *   *

"Hmmm?" Giraldus stirred in his sleep and smacked his lips in agitation. His dreams had suddenly become troubled, and the mole mumbled under his breath—something was wrong.

"Tysle," he called, wiping the drowse from his eyes. "Tysle, where are you?"

He shook himself and sat upright in a dreadful daze. Outside the small sleeping chamber, the jolly music was still playing, yet a bitter chill entered Giraldus's heart, and, for some unknown reason, he felt anxious.

"Tysle!" he shouted, and this time his voice was desperate and fearful.

Trembling, he clutched at the string and tugged on it. The lead was slack. The mole babbled frantically and heaved, gathering it in as fast as he could until great coils wound about the floor. Then, to his dismay and unending horror, he held the end of the string in his paws.

Where once Tysle, his faithful friend and guide, had been, the end of the lead was now shredded and smeared in fresh, sticky blood.

Giraldus threw back his head, and his despairing howl shook the mound. The mole's shrieks were like the approach of Hobb himself, and all merriment came to a sudden and bewildered halt at the sound of that fearsome baying.

Ysabelle was sitting beside Fenny and sprang to her feet at once.

"What manner of beast is that?" the captain cried, drawing his sword. "'Tis like a soul in torment."

Ysabelle turned a pale and worried face to him. "It's Giraldus!" she exclaimed. "What can have happened?"

The frightful screech was sent up again, and everyone rushed forward to see what was the matter.

281

They gathered before the entrance of the sleeping chamber, yet though the leper shrieked and moaned, no one dared to approach for fear of his disease. The woodlanders could only gasp and stare at what they beheld.

"Let me through!" Ysabelle demanded. "Let me through!"

She pushed her way to the front, and there she found him. The mole was on his knees, the bloody string still in his paws and clasped to his bosom. He did not hear the squirrel call his name, for grief overcame everything, and, as he rocked to and fro, his screams drowned out all lesser sounds.

"Giraldus!" she cried, staring at Tysle's shredded lead. "Where is he? What has happened?"

But the leper was too distraught to answer, and his bellowing continued to resound throughout the caverns.

Ysabelle stumbled backward, and her eyes sought for Vesper among the crowd. For a moment, she could not find him. There was Wendel, resting his cart against the wall, looking concerned and afraid, there was Fenny trying to push his folk back, and then she saw him. The young bat was at the rear of the woodlanders, and he was staring at the floor. When he lifted his head, he gazed across at Ysabelle and beckoned her over.

Squirming through the crowd, Ysabelle looked at what Vesper had found.

A hideously sickening trail of dark crimson stained the ground. "Blood," she whispered.

"See where the string has been dragged across the hall," he said. "From that dark tunnel it came. You stay here."

"Don't go in there!" she begged. "You don't know what might be lying in wait!"

"Tysle could still be alive," he fold her. "I must find out."

At that moment, Fenny was beside them, and his sword was in his paw. "Then I shall accompany you," he said grimly. "We will follow the trail together."

Ysabelle watched, afraid, as they crossed the hall to where the gory track passed into the unlit passageway. Silently, Wendel crept up beside her, and, with a glitter in his eye, the stoat put his paw comfortingly upon her shoulder.

"Oh, Wendel," she murmured, "what do you think has happened?"

"I know not," the evil creature said with practiced innocence. "I pray the little fellow is not too badly harmed."

They stared with wide eyes as Fenny and Vesper pressed themselves against the sides of the tunnel entrance, pausing to see if they could hear anything.

The bat shook his head at the mouse captain, and Fenny kissed the hilt of his sword.

Then they sprang. Into the darkness they charged, while in the hall the assembled and frightened woodlanders held each other nervously. Mousewives clung to their spouses, and terrified rabbits huddled in a quivering group.

They waited for what seemed an age, but no sound came from that grisly place, and Ysabelle drew close to the jester.

"What can be keeping them?" she asked. "There are no cries of battle. What are they doing? Do you think they have been wounded also? What manner of silent horror lurks in there?"

"Who can say?" Wendel softly replied.

The tension was too much for the squirrel maiden to bear. "I'm going to follow them," she said, pulling away from the stoat and rushing across the hall.

But before she reached the tunnel, Vesper came staggering out, his face a mask of horror and revulsion.

"Don't you go in there!" he uttered, catching hold of Ysabelle's arms and dragging her away.

"What is it?" she cried. "Did you find Tysle?"

Vesper shuddered and leaned against the wall as a wave of nausea washed over him. "Oh, yes," he said hoarsely, "we found him."

Ysabelle stared, but that was all the bat would say. Then Fenny emerged from the passageway, and never had the folk of the mound seen their captain in such a state of shock and despair.

"The–the little shrew," he stammered, 'the–little shrew has been–has been peeled!"

It took several moments for his words to register, and in that time no one dared to breathe–then everybody began speaking at once.

"Peeled!" shrieked a startled weasel. "But how can that be?"

"Bloody-boned?" squeaked a group of mice.

"It is impossible!" cried a hedgehog. "That would mean . . ."

Ysabelle covered her face with her paws. "Oh, Tysle," she wept.

"It means," shouted Fenny, finishing the hedgehog's sentence, "that we have a member of the Hobb cult among our number–perhaps more than one."

Wendel Maculatum let out a warbling wail. "Woe!" he yelled. "A murderer is here–we shall all be killed!"

The woodlanders were on the brink of uncontrollable panic. They began to shout in high-pitched voices, and accusations started to fly all around.

"It's them strangers!" they shrieked. "We never had no trouble before they came!"

"That's right. They did it. They killed him!"

"Silence!" Fenny roared. "It cannot be our guests. The Ancient himself has spoken with two of them."

Suddenly, the despairing squeals died down as, from his shallow cave, Giraldus came.

The mole was terrible to see. His face was ashen, and madness shone in his squinting eyes. With the bloody string still in one paw and his staff in the other, he shuffled through the frightened woodland folk, the warning bell tolling loudly.

In the center of the great hall, the leper came to a stop and raised the shredded lead for all to see.

"Who has done this?" his croaking voice demanded. "Who is responsible?"

No one could look at him; so awful a specter of grief had the pilgrim become that they cast their eyes downward.

"What, no one?" he thundered. "Did none of you see who it was? Whose foul claws are steeped in my Tysle's blood? What monster has robbed the most faithful friend I ever had of his dear, sweet life? Tell me! I must know—I must be avenged! When I discover who committed this heinous and filthy crime, I shall tear out the villain's throat with mine own teeth!"

Ysabelle could not bear to see him so full of despair. Compassionately, she rushed forward, and, ignoring the cries of horror around her, bravely took the leper's blood-stained paws in hers. "Giraldus," she cried, "please, come and sit with me. I will pray with you for Tysle."

"Pray!" the leper screeched. "What use is that? Where was the Green when Tysle's skin was slit from his body? Why did the Green not strike the killer down? Why does He not reveal him unto me now that I might perform that task?"

He thrust Ysabelle from him and tore his bag of holy relics from his belt. "I have worshipped a false deity!" he roared. "Now do I cast thee aside—no more shall I be the gull!"

From the bag, he snatched the bottles of holy water that he had taken from the shrines he had visited and, with a ferocious scream, hurled them against the wall, where they smashed into thousands of twinkling fragments. Then he tore into tatters the collections of leaves, and, with a tremendous snarl of rage, took out the special purse and emptied the grain of wheat into his palm.

"From the crown of the Green art thou supposed to have fallen!" he bawled. "I spit on thee now—and all your works!"

The mole spat, then closed his fingers about the grain, intending to crush it into dust, yet his paw was shaking, and his face twisted with anguish.

Tysle!" he cried as the rage-born strength left him and he sank to the floor, tears streaming down his face.

Once again, Ysabelle cared nothing for the horrors of his disease and put her arm about the mole, then held him tightly. "I'm so sorry," she wept. "I'm so sorry."

Giraldus opened his fist and let the grain of wheat fall to the floor. "Oh, Tysle," he uttered, choking on his tears, "did you really think I could not tell the ruined state of the shrines? Did you really believe I thought that orchard was fair to see? Most loyal and devoted of friends, good-bye." And his voice was lost amid the racking grief.

Vesper turned to Fenny. "What is to be done?" he asked. "The killer of Tysle is still with us."

The mouse scowled and glared at all his folk. "I cannot believe one of them is responsible," he muttered, "yet who else is there?"

Just then, an urgent hammering sounded upon the door of the main entrance. Everyone spun around as a scared-looking sentry came charging inside.

"Captain!" he cried, racing toward Fenny. "The Hobbers—they are on the move."

"Hobbers!" the woodlanders repeated in fear.

"Where are they?" Fenny asked.

"Not far," the sentry replied, "but so many—never have I seen such a hellish host. From every bolt hole and loathsome grot they come."

"They are coming here?"

"Directly—as if they know precisely where we hide!"

Fenny stamped his feet in anger. "How can this be?" he shouted. "How can they know this?"

"Who can say?" the sentry answered. "Yet upon the night air a vile stink hangs. That, I deem, is what draws them—like flies to a rotting carcass they are gathering."

The captain strode before his people and shook his fists in his fury. "We have been betrayed!" he stormed.

"What can we do?" the woodlanders squeaked in dismay.

"Take up your weapons!" Fenny declared. "The time of hiding is finally over. We must fight the enemy on our very threshold. To arms! To arms! Barricade the main entrance and seal the others so we may have more time!"

As the terrified folk rushed to arm themselves, Fenny spoke quickly to Ysabelle, who was still trying to console Giraldus.

"Now we must part," he told her. "This is your only chance. Go swiftly from this place before the battle commences. Your mission is too vital for you to remain here."

"But what of you?" she cried. "You and your folk must come with us."

"We cannot leave now!" he said. "The Hobbers would pursue us to our doom. Yet if we can hold them back just a little, then you have a chance. Flee now while you may!"

Suddenly, the sound of many fists battered against the door, and the muffled shrieks of the Children of the Raith Sidhe screamed on the other side. "There must be hundreds of them out there," Ysabelle breathed. "Listen to their evil voices."

"Where is that barricade?" Fenny roared. "Hurry!"

The woodlanders hurried to the entrance, bearing chairs and tables in their arms, and stout beams were hauled out to brace against the heavy door.

Horrendous sounds of splintering wood filled the hall as the might of the unholy mob pushed against it. Inside, everyone waited, spears and swords poised in readiness, the foul shouts of the Hobb cult filling them with terror, for the whoops and shrieks called for death and promised murder.

Fenny turned again to Ysabelle and pointed to one of the tunnels that led from the hall. "Go quickly!" he cried above the din. "That way will lead you to the far side of the mound."

Suddenly, the earth trembled, and soil rattled down from the vaulted ceiling. All eyes gazed upward as a frenzied scrabbling noise rumbled above them.

"They are digging their way in!" someone wailed.

Fenny ran over to where Vesper stood with a knife in his grasp. "Moonrider!" he roared. "Take the maiden!"

Vesper took hold of Ysabelle's paw. "Fenny is right!" he yelled. "We must leave!"

"But Giraldus!" she protested, pulling away. "Help me with him!"

The bat glanced across to where the studded door was already buckling, while overhead the soil was raining down. "Come on!" he told the mole. "Hurry!"

"Please, Giraldus!" Ysabelle insisted. "You must come!"

The leper blinked and wearily shook his head. "I cannot," he murmured. "What use am I now? I want no life without my guide. Let me be. Let me die here!"

Vesper shook the mole harshly and shouted at him. "How dare you pity yourself!" he snapped. "Is that what Tysle would wish? Would you see all his hopes vanish because of your self-ishness? Stir yourself—he would not want you to perish here!"

Giraldus stared at him dumbly, then he rose and a spark of his old fire burned in his blind eyes. "Lead me," he said, holding out the string.

As the mound quaked and clouds of earth burst from above, Vesper took it and gave a solemn grin. "Forward, forward," he cried.

Ysabelle looked about them. "Wendel!" she called. "Wendel! Where are you?"

From out of the confusion, the jester came hurrying. A look of panic was on his face, and under his arm he carried a small black prop box.

"Mistress!" he whined. "We are beset by enemies, outside and in! What shall become of us?"

"Come with me," she told him. "Fenny has shown us a way of escape."

"Has he indeed?" the stoat muttered with the faintest of smirks upon his face. "Then most certainly will I join thee."

The mouse captain saluted as they raced for the tunnel. "May the Green guide you!" he called. "Let the Starwife reign once more!" Then, as his folk waited to face the enemy, he whirled around and shouted his name at the top of his voice.

Vesper pulled the mole down the passageway, and close on their heels came Ysabelle and Wendel. But before he entered, the stoat clawed a curious sign beneath the archway, and, with one final look at the woodlanders, he followed the others.

Behind him the hall shuddered as the soil gushed down. One of the pillars swayed and toppled, falling with horrible violence. Then, with a rending crash, the ceiling collapsed.

Into the ruined mound, the Children of the Raith Sidhe surged. Huge badgers scooped aside the earth they had gouged and came lurching among the woodlanders with their jaws snapping and claws outstretched.

"In the Ancient's name!" the woodland folk cried as the battle commenced. "Death to the Hobbers!"

Spears flew, plunging into the tough hides of the ferocious badgers, but the wounds only maddened the creatures, and many brave defenders fell before them.

Into the broken hill, more of the infernal black tide leaped, and their weapons came slicing through the choking air, ripping and tearing through fur and flesh.

Then, finally, the door burst asunder and the woodlanders were faced with foes on all sides.

At the front of his folk, the mouse captain wielded his sword, meeting all comers with a deadly sweep of steel. A long-fanged rat staggered back as Fenny thrust his blade into the creature's side; then a leering hedgehog sprang forward, holding a mace above its ugly head. Fenny jumped nimbly aside as the iron-spiked cudgel came crunching down and, with a swipe of his blade, lopped off the attacker's claws. Shrieking madly, the hedgehog fled, but in its agony the creature strayed into the path of the badgers and was instantly slain.

289

The folk of the mound fought valiantly; though the Hobbers raged and volleys of poisoned darts slaughtered many, they struggled courageously on. With their fearless captain at their head, they were prepared to do battle to the last, and his name was a rallying cry for them all.

"FENNY!" they roared. "FENNY!"

With the night airs flooding the open hall and the stars glittering high in the heavens, the battle thundered on, and the bloody heaps of dead swiftly mounted.

*　　*　　*

Running for their lives, the escaping travelers heard the roof cave in, and the tunnel in which they ran shook alarmingly.

"The Hobbers have broken through!" Ysabelle cried. "We must hurry."

Through dimly lit passageways they hurtled. Vesper directed Giraldus as best he could, and the mole lumbered along, paying no heed to the scrapes and cuts that grazed his stumbling steps.

With blood pounding in their veins, they heard the clashes of steel against steel as the uproar of the fighting and the yells of the invading hordes echoed throughout the underground.

Ysabelle tore after Vesper and Giraldus. To flee was her only instinct—to get out of this gloomy place and leave the savage Hobbers far behind.

The tunnel snaked in irregular twists deep into the earth, and, gradually, the sounds of the terrible battle grew fainter till they were only indistinct noises and muted vibrations on the still air.

Yet the group dared not slow down, and they continued to speed through the shadows until Ysabelle's heart missed a beat. The shrieks of the enemy were growing louder again.

"The Hobbers are pursuing!" she shouted to Vesper. "Can we not go faster?"

"I told you to leave me behind!" Giraldus boomed. "'Tis I

who impede your escape. Leave me now—go on. I shall follow as best I can."

"We shall leave no one!" Ysabelle told him. "Is that not so, Wendel?"

But no answer came from the stoat, and, when Ysabelle glanced over her shoulder, she found that the tunnel was deserted.

"Wendel!" she cried. "Vesper—the jester is missing!"

The bat brought Giraldus to a halt, and they turned to see what had happened.

"He must have stumbled and fallen," Vesper said. "Did you hear nothing? How far back can he be?"

Giraldus cocked his head to one side. "The children of Hobb are drawing near," he proclaimed. "We must find our companion quickly."

"Remain here," Vesper told them before scampering off—back the way they had come.

Turning a corner, the bat skidded and fluttered around before galloping back to the others.

"What is it?" Ysabelle asked. "Why have you returned?"

"Something approaches," he told her. "A hellish light is coming toward us. I did not wait to discover what it was."

"Hobbers!"

"It cannot be them—not so swiftly."

Even as he spoke, the passage grew brighter as a fiery orange glow spread over the walls and a hollow chuckle rang in their ears.

Two dazzling eyes that dripped with flame came blazing forward, and Ysabelle clutched Vesper for support as they beheld the bearer of the Hobb lantern.

With the evil, crackling torch in his fist, Wendel Maculatum strode closer. The murderous stoat had arrayed himself in the revolting mantle of the bloody-bones and, so skilled was the needlecraft, it was as if he had divested himself of his own outer layers of skin and fur. Now, bunched sinews of rippling flesh covered his shoulders, and loose tendrils of vermilion ribbon

291

dangled from his arms like strips of muscle. The gruesome illusion was aided by the hellish torchlight that played over the silken stitches until they glistened like dark veins in fresh, raw meat.

Beneath the ghastly mask, a malicious sneer disfigured the high priest's lips.

"At last, I have you," he gloated. "Alone, in the deeps of the world, you are mine."

"Wendel!" Ysabelle cried. "I–I don't understand."

The stoat laughed scornfully. "Most stupid of fools!" he spat. "How easy it has been for me–how simple thou made my work."

"But–but you saved me!" she protested. "From the bats–you protected me!"

"I saved the Acorn!" the bloody-bones retorted. "I did not want the forces of Hrethel to take it. The amulet I needed for my Lord." He slid a blood-stained knife from a gash in the false flesh and held it threateningly before Ysabelle's face.

"Now," he hissed, "your paltry life is ended."

Vesper put his wing about the squirrel, and his eyes flashed angrily at the evil stoat. "If you touch her, I will kill you!" he snapped.

At that, Wendel sniggered and produced his jester's headdress, shaking it at the bat until the bells jingled madly. "Remember thy doom, Moonrider!" he laughed menacingly. "Thou canst never escape it–I shall make sure of that. Whatever happens, a curse uttered by the high priest of the Infernal Triad will always seek out its prey."

"I have no fear of you now," Vesper told him. "You will not be able to kill us all."

"Ha, ha!" came the wicked reply. "I have no need to put myself at risk. Hearken to that stampede. That is the sound of my followers approaching–it is they who will kill you."

Furiously, Giraldus struck the wall with his fist and roared. "Then 'tis you!" he accused. "You were the one who butchered my Tysle!"

The high priest tittered. "Well," he taunted, "the little runt always did want me to carve him."

A horrible scream issued from the mole's throat, and the sound made Wendel jump back in amazement. Giraldus was filled with wrath, and he lunged forward with his staff. The lantern was knocked from the stoat's claw, and the mole's massive paws grabbed him by the neck, squeezing until Wendel's eyes bulged from their sockets.

"Let me go!" he rasped, fighting for breath.

"Giraldus!" cried Ysabelle. "Stop it!"

"Do not halt me in this!" he rumbled. "I will have the life of this heathen filth—I will be avenged for Tysle!"

Vesper tried to pull on the leper's arms, but Giraldus was strong, and his diseased muscles locked like iron.

The high priest's lips turned a deathly purple, and his struggles grew less as the seconds rolled by.

Then Ysabelle stared up the tunnel and yelled, "Giraldus, you must stop—the other Hobbers are almost upon us."

Harsh cries now blared all about them, and, in a matter of moments, the passage would be swamped by hundreds of Hobbers.

"This vile rogue will die before they arrive!" the mole roared.

But Ysabelle pleaded with him, and Giraldus threw the high priest to the ground in disgust.

"Quickly," she told Vesper, "help me remove the ghoulish vestments from him."

"To what purpose?" he cried.

"Just do it! There is but one meager chance!"

Hastily, they tore at the bloody-bones, dragging the crimson sinews from the stoat's body. Then, without hesitation, Ysabelle pulled the grisly raiment over her head and snatched up the Hobb lantern.

"What are you doing?" objected Vesper. "You cannot wear that! It is a symbol of horror and evil!"

"We have no choice!" she snapped. "Listen—they are almost here!"

The terrible clamor of the pursuing Hobbers raged furiously, and, pulling the hideous mask down over her face, Ysabelle hurried toward the approaching enemy.

At the leper's feet, Wendel stirred. In a temporary daze, he remained motionless, until the situation became clear to him and he realized what the squirrel was about to do. Grinding his teeth, he sprang after her, but Giraldus was ready and grabbed the stoat by the ears, clapping his paws roughly over the villain's mouth.

"Please," he whispered, "please do make a sound and try to warn those pagan scum, for then I shall gladly snap thy scrawny neck."

Wendel's eyes roved wildly up at the mole and knew that he spoke truly.

Down the passageway the surging mob came. Huge brown rats led them, and all carried Hobb lanterns in their claws. With bloodlust consuming each heart, they charged, eagerly following the scent that their high priest had put down for them. Then, in a tumbling mass of arms and blaspheming oaths, those at the front came to an abrupt halt.

Standing before them, with its claw raised, was the bloody-bones.

The rats slavered and sniffed. What was the high priest doing?

"Stop!" the macabre figure commanded as the foremost rat took a step closer.

The Hobber obeyed, but his eyes swiveled suspiciously, and a long, pointed tongue slid from his jaws to lick his snout. "What are thy orders?" it asked with a wheedle. "Why didst thou lead us down here—are there more dainties for our bellies?"

Behind him, another ugly rat brandished a sword and demanded the same. "We don't want to have missed all the fighting above fer nothing!" he snarled.

"Show us fresh meat; let us rend out gizzards and gut our foes till their livers squeak!"

The other Hobbers cheered their appreciation of that and gazed curiously at the silent bloody-bones.

Under the mask, beads of perspiration trickled down Ysabelle's brow as she sought for something to say to these nightmares. Staring out through the narrow slits of that vile mask was a horrendous experience, and all her instincts screamed at her to tear the infernal disguise off. Yet if she had done that, the Hobbers would have slaughtered her immediately.

"Go back!" she eventually cried in as deep a voice as she could manage. "Return to the upper levels!"

The rats stared at her dubiously. "Why did ye lay the trail if'n yer didn't want us?" one of them squawked.

"Dare you question the servant of the Lord Hobb?" Ysabelle declared. "Only to me are his dark designs revealed."

That cowed them, and the rats fell back, muttering to each other.

"Begone!" she said. "Go, I say!"

Grudgingly, the Hobbers turned and began to traipse up the tunnel, yet Ysabelle was not certain she had convinced them.

Taking a cautious step backward, she waited until the rats were out of sight, then spun round and fled.

"Hurry!" she told Vesper and Giraldus. "I feel sure they will return."

"What of this?" the mole asked, shaking the stoat in his paws as if he were a doll made of rags.

"He must accompany us," Vesper said. "We cannot leave him here. He would only run after his followers and bring them back again."

"He would find that an impossible task if he were dead," muttered Giraldus.

"Come," said Ysabelle. "Let us be gone."

So they set off down the passage, and, as she ran, Ysabelle

gladly tore the cadaverous disguise from her body. Giraldus bounded blindly along, dragging the high priest with him, and it did much to lighten the mole's spirits to know that the evil creature was in extreme discomfort.

"Quickly," Vesper urged, hopping around a sharp bend, "it cannot be far now."

They ran as fast as they could for some minutes, then the tunnel curved again, but when they turned the corner, Vesper cried out in dismay.

"It's blocked!" he howled. "The way is sealed—the roof has caved in here also."

Sure enough, directly in front of them, one of the tunnel's wooden support beams had splintered and now lay buried beneath a wall of soil. The rubble completely covered the path, and their escape was cut off.

"We are trapped!" uttered Ysabelle.

Wendel laughed at them. "Idiots!" he said with scorn. "Your paltry efforts have come to naught, and now mine followers shall hunt you down."

Giraldus gave the stoat a resounding slap, and one of Wendel's sharp teeth flew from his mouth. "Be silent," the mole told him. "I need to think and collect my bearings." Taking up the shreds of Tysle's lead string, he bound the high priest and thrust him roughly against the wall.

Behind them, another wooden beam gave an ominous creak, and loose soil trickled down from the sagging ceiling.

"Listen," breathed Vesper," the entire tunnel is on the verge of collapse."

"What can we do?" asked Ysabelle fretfully

Giraldus closed his eyes and stepped up to the wall of earth that barred their way.

"Hmmm," the leper murmured, his bandaged fingers playing over the immovable surface. "If mine wits are not addled, I would say that this barrier is only one spring worm in depth, and beyond it lies the outside world."

"Are you certain?" asked Vesper.

"Never doubt a mole beneath the ground, young batling!" he advised with a rumble. "Now, I think the time has at last arrived for one final excavation—stand back!"

"What of the roof?" Vesper persisted. "Will it hold, do you think?"

Giraldus ran his paws over the bulging ceiling of earth and tutted. "Not long do we have—the delicate balance of the warrens has been destroyed. I must work swiftly."

Using his considerable strength, the mole heaved on the buried beam and dragged it from the rubble. Then he wedged it beneath the remaining support and hoped the makeshift pillar would suffice until they were clear.

"Now," he said, "stand aside."

Blowing upon his leprous palms, the mole then spread his arms wide. "Forgive this thy servant," he muttered under his breath, "for he is a rash, loose-tongued old sinner. Yet give unto him one final ounce of strength that he may be the saving of his friends and fellow travelers."

Gritting his teeth, he dived at the soil.

Breathlessly, Ysabelle and Vesper watched as the mole shoveled heap after heap of earth from the path. For Giraldus, it was an agonizing time. As he delved and tore, tremendous pains rifled up his arms, and he was compelled to keep his jaws clenched to prevent himself crying out.

Swiftly, the tunnel began to clear, and, while they watched, no one paid any attention to the trussed and tied Wendel.

With his eyes fixed upon the laboring back of his immense guard, the stoat wriggled in his bonds and feverishly gnawed them with his teeth.

"Uuuurrggghh!" Giraldus cried as one of his fingers was torn from his paw. "A plague on this illness!"

Yet it did not stop him toiling, and suddenly a draft of cool night air blew into the passageway as he finally broke through.

But Wendel had also been successful. As soon as the last loop of the string broke in his jaws, he leaped away, yelling at the top of his voice.

"Children of the Raith Sidhe! 'Tis I, your high priest! Come—there are enemies here! I need your aid!"

Vesper pelted after the escaping stoat and flung himself upon Wendel's back. The two went tumbling down the tunnel, punching and kicking wildly, each desperate to restrain the other. The young bat fought as best he could, but he was no match for the high priest. His claws were vicious and sharp, and his limbs were lithe as any eel.

Pinning the Moonrider to the floor, Wendel reared his head and opened his savage maw to bite out his opponent's throat. But, just as the high priest came snapping for the exposed flesh, Giraldus lumbered up to them and yanked the stoat backward, leaving his teeth to clamp shut on empty air.

Vesper coughed, and Ysabelle helped him to his feet as deadly, answering shouts came echoing toward them. The Hobbers were already returning.

"Worms!" cackled the stoat. "You shall not leave this place alive!"

Giraldus slammed him against the wall, and, as the tunnel juddered threateningly, he turned to Ysabelle. "Take the batling and go!" he thundered. "The way is clear now! I shall not be detained long with this vermin."

The squirrel maiden dragged Vesper to the freshly dug exit, and, with a worried glance back at the leper, they quickly crawled through it.

Outside, the night was chill, and the frosty stars blazed white and cold overhead.

The clamor of the continuing battle drifted over the broken hill, and Ysabelle wondered how Fenny and the other woodlanders were faring. Surely, against the evil forces of the Hobb cult, they could not hope to succeed.

Quickly, she stared back into the tunnel—what was keeping Giraldus?

"Hurry!" she hissed.

But within the gloom of the passageway, with his arms tight about Wendel's struggling form, the mole merely bowed. "I shall not follow!" he said. "Not this time—Giraldus the pilgrim has a score to settle."

"Forget the high priest!" Vesper told him. "You belong with us!"

"Nay!" the mole protested. "I belonged with Tysle, and he is no more. Yet, who knows? Where the shrew led me I have always followed. Perhaps my faithful guide shall direct me one last time."

As Ysabelle and Vesper stared, he lifted the stoat into the air and cracked his head upon the earthen ceiling. Great fissures split the curving walls, and Wendel screamed, his claws raking the leper's face. But Giraldus felt nothing.

The high priest was flung to the ground, and, with a bellow of rage, the mole leaped on top of him, striking the evil creature with his massive fists.

This time it was Wendel who was outmatched, for Giraldus was bulky, and his muscles were powerful.

Beneath the leper's leaden weight, the high priest could do nothing, and blow after blow rained down upon his bruised and battered face.

Yet the stoat was sly and countered his assailant's strength with low cunning and agility. With the speed of a venomous serpent, Wendel's head twisted and turned, dodging most of the punches, then he snapped and bit hard on the leper's paw until blood flowed and a thumb was wrenched free.

Giraldus roared in agony, and the high priest wriggled beneath him, slithering to free himself.

Suddenly, he was on his feet again, and, as the mole

searched blindly for him, Wendel lashed out. A brutal kick fell in the mole's stomach, then another struck him on the side of the head.

Giraldus slumped against the wall, and Wendel gave a hideous, shrieking laugh, throwing dirt into his victim's face. As the leper spluttered, the stoat snatched up a splintered shard of wood and rammed it deep into his shoulder.

"Aaaarrrgghh!" Giraldus wailed, clutching the gushing wound.

Wended nipped around him, flinging stones at his enemy. Then he caught hold of a length of Tysle's string and wrapped it swiftly about the floundering pilgrim's throat.

"Now, blueskin!" he hissed malignantly, "feel thine own breath throttled from thy body." With a savage grunt, he heaved and twisted on the noose. Gasping, Giraldus tore at his neck where the cord bit deep into his skin.

Outside, Vesper and Ysabelle stared helplessly at the bitter duel.

"I'm going back in there!" the bat cried. "He needs help!"

"It's too late!" the squirrel wept. "Look!"

In the tunnel, Wendel crowed in triumph as the strangled mole fell limply to the floor.

"Giraldus!" Ysabelle sobbed.

"So does the Lord Hobb punish those who stand in his unholy way!" the high priest chuckled. He stared at the body of the mole for a moment, spat, then raised his face, his eyes glinting at Vesper and Ysabelle.

"My dearest friends," he sniggered, "where do you think you are going? You shall never escape me!"

And then the tunnel was filled with the uproar of his followers as they came pouring in, knives and spears flashing, all ready for murder.

Casually, Wendel lifted his claw and pointed through the opening. "Get you out there and kill them," he said softly.

With a terrible scream, the rats dashed forward. Yet, even as the stoat flung his head back to laugh, the eyes of Giraldus flickered open.

Feebly, the mole pulled the string from his crushed and bleeding throat and wound it secretly about the makeshift pillar that he had wedged beneath the remaining support beam. With a final look in Ysabelle's direction, his once resonant voice now croaked for the last time.

"Green be with you!" he called, and, summoning all his dwindling strength, he gave a tremendous heave.

Wendel's joyous laughter died on his lips as the pillar fell and his followers shrieked as they scrabbled for the exit. With a thunderous explosion of earth and stone, the wooden beam gave way, and the tunnel roof collapsed on top of them all.

Soil and dirt blasted outward, drowning the startled screams of the Hobbers and knocking Vesper and Ysabelle off their feet.

When they raised their heads, the side of the mound was a sagging heap of rubble, and not a trace of the mole's entrance could be found.

"Giraldus," Ysabelle murmured. "Oh, Vespertilio, they're all crushed under there, buried alive."

Vesper looked about them. "Come on," he said. "Giraldus did it so we could escape. Already, the curious are coming to investigate what has happened."

The night was filled with angry voices as patrolling Hobbers came scampering from the surrounding trees, their swords shining in the darkness. Ysabelle and Vesper bounded over the grass, but there was nowhere to run to.

"It's no use!" she cried, looking behind them to where fierce rats slid down the ruined mound. "They have us trapped."

Vesper knew she was right, and the enemy closed gleefully round them. "Quick," he cried, "hold on to me."

With a beat of his wings, the bat rose into the air, and, before Ysabelle could gasp her surprise, she had wrapped her arms about him and was lifted from the ground.

Up they flew, leaving the astonished rats to shout oaths and brandish their Hobb lanterns. Some tried to hurl their knives after them, but they all fell wide of the mark, and the Children of the Raith Sidhe tore at their ears and screeched in impotent fury.

Ysabelle and Vesper gave grateful sighs of relief as the bat veered over the forest, leaving the devastation of the mound far beneath them. Out under the glimmering heavens they flew, out to where the land of Greenreach rose steeply in the dim distance.

But the danger was not over, for as they soared above the treetops, Ysabelle could see a dark mass gathering behind them, and the night was filled with many desperate cawing calls.

"No," she breathed. "Vesper, you must hurry."

"What is it?" he cried, unable to turn around.

"The carrion birds," she answered.

Above the glare of the Hobb lanterns, hundreds of gore crows, ravens, jackdaws, and magpies were circling and shrieking. It was apparent that the rats were telling them what had happened, and, with a thrash of their ebony wings, the hellish birds tore through the night sky in wrathful pursuit.

AT THE KING OF TREES

Over the starlit forest, Vesper and Ysabelle flew. The bat furiously beat his wings, but his exertions were almost too much to bear.

"I cannot continue for much longer!" he cried. "My shoulder aches already!"

"You must!" the squirrel told him. "The crows are not far behind–they will tear us to pieces."

Vesper gazed at the dark shape of Greenreach ahead and knew that he could never reach it.

With her arms about his neck, Ysabelle saw the black clouds of carrion birds chasing them, but, with every sweep of his wings, she could sense how tired Vesper was becoming.

Gradually, the evil birds were gaining, advancing with every passing second, and their blood-curdling cries trumpeted across the starry heavens.

"Strike them down!" they shrieked. "Tear and rend with claw and beak!"

Despite his fear, Vesper's wings began to beat more slowly.

"Oh, please," Ysabelle cried, "just a little way more! If we could only reach the holy land!"

"I cannot!" he wailed. "The strain is too great. Forgive me, my princess, forgive me!"

With a sickening lurch, they toppled from the sky and spiraled downward. Swiftly, the forest rushed up to impale them upon bitter twigs and dash their bodies against its mighty boughs. But even as the new leaves brushed against the squirrel's tail, with a shout, Vesper caught a breeze in his leathery wings and skimmed shakily over the treetops before sweeping down between the branches.

Through the shadow-filled woods they unsteadily flitted until it seemed that the pursuing carrion birds had lost track of them beneath the screening trees.

No harsh, cawing voices could they hear, and, though they were both relieved, Vesper was exhausted.

We must alight," he panted. "I fear my damaged wing was not healed as much as I did think."

"But we are so near," Ysabelle urged. "Only a few leagues more, and we shall be there!"

The bat shook his head. "I wish I could," he lamented, "but I am no mighty Knight of the Moon, only a weanling. Oh, Ysabelle, to have failed here at the end—I am sorry."

She hugged him tightly. "Do not despair," she said. "We can complete the remainder on foot."

He managed a rueful grin, then, suddenly, from out of nowhere, a black shape dived through the leaves of a sycamore and raced straight for them. Before Vesper had a chance to act, the creature bore down on him; a gnarled talon flashed out and struck the bat across the face.

Emitting a frightened yell, Vesper plummeted down, spinning and tumbling out of control.

Ysabelle held on grimly, and, though he tried to regain his balance and mastery, there was nothing the bat could do.

The ground raced up to them, and they crashed with a sickening thud.

Ysabelle rolled helplessly down the sloping lawns, but Vesper crumpled into a fearful heap of wing and fur and lay still as death.

The cold, crackling voice of the crow rang overhead as it fluttered in a wide circle, delighted at the violence it had wrought. Then, with one red-rimmed eye trained upon the corpse-like figure of the bat, it spread its feathers and descended.

"Victuals," it cawed, "sticky treats for me. The others won't get none. They didn't spy the beasts below the trees. Only I did that, and I shan't open my beak to tell them, oh, no."

Hovering above Vesper, it reached out with a scaly claw and tentatively turned him over. The bat made no resistance and lolled limply to one side.

"Hoo, hoo," squawked the fiendish bird, "the nasty dizzard is dead. Ooh, delicious corpse flesh! Shall I peck out the eyes first, or guzzle the entrails?"

It landed on top of Vesper, and its midnight feathers smothered his face. With its cruel talons stretched wide, the crow pinned the motionless form to the ground and stared covetously at its catch, musing on where to begin.

"Entrails," it decided greedily. "No, no, too hasty, too hasty! Sup first on the heart's blood—that rich, heady mead—and carouse a while in the sweet darkness."

Plunging its head down, the bird shoved its sharpened beak onto Vesper's chest and tore out a mouthful of fur, which it spat distastefully upon the ground. Then it lunged forward a second time, only now to pierce the plucked skin and suck up the young bat's blood.

Without warning, a wild creature darted from the shadows, and fierce paws gripped the crow's tail feathers, tearing the quills out by the roots.

"Get away from him, you foul Hobber!" came a fearless voice.

The bird screeched in pain as it whirled round to face its attacker, but a fallen branch came swinging toward it and struck the crow across the back.

Flapping its wings in terror, it twisted and swiveled its sleek head, yet the insane nightmare was too quick. Again, the brandished branch was singing through the darkness, this time hitting the bird's beak, which gave a horrible crack and broke as easily as an eggshell.

"Aaaaaiiyyeee!" it screamed, feathers flying all around. "Aaaaaiiyyeee!"

Reeling backward, it staggered from Vesper's body, and, with blood pouring from its wounded face, took to the air in blind fear.

Ysabelle did not wait to watch it soar from sight. Throwing down the branch, she raced to Vesper's side and cradled his head in her paws.

"Vespertilio!" she called, "Vespertilio!"

The young bat made no answer, and, with trembling fingers, she touched the bald patch upon his chest.

"Green be praised," she whispered, for there she had felt a faint heartbeat.

Tenderly, she brushed the fringe from his brow and examined the bloody rents that the crow's claws had ripped into his face.

A terrible feeling of despair overwhelmed her. Was this the end? Had they come all this way and through so many dangers for it to finish so bleakly?

For some time, Ysabelle knelt at Vesper's side, holding his head and repeating his name, but only the sounds of the still night filled her ears, and an unhappy tear rolled down her cheek.

Now was the time for grief; all the sorrow she had kept hidden flowed from the maiden unchecked. Never had she thought that such a ravening emotion could so utterly consume her. Unrelenting and unquenchable sobs seized her absolutely, and they pulsed through the forest, beating out a mournful lament on the night air.

For many days now she had tried to be strong. Since the Acorn had come to her, Ysabelle had striven to do her duty with honor and in a manner befitting one of royal blood. At that moment, however, she felt woefully small and unsuited to the vast and mighty office the amulet had bestowed on her. There, in the dark woods, she was simply a girl, and the awful majesty of the life she had accepted seemed a whole world away.

Beneath the unlit and shadow-enshrouded trees, something heard her plaintive weeping. It was cloaked all in black and seemed to be a part of the darkness itself, a part that had been given tangible form and substance and that now moved stealthily toward the unsuspecting squirrel maiden and her unconscious beloved.

A deep hood covered the face of the stranger, but within its void two eyes regarded the forlorn Ysabelle as she continued to pour out her grief. Countless tears fell on the ground, glimmering briefly in the cold light of the stars above.

Closer to her the tall figure was drawn, making no noise as it drifted through the grass. Ripples of darkness curled about the folds of its cloak as it moved, and waves of shadow spread in every direction.

Not until the cloaked stranger was dangerously near did Ysabelle notice it. With a start, she looked up to find the mysterious newcomer standing almost by her side. Fearfully, she searched for the fallen branch, but the weapon was out of reach.

Wild thoughts crowded into her mind: the figure was like the fanciful descriptions of Death, and she clung to Vesper more desperately than ever.

The hooded form made no further move, content for the moment merely to watch the maiden a little longer. Yet the still silence made it seem all the more sinister, and Ysabelle felt as though she had at last encountered a foe from whom there was no escaping.

"Have you not gathered enough this night?" she cried. "First Tysle, then Giraldus! How many more of the righteous must you collect? What of the enemy—why do you not harvest from their number?"

The stranger took a step closer, and at last it spoke. "A strange spectacle is this," came a sharp and bitter voice. "What sign or wonder have I discovered in the haunted realm of night?"

Ysabelle held Vesper tightly as the cloaked form glided toward them with one paw outstretched.

"Keep thy distance," she warned.

307

Gentle laughter issued from the depths of the all-concealing hood. "I mean you no harm," said the voice. "I was simply trying to ascertain whether you were real or no. Unearthly visions have mocked me before now. Are you two phantoms sent to cheat my senses?"

The squirrel drew away from the reaching fingers as they tried to touch her.

"I am no spirit!" she insisted–then remembered when she had said that before, and to whom. "Who–who are you?" she stammered. "It cannot be! Wendel–is it you come back from the grave?"

The figure lowered its arm and drew itself up. "Neither of us is certain," it said, "what tricks the misery of life can play–I see that you have much sorrow behind you."

"In front of me also," Ysabelle replied.

The cloaked stranger regarded her for a moment, then stooped over Vesper.

"Thy companion is injured," it said. "He must receive help if he is to live."

Ysabelle stared aghast at the bat and turned pleadingly to the newcomer. "Oh, please," she cried, "whatever you are, whether a shade of the unhappy dead or no, will you not aid me?"

"You beg me to help you?" the voice echoed. "Then I would also be assisting a Knight of the Moon."

Ysabelle frowned, and, as she watched, the stranger slowly drew the hood from its head.

"You–you are a squirrel!" she spluttered, overjoyed beyond belief.

"Thus do you see my dilemma," returned the other. "Are not the Moonriders our despised enemies? So, when I came across thee, I did greatly wonder. A maiden of my own race, nursing one of those accursed rats with wings!"

"You do not understand!" Ysabelle told her. "You cannot know what has passed between us and what we have learned. Please, it there anything you can do for him?"

The cloaked squirrel glanced up the sloping lawns, and the white starlight shone over her gaunt face, glinting in the silver circlet she wore on her brow. "It is dangerous to remain here," she said in a hushed whisper. "If we are caught, they will punish us. You crave the bat to be attended to, then we must go now."

"Wait," Ysabelle called. "I do not understand. Where are we? What help is there—who are you afraid of? Is it the Hobbers?"

"So many questions," said the other, peering nervously into the dim shadows around them. "Did you not know that you lie at the foot of the slope of Greenreach?"

"The holy land!" Ysabelle marveled. "But that is excellent tidings!"

She caught her breath as the enormity of what lay ahead dawned. It was almost over—all the suffering and terror was nearly at an end. The maiden could hardly believe it; this was the time she had anticipated and blindly looked forward to since the fall of the Hazel Realm, yet now that she had arrived, many unexpected fears reared to trouble her.

The time had finally come when she would have to accept the full power of the Starwife. No longer could she be just Ysabelle. Now she had a land to govern and all the daunting responsibilities that that entailed. The liberty she had experienced since the night she had escaped from the Ring of Banbha seemed to vanish. She was left stripped of her freedom, and only long years of a lonely reign stretched out before her.

Lowering her head, she gazed sadly at the bat and slowly stroked his hair. "Oh, Vespertilio," she called to him, "most courageous of Moonriders, you did make it to the holy land after all. We did cheat the Hobbers."

"I know not why you speak of childhood ogres," the standing figure announced. "Only one enemy do we have. The forces of Hrethel have conquered this place and encamp about its border, keeping a close watch on all who come and go. They are as yet ignorant of the secret ways that are known to only me, and I have roamed quite freely these past days in the hope of finding help. Yet all my hopes have proven vain. No aid is there, and Hrethel will remain victorious."

As Ysabelle listened, she felt her terrible destiny bind her tightly. The time had come; she must disclose her identity to this squirrel. It was her solemn duty to complete the mission her mother had entrusted to her.

Resting Vesper's head upon the grass, she rose from her knees. "Do not despair," she said grimly, "help has indeed come at last, for I bear with me that which has imbued the Handmaidens of Orion with majesty and might from the dawn of days." Gingerly, she lifted the Silver Acorn, and immediately the stranger gasped.

"The amulet of the Starwives!" she breathed in reverence. "Hope beyond all reason and daring has come to us! We did think the device lost—what chance brought it into thy keeping?"

"The Acorn came to me by the strangest means," the maiden told her. "A falcon had possession of it, bearing it no doubt from the wreck of this land. Yet the legions of Hrethel did kill the messenger in the sky, and so the Silver fell into my own paws."

The other squirrel curtsied humbly. "Then truly art thou the chosen one," she declared. "The successor has been decided by greater councils than ours. You are now my sovereign, and I rejoice to be the first to bow to thee, my lady." She stared excitedly, then seemed to be in perplexed embarrassment. "But forgive me," she ventured. "May I know the name of my new mistress?"

"I am Ysabelle, daughter of Ninnia and last of that royal house."

"You must take the amulet to the Starglass at once!" the cloaked figure said. "Only then can you rid the land of the Moonriders."

"What about Vespertilio?" Ysabelle asked. "I cannot leave him here!"

"Does the Hazel Realm love the company of bats so much that it would see the downfall of us all?"

Ysabelle knelt beside him one again. "I shall not leave him," she said flatly.

"This is madness! Neither you nor I can carry your companion so far up the hillside; here he must remain! At least for a little while. As soon as we reach the Hallowed Oak, I shall dispatch a sentry to fetch him."

"The oak still stands?" asked Ysabelle. "I did think the forces of Hrethel would have reckoned its destruction uppermost in their designs."

"Stand it does," returned the other, "and there are still a few like myself whom the bats did not slaughter. Do you not see how urgent is the need for you to come with me? Please, my lady! Too long has this realm been without a Starwife. Think of thy subjects and the holy destiny that awaits thee. If you are in truth the daughter of Ninnia the Wise, you must see where your duty lies."

Ysabelle was confused. Her heart demanded that she remain, but her reason reproached her for abandoning her mission. She did not know what to do. Surely it was best to watch over Vesper?

"Yet that time could be better spent taking the amulet to the Starglass," she told herself. "What comfort can you give him if the world is plunged into the despair the Ancient predicted?"

"My lady?" implored the squirrel beside her.

Ysabelle nodded. "You are right," she said. "Fates other than his and mine are depending on me. I will go to the Starglass." But before she set off, the squirrel maiden kissed Vesper's forehead, then hid him beneath a covering of leaves. "It will not be long," she vowed. "I will return for thee."

"Hurry!" insisted the stranger. "Let us ascend the hill as fast as we may." She swirled the cloak about her and began walking briskly back into the shadows.

With a last, lingering look at Vesper's concealed form, Ysabelle caught up with her. "Good friend," she said, "may I presume upon thee to learn how thou are named?"

The other pulled the hood over her face once more. "Call me Morwenna," came the short reply.

*   *   *

And so Ysabelle was parted from Vesper, and she melted into the darkness on the slopes of Greenreach.

For some distance the ground rose in a gentle incline, but beyond the crowding trees, Ysabelle could sense some vast, brooding shape looming before her. Then the land lifted sharply, and the shoulders of the blessed hill climbed steeply beneath her feet.

It was not long before she became aware of the devastation the Moonriders had brought about. At first, Ysabelle's nostrils tingled with the acrid reek of burned timber and she could taste a bitter tang on the cold air. As she followed the cloaked and silent figure before her, she noticed the grass she walked on was withered and brittle, as though scorched by fierce heats. Presently, the undergrowth disappeared completely, and bare soil took its place.

Morwenna seemed to disregard all need for secrecy and marched up the hillside quite openly. Ysabelle found this alarming; surely they ought to be seeking cover? Upon that naked hillside, she felt increasingly aware that anything could see them, and she craned her neck to stare at the open sky above. The fear that either a gore crow or a Knight of the Moon would come swooping down was constantly with her, and she found her new companion's brazenness impossible to understand.

The trees that now reared on either side of her were blackened and dead. Charred specters of once glorious birches and hornbeams raked the sky with ugly stumps, and the only foliage that bloomed upon their ghastly branches were ragged leaves of ash.

Ysabelle was shocked at the extent of the destruction. Surely no mortal creature could have so afflicted nature's work. It was as if the sun itself had visited the hill with a tremendous fireball, for nothing living remained. No blade of grass, no green shoot, and no spring bud had survived; all was lifeless, and the earth had crackled into soot and cinders.

It was the most desolate landscape imaginable, a glimpse of Hades and the mournful ravages of the Pit.

"It is a nightmare we walk into," she said to Morwenna. "How dismal and grim a place this is."

The hood turned to her. "Yes," she replied, "the fire eggs were most efficient. Their targets blazed for two whole days, and the pall of black smoke could be seen for many leagues. All of the sacred groves were utterly consumed and are now tangles of charcoal that crumble before the slightest breeze."

She paused and pointed to a dark mass of withered boughs. "Once, that coppice was the fairest place in all Greenreach," she lamented. "There, the virtuous blossom lingered on the bough throughout the seasons, and the enchanted fragrance was stronger than wine to the senses.

"Now the land is a grievous desolation," she said, drawing the cloak about her and resuming the climb. "An abode only of ghosts and memories too painful to rake from the ashes."

Ysabelle clasped the Silver Acorn in her paw. "Can even this possess the strength to heal it?" she asked.

"It must," Morwenna told her. "The amulet is more powerful than perhaps you realize."

Ysabelle thought she detected a curious edge in the cloaked squirrel's voice but could not understand what lay behind it, and they trudged on in silence.

The barren, blasted hill continued to tower into the heavens, and Ysabelle grew more uneasy the further she ascended. That familiar feeling of being watched prickled the nape of her neck, and she stared into the shadows around her. But the darkness pressed too heavily upon the holy land, and her eyes could see nothing.

Morwenna observed her disquiet. "Is aught amiss, my lady?" she murmured.

"I do not know," said Ysabelle, "yet I feel as though we are under the scrutiny of many eyes."

"Perhaps it is the ghosts I spoke of," came the reply. "Green alone knows how many perished in the flames."

The cindered soil under their feet was warm and smoldering now. From gaping cracks in the ground, trails of smoke curled slowly into the night. Absently, Ysabelle followed the winding course of one smoky thread, and a cry of horror issued from her lips.

"In the trees!" she gasped. "Look!"

Silhouetted against the stars, the spindly frames of the blasted trees could be clearly discerned. Yet among the clumps of ash that draped across the blackened boughs like tattered war banners, small figures crouched and glared down.

"Bats!" Ysabelle breathed. "There are hundreds—no, thousands—of bats, all around us!"

Morwenna pulled her close. "Be silent, my lady!" she hissed in her ear. "The forces of Hrethel might not harm us. Come quickly."

She compelled Ysabelle to hurry, yet the squirrel maiden could not take her eyes off the countless Moonriders who returned her gaze without stirring from their perches.

"I do not understand!" she muttered. "Why are they letting us continue? Why have they not attacked?"

"It is better not to question such good fortune," came the fretful reply. "Let us pray we reach the Hallowed Oak in safety."

Ysabelle wished she had obeyed the instincts of her heart and stayed behind with Vesper. This was complete and utter madness; they were marching deeper into the enemy's territory—but why?

"I beseech you to trust me," Morwenna muttered. "This is the only route–I swear."

Through a pool of cold, feathery ash she led the maiden, and the summit of the hill drew near. Breathless, Ysabelle longed to turn and flee, but she knew that was impossible now–it was too late to go back. Although the bats had allowed them to come this far, she knew that as soon as she tried to retrace her steps, they would rise from the trees and attack.

"My lady," Morwenna's voice interrupted her chaotic thoughts, "behold!"

She lifted her paw, and, in spite of her fears, Ysabelle stared at the wondrous spectacle that reared before her.

There, within a ring of charcoal twigs, was a magnificent and astounding spectacle. Upon the top of the blessed hill rose a flourishing oak tree, the like of which she had never seen before. It was twice the height of the central oak in Coll Regalis, and its girth was five times as wide. Amid all the scorched and cindered waste it soared into the sky, like a flame of hope besieged by fear and despair.

Ysabelle could not believe her eyes, yet the constant dread of the watchful enemy made it impossible for her to feel any relief at the sight. The hope that she could fulfill her mission flickered briefly in her breast, but one glance at the glaring Moonriders made her doubt they would ever reach that king among trees.

"It's beautiful," she said. "Yet how did it escape the flames?"

"Rohgar thought it prudent to leave well alone," Morwenna replied in a low whisper. "Even he dares not challenge the ancient powers that are twined about the holiest of oaks. It would take a force greater than his winged rabble to harm it."

"And the Starglass is still in there?" Ysabelle asked uncertainly.

"It is. The Moonriders are fearful to even tread within the oak; they have not ventured to assail the royal chambers or take the Starglass by force."

Ysabelle peered up at the tree's graceful and stately branches. It was like a fountain of crystal-clear water that spouted magically in a parched desert.

Her excitement dwindled as she saw many Knights of the Moon on guard around the trunk of the Hallowed Oak, standing sternly about small campfires. Screechmasks covered their heads, and armored gauntlets were upon their feet. Ysabelle feared those creatures more than she dared to admit, and she found that strange, for were they not of the same race as Vesper? It was a confusing and unwelcome thought, and she thrust it to the back of her mind, focusing on the present situation alone.

"Are you certain all will be well?" she asked nervously. "Will those guards not challenge us? How shall we pass through their ranks?"

"Do not concern thyself with them, my lady," said Morwenna, trying to conceal a tremor in her voice. "Remain here; I shall speak to their general."

"But what will you say?" Ysabelle demanded. "Why have they allowed us to come this far without attacking? It is as if they expected my arrival. There is much you have not explained: did they send you to bring me here? What dreadful hold do they have over you?"

Morwenna cast back her hood, and her face seemed anxious. "Calm thyself, my lady," she said, biting her lip. "I intend to answer all thy questions, yet this is not the time. Wait until we gain the safety of the oak—then we may talk freely. Oh, if we can but close the doors behind us!" She pressed her paw to her forehead as if she was about to faint, and Ysabelle reached out to support her.

"What have they done to you?" she asked. "Is it so appalling you may not speak of it? Let me help you if I can."

Morwenna thanked her but added, "Only once we are inside can you know my woe."

With that, she strode over to the ferocious-looking enemy, leaving Ysabelle to wait in uncomfortable silence. Standing, awkward and greatly ill at ease, she saw Morwenna greet the largest of the Moonriders, yet she could not catch what words passed between them.

The frightful and repulsive war helmet of the general turned and stared across at the maiden, who at once felt the hostility and malice flow out from the narrow eye slits.

Ysabelle's face clouded over as doubt and foreboding filled her. She grew certain that this was an elaborate trap and that the unfortunate Morwenna had been used by the bats to lure her into it. Oh, how she longed to be far from this horrible place!

In spite of herself, she gave a small laugh. "To think," she murmured, "that the destination I had been so anxious to reach should prove to be the one place I have no desire to be."

Her ironic musings were soon dispelled, for Morwenna was already returning.

"Most excellent news," she said. "I have persuaded them to let you pass inside the oak."

Ysabelle shook her head. "Would you truly lead me farther into the jaws of the enemy?" she asked. "They must have threatened you most cruelly."

Morwenna turned pale. "Please," she sobbed, "I cannot talk of that. Oh, my lady, if you care for the lives of we who are left, you will follow me." She glanced over her shoulder and shivered. "Beware," she whispered. "Rohgar watches us; he must not suspect you are wise to the danger."

Ysabelle closed her eyes. "What a fool I have been," she berated herself.

"Perhaps not," the other said quickly. "There is still a way to outwit them. The Starglass can still be reached if we are cunning enough."

The maiden sighed resignedly, not daring to hope anymore, yet what else could she do? "Very well," she murmured. "Guide me to the oak; complete the plan of the Moonriders."

317

A grateful smile flashed over Morwenna's wedge-shaped face. "Oh, thank you, my lady," she said, "and when we are within, I shall speak to my sentries. They will seek out thy injured companion."

"Then let us be swift—you did say that Vespertilio might not survive!"

Morwenna showed her teeth as she grinned again. "Perchance I was a little hasty in the diagnosis," her syrupy voice admitted. "A few minutes more will do no harm to him, I am sure."

Taking the maiden by the paw, Morwenna walked quickly over the soot-covered ground to where the guards stood in rank upon rank of glittering armor.

Each screechmask turned toward Ysabelle as she approached, and she was horrified to be so close to them. The bats shuffled on their gauntleted feet and cleared a path through their number straight to the entrance of the immense tree.

Within the eye slits of the hideous helmets, the Knights of the Moon glared at their reviled enemy. Here at last was the one they had so desperately been seeking, and their gaze burned on the blood-tarnished amulet about her neck.

One of the older creatures moved without warning, shifting his weight and gouging the cinders with is steel talons as the two squirrels passed. Ysabelle winced and stared at him warily. The force of the Moonrider's hatred blazed in his eyes, and, for an instant, she thought he would lash out at her.

Through the remaining groups of guards they went. The crackling flames of the campfires danced over the screechmasks and lent them a semblance of life so that a host of gibbering demons seemed to surround the two squirrels.

By the time Ysabelle was taken to the great entrance, her nerves were overwrought; this was all wrong. She glanced upward at the oak, which now towered over her, and so high did it stretch that Ysabelle felt like an ant at the feet of a giant. This mighty tree was part of her holy inheritance, yet remembering that did little to ease her fears. With her head thrown back to glimpse its topmost branches, the wild thought came to her that the oak would come toppling down and smash her into the earth. Ysabelle felt her knees buckle, and her head began to swim.

"Come, my lady," Morwenna urged, and the harshness of her voice was like a slap to Ysabelle's senses.

In front of them, an ornately carved doorway reared: its handles were of gold, inlaid with silver, and fashioned in the shape of stars. Morwenna placed her paw upon one of them and pushed.

The door swung open, and Ysabelle found herself standing in the grand hall. It was completely deserted, and the sound of their footfalls echoed grimly around them. In other circumstances, the maiden would have admired the beautifully decorated chamber, but her predicament allowed for only two emotions—fear and dread.

Silently, Morwenna closed the door behind them, and her gaunt face was wreathed in a most unpleasant smile.

"Unbounded was the craft and skill of our folk," she declared, indicating the carved walls. "Now, all this is thine, my lady."

Ysabelle looked at her desperately. "Summon thy sentries!" she said at once. "Before I am taken and tortured by the waiting bats, send them for Vespertilio!"

"Tortured?" uttered Morwenna in surprise. "There shall be none of that. No bats will harm thee here, my lady. Did I not say that they dare not enter the Hallowed Oak?"

"Is this not a trap of their devising?" the maiden mumbled.

"Most assuredly not. Why didst thou think I would take part in such a base deception?"

"But outside, you did lead me to believe it was so."

"I think thy fancy hath got the better of thee," Morwenna said. "But ought we not repair at once to the Chamber of the Starglass?"

Ysabelle looked at her curiously. If she had been wrong about the trap, and she sincerely doubted that, her arrival here had been far too easy. "No," she said cautiously, "call the sentries before we proceed any further. I am worried for my friend."

"But mistress," the other replied, "at present they are all stationed with the Starglass, and through the thickness of the chamber door, I have little chance of being heard, no matter how hard I try."

Ysabelle relented, although a dreadful suspicion began to dawn. "Very well," she said. "Take me there."

"This way," Morwenna replied, striding to the far left of the grand hall. "The chamber lies through here."

Ysabelle collected her wits and resolved to discover what strange game Morwenna was playing with her. Warily, she looked through the archway that the other indicated. "It is a flight of stairs," she said in mild surprise. "They lead downward, yet I thought the chamber would be above the ground, not below."

"Ah," muttered Morwenna, "it was, but I did instruct the sentries to bear the holy Starglass to the fastness of the tree's root chambers for safety's sake."

She began to descend, the hem of her cloak brushing the steps behind her. Ysabelle found Morwenna's explanation difficult to believe, and her suspicions grew stronger within her.

Cautiously, the maiden crept after, aware that she was walking into danger, yet how else was she to discover the truth?

"Tell me, my Lady Morwenna," she said as they descended the winding stairway, "what happened that night when the Moonriders attacked?"

"Did I not already state that the fire eggs were most cruelly efficient?"

"You misunderstand," Ysabelle interrupted. "What I should like to learn is how the attack was possible? What happened to the defenses woven by the last Starwife?"

"Ah," the other sighed mildly and without a hint of remorse or regret, "my poor former mistress. She had been so very ill for such a long time. Very old and frail was she, and, when the Knights of the Moon invaded, it proved too much."

"But how were they able to invade?"

They had reached the foot of the steps, and, taking up a candle staff, Morwenna lit it from a lantern flame.

"Henceforth we must descend into the grottoes beneath the oak," she told Ysabelle. "That is where I did think the Starglass would be most secure."

Unlocking a small door, she passed inside a dry, earthen tunnel, and, with a last, nervous look around her, Ysabelle went in after.

The guttering candlelight sent their shadows dancing around the narrow way, and Ysabelle's unease mounted. From the legends she had heard about the Starglass, it was too large to have been carried down here. Morwenna was leading her to some unknown destination for reasons and motives all her own. Ysabelle tried to calm her fraught nerves; that dissembling squirrel possessed the answers to all that had happened, and she determined to discover what she could.

"You did not answer my question," she said.

The Lady Morwenna turned her most servile and fawning face upon her. "How can I know such things," she declared, "when even my mistress was at a loss to explain it? The mystery still remains. Perhaps the power of the Starglass was waning as the old Starwife died? Who can truly say?"

"My mother thought it was traitor's work," Ysabelle pressed daringly. "Would you know aught of that?"

The implied accusation seemed to wash over Morwenna completely. "No doubt your mother was wise in many ways," she replied blithely, "yet I fear her much-vaunted and doubtless exaggerated wisdom was at fault touching this."

"I think not; never have I known my mother to be wrong."

"Have a care!" Morwenna said abruptly.

Ysabelle caught her breath—had she gone too far? Was the other squirrel threatening her?

Yet when Morwenna turned, that ingratiating smile was still fixed to her face. "You must tread with caution," she explained. "The passage here becomes dank, and mud covers the pathway."

From then on, Ysabelle was forced to keep a close eye on the ground. It was not easy, for Morwenna's candle failed to illuminate the squelching road, yet the other squirrel hardly seemed to need its light. Hurrying swiftly ahead of the maiden, she ducked beneath curtains of fibrous roots before they were even caught by the feeble flame.

Ysabelle knew that she had made a grave mistake coming down here, but she could not turn back now, for the blackness behind was absolute, and, when she glanced over her shoulder, it was like looking down the throat of some immense fiend of darkness that was ever trying to swallow her.

"My Lady Morwenna," she called to the receding figure, "was it really wise to bring the Starglass down this far?"

A mocking chuckle came back to her, and Ysabelle wished she still possessed the knife of the high priest.

"Not far now," Morwenna's voice assured her. "The chamber is very close."

Ysabelle drew a paw over her forehead. What had she done? She had been fool enough to follow this deceitful creature and had become utterly ensnared by her lies, abandoning Vesper to the perils of the wild night. The maiden was furious with herself; here, at the very end of her journey, she had been tricked.

"Here our descent finishes," said Morwenna, coming to an abrupt standstill and flourishing the candle before a low doorway. From a belt around her waist, she took a ring of keys and fitted one inside the lock. The moldering door creaked open, and she stepped inside.

"Enter, O Starwife," she hissed.

Ysabelle's scalp crawled. The chamber beyond was pitch dark, yet a damp, stale smell flowed from it, and, for a moment, she was beside the haunted mere once more.

"I cannot go in there," she said.

"But you must," Morwenna insisted, beckoning with a finger that ended in a long, curved claw.

Ysabelle took a step backward. "No sign of the Starglass can I see," she muttered, "nor the sentries. Where are they?"

"Oh, they are here," the other said with a faint snarl purring in the back of her throat. "Come and see. Tell them of thy stricken friend."

"Where have you brought me?" the maiden asked, staring fearfully into Morwenna's heavily lidded eyes.

"To a most lovely corner of the realm," came the chilling response. "This is where the survivors of the Moonriders' assault were brought, and where you can at last greet thy new subjects."

Ysabelle was breathing hard now. She knew it would be madness to step over the threshold of that vile chamber. There was something unclean and terrifying about the impenetrable blackness that seemed to seethe and swirl beyond the candle flame.

"Do not keep me waiting," came Morwenna's cruel voice. "Do you not wish for the Starwife to accede to the throne?"

The way she said it left Ysabelle in no doubt exactly whom she meant.

"You betrayed them, didn't you?" she said. "You were the one!"

Morwenna stepped back through the doorway, and Ysabelle pulled away from her. "Oh, the poor little maiden is affrighted!" she declared with feigned concern. "Come, take my paw, let me guide you inside."

"How did you break the defenses?" Ysabelle cried. "What evil arts caused the Starglass to fail?"

A light, careless laugh broke from Morwenna's thin mouth. "Such fancies," she sighed. "Here am I, doing my utmost to help you, and all you can do in return is lay such callous treacheries upon me."

She took a step nearer, and Ysabelle stumbled out of reach. "What did Hrethel promise you?" she asked. "What possible rewards could justify such abominable treason?"

"Hrethel?" echoed Morwenna innocently. "You think I labored all those detestable and loathsome years simply for the benefit of that wizened bat?" Her voice rose until it became a shriek, and she pounded the candle staff on the ground in anger, finally casting aside the last vestiges of pretense.

"He and his wretched forces were simply my instruments!" she snorted. "And how well I used them, how easily were they deceived by my great art and their own lusts. Didst thou really think I brought about the ruin of Greenreach merely for them? Soon they shall be swept aside and perish in the eternal fires!"

Ysabelle shuddered at the sound of that voice. It was totally consumed by evil, and she continued to retrace her steps backward. "Then why did you do this?" she cried.

Morwenna's eyes threw back the light of the candle and came stabbing through the darkness at her. "I did it for my Lord!" she proclaimed. "I did it for He who was unjustly banished from this world by those who usurped Him. Now that mighty majesty shall come forth and govern a new darkness, every creature will worship Him, and despair reign over all."

"Hobb!" Ysabelle murmured. "You are a worshipper of Hobb!"

Morwenna faltered, and a curious expression crossed her face. In one quick movement, she removed the circlet of silver from her brow and held the candle near so that the maiden could see. There, upon her forehead, was a tattooed image of a staring eye.

"I am the priestess of Mabb!" she spat. "When my Lord emerges from the imperishable darkness, He shall release my true mistress from her long imprisonment, and I shall serve them both!"

"You are insane!" Ysabelle yelled.

"Oh, no," the other replied softly. "My mind is clear–I know precisely what I am doing." She stepped closer, and her paw stretched out. "Such a pity about the high priest," she muttered, "yet Wendel was always rash. He will not be missed—another will rise to take his place. I congratulate you on the good fortune that has followed you from your squalid homeland; many times have you confounded my designs, yet no more, alas. Here I command, and thy fate is sealed."

Swiftly, she snatched Ysabelle by the hair, and the maiden screamed in pain and terror, trying to pry away the claws, but Morwenna's grip was tenacious and strong. Desperately, Ysabelle lashed out and struck her across the face.

The priestess fell back, outraged and astonished at the ferocity of the blow.

"How dare you!" she screeched. "How dare you raise a paw to me!" Bristling with graceless indignation, she shoved Ysabelle against the wall and tightly twisted her claws in the long tresses. "Too many drab, dreary years have I toiled in the service of others to let my plans slip now. Did you really think a paltry beggar from the crude, peasant-filled waste of the Hazel could replace me?"

She gave the tangled locks a vicious tug until tears sprang from Ysabelle's eyes, then her fingers closed around the Silver Acorn, and she pulled it viciously from her neck.

"No!" wailed Ysabelle. "You cannot take that! It belongs to me!"

Morwenna cackled. "The amulet is mine!" she hissed. "There shall be no Starwife but me!"

Clenching the Acorn in her claw, she dragged Ysabelle toward the dank chamber and shrieked, "The time has come for my darlings to feed!"

Fiercely, she hauled Ysabelle into the dismal grotto, then gave her a rough push that sent her slithering over the muddy ground.

"Come, my pretty ones!" Morwenna crooned, holding the candle high above her head. "See what new morsel I bring!"

Ysabelle stared about her, expecting the shadows to be filled with hellish rats with knives and cudgels in their fists, but there was nothing, and all that happened was a distant gurgle that issued from the far darkness. Morwenna gave a satisfied smile, then strode to the rocky wall and lit a torch mounted there.

It spluttered into flame, and, by its greater light, Ysabelle could see that she stood upon a slimy shore that dipped into oily black water—yet upon that slippery bank, she saw a sight that churned her stomach and froze her blood.

Scattered all around were hundreds of chewed and crunched-up bones—the grisly, skeletal remains of some horrendous, carnivorous feast. Ysabelle cried out, for grinning from the mire was the skull of a squirrel.

"Is this what became of the survivors?" she shouted. "What poison flows through your veins—what diseased canker pulses inside your breast?"

Morwenna held the Silver Acorn aloft and twirled it in the firelight. "Even in the throne room, I could hear their screams as my pets devoured them," she murmured. "I wonder if thy piteous wails will carry so far?" Then, gazing at the dark water, she added, "It has been two whole days since last they dined. I am certain your end will be a swift one—alas."

With that, she returned to the doorway, pausing only to listen to the faint splashes that drifted ever nearer to the shore.

"I am not afraid," Ysabelle called defiantly.

Morwenna looked at her in mild amusement. "Not yet, perhaps. You are still very much the little royal princess, stiff necked and proud. How many of those have I seen in my drudging years? Yet all are gone now; they either burned or were brought hither. How my ears were amazed to hear their ignoble shouts and screams." She chuckled ever so faintly. "Soon you, too, will squeak as they did before you—squeak and squeal until your lungs rupture."

"You will not hear me cry out," Ysabelle swore. "I shall not satisfy thy black heart by shrieking for mercy!"

Morwenna put her claw on the iron handle of the door. "Most commendable," she said sourly, "but you really are no different than the others. When the time comes, I shall hear you sing as they did." A sudden thought seemed to take her, and she gave a hissing snigger.

"Oh," she cried, "perhaps you hope to be rescued? Ah, my dear, vulgar peasant urchin, how simple thou art. Tell me that you do not put thy faith in the churl-filled forces of thy mother's stinking and noisome land!"

"How do you know of them?"

"I shared all that Wendel knew. Oh, yes, I know that thy dispossessed army of paupers will strike, but, you see, so do the Moonriders. As we speak, they are preparing for battle—why do you think they wore their ridiculous tin pots on their ugly heads? Not to greet thee alone."

"As for the other squirrel houses, thy arrogant mother was deluded. Never will they open their borders to take up arms and venture to march here. We have all been sundered too long; why should they hazard such a risk? No, only two armies will do battle this night, and, when the dregs of both are spent, the Children of the Raith Sidhe shall destroy any in their path!"

"No!" cried Ysabelle.

Morwenna sneered, then pulled the door shut.

Hearing the key turn in the lock, Ysabelle came sliding through the mud and beat her fists upon the door.

"Wait!" she shouted. "Morwenna!"

No sound came from the other side, and Ysabelle slumped against the sealed entrance in despair.

On the surface of the dark water, a large bubble burst, and she stared across to see what had caused it.

"Save me," she whispered. "Green save me."

A pair of bulging, golden eyes swept toward the shore, and, as a repulsive, wart-covered head rose beneath them, they swiveled round to glare at her.

Ysabelle ran to the burning torch, but it was fixed into the rocky wall, and, when next she looked round, two further pairs of eyes were sailing out of the blackness.

Onto the shore the first of Morwenna's disgusting pets lumbered. Its bloodless lips gaped open as it gazed greedily at the squirrel maiden, and an enormous tongue flicked out like a whip of flesh.

Ysabelle hurried back to the door and screamed for help, but Morwenna had gone, and there was no one to hear her.

*　　*　　*

Throughout the trackless and gloomy forest, an atmosphere of expectancy and tension thrilled and charged the deep shadows.

Beneath his covering of leaves, Vesper slowly unfurled one wing and gave a weary groan. Gradually, the young bat stirred, but before he had a chance to look about him, a searing pain stung in his cheek, and he delicately touched the wounds that the gore crow had torn in his face.

Vesper sucked the air sharply through his teeth and grimaced. "A fine sight thou must surely be," he grumbled to himself, "scored and slit like the pastry crust of a pie."

Covering his head with his wings, he gave another groan. "What dull hammering throbs under my skull, and why does mine chest burn and plague me?"

His complaints suddenly disappeared as his face reared from the leathery membranes of his wings and he stared about the dark woods, aghast.

"Ysabelle!" he cried. "Ysabelle, where are you?"

Quickly, he staggered to his feet, brushing away the leaves that clung to him, his tongue clicking all the while to pierce the surrounding shades of night.

No sign of the squirrel maiden could he see, and there was no clue as to where she had gone.

"Ysabelle!" he called. "Ysabelle!"

Countless possibilities as to what had happened flooded into his throbbing head. What if the gore crow had carried her off to devour in seclusion? What if she had run away in terror and had fallen and injured herself? What if–

"Stop this," he berated his fevered imagination. "Jumping to wild fancies shall achieve naught but a greater pounding on the skull than already exists. No, you must be calm, Vespertilio. Think wisely, for tearing about the forest is no solution."

He gazed at the leaves that had covered him and nibbled his wispy beard. "That is a proof that someone cared enough to try to conceal me from hostile eyes," he muttered. "Only Ysabelle would do that. If she had time to contrive such a screen, then surely that shows she was not taken by force and went from here of her own free will.

"The question remains, however," he mused, "what am I to do now? Did she mean to return? And how long was I lying senseless? Perhaps she departed only a short while ago."

He scowled and rubbed his chin thoughtfully. "Then am I to wait here?" he asked himself. "Would it not be better to scout the land? From the air, I might catch a glimpse of her."

That decided the matter for him, and Vesper stretched out his wings to see if they, too, had suffered any damage from the crow's attack. Gingerly, he shook them, then caught the air between his fingers and rose gently from the ground.

Flitting in a cautious circle to begin with, the bat tested the strength of his shoulder and was satisfied that it would bear him safely. Then he beat his wings more rapidly and shot up through the branches and into the heavens.

With the high air currents ruffling his fur and cooling the stinging cuts that marred his face, the bat gazed in surprised wonder at the vast bulk of the blessed hill that reared from the forest.

"Then we did reach her holy land," he breathed, and at once Vesper realized that there he would be sure to find her.

Fluttering his wings, he wheeled a wide arc in the starry sky and swooped toward the land of Greenreach.

The dark shape of the hill rose beneath him as he flew low over the steep slopes.

"Ysabelle!" he called, peering into the veiling gloom.

But the young bat's voice dried in his throat as he witnessed for the first time the destruction his kind had inflicted upon the land. The blasted trees lay stricken and mutilated all around, and Vesper felt deeply ashamed.

The grievous sight wrung his heart, and he wondered what Ysabelle had thought when she had looked upon the charred wilderness. Perhaps that was why she had not returned; what if the maiden now despised him?

With these wretched notions weighing heavily on his spirits, he flitted miserably over the devastation.

"Hold there!" bawled a commanding voice.

Vesper was shaken from his thoughts and fluttered to a surprised halt. "Who is it?" he cried.

From out of a knotted web of cindered branches, a Knight of the Moon came flying. He was almost twice the size of Vesper; a fearsome screechmask covered his head, and the outstretched wings were painted with flames and images of the moon. Snarling, the bat zoomed about Vesper, glaring and squinting at him.

"What is this?" he barked. "A puny weanling come to play at battle! Declare thyself and thy errands here."

"I am Vespertilio!" he obeyed. "Son of Indith and Novatus of the ruined tower and second colony. My errand is a most urgent one. I must speak with—"

"Novatus?" broke in the fierce Moonrider, eyeing him with suspicion. "He was a courageous warrior and died in great honor. If thou art in truth of his blood, name me his battle helm."

"Terrorgrin," came the instant response.

The bat flew beside him and gave Vesper a hearty clap on the back. "Welcome friend," he said. "Thou wilt pardon my mistrust, but 'tis a deadly time, and I have mine orders from Rohgar himself."

He fluttered down to the gnarled and blackened branches and beckoned Vesper to follow him.

Alighting, the Knight of the Moon removed his screech-mask and scratched his ears. He had a strong-looking face with many old scars across his snout, and a tuft of fox-colored hair sprouted on the top of his head.

"Aldwulf am I called," he said as Vesper landed at his side, "and this grim helm is Warbrow. Now, relate unto me the unusual chances that bring thee here, for I know thou art too young for combat. Yet what caused those vicious cuts upon thy face and that raw wound in thy chest? Hast thou encountered the enemy?"

"I have come not to fight," returned Vesper, "but to find . . . someone." He stared nervously at the other bat and tried to muster the courage to say what he must.

Aldwulf snorted at his hesitation. "I perceive what has brought you here!" he roared. "Why, do I not have two fine sons of mine own reaching thy years. Mischief doubled are they–is it thine intent to observe the final battle? Aye, my offspring have tormented me with the same desire. The art of the pouch bombers is fine indeed, yet the field of combat is no place for idle spectation."

"No!" Vesper cried. "I have not come to view the battle either–" Frantically, he gripped Aldwulf's shoulders, and his eyes grew wide. "What battle do you speak of?" he asked. "Why art thou bedaubed with paint? Who art thou preparing to fight? Have the Hobbers assailed this hill?"

The Moonrider pulled away from him. "What riddles are these, child?" he murmured. "'Tis the tree worshippers we ready our legions for. Didst thou not know that a host of those foul tree rats are marching toward us?"

"The army of Ysabelle!"

"'Tis the enemy!" Aldwulf snapped, raising his eyes to stare into the night sky as dark shapes coursed overhead. "Behold!" he yelled. "There fly the pouch bombers with their fiery burdens. That pack of barbarous savages will soon know the meaning of terror."

Vesper gaped upward, and as he stared, he could see other squadrons gathering in the heavens. "You must stop this!" he demanded. "You know not what is truly happening! The squirrels are not our foes!"

"What treason is this?" Aldwulf cried. "If thou wert not so green in years, I would smite thee with mine fists! Bite thy mutinous tongue—no pity shouldst thou feel for that heathen dross! Death is too blessed a gift for them, and if there were another fate I could deliver, I would not hesitate. All should perish, and so they shall."

"You must listen to me!" Vesper shouted. "You all must. This is not how it should be—the Hobbers are the true menace!"

Aldwulf grabbed him by the throat and bared his fangs. "Avaunt!" he spat. "No craven weanling shall utter such filthy lies in my hearing. Go join the other cowards and collect chiff-chaff eggs!" He thrust his screechmask back over his head and started to beat his wings, leaving the spineless youngster behind.

"Wait!" Vesper begged. "I have spoken with the Ancient! The messenger of the Lady—please, you must listen!"

But the warrior soared away in disgust, his talons glittering a trail of silver light beneath him.

Vesper rose to follow, but Aldwulf was speeding toward a vast legion of Moonriders mustering in the sky, and the young bat's nerve wavered. The Moon-Sent Angel had been wrong to choose him; no one would ever believe what he had been entrusted to say.

As he hesitated, high in the chill airs a trumpet blast blared from the forest and rang in his ears. The army of the Hazel Realm had arrived at last.

Vesper's stomach lurched—he was too late.

Thundering shouts came echoing from above as the forces of Hrethel roared for blood, and, flying from legion to legion, the large form of General Rohgar called out his final instructions. Suddenly, he shot upward, giving the signal to the pouch bombers, and, with terrible shrieks, the bearers of the fire eggs veered away from the main host.

Upon the ground, the mighty army that had set forth with Ysabelle from the Hazel Realm drew their swords and raised their spears as the holy land loomed before them. Vesper could just make out their shadowy number far below, and his pity went out to those who had once held him captive as the pouch bombers spiraled down.

Soon, the first explosion would erupt at the foot of the blasted hill and the carnage would begin.

"There must be something I can do!" Vesper wailed. "I have to stop this!"

Thrashing the air desperately, he raced toward the huge cloud of Moonriders, yet they were already swarming after the pouch bombers to assume attack formations. In a moment, the first of them hurtled past Vesper as he shouted at the top of his voice, trying to make them hear him.

"Clear the way!" shrieked a furious Knight of the Moon, who sent Vesper spinning as he rocketed hazardously close.

"Wait!" Vesper yelled until he was hoarse from shouting. "This is wrong—listen to me!"

The immense host swooped over the hillside and circled round the lower slopes, where the army of Coll Regalis waited defiantly.

Ysabelle's faithful border wardens strung arrows to their bows as the tremendous cloud of winged enemies blotted out the starlight.

Since their sovereign had been taken from them, the highest-ranking royal guard had assumed command. Warden Mugwort he was called, and, by his strength of will, the forces dispersed by the Hobber attack had mustered and continued the solemn march to Greenreach.

Now he strode to the front of the thronging mass of black and red squirrels. Holding his sword high in a gesture of challenge, he called to the assembled force.

"We stand before the holy land!" he shouted gravely.

"Let us offer our prayers to the spirit of the Green and hope that wherever our Lady Ysabelle now resides, she will be proud of us this night."

At the rear of the troops, a small figure wept into her cap as Mugwort continued.

"From darkness into darkness we have come, yet let valor and courage light our way now. Above us the enemy are poised to strike, and we are but few in comparison. Our kindred of the remaining houses have proven faithless, so, in the name of the Hazel Realm alone, let us show these winged rats what it is to battle bravely. With their lives shall they pay for defiling the holy land!"

A resounding cheer was sent up, and a volley of arrows flew into the sky as a sign of defiance to the reviled flying vermin.

With scornful laughter, the first phalanx of pouch bombers dived down. "The flame of victory is with us!" they sang. "Let us scorch the earth with our fierce flowers!"

Numb with horror, Vesper could do nothing but watch as the first pouch fell to the ground and a ball of red fire erupted in the midst of the squirrel army.

"I have failed," he murmured dismally. "Now there is no hope left. The Children of the Raith Sidhe will be the only victors, and the world will be plunged into eternal suffering."

Another explosion burst into the night, and the ferocious flames tore upward. Even from where he despondently fluttered his wings, Vesper could feel the unbearable heat singe his fur, yet despite this, a freezing chill crept over him. He was witnessing the end of everything. The only forces capable of purging the forest and ridding the land of the Hobbers' threat were annihilating one another.

The young bat trembled as, far below, the slaughter commenced. Squirrels burned in the dreaded flames and Moonriders plummeted to the earth, pierced by many arrows.

As the fire eggs continued to blast and shake the ground, Rohgar's voice bawled the order and his legions plunged downward, their razor-sharp talons outstretched.

"Forgive me," Vesper whispered. "I did all I could, yet it was in vain."

He could stand it no longer. Torn with remorse and filled with the dread of what was to come, the bat turned from the carnage that raged below and flew away.

"Oh, Ysabelle," he wept, "where are you?"

THE FALL OF THE OAK

The Lady Morwenna hurried up the steep stairway, clutching the Silver Acorn tightly to her bosom. This was the moment she had waited for, the only delicious dream that had kept her in the Starwife's service all those tiresome and humbling years. Now, a power older than the foundations of the world would be hers to command and wield. Under the Infernal Triad, she would have complete mastery over the creatures who survived the tumult that would shortly lay everything to waste.

Up she sped, pausing only to hear the sounds of battle echoing from outside the Hallowed Oak. Soon, those meager forces would be overthrown by Hobb's followers, and true darkness would be reborn.

Hastily, she climbed the sacred stair, and, with her breath rasping from her chest, she stood at the entrance to the Chamber of the Starglass.

It was exactly as she had left it. Her old cloak, embroidered with powerful charms and black enchantments, still covered the great device, and the circular room was filled with shadow.

Morwenna waited to catch her breath before entering. She had endured much for this one moment, and she wanted to savor every instant.

"At last," she panted, "all my struggles and hardships are ended. The old life shall wither, and the new will begin."

An exultant expression lit her bony features as she stepped across the threshold.

In her fist, the Silver Acorn tingled and pulled her toward the center of the chamber.

"The Starglass," Morwenna breathed. "It calls to the Silver, and the metal hearkens to the summons." She closed her claws about the precious symbol of the Starwives to prevent it flying from her grasp and stepped nearer to the covered glass.

"Have patience," she crooned to them both. "You shall greet one another presently, and I shall rule each."

The closer the Acorn came to the Starglass, the more agitated it became, and Morwenna strove to control the violent tugs that wrenched her forward. Finally, she held the amulet above the dark spells sewn into her cloak, and through her claws, a pale radiance welled up.

The silver of the talisman glimmered, shining from the tarnished metal, and the light grew in intensity until it filled the chamber with a harsh glare. Beneath the embroidered cloak, the Starglass rippled, and the black material billowed as power surged from its immeasurable depths.

A triumphant laugh issued from Morwenna's lips, and she took hold of the cloak to drag it from the magical device. Then she froze.

"But wait," she reproached herself. "If I uncover the Starglass, the walls of defense shall spring back around the hill. I would not be able to break the sorceries in time for the arrival of the Worshippers of Hobb. They will be unable to invade, and those who stand in our way will survive!"

Her claws twitched away from the cloak, and she staggered back to the doorway.

"I shall not be thwarted!" she cried. "When the black tide pours from the forest, I shall return."

The Silver Acorn grew dull once more behind the immovable bloodstains as Morwenna fled down the sacred stair. In the deserted chamber, the Starglass became still, and the cloak continued to suffocate its magic.

*   *   *

Ysabelle shrank against the damp and dripping wall. Two bloated and glistening toads stalked her, and behind them she could see another emerging from the scummy water.

Over the bone-strewn mud, the misshapen, squab-faced monsters came squelching. Splaying their webbed claws wide, they swaggered after the squirrel maiden, their bulbous eyes almost popping from the livid sockets. Their mistress had fed them well; on tender young flesh they had gorged, satiating the brutal appetite that always festered and inflamed their putrid bellies. Yet their last victim had been sent to them days ago, and they had since picked the bones clean and sucked out the final dregs of marrow. In the dark water they had waited, the hunger growing once more, until they did think their benefactor had forgotten them.

Now, however, a fresh morsel had been given, and their ravening mouths dribbled greedily as they approached.

Ysabelle looked from one hideous toad to another and knew there was no escaping them.

A long tongue lashed from the nearest slime-oozing beast and flicked across Ysabelle's arm. She cried out in revulsion and terror, then the tongue came snaking for her again, this time slithering around her tail before it snapped back inside the wide, gaping mouth.

The second toad snorted a snotty bubble from its nostrils and sidled closer. An odious grin split the squat head, and the green lips parted as it prepared to strike. Eyeing the squirming bait and carefully selecting the tenderest cut, it inhaled as though relishing a sumptuous and mouthwatering scent. Indeed, saliva did slobber from the ogre's jaws as its own tongue unraveled and shot out.

The squirrel screamed as the fleshy pink rope wrapped tightly about her waist, constricting and forcing the breath from her body. Another tongue caught hold of her wrist, gripping fiercely until her fingers throbbed and she squealed in pain.

With their luminous eyes swollen and projecting more than ever from their glutinous heads, the creatures gurgled and slowly began to draw Ysabelle to them.

"No!" she protested, slipping on the mud as the whips of muscle dragged her forward. But there was nothing she could do, and when a third tongue twisted about her—this time squeezing around her neck—all Ysabelle's cries were strangled into a choking silence.

The unclean beasts bobbed excitedly as they trawled their catch in. Their webbed claws slapped the mud with malevolent glee, and the squirrel was pulled to her knees. The fattest and most deformed of Morwenna's beauties waddled up to her; its sticky tongue retracted swiftly into the twisted mouth, and it brought its stinking face close to hers.

Ysabelle tore at her throat as she struggled for breath. The grotesque nightmare licked its cold lips as it reached up a clammy claw, enthralled and captivated by the luscious delectable. It clutched at her, running its slime-dribbling fingers zealously through her fur. The other toads gave guttural croaks and belches as it opened its monstrous mouth and lunged to snap and bite.

Ysabelle closed her eyes and shuddered.

Suddenly, the moldering timbers of the door splintered, bursting asunder as a raging fury came crashing into the dismal grotto.

Morwenna's pets blinked in surprise and splashed in the mud, wild with dismay.

"Begone!" commanded a voice that boomed throughout the cavern. "Release her!"

The toads cringed and flinched as the hateful intruder charged at them, rising into the stale air, beating them with its wings and lashing out at them like a thing demented.

Gulping their tongues back into their throats, they shuffled away from the squirrel and slithered down the bank to the safety of the water.

Ysabelle gasped as the air filled her lungs, and she rubbed her bruised neck. "Vespertilio!" she cried. "I never thought to see you again!"

"Nor I you," the bat said, taking her by the paw and helping her up, "till I did hear thy voice calling. But be quick—little time is left to us."

"Where is Morwenna?"

"Who? When I entered this mighty oak, I did meet no other. Is she a friend of yours?"

"Hardly that!" she replied. "She is the cause of all this madness and has taken the Acorn from me!" And, running from the cavern, she hastened through the passage behind the shattered doorway.

From the chill water, the forlorn toads gazed miserably at Vesper as he hurried after her, and each began to howl retching wails.

Up through the narrow tunnels, Ysabelle ran until she reached the entrance to the Hallowed Oak and passed within, swiftly climbing the stairs beyond.

But on arriving at the grand hall, she hesitated: a fearful clamor was issuing through the great doors, and, with cautious steps, she ventured toward them.

Vesper flitted behind her, flying over the winding stairs, and came gliding into the hall, alighting at her side.

Ysabelle stared out at the withered hilltop, and hellish lights starkly lit her face.

Vespertilio," she breathed, "what riotous uproar is that? What are those flames that blister into the heavens yonder?"

"Princess," he began, "thine army has arrived. That is the sound of my kind destroying the forces of thy mother's realm."

"My army?" she repeated. "Why do they engage so soon? Have the other squirrel houses joined them?"

"They have not."

Ysabelle held onto the door as her hopes were dashed. "Then all is lost," she murmured. "Every one of my royal guards will be slain; against your fire eggs they are defenseless. The Knights of the Moon have conquered."

Vesper cast his eyes down guiltily. "No, we have not," he muttered, "for only the Hobbers shall be victorious. Our triumph, shameful though I find it, will be short lived."

The maiden reached out for him, and he took her paw in his wing. "Without the amulet, there is naught we can do," she said sorrowfully. "The battle will rage until no more blood can be shed, and a darkness with no chance of dawn shall creep over the land."

In stricken silence, they watched the fierce red flames blast upward, and the clashing of steel against steel rang in the infernal night.

The scarlet fires of those warriors he had once so admired were reflected in Vesper's dark eyes, and remorse wrung his spirit until he felt as hollow and desolate as the scorched realm about him.

Unfurling one wing, he spread it about them both, as if to shield them from the horror to come. As he did so, Vesper's thumb brushed the strap fastened over his shoulder, and he tugged at it irritably. The leather bag at his waist gave a jerk, and Vesper stared down, amazed at his own stupidity.

"Ysabelle!" he cried. "Come—before it is too late!"

Dragging her from the vast tree and out into the troubled night, the bat bounded over the hill to where a small, neglected campfire brightly crackled.

"What are you doing?" she yelled above the thunderous din. "There is naught we can do—the span of this world is ended!"

Vesper tore the bag from about his shoulders and wrenched it open. "Not yet!" he declared. "There may still be a way!"

341

Stepping up to the flames, he held the gift of the Ancient aloft and, glancing desperately at Ysabelle, poured the powdered contents into the fire's heart.

On the slopes of Greenreach the bitter war rampaged, bloody and savage. The squirrels of Coll Regalis had lost many of their host to the scalding flames of the pouch bombers, and countless archers had fallen before the steel gauntlets of Hrethel's forces. The standard-bearer had been one of the first to die, and his lifeless body smoldered in the terrible heat, sprawling across the banner he had once been so proud to carry.

The Knights of the Moon plunged among them, ripping and slicing with their talons. Yet they, too, suffered losses; nigh on a hundred slaughtered bats lay on the battlefield, stuck through with arrows and spears or hacked by swords. The withering grasses were dyed crimson, and the soil had turned into a mire of gore.

All around, trees blazed like gigantic torches and choking plumes of poisonous smoke flooded the air, forming an immense ceiling of fumes that blanketed the entire sky.

Courageously, the squirrels fought on, brandishing their glittering blades and striking whenever the enemy swooped to tear at them, yet they knew that their numbers were dwindling.

Despair and vengeance drove them, repaying the bats as viciously as they could for the loved ones they had left behind in the Hazel Realm, those innocent families that the Moonriders had ruthlessly murdered in their hunt for the Silver Acorn.

"In the name of the Hazel!" Warden Mugwort roared, cleaving a wounded bat in two.

Boldly he fought, and with each drop of blood that he spilled, he called out the names of his dead children.

"For Penda! For Sorrel! For Bellinia!"

Leaping over the fallen corpses of both races, he swung the blood-soaked sword over his head to await another assault—yet none came. All across the battleground, Ysabelle's forces were left swiping at empty air and firing arrows into blank emptiness. For some unaccountable reason, the bats had gone.

Amid the inferno of burning trees, the squirrels stared in bewilderment into the smoky heavens. Flying with great urgency from the field of combat, every Knight of the Moon was returning to the hilltop of Greenreach, as though summoned by a single command that none could ignore.

The army of Ysabelle looked up at that which drew their foes and shook their heads in wonder.

Rising from the lofty hill, a huge pinnacle of purple flame towered into the sky. The violet brilliance seared through the dense reek of the blazing woods, setting to flight all the midnight shadows.

The like of its glory had never been seen on mortal lands and would only be glimpsed again nearly a thousand years hence.

It was a dazzling beacon, shining like a fierce pillar of hope through fear and doubt, and in the heart of each bat it called to them. Irresistibly, the winged legions swarmed toward it, too awestruck to utter a sound, and even the fearsome General Rohgar let the vivid magnet guide him without question. The purple flame seemed to speak to every single one of them, promising lost delights and offering forgotten dreams. It was a magnificent, worshipful spectacle, and they sped over the hillside as fast as their wings could bear them.

Warden Mugwort lowered his sword in disbelief, dumbfounded that the enemy had withdrawn so unexpectedly. Then a grim and determined expression stole over him, and his knuckles shone white about the hilt.

"After them!" he yelled. "Follow those retreating craven vermin!"

Jeering challenges, the army of Ysabelle stormed up the hillside to where the needle of flame reared into the sky.

With his face buried in his wings, Vesper stood at the squirrel maiden's side. The ferocity of the mysterious powders had taken them both by surprise. As soon as the young bat had sprinkled them into the campfire, they had sparked and spat, immediately changing the tongues of flame from yellow to brilliant purple. Then, with a burst of glimmering, amethyst stars, the fire had streaked upward, shooting into the night until a radiance as harsh as day illuminated the Hallowed Oak and the scorched trees around it.

Covering her eyes, Ysabelle held onto Vesper, and both wondered at the mighty force he had unleashed.

With the light of the beacon bleaching all color from his furry face, Vesper felt the urge to fly upward and spiral about the flame. But he gritted his teeth and, with Ysabelle at his side, mastered the insistent summons and stared into the sky.

Racing toward the splendor of the tapering flame came an enormous cloud. The bat swallowed timidly and gave Ysabelle's paw an anxious squeeze.

"They are coming," he whispered. "The legions of my folk have been called from the battle.

The squirrel smiled encouragingly. "Now, fulfill the destiny the Ancient envisaged for you," she told him. "You have their attention, but the doom of all still hangs in the balance. It is a slender thread. Do not fail, Vespertilio; the fate of us all depends on you."

"My thanks for that," he answered ruefully. "Now my nerves are more unsettled than ever."

Ysabelle looked steadily into his eyes. "I have faith in you," she said. "This is your hour. Seize the chance and put a final end to the evil war."

Her confidence inspired him, and he gazed upward where the first of the Moonriders were congregating about the intense light, fluttering around it like giant moths.

When the entire host of bats had gathered above the hilltop, the draft from their thousands of beating wings blew down upon Vesper and Ysabelle's upturned faces. As it streamed through their hair, the young bat took his leave of her and slowly rose into the air.

Up he flew, and as he soared beside the blinding tower of light, his mind reeled, trying to think what to say. How could he ever reconcile his race with Ysabelle's?

Vesper climbed swiftly, close enough now to recognize he screechmask of Rohgar among the mighty host, and he cleared his throat to greet him.

"Hail, Rohgar, heroic warrior of countless battles. I welcome thee!"

The huge noctule wheeled around, and the enchantment that had lured him and so beguiled his wits faded, leaving him confused and angry.

"What sorcery is this?" his voice thundered within Slaughtermaw. "Where are the paltry forces of the tree worshippers?"

His wrathful cries shattered the mesmeric spell that entranced those around him, and they, too, glared sternly about them.

"Who art thou?" Rohgar demanded of Vesper. "What black art fetched us hither?"

"It was a gift of the Ancient," came the proud reply, "and I am the one he chose to–"

Before he could finish, one of the other Moonriders chanced to look at the ground, and there he spied Ysabelle, standing alone and defenseless.

"General!" he shouted. "Behold, is that not the heathen savage our agent withheld from us and guided inside the oak?"

The noctule peered down and laughed within his screechmask. "Verily, it is the same," he said. "'Twould seem the treacherous lady hath done with her and thrust the maggot out to please us."

He stretched out his legs, and the steel talon looked like white flames before the light of the beacon. "Now she is ours!" he called. "Let us shred her vile being into a thousand ribbons!"

Shrieking with eager joy, the Knights of the Moon followed their general as he dived, plummeting for the kill.

Vesper was horrified. "You cannot!" he wailed, staring down at the vulnerable figure of Ysabelle.

Screaming with fear and rage, the young bat swept his wings behind him and hurtled toward the ground. With the wind tearing at his plunging body, he raced past Rohgar and reached the maiden before any of them.

Hastily, he leaped in front of her and spread his wings wide. If they were going to kill Ysabelle, it would have to be through him.

Rohgar came streaming through the night straight for them, while behind, the multitude of bats poured after.

The talons sliced the air; Ysabelle clung desperately to Vesper, and Rohgar bore down. The blades glinted before Vesper's eyes, but just as he closed them and braced himself for the onslaught, the noctule swung upward in a wide circle.

"What deception is this?" Rohgar screamed. "Why dost thou defend that rat of the trees?"

The legions that swooped after settled upon the mutilated branches of blackened trees, and their displeasure seethed.

"You have betrayed thine own kind!" they accused.

"I have not!" Vesper shouted defiantly. "The squirrels are not our enemies! We have all been betrayed!"

Rohgar charged at him and pressed Slaughtermaw into the young bat's face. "Stand aside, thou most wanting of lackbrains! That stinking witch is mine for the killing!"

But Vesper was not daunted and bravely stood his ground. "Listen to me!" he cried. "All of you! Other powers are at work here. Evils that you are ignorant of."

"If thou wish to be skewered along with that filth, then so be it!" Rohgar snarled, raising his talons to Vesper's throat.

Suddenly, a horn sounded, and all eyes turned to the rim of the hill. Brandishing their weapons in challenge, the army of Ysabelle surged forward, and for a moment all was confusion.

"Vesper!" Ysabelle cried. "The battle is to commence all over again!"

"No, it shall not!" he said firmly.

Using all his strength, he shoved Rohgar aside and pulled the squirrel after him. Out before the ranks of the Moonriders they ran, dashing headlong into the vanguard of the squirrel troops.

The royal guards at the forefront stared in amazement as they saw their sovereign rushing toward them, yet they gripped their spears, ready to slay the evil bat that held her.

"Now!" Vesper shouted, skidding to a standstill and whirling Ysabelle round.

The squirrel stared around them. To the left, the hordes of Moonriders shrieked their war cries, and to the right, her own warriors were preparing to resume the battle.

"What shall we do?" she cried.

Vesper took hold of her shoulders, and a mad gleam danced in his eyes. With the purple flame of the magical beacon shining lustrously over his face, he gave a toothy grin and said tenderly, "Kiss me."

Before Ysabelle could resist, he had pulled her close and pressed his lips against hers.

Squirrels and bats stumbled over each other as they beheld the unbelievable sight, and a ghastly, appalled hush descended.

Knights of the Moon sank to the ground, disgusted and horrified at what they were witnessing. Gallant wardens rubbed their eyes in disbelief, then threw down their weapons, dismayed.

The stunned quiet deepened, with only the crackle of the enchanted fire to disturb it. Then, with a splutter, the burning logs crumbled and the beacon that had drawn the bats faltered. The purple flames perished, dwindling down and changing back to yellow until they, too, guttered and all was dark.

Vesper and Ysabelle turned and faced their separate armies.

"Now you will hear me," the bat said, "for my words shall shape the future of the world."

A bewildered murmur of revulsion rippled through the astounded legions, yet all waited on the young bat's explanation for this unnatural union.

347

Choosing his words carefully, Vesper began—leaving out nothing. He told the gathered forces what had occurred since his capture by Ysabelle's guards. At first, his voice was small and unsure, but as the tale grew, it became filled with power and might until it resounded over the hilltop, and all who heard the young bat marveled.

Gravely, his audience listened, hearing of the horrors that had pursued him and the squirrel maiden through the forest. Never had Vesper spoken with such force, and his impassioned speech moved many, and their hearts began to doubt the wisdom behind the holy wars. Ever his voice urged them to put aside mistrust and hatred, for they were only serving the ends of the true enemy.

Into his tale Vesper wove themes of hope in the midst of despair, and valor in the face of terror. The Knights of the Moon who hearkened to him removed their screechmasks and gazed guiltily across at the strength of the Hazel Realm. But there remained those who refused to believe, and their black enmity smoldered still within their breasts.

The royal guards of Ysabelle stared at their queen in wonder as the fearful account of the past days unfolded. The red squirrels, always quick to mirth and swift to tears, sniffed and wiped their eyes at the perils that she had endured, yet their black kindred listened stiffly and with grim expressions. Warden Mugwort kept his paws clasped about his sword, watching for the first sign of treachery on the part of the bats, his loathing for them still untouched by Vesper's beguiling and eloquent telling of events.

At the point where the mouse captain had taken them to meet the Ancient, an astonished gasp escaped from the Moonriders when the identity of that venerable being was revealed.

"The Messenger of the Lady!" they breathed. "The weanling has conversed with the Herald of the Moon!"

Their beadlike eyes gleamed fiercely as the story rolled on, until Vesper told them the name of the one who had truly stolen their birthright.

"Hrethel!" repeated Rohgar, enraged at the young bat's insolence. "How dare you accuse our great Lord—always has he been anxious to restore our gifts! Thy madness is finally proven!"

Infuriated, the noctule raked the ground with his talons, but as he stared at his legions, he could see that they were not so certain of Hrethel's innocence.

"What is this?" he shrieked. "Can you doubt our good Lord on the rambling words of a crazed fool?"

The Moonriders eyed him uncomfortably. "Yet it would explain much," answered one. "Have we not wondered why the Warden of the Great Book had locked himself away with his charge? Why does he no longer attend the councils, and why does he suffer none to enter his chamber?"

"His actions are not for us to question!" Rohgar snapped.

"I put my trust in the Ancient," the other replied.

"The Ancient!" bawled Rohgar. "Only that fool's word do we have that he exists. How are we to know he is not deceiving us? For myself, I do not believe any of this fantastic deception. The tree rats are our enemies, and always shall be!"

From his warriors, the general received some approval, but the majority of the bats shouted them down. Rohgar glared around him. "Am I besieged by faithlessness?" he cried. "Where is the honor of we Moonriders?"

Vesper moved to approach him, but Ysabelle held him back and advanced in his stead.

"My lady!" Warden Mugwort called behind her.

But the squirrel maiden ignored the warning and stepped up to the huge winged shape of the wrathful general. There, she looked fearlessly into the eye slits of Slaughtermaw and said firmly, "By the spirit of the Almighty Green, all that Vespertilio has told you is true."

Within the screechmask, the noctule snarled; he could slay this miserable wretch so easily. Yet as his gauntlets twitched and the blades scored the cindered earth, a curious light blazed in the

349

squirrel's eyes, and Rohgar—mightiest general and fiercest of all Knights of the Moon—felt his heart quail inside him, and his anger was quenched. Silently, he removed the helmet from his head and gazed at the ground, abashed.

At the forefront of the Hazel forces, Warden Mugwort loosened his grip on his sword and sought for the strength to forgive.

From the rear of the squirrel army, a high, frantic voice piped up as the royal guards were pushed aside.

"Move thy hulking bulk!" it cried, squirming to the front. "I must get by. Oh, M'lady, oh, my poor heart—it flutters so."

Ysabelle turned and gazed into the center of her troops. A delighted smile lit her face, and she gave a grateful laugh.

"Griselda!"

From the ranks of the squirrels, the small mouse came. The brim of her ill-fitting cap had been tucked underneath to keep out of her eyes, and in her paws she still clutched the shield and tiny knife that one of the wardens had given to her.

"Oh, M'lady!" she blubbered, tears coursing down her face. "I knew you were safe. I knew it, I did. I said it all along!" Scampering toward Ysabelle, she threw down her war gear and flung her arms abut the maiden's neck.

Vesper grinned as they greeted one another, but there was still much to be done, and he saw that all eyes now looked to him and Ysabelle.

"What are we to do now?" asked Warden Mugwort.

Rohgar lifted his head and peered through the night, across the dark shape of the great river, out to the invisible walls of the city in the distance.

"We must fly to the Chamber of Hrethel," he growled. "He must be forced to return our birthright. The Great Book must be wrenched from him and restored to the other members of the council."

A murmur of agreement flowed from the other Moon-riders, but Vesper spread his wings and shook his head vigorously.

"Have you not heard me?" he cried. "Hrethel must wait—let him gloat over his precious pages a while longer. The Children of the Raith Sidhe must be our first concern."

From high above them, a cold voice rang out, and it laughed disdainfully at them all.

"Vain, empty words!" it shrieked. "What a shallow threat thy numbers are!"

Everyone stared upward. There, in the topmost branches of the Hallowed Oak, stood Morwenna, and her gaunt features were twisted with her hatred for them all.

The royal guards gazed at her in disbelief. For around her neck the Silver Acorn gleamed dully.

Morwenna regarded them with scorn and derision. From her high position they seemed like insects, and she chuckled at that, for she would certainly crush each and every one.

"Who is that?" asked Griselda fretfully. "Why does she wear the symbol of the Starwives?"

A look of immeasurable contempt crossed Ysabelle's face. "That is the traitor who brought about the destruction of this fair land," she spat. "It was she who allowed the Moonriders through the defenses."

"That creature is in league with Hrethel!" declared Rohgar.

"Oh, no," Ysabelle told him. "She has a far more sinister ally."

The noctule bared his fangs and seized his screechmask once more. "Gladly shall I slay that foul deceiver!" he exclaimed, donning Slaughtermaw and rising into the air.

Morwenna's harsh voice mocked him as Rohgar bolted upward. "Miserable worm!" she shrieked. "Too late are thou— much too late!"

The general shot straight for her, soaring through the stately branches of the oak, his talons glinting in readiness.

When he was barely a yard away, Morwenna hissed and opened her arms wide.

Suddenly, from the dark night, many black shapes darted. Surging from the shadows, they fell upon Rohgar and surrounded him in a frenzy of feathers and hellish squawks.

Upon the ground, everyone watched helplessly as dozens of crows and ravens viciously mobbed the general, tearing with their claws and stabbing with their beaks.

Rohgar's voice roared at them, and his gauntlets flashed red in the sky, yet there were too many. With an agonized wail, Slaughtermaw was wrenched from his head, and, in a moment, the bat's lifeless body tumbled down after it.

"Now do you see your failure," Morwenna called, "for the final battle is begun, and darkness shall consume all!"

Her cloak swirled about her, flapping madly as a thousand carrion birds descended from the heavens and swooped upon the hilltop.

Harsh cries rent the air as the armies scattered before the brutal assault. Moonriders desperately tried to take flight, but savage claws came ripping at their wings, and they spiraled helplessly down. Squirrels panicked in the ferocious onslaught, and many of them ran blindly and with no weapons to defend themselves.

"Stand and fight!" Vesper yelled, snatching up the tiny knife Griselda had dropped. "Ysabelle, call to your archers!"

The squirrel looked quickly at the band of black squirrels who alone had stood their ground. Under Warden Mugwort's orders, they were already stringing their bows, and the arrows of Coll Regalis went singing into the feathery hordes.

Recovering from the surprise attack, many of the other squirrels were regrouping, and a legion of bats had managed to rise into the air to deal with the infernal birds in their own element. And so the bloodiest of all battles commenced.

High above them, Morwenna laughed to herself; the foes of Hobb had not seen the full might of her followers yet. She raised her claw to give the signal, and at once the terror of her enemies doubled.

All about the hilltop, a sea of fiery faces reared, flames dripping from their gaping mouths. A horrendous mass of evil creatures flourished their Hobb lanterns and came charging forward, screaming foul oaths and curses.

Before the squirrels or bats knew what was happening, the ravening tide was upon them. Rats without number surged at the squirrels with poisoned spears in their claws and daggers clenched in their sharpened teeth. Swords rang and shields buckled, maces crunched into skulls, and arrows plunged through skin and hide.

In the air, the jackdaws and ravens flew against the Knights of the Moon in a blizzard of feathers, and huge rooks tore at the screechmasks with claws as bitter as steel and just as deadly.

Surrounded by the ringing battle, Vesper remained on the ground, thrusting his knife into any Hobber that leaped before him. Tirelessly he fought, parrying the terrible strokes that lunged at his flesh and slicing where he could in defense. At his side, Warden Mugwort swung his sword, notching it on the iron breastplate of a vile hedgehog who winded the squirrel by a swift blow to the stomach. Mugwort crumpled in two, and the gleeful creature raised its mace to dash in his brains.

But Vesper rushed in and stabbed the Hobber in the side. The warden gave him a grateful look, then wielded his sword more furiously than ever and cut a bloody swath through the invaders. Side by side, the age-old rivals of bat and squirrel fought against the true enemies of light and reason, and in those desperate moments the rift between the two races was forgotten.

As the horrific battle raged about her, Ysabelle stared at the uppermost branches of the Hallowed Oak. There, Morwenna haughtily shrieked her commands, instructing the Children of the Raith Sidhe and guiding them toward the inevitable victory.

A wintry calm entered Ysabelle's soul as her hatred for that artful traitor swelled, and she knew what must be done.

Swiftly she ran to the great entrance, leaving her nurse to patter after her.

"M'lady!" Griselda squeaked. "Whither art thou going? Come back!"

Through the grand hall Ysabelle stormed, almost flying up the staircase that spiraled inside the gigantic trunk of the mighty tree.

At the Starwife's bedchamber, the maiden hesitated. The shutters of the window had been thrown wide open, and in an instant she had crossed the room and gazed out.

Below her, all was chaos. Her army was beleaguered on every side. The number of Hobbers was beyond anything she had imagined, and the flames of their lanterns formed a great ring of fire about the squirrels. In the sky, the carrion birds were reveling in the deaths of countless bats. The Knights of the Moon were no match for the unbounded hordes that flew against them, and their battered bodies fell into the confusion beneath.

Ysabelle lifted her eyes from the sorrow around her, up to where a branch twisted gracefully from the tapering trunk and upon which a tall, cloaked figure stood.

Hurriedly, the maiden clambered out of the window and, clinging to the bark, began to climb. With the ground dwindling into the distance beneath her, she pulled herself up until the bough was directly over her head. Pausing only to catch her breath, and with the rumble of the battle rioting in her ears, she caught hold of the graceful projection and swung herself round, expertly leaping up until her feet were planted firmly on the branch.

Not far away, standing aloof amid the rustling twigs and new budding leaves, Morwenna's heavily lidded eyes shone across to her.

"My beautiful emeralds must be sadly disappointed," she said. "I was so hoping they would find you to their taste."

Ysabelle edged along the bough. "The amulet!" she demanded. "Give it to me!"

The other wrinkled her snout in disdain. "The audacity of the whelp," she hissed. "Is that the courtesy due to the Starwife?"

"Thou art no Handmaiden of Orion!" denounced Ysabelle, staring at the tarnished Acorn. "Why! You have not brought it to the Starglass!"

Morwenna's claws clutched at the Acorn. "Alas," she admitted, "that much is true, yet there was a reason." She peered down at the seething forces far below and gave a throaty laugh. "But the purpose of that hath now been achieved," she announced. "The worshippers of Hobb are all here. See how they swamp thy meager brigands. The Children of the Unholy Darkness shall rout thy friends and trample them under foot and claw. A fine, gorging feast shall they enjoy. This blessed hill will become a mountain of the dead, for corpses too numerous to count shall be piled here."

Stealing a glance at Ysabelle, she sniggered. "Now, the time has come for me to join the Silver with the Starglass. The spells of smothering have served their purpose."

Morwenna strode over the branch, her steps deliberately heavy, and the precarious road swayed alarmingly.

"Thou art standing in mine way, peasant girl," she purred, causing the bough to shudder even more. "Am I to hurl thee from this deadly place?"

Ysabelle staggered backward as the branch bucked and jerked. "I shall not let you take up the Starwifeship!" she shouted.

"Then thy bones will be shattered against the tree as thy body plummets into the midst of thy misguided and foolhardy companions below."

Morwenna advanced, her hooded eyes flaming as brightly as any Hobb lantern. With her cloak billowing in the high breezes, she raised her claws and stepped nearer.

Suddenly, a pouch bomber came shooting beneath the branch, pursued by a screeching gore crow. The bat swerved, veering around the enormous trunk, but the bird tore unerringly down, and before the Moonrider could check himself, they collided and smashed into the side of the tree.

A tremendous explosion ripped through the bark as the fire eggs the bat carried burst into devouring flame.

Ysabelle was thrown off balance and almost fell to her doom. But as the fierce ball of flame scorched the leaves behind her and leaped into the midnight sky, the priestess of Mabb came steadily closer. "The end of all that you find good is here," she said softly.

The maiden backed away, then Morwenna gasped and her claws flew to the amulet about her neck.

"It burns!" she shrieked. "The Silver burns!"

Ysabelle stared in horror as a stream of acrid smoke poured from Morwenna's fist. The squirrel writhed in pain and tore her claw from the Acorn. "What is happening?" she whined. "The bloodstains—they swirl and move over its surface! The amulet glows like an ember!"

"No," Ysabelle muttered, "please, no."

A shrill scream issued from the hilltop, cutting through the uproar and the sounds of death that filled the night.

Through the fire and smoke, the two squirrels stared down. The battle was floundering; the Hobbers were hastening from the fray, hotly pursued by the royal guards.

A mad fear seemed to have dismayed them all, and the fighting ceased as they cleared a wide space before the Hallowed Oak as if horribly afraid of some new, unseen terror.

As Ysabelle watched, an ugly crack streaked over the ground and a hiss of sulfurous steam gushed from its depths. Morwenna put her claws together and held them to her mouth, trembling with anticipation.

From deep beneath the earth, a vile roar came bellowing, and in the sky, the carrion birds squawked in fear and sought safety amid the concealing foliage of the Hallowed Oak's branches. As the trumpeting roar reverberated across the heavens, the Knights of the Moon hovered in the air and their screechmasks gazed down in bewilderment. The frightful shriek pierced Ysabelle's spirit, and she almost fell from her lofty perch in dread of that familiar sound. She called to the Green for mercy.

"But it is only the second night," she cried. "Not so soon–not so soon?"

The hideous, blaring roars grew louder until every creature stopped its ears and the hill shook beneath them. Jets of sulfur blasted from the fissures that now gaped before the mighty tree, and the oak shivered from the lowest root to the topmost branch.

Ysabelle fell back against the trunk and wept dearly as the Hallowed Oak quivered uncontrollably, and her eyes stared at the soil that blistered and bulged through the spitting fumes.

"My Lord is coming," exalted Morwenna, the Acorn gleaming around her neck, singeing the fur at her throat. "His Dark Majesty approaches!"

From the steaming earth, to the terror of all, the god of the rats, the Lord of the Raith Sidhe, slowly emerged.

Two massive horns punctured the tormented ground as the Master of the Pit reared into the waking world and the roots of the mighty tree flew apart as he crashed through them.

All around the hill, the Hobbers screamed as the huge head rose before them, blurred and shimmering behind a screen of vicious heat that incessantly poured from the unlit, lower regions of the earth. Lanterns wrought in his venomous image were thrown down as the rats tore at their hair and writhed in anguish at the malignant spectacle that manifested before them. Then their Lord's fiendish eyes blazed in their direction, and many terrified creatures slew themselves to escape his awful countenance.

Vesper recoiled and staggered into Warden Mugwort. Fear had seized them both, for the face that rose from the soil and glimmered through the heat haze was a vision of pure evil.

The horns that twisted from the forehead of the titanic apparition curved high into the night, and even from where he stood, Vesper could see they were steeped in blood. A matted tangle of fiery-red hair grew between the horns, forming a phosphorescent mane about the contorted, hellish head.

Beneath the wiry brows that arched into barbed points of ginger bristle, Hobb's eyes balefully shone on the world that had been denied him for so long. His pupils were as dark as the bottommost pit, and flames of war rimmed them, piercing into the hearts of the cowering onlookers, inspiring them with dread and despair.

Bellowing roars boomed from his gaping maw. It was a vast tunnel of flesh, edged by long, yellow fangs, and the spittle that poured from the dark blue lips was the color of blood.

The immense, rat-shaped fiend drew himself farther from the ground. A garland of skulls hung about his neck, and as he towered over the hilltop, a forked tail came ripping through the ashes and lashed about the oak tree, stripping the bark from the trunk and splintering the great doors of the entrance.

Out from the Pit the Lord of the Raith Sidhe climbed, his cloven hoofs stamping on the earth, and with his head thrown back, he beat his claws upon his chest, free at last.

The Hallowed Oak gave an ominous groan, and jagged splits ripped through the trunk as the gigantic tail pounded it and the poisonous fumes ate into the tree's fibers.

In the upper branches, Ysabelle turned her face from the awful vision and gripped the bark desperately as the tree shook and trembled.

Morwenna was jubilant; gazing down as the two horns came rearing up, she threw her arms open in greeting. "Welcome, my Lord!" she shouted. "Thy servant has prepared the way for thee. Welcome to the unhappy world once again!"

The curling, tangled mane rose before the cloaked squirrel, and behind the shimmering haze, the fire-rimmed eyes lifted high overhead as she made a humble bow.

Ysabelle howled when she beheld that terrifying face; the stench of Hades flowed from the open maw, and the light from the infernal gaze bathed the branch a lurid crimson.

With the amulet blazing at her throat, Morwenna laughed. "I have done this!" she declared. "For thy unholy glory and for that of thy consort, my Lady Mabb, I have worked unceasingly to bring this moment into being."

The terrible mouth of the Lord Hobb stretched into a macabre grin, and the malevolent fires burning in those eyes grew brighter than ever as, slyly, they swiveled from Morwenna to Ysabelle.

A hideously gnarled claw reached up, and Ysabelle screamed. This was it. Wendel's curse had come true; Hobb was going to claim her.

Morwenna cackled as the misshapen talons came groping through the choking, sulfurous air. "Send her to the Pit!" she squealed. "Let her know the misery of thy imprisonment and through eternity suffer a thousand torments!"

Ysabelle cringed from the huge claw, and Morwenna made to bow again, but something was wrong; Hobb was reaching not for the maiden, but for her.

"No," she shrieked. "I am the one who released you!"

Terrified, she realized her mistake and tried to tear the symbol of the Starwife from her neck. It was the power of the Acorn that had summoned her diabolical master, and, by invoking his dreaded name, his own high priest had cursed the bearer of the amulet.

In her horror, Morwenna fumbled with the chain, but it was too late, and she could not remove it. A fetid reek blew upon her as the ghastly head drew near and the unclean claw closed about her cloaked body.

The priestess screamed when the talons squeezed. "You are mistaken, Lord!" she ranted. "Spare me!"

With imploring squeals still on her lips, Morwenna was plucked from the branch and dragged into the swirling heats, her limbs flailing in the cloying fumes until she was brought before the demon's jaws.

Screeching, she threw up her arms, but her earthly life was over. The fiery eyes mocked her, and, from the dark throat, a cloud of sulfur blasted the struggling figure in the fiend's grasp.

Morwenna's screams cut the night as sheets of flame tore through the choking fumes.

The shrieks of the treacherous squirrel died as her body crackled and burned, writhing in the ghastly furnace.

When the noxious fog began to clear, only ashes and smoking dust remained in her Lord's evil grasp, and an empty black cloak twirled forlornly on the breeze until it snagged on the nearby branches.

Ysabelle's heart banged against her rib cage. It was Morwenna's soul that had been sent to the far reaches of the Pit. Gazing at the cloak that smoldered close by, she knew that that fate had been meant for her. Then the squirrel's eyes caught something bright spinning through the air like a falling star, and she stared impotently as the Silver Acorn dropped to the ground.

Now, Hobb turned his attention to her.

With the light of the underworld radiating from those baleful eyes, he blew Morwenna's ashes from his claw, and his putrid breath smote Ysabelle as if she had been struck a violent blow.

The squirrel almost fainted dead away, but the glare of that foul apparition held her, and she could only balk as the talons reached toward the branch once more.

Suddenly, a draft ruffled her fur, and Vesper's voice came shouting from above.

"Hold on to me!" he cried.

Before Hobb could snatch at her, the squirrel had gone. A fierce bellow issued from the immense nightmare as he saw a young bat bear his second victim into the sky and out of danger.

But now the night was filled with angry voices as the Knights of the Moon showed their mettle and zoomed toward the rat god's monstrous head, mustering their forces above him.

Before his very face they flew, striking with their gauntlets at the blood-matted fur and slashing the foul flesh of his venom-dripping snout.

"In the name of the Lady!" they called defiantly.

The Lord Hobb rained poison and fire upon them and many bats were shot down, spinning helplessly in screaming bundles of flame that exploded when they hit the ground. Yet still the others harried the deadly creature that dwarfed the blessed hill, daring to bite him with their steel talons and shouting challenges as they dived past his towering form.

The legions of Moonriders were as gnats to the unholy Lord of the Raith Sidhe, yet their incessant stings inflamed him and he roared in fury, bringing his fist smashing down against the trunk of the Hallowed Oak.

With a thunderous creaking of timber, the tree toppled and went crashing through the air.

The squirrels and Hobbers who had remained, staring up at the apparition in abject terror, hurried from the hilltop as the roots of the oak tore from the ground and the gigantic tree tumbled down the hillside, claiming many lives in its calamitous destruction.

Holding grimly onto Vesper, Ysabelle saw the magnificent oak smash down the slope, throwing up tons of earth in its wake. Beneath them the foul demon bellowed, its fiery breath streaking through the darkness and withering the Knights of the Moon who plagued him into ashes.

The world shook as Hobb pounded his hooves and the forked tail thrashed about him.

Ysabelle gazed below and spoke quickly into Vesper's ear.

"Take me down," she said grimly, "to the very feet of that abomination."

The bat stared at her, yet he knew the maiden too well to argue, and, with a sweep of his wings, they descended.

Past the twisting horns they flew, past the fearful countenance and the necklace of skulls. Catching the wind in his wings,

Vesper narrowly dodged the tail as it whipped toward them, and they landed on the ground without injury.

As soon as her feet touched the earth, Ysabelle raced over to the cloven hooves, not daring to look up at the towering nightmare, and snatched the discarded amulet to her bosom.

"Hurry!" she cried, wrapping her arms about Vesper's neck. "To the fallen oak!"

Beating his wings, the bat rose from the ground and sailed through the tortured night, out over the hillside to where the mighty tree lay broken in its ruin.

The massive trunk was shattered, and the decorated chambers that the craftworkers of Greenreach had toiled over were exposed and demolished. A section of carved stairway poked from a gaping, jagged hole in the wreckage, and, over the oak's fragmented corpse, small fires blazed where the silver lanterns had spilled their oil and flame.

Over this devastation Vesper flew, and Ysabelle scanned the dismal sight keenly.

"There!" she exclaimed. "Take me down there!"

The bat obeyed, and they alighted far from the main bulk of the crippled oak.

Through the shattered tangle of torn twigs and branches, Ysabelle hurried, striving to reach what she had seen lying upon the grass.

There it was: the dark circle of the Starglass, thrown clear from the fractured tree, darkly mirroring the smoke-filled sky.

The amulet was still hot in her paws, but she had borne the pain in silence; now, the metal began to cool as it drew her forward.

Vesper stared at the Starglass in wonder, for already its surface was shimmering.

Ysabelle held the Acorn by its chain and breathlessly brought it over to the magical device.

The black glass rippled and churned, and within the amulet, an answering light welled up.

"Now is the time!" Ysabelle cried. "Now do I accede to the throne and claim my place as Handmaiden to Orion!"

Hesitating at the last instant, she gazed back at Vesper, and tears brimmed in her eyes as she murmured in a meek voice, "Good-bye, my love." Then she returned to the enchanted device and called out, "May this new vessel serve you well!"

The stars in the heavens shone fiercely through the blanketing smoke, and their brilliance burned in the churning depths of the Starglass as the maiden lowered the Silver Acorn. Cold, white flames licked over the bubbling glass, leaping up to dance around the glowing amulet.

A high-pitched, sonorous note rang in Ysabelle's ears, and a wintry chill passed into her fingers, searing up her arm until she spluttered and a halo of silvery light shone around her. Vesper stood back as the icy fires enveloped the squirrel entirely. The power that beat from the Starglass was blinding, and he protected his eyes with his wings as Ysabelle became a pure white, dazzling flame.

Then, abruptly, all was dark.

Vesper rubbed his eyes, but it was few moments before they adjusted and he was able to see again.

The Starglass was calm and still once more, and, standing beside it, Ysabelle turned a resolute and solemn face to the young bat. In her paw, the Silver Acorn gleamed brightly, cleansed of the blood that had sullied it, and she fastened the chain about her neck.

"What happened?" Vesper muttered.

"I accepted the high office," she replied with a cool dignity he had not seen before, "and the power is now channeled through me."

"But–but, what does that mean?"

"The Starwifeship is truly mine," she told him, "and all that it entails."

A ferocious bellow sounded upon the nearby hilltop, and Ysabelle's face grew hard. "Take me back," she demanded.

Vesper began thrashing his wings, and the Starwife held onto him as they climbed into the sky.

About the blessed hill, the Lord Hobb roared. Destroying flame blasted from his jaws, remorselessly burning those who had worshipped him alongside the squirrels of the Hazel Realm. The tumultuous clamor of the shrieking multitude was terrible to hear, yet cutting through all the chaos came a clear and strident voice.

"Lord of the Raith Sidhe!" called Ysabelle, letting go of Vesper and dropping to the ground as he swooped down. "Hearken to me, the bringer of thy doom!"

The dreadful visage of Hobb turned to her, and his fire-rimmed eyes blazed with triumph.

But the Starwife was not afraid, and she held the symbol of her office aloft for all to see.

Steeped in the hellish glare of the infernal presence, the amulet gleamed. Pricking through the haze like a frosty white star, it shone within the baleful light, glimmering with might and purity.

"The world has no use for thee!" Ysabelle proclaimed. "Long ago thou wert shuttered from the living, and must be so again!"

A chilling noise issued from the hideous fiend above her, and those that heard it realized, with a shiver, that Hobb was laughing.

Fearfully, Vesper rushed to the squirrel's side and took her by the paw. "This is madness!" he cried. "Let me bear you from this foulness!"

But with a determined look on her face, she pushed him aside and repeated her warning to the monster above.

"The time of darkness is gone!" she shouted. "Never shalt thou trouble the world again!"

The scathing laughter subsided, and. for the first time in many ages, the demonic god of the rats spoke.

To hear his sepulchral voice was like being torn and cut by knives, and some of those Hobbers who remained shrieked and fell upon their swords to drown the insidious horror of that evil sound.

"NEVER SHALL I BE RETURNING TO THE LOWER DEEPS!" he rumbled. "NO LONGER CAN THEY HOLD ME! THINE SPARKLING JEWEL DID FREE ME OF THEM FOR ETERNITY. NO, NOW THE LORD OF THE UNDERWORLD HATH DOMINION OVER THE UPPER REALMS.

"DARKNESS AND DEATH WILL I SPEW FORTH, AND THE LUST FOR SLAUGHTER WILL CRAWL INTO EACH PITIFUL CREATURE'S MIND."

Ysabelle almost swooned before the force that was in that unearthly voice, but she roused herself and strode defiantly forward with the amulet in her paws.

"Not to the Pit that is broken do I consign thee!" she cried. "But to another confinement–of my own devising!"

"NEVER!" the Lord Hobb arrogantly scorned. "THERE IS NO FETTER IN ALL CREATION STRONG ENOUGH TO BIND ME. I AM FREE, AND THY HAUGHTY WORDS CAN INFLICT NO HARM."

"Though the fastness of the world's dungeons is breached," Ysabelle called, "I cannot permit thee to stalk the troubled earth and bring forth thy consort and the trickster. Begone from here, Beast of the Poisoned Seas!"

Behind the plumes of sulfur, the awful face contorted, and a ghastly sneer formed on the dark blue lips. "PRINCE OF THE DESPAIRING DEAD AM I!" he roared, "HEIR TO THE INNER VOID THAT WAS AND WILL COME AGAIN. CAST THY PETTY NETS ELSEWHERE, SQUIRRELING, FOR THY REIGN IS ENDED!"

A torrent of flames gusted from his mouth, but Ysabelle darted beneath him as the fires erupted where she had been standing, and, in a condemning voice, she pronounced his fate.

"Father of lies!" she called. "Hear my curse, and tremble! By the powers of this amulet you were summoned from the Pit, and to the Acorn thou wert drawn. Take now that which I give so freely. May thou have that which lured thee!"

As she finished speaking, the sulfurous jets that belched from the soil shivered and stirred before the night airs, and the Lord Hobb glared around him suspiciously. Quickly, the breeze grew in force until a fierce wind fell on the hilltop and the reeking yellow fumes were scattered throughout the sky.

With the gale tearing around him, the rat god heard a low rumble shake the heavens, which were suddenly ripped asunder as bolts of lightning jagged over his repulsive head.

The amulet in the Starwife's paws crackled with magical force and the stars blazed in the firmament as the power waxed steadily.

Ysabelle closed her eyes as the full might of the Silver Acorn seared through her and her voice rose in unbearable anguish.

Bawling, the Lord Hobb raised a cloven hoof to crush the squirrel beneath him. Yet, even as he brought it smashing down, a streak of lightening struck one of his horns, which burst into white flame, and a pall of livid green smoke spluttered into the flashing sky.

Never had the Lord of the Raith Sidhe known such pain, and he screeched in convulsing torment as the fire burned and scorched.

"WITCH!" he roared. "WHAT HAST THOU DONE?"

Arcs of blinding energy raged about the titanic fiend, bristling down his forked tail and wreathing around his deformed head.

The Starwife shuddered as the lethal forces locked within the amulet flooded out, lashing against the demon with unstoppable fury. The awesome might of the Silver Acorn coursed through Ysabelle's entire being, charging through every sinew and streaming forth to enmesh the Lord of the Underworld in a cage of dazzling stars that blistered and devoured him.

"NOTHING CAN HOLD ME!" he raged through his agony. "I SHALL NOT SUBMIT!"

Ysabelle felt the strength draining from her as the energy relentlessly beat out and the lightning crashed around the towering figure above.

Hobb was now covered in white flame, and the gnarled claws that thrashed the air wove a frantic web of fire in the rampaging storm.

All around the hilltop, his followers and the squirrels gaped in terror as he bayed and shrieked. Then they rubbed their eyes as, gradually, a change stole over the evil creature. The flame-enveloped figure was slowly diminishing, dwindling behind the sizzling sparks and shrinking into the ground.

"NOOOO!" Hobb's resounding scream echoed.

An inferno of blinding heat and light erupted from the soil, and the fierce bolts of lightning that snaked from the amulet in Ysabelle's grasp whipped furiously about the land of Greenreach. Then all was dark, and the raging wind sighed into a calm and peaceful silence.

The hideous majesty of the Lord Hobb had utterly vanished.

Not a murmur disturbed the stunned quiet that followed, only the soft beating of leathery wings as Vesper landed at Ysabelle's side.

"You destroyed him!" he marveled.

The Starwife shook her head feebly. "He cannot be destroyed," she answered in a drained whisper. "The god of the rats lies yonder."

Nervously, Vesper flitted to where she pointed, but he could not see anything upon the ground. Then he gave a small cry and peered at a tiny object that lay upon the charred soil.

It was a simple acorn, the ordinary green nut of the oak tree, similar to the millions that grew in the forest. Yet, with infinite caution, Vesper picked it up and brought it reverently back to Ysabelle.

"There is the prison I wrought," she said with great strain showing on her face. "No other choice was there. An acorn called him, and by that was he doomed."

The young bat gazed at the small, round shape doubtfully. "I do not understand," he muttered. "Surely he can break free from there?"

"Do you not see?" she asked, putting her paw to her brow and swaying unsteadily. "Hobb is not merely trapped within the shell. His very being is locked within the nature of this, and, as long as it lasts, and a squirrel sits upon the Oaken Throne, so shall the term of his imprisonment."

"Then you must keep it safe," he replied, putting it into her paws.

"No, Vespertilio," she breathed. "The acorn must be buried. A tree must grow, and that oak shall flourish for over a thousand years. In every splinter of its timbers, Hobb shall be sealed and—and while a twig or leaf of it remains, the world—the world is—is safe." And with that, she slumped to the floor, exhausted by the forces she had unleashed.

But the danger was not yet over. All around the ruptured hilltop, the members of the Hobb cult were rising from where they had cringed and prostrated themselves. Madness shone in every staring eye, and, hissing and gibbering, they took up their weapons once more and stole forward.

With a sudden wail, they leaped upon the squirrel army, rending and hacking, butchering the royal guards with a wild savagery that was terrible to behold.

Cawing maniacally, the carrion birds dived upon the Knights of the Moon, and their armored bodies began to fall in a grisly rain.

As the madness and uproar seethed about them, Vesper took hold of Ysabelle and carried her over to where the roots of the ruined oak had been torn from the ground.

"Ysabelle," he called, laying her against the mangled tree, "can you not stop this?"

The Starwife opened her eyes wearily and gazed in despair at the carnage that rampaged around them. "I am too spent," she breathed. "I cannot wield the magic to protect our forces. I am sorry." Then her head fell to her chest, and she knew no more.

A guttural shout made Vesper whirl round, just as a hump-backed rat sprang for him. The young bat's knife flashed in his grasp, and a moment later the rat lay dead.

Yet the number of Hobbers was immense; their insane yammering traveled to the farthest shores of the great river and filled the wild expanse of the forest. Brutally, they swarmed over the defending forces, and, into the gaping fissures that scarred the earth, the hot blood of bat and squirrel gushed and flowed.

With his back against the Hallowed Oak, standing over the body of his beloved, Vesper slew many raving creatures. Yet always others leaped in to take their place, and he knew he could not hold out much longer.

Overhead, the Knights of the Moon were failing against the gore crows and rooks, whose beaks and claws were stained a bright and sticky scarlet.

Warden Mugwort called to his troops, rallying them to him and keeping the flames of their courage burning. Yet the army of Ysabelle was hemmed in on all sides, and with each second that passed, another of their number fell before the rabid Hobbers.

From the flanks of the shrieking enemy, a jagged dagger came flying. Mugwort cried out as the barbed blade plunged into his shoulder, and he tore it out fiercely. Yet even as he cast the repugnant weapon from him, a blackness closed over his senses. The dagger had been dipped in venom, and with a cry of anguish, he fell dead.

The squirrels around him yelled in dismay. Roars of victory erupted from their roiling foe as they surged forward in one violent charge. The forces of the Hazel Realm were swept aside, and the battle seemed to be nearing a grim conclusion.

Vesper was overwhelmed by the countless hordes. A shrilly squawking hedgehog rushed at him, swinging a cudgel above its spine-covered head. The young bat threw up his wings to defend himself, but his assailant delivered a terrible blow to his ribs and Vesper was thrown sideways.

With insanity shining in his eyes, the hedgehog lumbered up to Ysabelle and licked his teeth gruesomely.

Vesper struggled to his feet, but the blow had knocked all the strength from him, and he collapsed at Ysabelle's side just as the creature prepared to pounce.

Suddenly, a loud trumpet blast boomed over the hilltop, and the hedgehog gazed blankly around him. His squinting eyes bulged in terror at what he saw, and with a frightful yelp, he threw down his cudgel and waddled away as fast as his bowlegs could take him.

Vesper shakily lifted his head, and a cry of joy blurted from his lips.

From the forest, an immense host was marching up the hill. Never had such a force been assembled, for here were two of the remaining squirrel houses, and their mighty armies contained ten thousand courageous souls, all geared for war and eager for battle. Yet what made Vesper's heart leap inside him was the sight of those who came at the vanguard of the vast number.

With swords drawn, the surviving woodlanders from the ruined mound stormed up the hillside—and Fenny was at their head.

"Ysabelle," the bat called, "we are saved!"

The Children of Hobb uttered terrified screams as this new threat advanced. The clamoring rats tore blindly about the hilltop, stumbling over themselves, fighting each other in their fear. Before the vast host had arrived, many terrified creatures had already perished at the feet of their brethren.

As the woodlanders reared over the rim of the hill, a number of the crazed Hobbers rushed at them and were swiftly slain, while others fled down toward the flowing river and were drowned trying to escape.

When the glorious reinforcements rushed at the enemy, the battle-weary army of Ysabelle revived and continued their fight, refreshed and filled with hope.

Yet in the sky, the carrion birds were undaunted by the arrival of the unbounded legions and set about the Moonriders with more ferocity than ever. It was not until the squirrels strung their bows and shot volleys of arrows into the air that the crows paid them any heed. Each flurry of arrows brought threescore of the feathered Hobbers down, and they dropped like stones from the sky.

Screeching, the birds veered from the hill, but the Knights of the Moon pursued them unto the farthest reaches of the forest, and none escaped their vigilance.

The ensuing battle was brief and deadly; nearly all the Worshippers of the Raith Sidhe were destroyed, but some managed to flee with their lives and ran shrieking into the forest to lick their wounds and wait for another day.

About the hill of Greenreach, cries of jubilation rang out and the squirrels of the Hazel Realm greeted their long-sundered cousins.

But this rejoicing was marred with great sadness, for the cost of victory had been dear, and the tally of the fallen ran into hundreds.

With jubilant cheers mingled with wails of lamentation filling his ears, Fenlyn Purfote strode through the bodies of rat and squirrel, over to the huge roots of the Hallowed Oak, where Vesper and Ysabelle lay.

At first, he thought that both were dead, but as he drew closer, he saw the young bat stir and welcome him with a feeble grin.

"Hail, Captain," Vesper whispered. "Glad am I to see you again."

The mouse smiled, then looked at the maiden at his side. "Thy friend is pale," he observed. "The denizens of the Ivy House are skilled healers. Let me call them."

"No," said Vesper, putting his wing about Ysabelle, "the Starwife is fatigued—no more."

Fenny whistled through his teeth. "The Starwife!" he exclaimed, but before he could say any more, an anxious voice trilled behind him.

"M'lady!" squealed the mousemaid. "Don't fret none; I'll soon be with thee!"

As Griselda hurried from the midst of her mistress's army, Vesper made a desperate appeal to the mouse captain.

"Please," he asked, "keep that nursemaid from us for a while longer."

Fenny nodded and turned to lead the clucking mouse away from the tangled roots.

Alone with Ysabelle, Vesper drew her close and kissed her lightly on the forehead, and, as her eyelids fluttered open, the first rays of the morning sun edged into the sky.

YSABELLE

The celebrations lasted for many days, yet it was a time in which Ysabelle saw little of Vesper, for his people had one last score to settle and had besieged the chamber of the evil Lord Hrethel.

Having been the one to expose his dire treachery, and proving himself to be valiant and courageous, Vespertilio finally achieved his lifelong ambition and followed in the tradition of his forefathers. Now he, too, was a Knight of the Moon. As such, his duty had compelled him to encamp with the other survivors of the final battle about the lair of their last enemy.

Two whole weeks stretched by, and the Warden of the Great Book refused to come forth. Then, one evening, a messenger came from Greenreach, announcing that the new Starwife was to be inaugurated by her subjects. Eagerly, Vesper took the tidings to the new general, who somberly granted him permission to attend.

The following morning, Vesper flew out over the walled city, anxious to see his beloved again. The great river shone beneath him as he sped toward the blessed hill, and, as he drew nearer, he could see that the squirrels had not been idle.

The wreckage of the Hallowed Oak had been completely removed, and not a trace of the fierce burning that had so marred the land now remained. Saplings had been planted to replace the trees that had perished in the fury of the fire eggs, and already, the hill was covered in new grass and spring flowers speckled the lush expanse of green.

Excitement charged the air as he fluttered round. The banners of the combined squirrel houses flew in the murmuring breeze above hundreds of brightly colored tents, and, not to be outdone, the woodlanders had hastily sewn a standard of their own to set flying alongside those of their allies.

Preparations for the approaching ceremony were nearing completion as Vesper set down, and though the squirrels and mice greeted him warmly, they were too busy to hear the tidings of the great siege. Only Fenny stayed with him, and he sensed that the young bat was troubled and agitated about something.

Leading him from the bustling crowds, the mouse captain refrained from asking what ailed his winged friend and told him instead of the progress that they had made in his absence.

"Oh, aye," he declared, "'twill be a beauteous realm again—though not as fair as it was afore. Still, the folk who remain will deem it pretty enough, I'll warrant."

Vesper fidgeted and looked over his shoulder, but the mouse made no comment and continued mildly.

"As soon as we can, the woodlanders and me are setting off. This isn't the place for us. Now the Hobbers are gone, a sweet meadow is what we'll settle for, and nothing else." They had walked far from the excited noise, and Fenny laid his paw on Vesper's shoulder.

"You will be most welcome to join us," he said, "you and whomever you might want to bring."

Vesper stared at him; it was as if the mouse had read his thoughts.

"Say nothing," Fenny told him. "Stay here, and I shall send her to you. Best to speak away from that heady babble."

The mouse turned and strode briskly back toward the tents. Standing amid the pale lilac flowers, Vesper took a deep breath and waited. He was terribly nervous and gazed at the wondrous display before him, knowing that what he was going to ask would be extremely difficult. Impulsively, he lowered his eyes so that he would not have to look at the merry scene and walked uneasily round in a tight circle.

"Vespertilio!" called a voice.

The bat jumped, and his toothy grin lit his face as Ysabelle came regally through the grass toward him.

"I longed for thee to be here this day," she said, "but dared not raise my hopes. So, the Knights of the Moon have released thee from thy duties! I am glad."

"I would have come even if they had not!" he answered, running to meet her. "Nothing could keep me from your side."

The maiden laughed as they embraced. "Oh, there is so much to tell," she said. "A chamber has been dug beneath the earth by the woodland folk, and there they have set the throne salvaged from the ruined oak. Look at the flowers around us! Are they not beautiful? I believe the spirit of the Green has blessed this place anew. It is all so joyous that I doubt sometimes whether everything was as dark and grim as I remember. My heart has never been so light and free of care. Griselda is chiding me continuously."

"But times were dark," Vesper told her. "Never forget that. We lost dear friends upon that desperate road."

"I know!" she said. "I have not forgotten them. Have you seen thy mother? Was she not proud of thee? I knew she would be. If only my parents were here today. Oh, but is it not glorious?"

"Ysabelle," the bat interrupted, "I have something to say to you."

"It will be a most wonderful ceremony—such pageantry and pomp. Our cousins, those of the Fir, have brought many fine minstrels, and they play the grandest music."

"Ysabelle!" he cried again.

The squirrel blinked at him in surprise. "What is the matter?" she asked.

Do you not know?" he replied morosely. "Have you forgotten the time on the mound, and when we danced to humbler tunes than those thy cousins can play?"

The Starwife looked uncomfortable. "Of course not," she said, "yet that seems long ago to me now."

"Long ago?" Vesper repeated in misery. "Listen to me, Ysabelle! My every breath is thine. You order my waking thoughts and tantalize my dreams. These past weeks without seeing you or hearing your voice have been a desolation to me!"

"Vespertilio," she said with some reserve. "What game is this?"

"No game!" he wailed. "Hear me now. We must flee this place. Do not take part in the ceremony. Relinquish thy high office! Come with me—let us begin a new life far from here! Our devotion can overcome all obstacles; I know it can!"

Ysabelle recoiled in astonishment. The emotions that came flooding from the young bat frightened her, and she pulled away from his clinging embrace.

Vesper fell to his knees. "This is what I had hoped and dreamed for!" he wept. "It can be done—long and hard have I thought. If we can only find some lonely spot, we can be truly happy. Never has there been a love like ours."

"Oh, Vespertilio," she said sorrowfully. "I did not realize how deep thy feelings were. Of course I have affection for thee, but do you not see? You have thrown my mind into confusion—I must have time to think."

"There is no time—listen! The trumpets are sounding, summoning everyone to the ceremony. You must choose, my beloved—it is our only chance of joy!"

"But where would we go! We are of two different kinds. Folk would spurn us at every turn!"

"What does that matter? We will have each other—Fenny has said we may go with him."

Ysabelle glanced back at the tents and all the banners that flew above them. "But I am the Starwife," she uttered feebly.

"Let them find another!"

"I cannot! Vespertilio, you do not know the grave responsibilities that now burden me. From the day the falcon dropped the Silver Acorn and it fell into my paws, my destiny has lain outside the natural world. It binds me tight, and I can never escape it—I must not. Your proposal is rash and ill considered. It would never succeed, and we would grow to despise one another. Our cultures are far too different."

"Ysabelle! You love me—I know you do. How can you deny the happiness that would be ours?"

"Enough!" she cried, refusing to hear any more. "I am now the Starwife, Handmaiden of Orion, and as such must act with wisdom." Tears brimmed in her eyes as she stroked his hair, murmuring, "A squirrel of the royal blood and a Moonrider: it was a lovely dream, Vespertilio, but such fancies must melt in the harsh glare of day. The dream is ended now. I go to my inauguration and do not think I should see thee again. Come no more to this place. Do not seek me, for I shall not speak with thee again."

"But we mean so much to one another!" he spluttered.

"I am not permitted to love any mortal," she answered. "My duty comes above all things. Good-bye."

With tears streaking down her face, she spun on her heel and raced over the hilltop to where Griselda was waiting for her.

Vesper uttered an empty cry as she fled from him, and he called her name unceasingly until Ysabelle had vanished from his sight.

Surrounded by the swaying flowers, which rustled in the breeze, Vesper wept, desolate and filled with despair.

"What is this?" came a velvet voice. "Sadness on such a glad day of rejoicing?"

Vesper looked sharply behind him. "Who are you?" he asked, wiping his streaming eyes upon his wing.

Through the salty blur of his tears, he saw a cloaked figure rising from the grasses, and a mist of lilac petals floated about the folds of the dark material. A deep hood obscured the stranger's face, and no clue to his identity could Vesper glimpse.

"Why were you hiding there?" he sniffed. "Explain yourself."

"It is a fine morning and the sun, she shines most richly. I am afraid that I was sleeping when thy voices awoke me."

"What—what did you hear?"

"Enough to know how forlorn thou art. To go through one's existence so discouraged is not good, my friend."

The bat frowned and tried to look beneath the hood. "Do I know you?" he asked. "Your voice is vaguely familiar."

"I am but a fleeting visitor, come to view the crowning of one so great. Is it not pleasing to be present on such a day as this? I am exceedingly grateful to be here."

Vesper shook his head. "No," he murmured, "I have nothing to be thankful for. My life is in ruins. No joys are left to me—only dark despair." He turned to leave, but the other called him back.

"Thou hast my sympathies, Moonrider. Yet do not let us part on so bitter a note. My time here is also brief; wilt thou not drink a toast with a passing wayfarer? If not to the future that you see so bleak, then to the past?"

All Vesper wanted to do was to leave Greenreach far behind him, yet the cloaked figure was so insistent that he grudgingly agreed.

"I have about me a certain mixture that is honey to the tonsure," said the stranger, "a fine mead from a distant realm—come drink."

From a pocket in his cloak, he took a small bottle that flashed and winkled in the bright sunshine as he pushed it into Vesper's grasp.

Politely, he received it and put the vial to his lips.

Abruptly, the figure let out a mocking laugh. "Did I not say my curse would hound thee?" hissed the scornful shade of Wendel Maculatum. "Taste now the full bitterness of thy doom!"

Vesper gasped in horror as the empty cloak sank amid the flowers and the malevolent spirit fled back to its cold tomb. Only then, as he stared helplessly around him, did the young bat understand, and the curse was finally fulfilled.

*   *   *

Prattling constantly, Griselda led her mistress down to the chamber the woodlander had prepared. The route was lined with members of the squirrel houses, and all bowed as their new sovereign passed.

"Ooh, is it not a delight?" the mouse gabbled. "Such a day I never did see, M'lady. Who would have ever thought it? You the queen over all—does my heart proud, it does."

Ysabelle said nothing, and her features seemed frozen. Inside, all was turmoil, and she walked down the stairway as one in a trance.

"Oh, look, M'lady!" squeaked the oblivious maid. "There is that bold fellow I told you of, the one who asked me to step out with him. The very idea! Still, mighty pleasant and well spoken he is—one of them woodland folk, I believe. Says he is of the brown mice, and he won't be leaving with the others to search for that mythical land they are always speaking of. Intends to settle down by the Deep Ford yonder, and might he come and visit me with a view to getting better acquainted? In all honesty, I don't know what to make of him."

But Ysabelle was not listening. She was thinking only of Vesper, and, as the crowds cheered, it was his remote voice, and that alone, she could hear.

A host of memories shone in her mind when she stepped woodenly up to the throne, and, blazing fiercely in them all, was the young Moonrider.

Solemnly, the minstrels began to play, and the maiden sat mechanically upon the elaborately carved chair.

From the throng that flanked the raised dais, the prince of the Ivy House came. In his paws he bore the Silver Acorn, which had been entrusted to him for this most magnificent occasion, and he bowed to the Starwife before ascending to stand in front of her.

Ysabelle hardly noticed him; an image of Vesper flickered before her eyes, and she smiled faintly, remembering their times together. A delicious warmth kindled inside her, and with it, a tremendous ray of hope cleared all shadows from her heart, and at last she listened and knew what she must do.

"Sovereign queen," the prince gravely intoned, "in the might of the Starglass thou hast been tempered." As he spoke, the squirrel raised his arms and held the amulet above Ysabelle's head.

"Under the firmament thou wert tested and hath proven worthy. Accept now, before we who are gathered here, the symbol of thy peerless office. May the Green bless thee."

The minstrels grew silent as the prince began to lower the Silver Acorn, but, even as it descended, Ysabelle threw up her paw and pushed it aside.

"No!" she cried. "I will not accept it."

A startled murmur rippled around the chamber, and Griselda's cap fell from her head in her startled surprise.

"But, most noble monarch," the prince began, "the acceptance is made. This is a mere formality."

"I do not care!" Ysabelle replied, rising to her feet. "I have done my duty. What is there for me to look forward to now? A long, dismal life stretches before me. I would rather live from day to uncertain day, happy with my beloved, than commit myself to such a cruel and lonely sentence!"

The court was scandalized and uttered shrieks of protest. Only one figure refrained from voicing his displeasure, and a great, glad smile split his face from ear to ear.

"That's right," Fenny called. "You had me worried for a moment!"

Ysabelle stared at the mouse captain and laughed. "None of this matters now," she declared. "I must go to him. I must speak with him!"

Pushing past the horrified prince, Ysabelle tore from the throne and raced through the chamber, with Fenny's shouts ringing above all the clamor and her devotion to Vesper spurring her on.

"Green be with thee both!" the mouse called as she hurtled up the stairs.

Out into the fresh morning air, Ysabelle ran, her long, raven hair streaming behind her.

Past the brightly colored tents she hurried, her true love's name always on her lips.

"Vesper!" she sang. "Vesper, forgive me. I did not know what I was doing. Of course I love you. Don't leave without me. Wait! Vesper!"

Up to the place where she had left him, Ysabelle fled, and her heart nearly burst with the emotion that swelled inside her.

"Vesper!" she called urgently, scampering through the lilac flowers. "Vesper!"

Then the squirrel maiden juddered to a halt and stared aghast at the terrible sight that met her eyes.

"No," she whimpered, "Oh, please, no!"

A slight breeze ruffled through the flowers, and upon it she thought she could hear a faint, victorious chuckle. Ysabelle's knees buckled under her, and it was as if a bitter knife had pierced her heart.

There, with the tiny vial of blue glass still in his grasp, and the traces of its contents glistening upon his lips, her one and only love lay dead.

"Vesper," she wept desperately. "Oh, Vesper, forgive me!"

But the only answer came from the delicate bluebells that rustled and swayed around them.

ROBIN JARVIS writes: "Whenever I am asked where I get my ideas for books and characters, I always wish I could come up with some weird and wonderful answer. 'I dream them,' for example, or, 'I get inspired whenever there is a full moon.' But, unfortunately, neither of these is true. Like many writers, I sometimes base my characters on real people (or parts of real people) and sometimes they are the complete product of my imagination. But they generally all start as a sketch or drawing and then take shape as a character is developed around them.

"I started making sketches of mice because they were the smallest things I could think of to draw. When I sent them to a publisher, I was asked if there was a story to go with the drawings. At the time there wasn't, but I sat down and thought of a project visually and drew a story board as though I were making a film. I had envisaged it as a picture book, but it became a 70,000 word manuscript, and I've been writing ever since.

"I can't think of a better way to earn a living!"